continued . . .

THE
SHARPEST
BLADE

Sandy Williams

ACE BOOKS, NEW YORK

THE BERKLEY PUBLISHING GROUP
Published by the Penguin Group
Penguin Group (USA) LLC
375 Hudson Street, New York, New York 10014

USA • Canada • UK • Ireland • Australia • New Zealand • India • South Africa • China

penguin.com

A Penguin Random House Company

THE SHARPEST BLADE

An Ace Book / published by arrangement with the author

Copyright © 2013 by Sandy Williams.
Penguin supports copyright. Copyright fuels creativity, encourages diverse voices,
promotes free speech, and creates a vibrant culture. Thank you for buying an authorized
edition of this book and for complying with copyright laws by not reproducing, scanning,
or distributing any part of it in any form without permission. You are supporting writers
and allowing Penguin to continue to publish books for every reader.

Ace Books are published by The Berkley Publishing Group.
ACE and the "A" design are trademarks of Penguin Group (USA) LLC.

For information, address: The Berkley Publishing Group,
a division of Penguin Group (USA) LLC,
375 Hudson Street, New York, New York 10014.

ISBN: 978-0-425-26588-8

PUBLISHING HISTORY
Ace mass-market edition / January 2014

PRINTED IN THE UNITED STATES OF AMERICA

10 9 8 7 6 5 4 3 2 1

Cover art by Gene Mollica.
Cover design by Lesley Worrell.
Map by Adam F. Watkins.

To the coolest grandmother on the block.
I love you, Grandmommy.

ACKNOWLEDGMENTS

◆

First, I want to send out a big, heartfelt thank-you to all my readers. Your e-mails, Facebook messages, and your general enthusiasm for McKenzie and her friends have made this writing gig a wild, wonderful ride. I hope you find this book as satisfying an end to McKenzie's story as I do.

To my regular beta readers, Trey, Shelli, and Renee, you guys continue to rock. And to my new betas, Leah Lewis, Paris Hansen, and author Marika Gallman, thank you for your awesome feedback. Marika—your comments were perfect and hilarious!

I owe a debt of gratitude to my agent, Joanna Volpe, who always has my back, and to my editor, Jesse Feldman, who did a wonderful job of catching up with the series and who helped me bring it to a satisfying end.

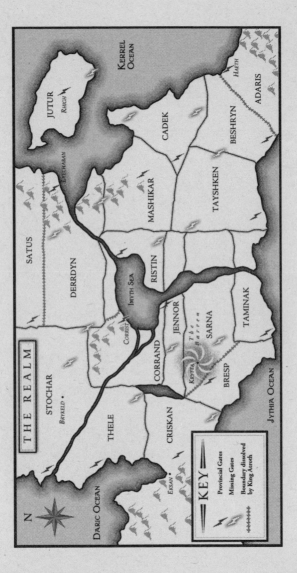

ONE

‒•‒

THE TIME IN the bottom right corner of my computer screen mocks me. I try not to look at it, but no one has come to the reference desk in over an hour, and I can stare at nothing for only so long. Even though this is only my fourth day working as a library clerk, I know every hour is going to drag. Theoretically, that should be a good thing. It means no one's swinging a sword at my head or aiming a gun at my chest, and I'm not in a situation where I'm forced to hurt or kill someone. The problem is if I'm not distracted by people asking questions, I'll be distracted by something else.

Or rather, *someone* else.

A flicker of emotion travels through the bond I share with Kyol. If I close my eyes, I can picture him perfectly, his firm, unsmiling lips and his dark silver eyes. His gaze is always steady and unwavering. He's one of the strongest men I know, and sometimes his presence unravels me, especially when chaos lusters spark across his face. It's hard to believe we haven't seen each other in three weeks. It feels like I've spent every day with him. I know when he's asleep. I can tell when he's sparring with his men or when he's talking to Lena, the Realm's queen. Right now, he's thinking about me. Probably because I'm thinking about him.

I force out a frustrated sigh because he's not the fae who

should be invading my thoughts. Maybe he wouldn't be if Aren were around, but there's been no sign of him or Lena or any of the rebels since I left the Realm. They're giving me space, time to live my life without interruptions from the fae. That's something I've asked for a hundred times in the last couple of years, but now that I finally have it, I'm going a little crazy. Not having any news from the Realm makes me restless.

Kyol's mood darkens when he senses my unease. I try not to let that affect me, but I fail, and a cloud settles over me just the same. *This* is one of the reasons I'm glad I haven't gone back to the Realm. Even though Kyol and I are in separate worlds, our emotions spiral off each other's until one of us is distracted enough to feel something else. It would be a thousand times harder to block him out without the In-Between separating us.

And the other reason I haven't returned? I lean back in my swivel chair and scan the quiet, calm library. This is the first time in ten years that I've been a normal human.

Of course, I'm not *completely* normal. If I were, I wouldn't see the pale, erratic lightning flitting across the skin of the girl who's coming in the library's door. Two of her friends are with her. I don't know their names, but I've heard them call her Kynlee before. She's shown up here after school every day I've worked. If she were human, I'd guess that she's fifteen, maybe sixteen years old. Her friends are definitely close to that age, but they're not fae. Kynlee doesn't really look fae either. She laughs and smiles like a normal American teenager. She's dressed like one, too, in jeans and a yellow crew-neck tee. The only thing odd about her clothing is the purple gloves that reach up to her elbows, but I understand their purpose: they keep her from skin-to-skin contact with humans.

When the trio walks by my desk, I lock my gaze on my computer screen to keep myself from staring at her chaos lusters. I'm almost certain her friends don't know what she is. Humans who don't have the Sight like I do can't see the lightning, but they would feel the hot, tingling sensation when it leaped to their skin. Or, in Kynlee's case, they would feel a surprisingly chilly sensation. Her chaos lusters aren't as bright as a normal fae's, which means she's *tor'um*. She has little to no magical

ability, and if this were the Realm, she and others like her would be considered the dregs of society.

After the *tor'um* and her friends take a seat at a table in the Teen section, my gaze ventures back to the time on my computer screen. Only three freaking minutes have passed since I last looked at it.

"You shouldn't scowl," the woman sitting next to me says.

"What?" I ask, turning toward Judy, my supervisor, even though I think I heard her clearly.

"It makes you look unapproachable."

Yep. That's what I thought she said. Surprising advice given that she's always scowling. Judy is a full-time librarian with twenty years of experience marked by gold stars on her name badge. Unfortunately, she happens to hate having degreeless library clerks like me manning the reference desk. But it's not my fault the city of Las Vegas had to make budget cuts, and considering that the most difficult question I've been asked today is "Where's the restroom," I'm pretty sure I can handle the job.

Planting a semipleasant expression on my face, I rest my folded arms on the edge of the desk and stare out at the bookshelves. At least the *tor'um* was enough of a distraction to break the cycle of emotion Kyol and I were close to being caught up in. He's not thinking about me anymore; he's concentrating on something else. What that something is, I don't know. We can't hear each other's thoughts or see what the other is doing, but we have a ten-year history together. Even without our magical life-bond, I know him well enough to link his emotions to his thoughts, and right now, he's not focused on my feelings. He's focused on his actions.

I feel myself frowning. I can't help it. Kyol is calm, but he isn't relaxed. My muscles mimic the tension in his. It's a strange sensation, one that makes me sit straighter in my seat. I don't think Kyol's worried, but he's heading somewhere that isn't safe.

I draw in a breath, then let it out slowly, trying not to let my emotions distract him. He was the previous king's swordmaster and is Lena's lord general. He's more than capable of taking care of himself.

Just like Aren is capable of taking care of himself.

A little stab of pain cuts through my stomach. I never thought Aren would stay away this long. I thought he'd come to his senses quickly, get over the life-bond, then come get me. The fact that he hasn't hurts, and I don't know whether to be pissed off about it or devastated. Most of the time, I'm both.

Still, I want to see him, but I can't get to the Realm on my own. Fae can fissure from any point they want to as long as they're not surrounded by silver, but I have to be escorted through a gate to survive the trip through the In-Between. Plus, if Aren wanted to see me, he would have found me already.

Which leaves only one conclusion: he doesn't want to see me.

I don't want to believe that because, if it's true, if he's letting this life-bond—a life-bond I didn't have any control over entering—break us up, then I was wrong about him. He doesn't love me half as much as I thought he did. He doesn't love me half as much as I love him.

I swallow down the lump in my throat and scan the library again, looking for something to distract me, but no one looks like they're lost or need help. There's not even a paper jam at the printer station. My gaze finally rests on Judy, who's flipping through a magazine. If she's doing that, then she shouldn't have a problem with me checking my e-mail for the hundredth time today. I've contacted every hospital in London looking for Shane, the Sighted human I left behind to save my friend, Paige. I lost track of him in a mass of panicked people at a concert, and I don't know if he escaped, died there, or ended up in the hands of the fae. The London authorities have assured me he never checked into a hospital, and I keep hoping he'll turn up somewhere safe.

As I'm reaching for the mouse, goose bumps break out across my skin. This is the only warning I ever get when a fae fissures into this world, so I stiffen, waiting for a flash of light. Several seconds tick by without anyone appearing in the library. I frown. Then I hear the soft rumble of the air-conditioning unit.

"Are you going somewhere?" Judy asks as she pulls on her thin white sweater. She's looking over the brim of her bifocals

at me, and I realize my hands are braced on the edge of the desk like I'm about to rise.

I clear my throat, then say, "I'm going to take a quick restroom break."

"Your regular break is in five minutes," she says. "You can wait."

If I really had to go, I'd get up anyway, but since I don't, I bite my tongue and sink into my chair. I really hate working with Judy, but hey, at least I have a job. And at least she's my biggest problem at the moment. It could be so much worse.

As if to confirm that last thought, my chest tightens as a new emotion surges over Kyol. It's not quite fear. He isn't hurt, and he's not fissuring in and out of a fight, but there's definitely some kind of tension running through his body. Maybe I was wrong about him being somewhere unsafe. He could just be sparring with someone or—

Kyol's pain hits me. It's so potent and solid, my chair flies back when I leap up. I try to build a wall between my emotions and his, but I'm disoriented—too off-balance to even stay on my feet—and he's too hurt to shelter me from what he's feeling. I stagger into an empty book cart, knocking it over and falling to the ground.

Someone hurts him again. It feels like someone's just punched me in the chest.

My vision blurs. I blink to clear it, then focus on the industrial-grade carpet beneath me, staring at the specks of white scattered through the blue pattern. Instead of blocking out what Kyol's feeling, I project what I'm feeling: the cool touch of the air-conditioned air and the solid, steady ground beneath my hands and knees. I don't think it helps. He's still hurting, and I'm a whole fucking world away from him.

"McKenzie?" Judy asks, standing over me.

I look up. Her face is blurry, but she sounds genuinely concerned.

"I'm okay." I force out the lie. I am not okay. I can barely think. If I'm affected this much by what's happening to Kyol, then he must be . . .

No, he can't die. I won't let him.

Kyol! I mentally scream. I've shouted his name in my head before, and even though he can't hear it, he can feel it. He's always sent a wave of reassurance in return, but there's no reassurance now. He's badly injured.

Another surge of pain washes through me. I squeeze my eyes shut as I reach up for the phone. My hand knocks the whole thing off the desk. I grab the receiver anyway, manage to hit "9" to dial out, but who do I call? Everyone who can help is in the Realm. How the hell am I going to get there?

After slamming the receiver down on its base, I look up. Kynlee and her two friends have shot to their feet and are staring at me.

The whole library is staring at me.

I don't have time to worry about it. I have to help Kyol, and I'm already on my feet and moving toward the *tor'um*'s table.

Kynlee's eyes widen as I stride toward her, but she doesn't move until I reach out to grab her arm. I manage to catch her gloved wrist.

"Hey!" the sandy-haired boy standing next to her says.

"I need to get to the Realm," I say. Kynlee's dark gray eyes widen even farther.

"What?" she squeaks.

"There has to be someone you can call," I say, taking my cell phone out of my pocket and shoving it into her hand. "Someone who can fissure."

"You can see . . ." She fades off, obviously figuring out that, yes, I can see the pale lightning on her skin.

"Call someone," I order, shaking her arm. She won't take my phone. I hear Judy calling my name, but her voice sounds as distant as the voices of all the other patrons murmuring in the background. I don't care that I'm acting like a freak; all I care about is getting to Kyol.

"I don't know anyone—"

"You have to!" I'm trying not to panic, but Kyol's fighting for his life right now. If she doesn't know a fae who can fissure me to the Realm, I won't be able to get to him in time to save his life.

I might not be able to save him anyway.

"You have to know someone," I say again, desperation leaking into my voice.

The guy standing to Kynlee's left—her boyfriend, maybe?—steps forward.

"I think you need to go," he says. There's a little too much uncertainty in his voice for me to really pay attention to him, probably because I'm a good decade older than he is. He's just a kid. So is Kynlee, I'm pretty sure. I shouldn't have a death grip on her wrist. I shouldn't even consider dragging her outside with me and—

"Okay," she says softly.

"Then call them now."

"No, I mean"—she glances at the guy—"I can do it. I can take you there."

My grip tightens on my phone. "But you're—"

"I know what I am," she interrupts. "But I can do it. Well, I can do it if you, uh, have an anchor. I've never been there before. Oh, and I don't know where a . . ." She looks me up and down. "Well, you're . . . you and I can't just, you know."

I'm human. She can't just fissure me to the Realm. She has to take me through a gate.

Beside her, her maybe-boyfriend frowns, understandably confused. "Kynlee?"

"It's fine," she says, turning to him with a forced smile. "I'll see you tomorrow, okay?"

She grabs her backpack.

"Are you sure?" he asks.

I don't hear her response to that. Tears pool at the corner of my eyes when agony surges through the life-bond. All traces of reason vanish from my mind. The only thing that matters is getting to Kyol.

Without any thought to the consequences, I pull Kynlee toward the exit.

TEN minutes later, when I'm pulling over on a deserted stretch of highway, I'm still not thinking of the consequences. I reach across the car to open the glove box and grab the small,

draw-stringed bag of anchor-stones I have stashed there. I overturn it on top of the dash, then shift through the stones. They're all opaque, almost like quartz, but they have different tints and weights. I find one that has a hint of red on one jagged edge. Lena gave me it before I left the Realm. It will take us to a safe house in the Outer City of Corrist, the Realm's capital. After that . . .

God, I don't know what happens after that. I don't know where Kyol is. I'll be able to tell his direction when I get there, but how long will it take to get to him? Will he be in Corrist or in some province a hundred miles away?

"That will take us to the Realm?" Kynlee asks, eyeing the stone.

"Yes." My answer is short, just like it was short with the other questions she asked on the way. I can't focus on anything but Kyol. He's weak and alone, and I swear he's just figured out what I'm about to do. Anger sparks along our life-bond, and if emotions were words, his would be yelling, "Stay the hell away."

The intensity in that unspoken order jerks me out of the semitrance I've fallen into. For the first time, I look at Kynlee and really *think* about what I'm doing. I'm not just planning to fissure with a *tor'um*; I'm planning to fissure with a teenage girl who might not know a thing about the Realm.

This is the stupidest idea I've ever considered. Fissuring isn't pleasant under the best of circumstances. Attempting it with a—

"Let's do this," Kynlee says. Then she's out of the car, slamming the door shut, and crunching across the dry, dead grass that lines both sides of the road.

"Hey, wait," I say, climbing out of my seat to follow her. Even though she's walking and I'm running, it takes a second to catch up. Fae, even fae who are *tor'um*, move faster than humans do.

"Where is it?" she asks, stopping next to the river that connects Las Vegas with the lake to the east. I assume she's asking about the gate.

I pinch the bridge of my nose. My head's pounding. I've never been prone to migraines, but I have one now. It's severe enough that I'm having a hard time focusing.

"I need to think about this," I say.

Kynlee strips off one of her long, purple gloves. "We're already here."

An alarm starts going off in my head. Why is she trying to convince me to go through with this? I'm a complete stranger. She doesn't owe me anything.

"Why are you so set on going to the Realm—"

My last word is more of a yelp. Kyol's moving. I can feel it in the way he braces against the pain. He's hurting so much he's not breathing—a big mistake when you need oxygen to fuel your muscles—and I can practically feel the strength draining from his body.

Reason flees from my mind.

"The gate's there," I say, practically throwing her at the blurred atmosphere on the bank of the river. She lands on her knees but doesn't hesitate to dip her hand into the water. She raises her palm to the sky, letting the water rain between her fingers. Each silver droplet glints in the sunlight. They seem to linger there, taunting me, drawing out the seconds and multiplying the panic ricocheting around in my chest. *Finally*, the drops solidify into a vertical slash of pure white light.

There's no room in my mind for second thoughts. With my anchor-stone in my palm, I clasp Kynlee's hand, then brace for the cold bite of the In-Between.

TWO

•-•-•

I'M PREPARED FOR the In-Between and the physical drain that comes from being led through it by a fae with little magic. What I'm not prepared for is the full assault of Kyol's emotions. His agony roars through me.

I drop to my knees, cover my ears with my hands as if that will somehow block him out. Holy hell, he's close. I didn't expect him to be in Corrist. The Realm is a big place, one huge continent divided into seventeen provinces, and I thought I'd have to have someone fissure me closer to him. The fact that I don't should save me some time, but not if I can't find a way to tune out his emotions.

Closing my eyes, I draw in a slow breath and concentrate on myself, on the fact that I'm not hurt. I'm whole and healthy. Whole and healthy.

On some level, it works. Some of my haziness lifts. I just need to maintain my focus. Keep Kyol out of my head and keep me in it.

Chaos lusters leap across my skin as I crawl across a wooden floor. The lightning only appears on humans in this world. It's bright and white, but barely lights up the room. I have to feel my way along a wall, trying to find a door or window or other source of light. My eyes are just beginning to adjust to the darkness when my hand finds a crevice that feels

promising. I reach up, fumble with the lock, then freeze when I hear a moan. I look over my shoulder, see a *tor'um* curled up on the ground.

Shit.

My sanity whooshes out of me, and Kyol's emotions whoosh back in. My head feels overloaded, and my heart thumps way too fast, a fact that makes me all the more aware of how slowly Kyol's is beating. The lull between each beat puts so much strain on my body, my lungs are having trouble expanding. It doesn't just feel like Kyol's dying. It feels like I am as well, and I have to mentally fight against the part of me that is okay with that, the part that's screaming that it would be better to be dead, too, than to live without him.

"My dad is so going to kill me."

The murmured words pull me back to the present. I focus on the *tor'um*, watch her slowly sit up as I try to remember exactly why she's here.

"Where are we?" she asks, her long, brown hair spilling over her shoulders.

I'm frowning. I can feel my forehead crease and my eyes narrow as I take in the empty, one-room house.

The one room *safe* house. That's right. When Lena gave me the anchor-stone imprinted with this location, she told me it would be stocked with weapons, food, and water. The walls are made of stone, but the floor isn't. There should be a few loose planks to pull up in the back corner.

And, more importantly, there should be a ward, a magical trip wire, set somewhere in here. If I break that, it'll send a signal to the ward-maker, and he or she will notify Lena that someone needs help.

I nearly trip over the *tor'um* in my haste to find it.

"What are you doing?" the girl asks. She has a name. I'm certain I knew it at one time, but it's so freaking hard to concentrate. There's only one name that matters, and he's dying a few blocks away.

I find a loose board, try to get my fingers beneath it. Goose bumps prickle across my arms. The ward is beneath the floor; I just need to get to it.

The *tor'um* says something else, but the board pops free,

and a telltale tingling runs through me before vanishing abruptly. The ward is broken. Thank God.

I jerk up another board.

"Hey, are you okay?"

I look up. The girl's hand is on my arm. She lets go when I meet her gaze, but my skin feels like ice where she touched me.

"I'm . . ." I squeeze my eyes shut. *Focus, McKenzie!*

"You need to stay here," I say. Then, when a sliver of clarity breaks through the fog in my head and I remember her name, I add, "Kynlee. Stay here, and when they come, tell them Kyol's less than a mile that way." I point to the west. "I'm going after him."

"Who are 'they'?" she asks.

A third board pops up. In the hole underneath is a midnight blue cloak. I throw it aside, revealing two small, lidless crates. They're filled with *cabus*—a foul-tasting fae drink that rehydrates and reenergizes—and magically preserved meats and cheeses. But lying between the crates is what I need: weapons.

"Who's Kyol?" Kynlee asks.

A sharp lance of pain strikes behind my eyes. Darkness spills through my vision. I brace my hand against the side of a building, feel stone that's rough and damp.

Damp?

I make myself focus. I glare at the crumbling mortar between the stones and realize I'm not in the safe house anymore. I'm outside on a street. Moonlight illuminates its craggy, uneven surface and the dirty, dilapidated façades of the buildings lining it have mold and moss growing between cracks. The rancid smell of sewage and decay clings to my lungs with each breath I pull in, and I have to fight down a gag reflex. This is *not* a good area of the city, and it's especially not an area in which a human should be running around in plain sight and alone.

But I'm closer to Kyol, and already, my feet are moving me forward.

My feet are insane, I think. They should be running toward the palace, toward help. These streets aren't quite empty—I pass a group of armed, young fae whispering and watching

me from across the street—and I feel more eyes on me than I see. More than once, a silver gaze peeks out of a darkened window, following my progress through the city.

I place my hand on the hilt of the sword that's buckled around my waist. Three steps later, I frown down at the weapon.

My first thought is, how the hell did I get it and the dagger that's sheathed on my opposite hip? My second is that this must be a dream. It's the Realm that's confused and groggy, not me. Any second, Kyol is going to come out of the door in front of me dancing a jig.

I laugh. Kyol isn't a jig-dancing kind of fae. I can't even see Aren breaking into a—

Aren.

His name centers me, and I cling to it, remembering his cedar-and-cinnamon scent and the way his lopsided grin triggers lightning inside me without so much as a touch. It's been three weeks since I've seen him. Three weeks since he pushed me away because of this life-bond. I have to get control of it.

I look again at the door in front of me. The building it's set into is a tall, three-story structure made of identical slate blue stones. Each floor has four square windows, but not an ounce of light comes out of any of them. Either it's completely dark inside, or the glass is painted black.

I try the handle, and when it turns, my feet take me inside, leading me closer to Kyol.

THE room I enter is magically lit, but the natural moonlight still visible through the open door is more comforting than the blue-white light from the orbs ensconced on the walls. It feels like I've stepped into the lobby of a hotel. That's the vibe I get from this place though hotels are extremely rare in the Realm, where fae can easily fissure back home to sleep in their own beds. But there's an elaborate, wooden desk to my left and a cluster of plush-looking blue chairs to my right. Behind them, a series of small squares within small squares decorates the wall, and a few feet to the left of that is a wide staircase. It narrows as it climbs to the next floor.

I draw my sword as I step farther into the empty room. Something is wrong about this place. It's too richly decorated to belong in a neighborhood like this. It's clean where everything else is dirty, soft where everything else is hard and sharp. The only thing the building has in common with the outside world so far is the smell. It gets worse as I make my way to the staircase. Kyol is up there somewhere. He's still weak and hurting, but I think he might be more . . . stable? That's the only word I can think of that fits. He's holding on to see me.

The warmth that swirls through me at that thought is laced with trepidation, and I almost lose focus.

I steady myself on the wooden handrail. Somehow, I'm already halfway up the stairs. I think my disorientation is Kyol's fault. He's fading in and out of consciousness, and I'm falling into and out of a walking coma.

I take another step, then another. The silence doesn't bother me until I'm almost at the top of the stairs. There should be a squeak or groan or something from the steps bearing my weight. Instead, I'm greeted by more silence. It's so unnatural, I deliberately tap my sword against the wall. The beige-painted surface completely absorbs the sound. Someone's used a rare magic here, one that absorbs the vibrations in the air.

Tightening my grip on my sword, I climb the rest of the steps.

At first, when I emerge onto the second level, it feels as pristine and untouched as the ground floor, but then I step onto the carpet. It's not plush beneath my sneaker. It feels soggy. When I look down, I know why. There are no bodies in the long corridor, but a ring of blood puddles up around my shoe as if I just stepped on a sponge. Fae disappear when they die, taking with them their clothes, armor, and anything they're holding or carrying on their bodies, but any blood spilled before their hearts stopped beating remains behind. That's what has happened here. Of course, I have no evidence that the fae actually died. As long as the building isn't protected by silver, they could have fissured out.

Or the blood could be from Kyol. He's not on this floor,

though. He's one story up, almost directly over my head. Surely, he couldn't have made it upstairs with an injury severe enough to saturate the carpet like this.

The staircase leading up is farther down the corridor. I wish it wasn't. I want to go directly to Kyol; I don't want to walk past the three open doors to get to the second set of stairs. This place sounds and feels like a tomb, and I'm afraid to peer inside any rooms.

The sticky, metallic scent of blood is getting to me, so I start breathing through my mouth as I make my way down the corridor. I'm not as freaked-out as I should be when the carpet continues to squish beneath my shoes. That's evidence that I've seen way too much violence in my lifetime. I hate this, the fear and tension running through me. I'd rather be back in the library, sitting behind a computer screen bored to death.

I grimace. Bad choice of words.

I'm nearing the first open door. It's on my right. I try to convince myself to keep my gaze focused on the stairs ahead, but my vision goes black again. When it clears, I'm staring at a large, silk-draped bed. It's in the center of the room, and lying on top of its sheets is a woman dressed in nothing but blood and gashes. Her eyes and mouth are open, the latter as if she was screaming. Or gurgling, rather. Her throat has been slashed open. I can see something white peeking out of it, some tissue or ligament or something. I don't want to know what it is. I don't want to see this.

McKenzie.

I don't really hear Kyol think my name, but he's trying to get my attention, projecting steadiness and reassurance in my direction. How he can do that when he's hurting so much, I don't know, but I use the strength he's lending me and turn away from the dead . . .

The dead *human.*

My gaze fastens on her face again. She's not fae. And the way she's been killed, her skin sliced open in long, wide cuts all over her body . . . I recognize this violence. She was tortured and killed just like the Sighted humans we discovered in London just under a month ago were.

My feet—my possessed, unreasonable feet—take a step inside the room. As soon as I do, the air beside me moves, sending goose bumps down my arms. My heart goes still one second later, just before I hear the whisper, *"Tchatalun."*

THREE

◆-◆

ADRENALINE JOLTS THROUGH me. I raise my sword as I spin, knowing only someone who wants me dead would call me *defiled one*. My sudden move surprises the fae. He barely fissures out of the way of my blade's path. Instinct tells me he'll reappear behind me, so I pivot again, slashing out as he steps out of the light.

His sword is drawn and raised. He deflects my attack as if he's swatting a fly and strides forward.

Kyol's fear spikes with mine. We both know I'll never win a sword fight against a fae, but I have no choice except to try.

I thrust my sword forward. My attacker steps left then his free hand darts out, catching my wrist before I fully register his movement. He shakes it hard, but I manage to hold on to my weapon with one hand and throw my fist at his face.

I'm off-balance—I don't even have my full weight behind the punch—but hate fills his silver eyes. Still holding my wrist, he shoves me into the wall. I go for his eyes, knowing I have only seconds to maim and kill him before he maims and kills me.

My nails scratch down his face. He hisses, shakes my wrist again, and this time, I lose my grip on my sword. It falls uselessly to the carpeted floor as the fae slams me into the wall again. My head hits so hard, my vision blackens. When it clears,

my attacker raises his sword to my shoulder. His blade is sharp, so sharp I don't immediately feel the skin peel away from my muscle as he slides it down my arm, following the path of one of my chaos lusters.

Agony surges through Kyol—he's trying to move, trying to make his way to me—and his emotions scream for me to run. I try. The blood sliding down my arm makes my skin slick. The fae loses his grip on my wrist, and I turn and run even though I know it's virtually impossible to escape.

I make it back into the hall, then into the next room. As I slam the door shut, I note there's another dead woman on the bed in here. I don't have time to process what that means; I'm trapped. There's no other door to exit through. There's not even a window.

Reaching down to my left hip, I take out the dagger that's sheathed there and wait for the fae to kick open the door. Instead, he slowly turns the knob.

I clench my teeth hard enough to make my jaw ache. I'm human. The fae is toying with me. He thinks he has all the time in the world to be slow and deliberate, but screw him. I grab the edge of the door as it's easing open, jerking it toward me as I thrust out with my dagger.

I'm aiming low—toward his groin since his torso is covered by *jaedric* armor. I end up slicing into his hip. Not a lethal wound, but he roars as if I've just struck his heart.

I think he roars, at least. Everything is still magically muffled, and I'm concentrating on the sword in his hand.

The door protects me from his enraged attack. His blade sinks into the wood, giving me the half second I need to strike again.

This time, I watch where I aim, and my dagger stabs up and under the *jaedric* and into the center of his gut. Then, as if I've done it a thousand times before, I twist the knife inside of him.

I don't flinch or look away when his eyes widen. I memorize his face, the sharp nose, his black eyebrows and eyelashes, and I note the name-cord braided into his hair. Light from a magically lit orb reflects off the cord's red and black stones just before his body disappears. His soul-shadow replaces it a second later. The white mist encircles my hand

and the weapon I'm holding, before it rises and gradually fades.

I stare down at my dagger's surprisingly clean blade. My hand isn't clean, though. It's red with the fae's blood.

Numb, I slide the blade back into its sheath.

"McKenzie." Kyol's voice is so weak, I'm not sure if it's in my head. I stagger against the wall, then use it as a crutch to inch back toward the hallway.

"Kyol?" I hear my own voice. The magical silence has lifted, probably because I killed the fae maintaining it.

I shouldn't have been able to kill him. I should be dead.

My hand leaves a streak of red across the wall. My arm throbs, but it's my mind that's truly hurting. It's being crushed by the weight of the life-bond.

"Kyol," I call again.

"Taltrayn!"

I step into the hall as his surname is called out. It's not until the fae steps into view that I recognize the voice's owner.

"*Sidhe*," Lena murmurs, grabbing my arm as I sway.

"Help him," I manage to say.

Lena lowers me to the ground, barks an order at her guards, then leaves my side.

I don't know how long I stay there, doubled over and digging my fingers into my knees. It feels like I'm crouched on the edge of eternity. If Kyol doesn't survive, I'll pitch over into an abyss. I can feel the life-bond drawing me toward it. I fight to keep my balance, and in my mind, I grab hold of the strand of light that connects us and pull. Kyol has to stay on my side of eternity. He *has* to.

At first, all I get from him is a loud silence, a static of a thousand weak emotions. Gradually, some of those emotions strengthen. One in particular snakes its way through the life-bond: concern. It's for me, of course. He's always so worried about me. I wish I didn't know that, wish I couldn't feel just how much he cares. If he hated me or at least cared a little less, my decisions wouldn't hurt him half as much as they do.

Bracing myself, I open my eyes and look up. My heart does a somersault when I do. Lena is kneeling beside him at

the end of the hallway, but his stormy gaze is focused on me, and it feels as if a tidal wave moves through the air. Kyol's always had a tangible presence. Without seeing him, you know when he steps into a room, and even injured like he is, he gives off the impression that he could annihilate an entire army with just one practiced swing of his sword.

And that's why it scares me to see him like this. Kyol was King Atroth's sword-master. He's Lena's lord general. He knows how to kick his enemies' asses, and I've never seen him hurt this badly.

Breaking eye contact, I use the wall for support and rise to my feet. God, I feel weak, like I'm the one who's lost half my weight in blood. My arm isn't bleeding *that* much. It's not a minor wound, but it's nothing near as serious as the injuries Kyol has.

I inventory those injuries as I make my way to his side. Lena's taken off his armor and cut open his shirt. Her long, slender hands are on his abdomen, and if the blood covering him is any indication, that's the wound that almost sent him to the ether. It's making him hold his breath now. My stomach clenches in sympathy when Lena puts pressure on the injury, but I'm thankful she's here. Lena and Aren are the only healers I know now. It's a rare magical ability that's in huge demand with all the violence in the Realm, and it's the only thing that's going to ensure Kyol lives now.

Seconds tick by. Sweat glistens on Lena's forehead, and her face is taught and pale. After she finishes with that wound, she takes his left fist in her hand and forces him to relax it. When he does, blood gushes from his mutilated palm. It's not just a deep cut; at least two bones are broken. Maybe more. A wave of dizziness passes over me as I crouch beside him.

"Steady," Kyol whispers. His eyes are closed again, but his right hand reaches for mine. I intertwine my fingers with his and move closer. A warm, solid relief runs through our connection. Being close to me makes him feel whole. It makes me feel whole, too.

My heart shudders at that realization. It's wrong. A month ago, Aren was the one who made me feel complete. The only

thing that's changed between then and now is the bond, and I won't let myself be manipulated by magic. I need to shut down my thoughts and feelings. I need to be clinical, objective.

But I need Kyol to feel better. I should slide my hand free from his, but I don't. I tighten my grip and lend him whatever strength I can. It's not enough. He grimaces in pain.

I can't stand to see him hurt, so I turn my attention to Lena. That's when I see the staircase behind her. Kyol is leaning against the wall at its base. When I first got here he was on the third floor. He's on the second now.

"You should have stayed where you were," I tell him.

"You should have as well," he replies evenly.

I watch his chest rise and fall with each breath he drags in. I was so afraid I'd get here too late, that I'd see him take his last breath and feel his heart beat for the last time.

"I couldn't," I say simply.

His mouth bends into a grim smile. "I know."

Beside us, Lena snorts, then mutters in Fae, *"Life-bonds turn Tar Sidhe into tor'um."*

That has the ring of a proverb to it. My translation: life-bonds make people do stupid shit. That's the only reason Kyol would attempt the stairs half-dead, and it's the only reason I'd let a—

Oh, crap.

I sit back on my haunches, my eyes wide.

Lena wipes the back of her hand across her brow, then meets my gaze. Somehow, she knows exactly what's leaped to my mind. "Do you want to tell him how foolish you were or should I?"

"She's okay?" I ask.

"She's fine," Lena says.

Kyol's brow furrows. "Who?"

"Kynlee," Lena answers. "The *tor'um* who fissured McKenzie from her world to ours."

"Tor'um?" Alarm jolts through Kyol.

"I wasn't thinking," I say in my defense. "I couldn't think."

"It should have killed you," Lena says, her eyes narrowing slightly as she studies me. She's not just throwing those words around; she really thinks I shouldn't have survived the In-Between.

"Maybe she's barely a *tor'um*?" I suggest. Regular fae have different levels of *avesti*, of magical reserves. It's possible *tor'um* could as well. After all, most of them can't fissure at all.

Kyol pulls his hand free from Lena's. It's healed now—*he's* healed—but he's weak from her magic and from blood loss. I can feel his muscles tremble as he releases my hand, too, then carefully rises to his feet. All thoughts of being killed by the In-Between vanish from my mind when he sways.

"Maybe you should rest a little longer."

He shakes his head. "I want you away from here."

The way he says that makes me frown. He doesn't want me here in this building, and for the first time, my mind is clear enough to process what I've seen. I remember the room downstairs, the lush, lobbylike feel of it, and I can visualize the room I was in. It didn't have any windows, just walls covered in silklike cloth and a large bed. The sheets were rumpled beneath the woman, but I'm certain she wasn't killed in her sleep. She was . . .

Shit.

"This is a *tjandel*," I whisper. I first heard that word just under two months ago. King Atroth's lord general threatened to send me to one if I didn't give him information on the rebels. It's a brothel where human women are imprisoned. Fae pay to have sex with them. They get off on the chaos lusters that leap to their skin when they touch, and some of them like tormenting the women, most of whom don't have the Sight. They don't see the thing that's raping them.

"This is the third one we've discovered," Lena says.

"The third?" I echo, disbelief leaking into my voice. "How many are there?" I thought there might be one, maybe two, because, really, how many fae can be demented enough to come to a place like this?

"I don't know," she says, wrapping her hand around my right wrist and inspecting my injured arm. I try to pull away. She's just expended a ton of energy healing Kyol, and the dark circles under her eyes indicate she wasn't well rested in the first place.

"Lena—"

She gives me a murderous look that *almost* makes me stifle my protest. "You look like hell. Your hands are shaking."

"My hands are shaking because I'm trying not to wrap them around your neck," she bites back. "Now stop being a fool and let me help you."

Fine. If she wants to further exhaust herself by healing me, she can go for it. I let her place her palm against the slash on my arm.

"We found the other two *tjandel* days after the humans were slaughtered," she says smoothly, as if she didn't just threaten to strangle me. "We were provided with a tip to this location."

"We thought they would be alive," Kyol says.

"Was this a trap then?" I ask, trying not to grit my teeth. Lena's magic burns as it heals. "Who gave you the tip?"

A few seconds pass before Lena answers, "Aren."

Aren. The pain in my arm suddenly subsides. Now, the hurt is lodged in the center of my chest.

"Where is he?" I should get an Emmy. My voice sounds completely normal, and I'm certain my expression doesn't change at all. Only Kyol feels the way my heart twists.

"Not in Corrist," she says, "or he'd have come the instant we heard you were here."

Would he? He hasn't fissured to Earth once in the last three weeks, and the last time I saw him, he was . . . crushed. I don't remember forming the life-bond with Kyol, but that didn't matter to Aren. He thinks I'm still in love with Lena's lord general, and that the bond will destroy any feelings I have for him. It won't, but I don't know how long it will take Aren to see the truth.

I don't know *if* he'll see the truth.

When Kyol draws in a breath, I realize my emotions are completely open to him. His aren't open to me, though. They're still very much there, but they're not overwhelming me like they were when I first entered this world. He's healed, and even though he's weak, he's strong enough to put his walls back into place.

I need to find myself some freaking walls.

Lena releases my arm. Her hands are still shaking. I don't think that's entirely due to the energy she just expended. It's getting to her, ruling the Realm and playing politics with the high nobles. *She* needs a three-week break from this world.

Kyol peels off the remaining shreds of his shirt. I lock my gaze on Lena. I know what Kyol's body looks like—muscular shoulders, chiseled chest, and strong, washboard abs. He's built like a warrior. I might have ended our relationship, but that doesn't mean I'm blind.

"The swordsmen who came with me," Kyol says. "Have they reported in?"

"No," Lena answers, her tone way too neutral. That catches my attention. I might not have been around for a while, but I doubt the number of swordsmen who've pledged loyalty to Lena has suddenly increased. She can't afford to lose any fae.

"Some still may, though." She accepts a clean cloth from one of her guards and methodically begins cleaning her hands. "Your attackers were concealed by illusions?"

Kyol's responses to questions like that one usually come quickly, and with military precision. This one doesn't. He hesitates just long enough to be noticeable—noticeable to me, at least—before he answers. "Yes. They were. This place felt wrong. I turned to order everyone to fissure out, and when I did, I must have bumped the fae who attacked me. His illusion broke, and I was able to redirect his attack."

He wasn't able to redirect it enough. His injuries prove that.

"You saw your attacker then," Lena says. "Was he an *elari*?"

Kyol's mental wall thins, but it holds. He very deliberately doesn't glance my way.

Lena lets out an annoyed breath. "I don't think she'll shatter if she hears."

"No," I say, facing Kyol fully. "I won't." And I'll kick his ass if he deliberately withholds information from me. He did that for ten years, and justified it by convincing himself he was protecting me.

His jaw clenches, and I'm pretty sure he knows exactly what I'm thinking.

"Yes, he wore the red-and-black name-cord that suggests he was an *elari*."

The fae who attacked me had a similar name-cord. I only caught a brief look at it, but there were two shades of red stones separated by black ones. Only the most prominent families keep tradition and wear them now. It shouldn't be too difficult to find out which family it is. As for the word, *elari*, I'm not certain I've heard it before, but it sounds similar to *enari*.

"You were attacked by a servant?" I ask, translating *enari* into English.

"A follower," Lena says without looking at me. "Already, a false-blood is opposing me, and his supporters are zealots."

A false-blood. I want to groan. Lena has a strong, legitimate link to the *Tar Sidhe*, the fae's magically powerful Ancestors, but not everyone who seeks the throne does. In the last ten years, when I wasn't reading the shadows of fae criminals, I was reading the shadows of false-bloods and their minions. They were considered felons, too, of course, but they created so much more death and destruction than the other fae I tracked. If a false-blood is responsible for what happened here, he'll be among the most violent and cruel I've ever encountered.

But if a false-blood is responsible for this, then most likely he's also responsible for the slaughter of the Sighted humans in London. The bastard used the same *modus operandi* in both places. The problem is *that* fae is supposed to be locked up in the palace.

"Lorn," I say out loud. "He's the one who's supposed to be behind all this violence, but if he's still under arrest—"

"He's not," Kyol says. His gaze locks on Lena. "She released him."

My eyes widen. "What? Why?"

"Too many of the high nobles were indebted to him," Lena says, glaring at her lord general. "The others, he was able to blackmail. I didn't have a choice."

I barely suppress a groan. "You caved to the high nobles? Again? Lorn's going to kill me, Lena."

"I don't think he'll actually kill you," she replies, expressionless. "Kidnap, threaten, manipulate, yes, but he'd see your death as a waste of a valuable asset."

"Great," I say. "I feel so much better now."

Lena closes her eyes in a long, most likely annoyed, blink. She's not a big fan of sarcasm. She's probably right about Lorn, though. He might not kill me, especially since his arrest was, apparently, so short. But three weeks ago, I was the one who suggested he might be manipulating things behind the scenes. He knew who was leading the remnants, but he refused to give us the name, and he outright admitted he profited from the war. Plus, I'm all but certain Lorn is the fae who anonymously gave us the London address where we found the slaughtered humans. There were just too many coincidences for Lorn not to be involved.

Still, it was all circumstantial evidence. It definitely wouldn't have held up in a U.S. court.

A little knot of guilt lodges itself in my chest. If Lorn is completely innocent in all of this, I'm going to feel like shit for falsely accusing him.

Kyol turns toward me. I don't look at him because I can already feel his censure. In his opinion, I have no reason to feel remorse for what I did. He's never liked Lorn, but Lorn has spies and informants everywhere. He knows the rumors behind every rumor, and if you pay him the right price, he can help you win a war.

"So there's another false-blood," I say, steering the conversation back to the subject that matters. "That's not the end of the world. Kyol and I have hunted false-bloods for a decade. We'll track this one down and take care of him."

No one responds to my words, and Lena's expression looks grim.

"What?" I ask.

"This one is different," she says. Goose bumps prickle across my skin. I don't think Lena's words caused them. My sixth sense is tingling.

"They're all different," I say absently while I frown into the open doorway on my right. The room's single bed is empty. No humans were killed there. That should make me feel better, but it doesn't.

"The others didn't kill like this," Lena says. "They weren't this cruel."

The fae who first pulled me into the Realm was this cruel.

Thrain might not have skinned humans alive, but he starved and hit me. He scared the hell out of me. I start to point that out, but I can't shake the feeling that something isn't right here.

Of course something isn't right, I tell myself. This is a *tjandel*, and humans were just slaughtered in their prisons.

Kyol notices I'm distracted. I feel him grow more alert. His gaze sweeps down the long corridor, and he takes a step closer to Lena. Or closer to me. I can't quite tell. It's his duty to protect both of us, but Lena is far more important than I am.

"No false-blood in the last century has had the support that this one does."

That statement makes my attention snap back to Lena.

"What do you mean?" I ask.

"We've lost—"

Something moves in my peripheral vision. I turn my head toward the staircase and see the light from a magically lit orb reflect off a fae's blade. He descends another step, then, just as I realize he's not one of Lena's guards, he lifts his sword.

FOUR

·•·

"**W**ATCH OUT!" I shout, grabbing Lena's arm.

The swordsman's blade is already arcing toward her. I can't get her out of the way in time, but Kyol's fighting instincts are insanely accurate. He's at the foot of the staircase, diving beneath the swinging sword and ramming his shoulder into the man's knees.

I lose sight of the fae when Lena's guards rush to protect her. By the time I get a better view, Kyol has one strong arm locked around her attacker's neck. His struggles to get free cease when Lena and one of her guards rest the points of their blades on the fae's cheeks.

His eyes widen with fear. *"I'm sorry,"* he blurts out. *"I thought you were one of them. I didn't know. I didn't know it was you."*

That's complete crap. The *jaedric* armor Lena's wearing has been bleached white, and long strips of blue silk flow down her legs, almost creating the look of a long skirt. It's definitely not the clothing that any normal soldier would be wearing, but even if her attacker is blind, I'd guess he was standing just out of sight on the stairs for at least thirty seconds. Maybe even a minute.

"You're not a follower," Lena says.

"Of course not," he replies, looking affronted, and I can practically see an idea form in his mind. His voice takes on

an overly innocent—and in my opinion weaselly—tone. *"I would never follow a false-blood. Only true Descendants like yourself should sit on the silver throne."*

"Why were you here?" Lena's question sounds like an accusation.

I feel my lip twisting. It's clear why he would be here.

"I was just . . ." The bastard looks at me and immediately shuts up.

I'm not sure when I drew my dagger, but my right hand is clenched around its hilt, and I'm holding it like I'm ready to use it. Add to that the fact that I'm covered in blood and lightning, and I can see why he might suddenly go mute.

If Aren were here, he'd make a comment about how terrifying the *nalkin-shom* looks. Kyol doesn't say anything; he just hefts the sleazy fae to his feet, then motions to one of Lena's guards.

"I can tell you what I saw," the fae says, as his hands are bound.

Lena turns her back on him. After the guards drag him down the hall, I ask her, "How did you know he wasn't an *elari*?"

"No name-cord," she says, sheathing her sword and crossing her arms over her chest.

"All the *elari* come from the same family?"

"No. They've twisted the tradition. The stones don't denote their ancestry. They're using them to show their allegiance to the false-blood."

She's definitely overworked. I can hear it in the slight edge of bitterness in her voice and see it in the set of her shoulders. Plus, she seems oblivious of the fact that she was just attacked.

"He tried to kill you," I say, nodding toward the fae as her guards manhandle him down the steps to the first floor. "Does everyone want you dead?"

She shrugs like it's a minor thing. "The bounty on my head surpassed the bounty on yours last week. Neither is a small amount."

Great.

Kyol picks up the captive fae's sword. Lena watches him slide it into his scabbard, then slip on the cloak a guard hands him.

"You reacted quickly to McKenzie's warning," she says.

He says nothing, but an emotion that feels close to uncertainty pokes a tiny hole in his wall. He *did* react quickly, especially considering how weak he still is.

Lena's mouth tightens.

"Escort McKenzie to the gate, Taltrayn," she says after a long pause. "You two need to talk."

WE make our way through Corrist's Outer City side by side, but we don't say anything for most of the walk. Lena sent only Kyol with me. For privacy, I assume. It's a cold night, so the cloaks she gave us aren't out of place. Even so, I watch the shadowed doorways and side streets, tense. Kyol isn't an inconspicuous man. He's well over six feet tall and broad-shouldered. I'm not fragile or small-framed, but next to him, I feel like I am. He's always treated me that way, like I'm something to be coddled. That's part of the reason I ended our relationship. He protected me too much. He still does.

A gust of wind blows down the narrow street, lifting my hood. I grab it quickly and keep it pulled low, hiding my face. It's never been safe to be a human in the Realm. We're all worth something to the fae, and thanks to Aren, I've developed a reputation as the best shadow-reader ever to breathe the air in this world. That part of the rumors Aren spread might be true, but the rest of it? I'm not a witch who's going to suck anyone's magic dry.

I don't realize it for several steps, but my mouth has curved into a small smile. As much as my exaggerated reputation annoys me, I can imagine the light in Aren's eyes as he crafted it. Rumor spreading is something he enjoys and excels at. He was able to convince the entire Realm that *he* was the fae who intended to take the throne from King Atroth, not Sethan, Lena's brother and Aren's friend. That protected Sethan and his supporters until the very end, and I have to reluctantly admit that my reputation has bought me a few seconds that ended up saving my life.

"You're doing well on your own."

I glance at Kyol. He's taken off his hood. We're near the gate, and the guards Lena's assigned to monitor it will want to see who's approaching.

I shrug. "I have a job."

"Do you enjoy it?" he asks. His voice is monotone, and his emotions are muted behind his mental wall.

"It's a paycheck." A *miniscule* paycheck. "I'm able to live on my own without help from the fae."

Half a dozen steps later, he says, "That's what you always wanted."

I answer with another shrug as the street we're on spits us out onto the flat, hard-packed earth that lies between the city and the gate on the river two hundred yards away. The silver wall that separates the Outer and Inner City is to our right, rising into the night sky and shining in the light of the moon. It's an oddly comforting sight. I've missed the Realm. I can't remember the last time I was away for so long, and even with the chaos lusters on my skin telling me I don't belong in this world, I feel more at home here than I did back in Houston. It certainly feels more like home than Las Vegas.

But I'll never be safe here. If the price on my head really is anywhere close to Lena's, fae will go out of their way to hunt me down. They'll risk their lives to take mine, just like the fae in the *tjandel* did when he attacked Lena. He was there to *enjoy* the humans. The *elari* killed the others who were there, but he happened to be an illusionist himself. They didn't see him. He could have escaped entirely if he'd fissured out, but he watched what the *elari* did and, once he learned Lena was there, he was blinded by potential profit.

We're halfway to the river. Three swordsmen stand guard on the silver plating that lines the bank. While we're still well out of earshot, I look at Kyol.

"You saw him, didn't you?"

He doesn't have to ask for clarification. He knows exactly who I'm talking about.

"I saw a shadow," he answers quietly. "An almost transparent image of the fae."

Lena thought so. *I* thought so. He moved too quickly to have just been reacting to my warning.

"You're seeing ghosts, and I'm fissuring with *tor'um*," I say. "I guess we can consider these positive benefits of the bond."

A wince of pain leaks through his mental wall, and I realize the implication of my words: if these side effects are the positive benefits, everything else is a negative.

"I didn't mean—"

"I know," he says.

"And I know you didn't have a choice," I tell him. "I know it was the only thing you could do, and that it shouldn't have worked, and if you were really thinking you would have—"

"It's okay, McKenzie," he interrupts again, more firmly this time. It's his way of telling me I don't have to say anything.

I feel like I have to say everything. The life-bond isn't easy for me, but it has to be worse for him. My emotions are too open. I don't have as much practice as he does at pretending to be hard and cold.

Because I know he's hurting, I change the subject. "Is this false-blood really different from the others?"

I'm almost certain the answer to that question is no, but he doesn't respond. My stomach tightens uncomfortably as we walk. I'm about to ask my question again when he draws in a breath to speak.

"Derrdyn Province has declared its support for the false-blood."

I stop walking. "The whole province?"

He looks back, gives me a single, solemn nod.

Lena's right. This false-blood *is* different. Sethan didn't even have a whole province declare support for him, and he was a true Descendant. Of course, Aren and the rebels kept his identity secret for as long as they could. Did this false-blood do the same thing?

"Who is he?" I ask. "Three weeks ago, he didn't exist."

"Three weeks ago, we were focused on Caelar and the remnants," Kyol says. He starts walking again, and I fall into step beside him. Caelar wasn't a false-blood. He was one of the king's swordsmen, and after Kyol killed Atroth, he organized the soldiers who opposed Lena taking the throne.

"We don't know the false-blood's name," Kyol says after a moment. "His *elari* call him the *Taelith*. It's an old word that means *anointed one*."

"Haven't they all thought they were anointed?"

"An entire province has never believed it before," he says, his gaze focused on the river. His emotions are locked down tight, but I feel an echo of sadness in him. Kyol loves the Realm. That's why he always put its needs before mine. It's always been a violent world—for my whole lifetime and for his—yet that hasn't discouraged him. He's devoted his life to protecting it, and in his quiet, steadfast way, he's always been optimistic about its future. He's clung to the hope that the bloodshed could end.

That optimism seems diminished now.

The urge to wrap my arms around him, or at least to take his hand in mine, is almost overwhelming. Instead, I pull my cloak tighter around my body.

We're almost to the river. I can make out the blur on its bank that marks the location of the gate. The guards aren't watching our approach anymore. They're focused to our right. I look that way and see Kynlee. She's walking toward us with two escorts. Trev is one of them. That almost makes me laugh. If I weren't protected by the fae he's pledged his loyalty to, I'm certain he'd be the first in line to collect the bounty on my head. He really ought to direct his anger elsewhere, though. I'm not the one giving him shitty assignments like babysitting *tor'um*.

Kyol doesn't say anything when he sees her, but an echo of the shock he felt when Lena mentioned a *tor'um* fissured me to the Realm leaks through our life-bond.

He looks at me.

"I know," I tell him, because what else can I say? I was completely out of my mind when I came here.

His emotions soften for an instant, but his hard, neutral expression doesn't change.

"They'll fissure you both back to Earth," he says, indicating Trev and the other fae with Kynlee. "If you happen to need me . . ."

He'll feel it if I do.

"I'll be fine," I say out loud.

He nods. When Kynlee and her escorts reach us, he says, "Good-bye, McKenzie."

I watch him walk away. One step. Two steps. Three. It feels like a gulf opens between us.

"Hey, Kyol," I call out.

He turns. The Realm's cold night air ruffles through his dark hair and wraps his cloak around his body.

"I'm really glad you're okay."

A month ago, fissuring between the Realm and the Earth twice within an hour would leave me disoriented for a few minutes. This time, I'm not even slightly dizzy. That's definitely a good thing, but it makes me uncomfortable, too. I'm not the same person I was a month ago.

The other thing that's making me uncomfortable?

Kynlee.

I watch the *tor'um* as she sinks into the passenger seat. Trev and the other fae brought us back to the Vegas gate so I could get my car, and even though she looks semi-innocent sitting there silent with her arms crossed, she can't be.

After starting the engine, I ask, "What is it you want?"

She toys with a tear in the fabric of her seat, not looking at me. "What do you mean?"

"Why did you fissure me to the Realm?"

"You asked me to," she says, like I was asking her to pass the salt at dinner.

"No, I asked you to call someone who could do it." My memory is murky, but I'm pretty sure that's true. "You volunteered too easily. You didn't even know what a gate looked like. Have you ever fissured before?"

"Yes," she says, looking up long enough to throw a glare my way.

I make a U-turn, then glance at her, my eyebrows raised.

"Once," she adds.

I stare a little longer.

"Three years ago," she mutters. "Across my living room."

I should so be dead right now.

"Traveling through the In-Between is dangerous," I tell her. "There has to be a reason you risked it with me. So, what is it you want?"

"I don't want anything," she says, sinking back into her seat.

"Kynlee."

"I don't," she says. "Look, I was just curious. My dad hardly ever talks about the Realm. I wanted to know what it was like. I've asked him to take me there; he won't."

"That's it? Seriously?"

"That's it," she says.

Great. I've aided and abetted a teenage rebellion.

"Your dad lives in Vegas with you?" I ask.

"Yeah." She stares out the passenger window.

I turn off the highway. "The city doesn't bother you?"

"The city?"

"The tech," I say. "The city's tech doesn't bother you?"

"Oh." She rolls her eyes. "That's why we live here. All the tech on the Strip makes the chance of a fae coming here and finding us practically zero. I get headaches sometimes, but I just pop a Tylenol."

I guess she doesn't have to worry about the tech damaging her magic. It's already wrecked.

Kynlee gives me directions to her neighborhood. It's close to the library, and it backs up to a newly renovated shopping center with a Walmart, a big electronics store, and several clothing chains. By the time I pull up to Kynlee's house, it's well after dark. Even though it's still hot as hell outside, I pull on the light sweater I keep in my car in case the library is cold. My pants are crunchy from the dried blood, but they're black, and it's dark. Someone would have to take a really close look to notice the stains.

"You can go," Kynlee says, when I get out of the car. "I'm fine."

I follow her to the porch anyway.

"Seriously, I'm fine," she tells me. "Thanks for bringing me home. See you later."

"I want to talk to your dad," I say, when she opens the door.

"That's okay. Thanks. Bye." Kynlee steps inside. I'm pretty sure she intends to shut the door in my face, but before she does, a man—a *human* man—steps into the entryway.

"You're late," he says, glaring at Kynlee. All I can do is

stare. I'd assumed her dad was fae. More precisely, I'd assumed he was *tor'um*. I used to think fae didn't live in my world— they just visited it and left after they got what they needed— but two months ago I met a group of *tor'um* who lived outside Vancouver. They were living fairly normal, human lives there. In the Realm, *tor'um* are looked down on and are all but shunned. At least they were when King Atroth was in charge. Lena accepts them, though. She and her brother were friends with the *tor'um* in Vancouver. In fact, Sethan died trying to protect them from Atroth's fae.

Of course, the reason Atroth's fae were there to begin with was because the *tor'um* were sheltering rebels.

I shake my head, dislodging thoughts of the Vancouver *tor'um* from my mind. This man can't be Kynlee's real dad— human and fae can't have kids—so he has to have adopted her.

"I'm sorry," she says. "I had to get another ride home."

"Who are you?" the man asks me.

"My name's McKenzie," I say. "I met Kynlee—"

"She works at the library," Kynlee says quickly. "I had to wait for her shift to end." She looks at me with wide, pleading eyes.

"Um." He's human, but he knows about the Realm. That means he has to have the Sight. He has to know what his daughter is. And if he's her legal guardian, he has a right to know where she was, doesn't he?

Her father stiffens. He looks at his daughter, then at me, then back at her again.

"Kynlee." His voice is low. "Where are your gloves?"

She's not wearing either of them. Her arms are bare, and the lightning striking across her skin is pale and erratic. Is it more frequent than usual?

It must be. He grabs her wrist as if that will help him inspect her *edarratae* more closely. "What have you been doing?"

Kynlee sighs in defeat. "I was just helping her, Dad."

"Helping her with what?" He eyes me.

Ah, hell. This is going to go so badly.

I clear my throat. "She fissured me to the Realm. I shouldn't have let her. I wasn't in my right mind, and I'm sorry."

He doesn't immediately slam the door in my face. He

peers up and down the street, searching for fae, I presume, then he shoves Kynlee inside, and says, "Stay the fuck away from my daughter."

If I had been standing one inch closer, the slamming door would have bloodied my nose.

FIVE

⋅—•—⋅

I T'S JUST AFTER 10:00 P.M. when I pull into my apartment complex and turn off the engine. Physically and emotionally exhausted, I climb the steps to my second-story apartment and unlock the door. My place is tiny—a six-hundred-square-foot, one-bedroom apartment in a bad part of town—but it was renovated just before I rented it, and I can actually afford the rent without help from the fae. It's mine—so is the used car I parked outside—and there's something satisfying in knowing that I can make it on my own.

"Sosch," I call after closing and locking the front door. The *kimki* has been living with me these last three weeks. I'm not sure if that's by choice. He showed up in the hotel suite I was staying in a few days before I moved out, and since a fae hasn't been in my new apartment, Sosch has been stuck with me. The only way he can get back to the Realm is by piggybacking through a fae's fissure.

I expect to find him curled up on my couch. He's not. He's on the kitchen counter—a place where I've explicitly told him not to be half a hundred times—and he's glaring at me like I haven't fed him in a week.

"I fed you this morning," I tell him, grabbing a box of Goldfish out of the cabinet. I pour the crackers into a bowl on

the floor. Sosch still doesn't look pleased. He holds grudges worse than any person I know.

Whatever. I'm too tired to cheer him up. I leave my keys on the counter, then walk to my bedroom door.

My *closed* bedroom door, I realize only after I've already started to push it open. I never shut it.

Instinctively, my muscles tighten, bracing for someone to come barreling out at me. The someone doesn't. He doesn't because he's tied spread-eagle to my bed.

What the hell?

The man is awake, his mouth is duct-taped shut, and he's glaring at me with murder in his left eye. His right eye is swollen shut. His lower lip is split, and I'm pretty damn sure I see blood on my sheets. He's had the crap beaten out of him, and I don't know whether I should cut him free, take the rag out of his mouth, or just leave him completely alone.

Something clatters to the floor in the bathroom on the other side of the wall. I curse under my breath, quickly pull the bedroom door shut, then dart to my couch, where I've hidden the sword that Lena insisted I keep. I get it unsheathed and spin toward the bathroom just as the door opens.

Lee, a human who quickly ended up on my shit list when I met him a month ago, steps out. He stops when the point of my sword touches the middle of his bloodstained shirt. His dark brown eyes look at the long blade, then his gaze meets mine.

"How did you find me?" I demand. "And who the hell have you tied to my bed?"

His eyes narrow. I have no idea why. If he thought he was going to just show up and tie a man to my bed without me asking questions or taking precautions to protect myself, he was wrong. He's lucky I didn't skewer him on sight.

"There's no need for that," he says, indicating my sword with a duck of his chin. When he makes a move to swat it out of the way, I turn the blade so that its edge, not its flat end, meets Lee's hand. Fae keep their swords sharp. It cuts into his fingers even though his touch was light.

He pulls his hand back, cursing and clenching it into a fist.

"I think there is," I tell him, pressing the blade's point

forward. Lee's a quick learner. He takes a step back to prevent me from drawing blood again; and then, he sways. That's when I notice he's keeping his right arm pinned against his side.

"I'm hurt," he says, moving his arm just enough to make me look closer. It's the perfect distraction. In my peripheral vision, I see his other hand reaching behind his back.

I could shove my sword forward, aiming between his ribs. A two-handed thrust with my body weight behind it would slide the blade all the way through. The thing is, I hate hurting people, and I am not, by nature, a killer. Lee must be gambling on that because he doesn't look worried when he pulls out a gun and levels it at my chest.

Alarm spikes through me. It's so sudden and potent I'm disoriented for a moment. Having a gun pointed at me makes my heart rate go into overdrive. It takes no effort, no skill to pull the trigger and end a life, but logic tells me Lee doesn't intend to kill me. He's here because he wants something, so I don't have a reason to be *this* worried. The fear moving through me isn't entirely my own.

"What do you want?" I ask, trying to shut my emotions off from Kyol.

"Is this the way you want to have this conversation?" Lee counters. "Or would you rather put away the weapons and have a seat?"

His forehead is covered in a sheen of sweat. I look at his side again, to the arm he has pressed against it. There's more blood on him than on the man in my bed. Lee wasn't lying about being hurt.

"Fine," I say, lowering my sword. "Let's talk."

I almost choke on that last sentence. Kyol's here. Well, not *here*, but he's in my world, in Vegas. Back in the hotel room I used to stay in, I think. I never told him I moved.

I'm fine, I try to project. Kyol should be resting and recovering from his injuries; he shouldn't be here in a city filled with tech. *Go back to Corrist.*

My emotions must not be speaking clearly. He doesn't fissure out. He's on his way to find me, using the bond like I used it in the Realm to find him.

I let out an exasperated breath, making sure he feels every

ounce of my annoyance. We've been apart for, what? Less than two hours? How much trouble does he think I could get into in that time?

I think calm, safe thoughts as I make my way to my couch and sit, hoping he'll figure out I don't need him.

Aside from a cheap coffee table and the even cheaper breakfast table with chairs, the couch is the only piece of furniture in the main living area of my apartment. Lee puts his gun away and makes a move to sit on the couch's other end. Sosch beats him to it.

Lee rethinks sitting.

"What is that?" he asks. He's breathing hard. I think he's trying to act like he isn't as hurt as he is. I refuse to acknowledge the sympathy that wants to bubble up in me. If Lee wants to pretend he's not seriously injured, I'll let him.

"My guard dog," I tell him. "Who's in my bedroom?"

Lee raises an eyebrow in my direction, maybe to see if I'm joking. I'm not really. Sosch has, in a roundabout way, saved my ass a couple of times, and it's clear he doesn't like Lee. He has good taste.

Realizing I'm not going to elaborate, Lee finally grabs a chair from the breakfast table and all but collapses into it.

"He's a vigilante," Lee says. My grip tightens reflexively on the hilt of my sword. Lee's father is—or rather, was—the leader of the vigilantes. Nakano's other son, Naito, who's a human shadow-reader like me, killed him in Boulder a month ago. It was revenge for killing Kelia, his fae lover and the first rebel I considered a friend, but Nakano was a cruel man bent on eradicating the fae. He'd gone so far as to create a serum that gives humans the Sight so he could build his own personal army. He didn't give a damn that the serum kills anyone who takes it six months later.

Lee has less than three months before the serum kills him. And my friend, Paige, has only a little more than that. Lee injected her with the serum because she was my friend. He knew I was involved with the fae, that I could lead him to his brother, and he didn't care who he had to use to get what he wanted. He was determined to kill Naito so that he could finally gain his father's approval.

"Why have you tied a vigilante to my bed?" I ask, sounding relatively patient instead of extremely pissed off. The only reason I'm able to manage that tone is because Lee couldn't bring himself to kill his brother when he had the chance.

"His name is Mikhail Glazunov. He was my dad's friend, his second-in-command. He's in charge of the vigilantes now."

And he's in my apartment. The way he looked at me when I opened the door . . . The vigilantes are all filled with hate. I don't want Glazunov here. I especially don't want him in my bedroom.

"Start explaining," I say in a voice so cold, Lee looks like he might be rethinking his decision to come here. Even Kyol feels the chill. He sends assurance through the bond, telling me without words that he'll be here soon and will take care of this.

I don't need him to take care of this. I need Lee to grab the vigilante and get the hell out of my apartment.

Lee clears his throat. "Glazunov . . ." He takes in a shaky breath. "Let me start this differently. I know that what I did to Paige was wrong. I didn't think the serum would hurt her because it didn't hurt me. I wasn't thinking about the future. I made a mistake, and I am sorry."

"You're sorry," I echo. "That makes everything okay. I'm just supposed to listen to you and—"

"I know my words don't make it okay," he cuts in. "But I'm trying to fix things. I need to talk to Paige. She has the serum research. Glazunov helped develop it. He might be able to find out what's wrong with us."

"He can find out what's wrong with you somewhere else. Why tie him to my bed?"

"He doesn't exactly want to be here."

"So take him away!" I yell as I stand.

Sosch darts to the arm of the couch. I feel bad for startling him, but I can't stand the fact that Glazunov is here. I can't stand the fact that Lee is either.

"You want to help Paige, don't you?" Lee asks, ignoring my outburst. "I was hoping you'd know a way to make him help us. I know fae have different magics. Can someone coerce him?"

I snort. "You hate the fae, and yet, you want to use their magic?"

"I was raised to hate them," he says. "I don't. Not anymore. But I don't trust them either."

"Funny. I don't trust you."

"Do you know a fae who can help or not?" he asks. He's annoyed. Good. I am, too.

"Why don't you ask the remnants for help?" That's who he was with the last I heard. Caelar and the others were all camped out in the Corrist Mountains just before they attacked the palace a month ago.

"I can't find them." He uses the back of his hand to wipe a rivulet of sweat from his brow. "When they learned what I did to Paige, they were pissed. They fissured me to Houston and told me to stay away from her. That hasn't been a problem because she's staying away from me. I went to her house, talked to her landlord, called some of her friends. No one's heard from her."

I cross my arms, making sure my go-to-hell look doesn't waver. It doesn't stop him from asking his next question, though.

"You haven't heard from her, have you?"

My expression doesn't flicker, but inwardly, I cringe. I have heard from her. Three weeks ago, I left messages on her cell phone, her home phone, at the bar where she used to work, and with several of her friends. She finally got in touch with me after a few days, and we've been talking a few times every week since then. The conversations were awkward in the beginning. We're on opposite sides of the war. Paige respects and trusts Caelar and the remnants, and since Lena's been hunting them down these past couple of months, Paige has no desire to see her on the throne. She won't tell me anything about the remnants except that she talks to Tylan, Caelar's brother, almost every day.

Of course, it's been almost a full week since I last heard from her. She's working with a chemist to analyze and dissect the Sight serum research we took from the vigilantes' compound. As far as I know, they haven't made any progress on finding out why it's fatal.

"You have, haven't you?" Lee asks.

"No," I tell him. It's not technically a lie. I haven't heard from her in almost a week now. Plus, I don't owe Lee the truth.

"Really?" His shoulders slump.

I start to make a smart retort, but stop on the first syllable. His question wasn't sarcastic. It didn't even sound like a question. It sounded more like his hopes were being crushed. Suddenly, he looks twice as pale as he did before.

Damn it, I don't want to feel one ounce of sympathy for him. I bite my lip to keep from asking him if he's okay.

"You've been looking for her, though," he says. "That's how I found you. You called the bar where she works. Your number showed up on the caller ID."

"They gave you my number?" It never occurred to me to conceal my identity or to use a public phone when I called. I'm used to hiding from fae, not from humans.

Lee nods, then winces as if the motion was too much for him. "They knew me. I showed up there a few times before to talk to Paige."

He's breathing even harder now. The conversation is wearing him out.

I stand. He does, too, and his hand goes behind his back to where his gun is.

"I was going to get you a glass of water," I say.

"I'm fine."

"You don't look fine, Lee."

"Are you close to finding her?" he asks, wiping his hand across his face again. "Will you let me know when you do?"

I'll talk to Paige about it. She's justifiably pissed at Lee, but if working together helps save both their lives, she might have to cave and speak to him.

Out loud, I say, "I'll think about it if you get Glazunov out of here."

Something flickers through his expression just before he meets my gaze. "There's another reason I'm here."

"Another reason besides the fact that you're bleeding on my floor?" A few drops have splattered on the fake hardwood. At least it's not carpet, but he seriously needs to get to a hospital.

"I need you to watch him for a few days," Lee says.

One second ticks by. Two. Three.

"Excuse me?" I couldn't have heard him correctly.

"I don't have anyone else I can trust him with," he says.

"You can't trust him with me!" I yell.

"I have to," he says. "Look, the . . . the vigilantes. Whatever you want to call them. Some of them died at my dad's compound but not all of them. Not most of them. And the lead chemist who created the serum is still alive. I found out where he is. If he and Glazunov have their research, and if they work together, it's our best chance to find a cure."

"No," I say, shaking my head. "Absolutely not. I'm not babysitting a man you've kidnapped, a man who probably wants me dead."

"I'm leaving him here, McKenzie," Lee says, leveling his gaze at me. "I won't be gone more than three days. All you have to do is feed him and give him some water."

He's serious. He's going to walk out of here and leave that man tied to my bed. I won't be able to just let Glazunov go. If he doesn't try to kill me immediately, he can come back anytime. He knows where I live. And if I call the cops instead, I'll have to explain how he ended up tied to my bed.

"You don't have a choice on this," Lee says.

Those words make my resolve turn to steel. I'm sick of people taking away my choices. I'm not putting up with it anymore.

I give a short, humorless laugh as I pace past the couch.

"I'm sorry," Lee begins. "It's the only . . . Where are you going?"

I don't answer. I reach my front door, turn the knob, then swing it open. As soon as Kyol crosses the threshold, I say, "He has a gun."

SIX

◆•◆

K YOL DISAPPEARS INTO a flash of light. By the time I turn
back to the living room, he's behind Lee, taking the gun
out of a holster hidden under his shirt and tossing it onto the
couch. A second later, he has Lee's arm twisted behind him
and a dagger against his throat.

"Are you hurt?" Kyol asks, not taking his attention away
from Lee.

"No," I tell him. "Just pissed off. He has a vigilante tied up
in my bedroom."

"Christ," Lee says, flinching when Kyol puts more tension
on his arm. "I'm just trying to save Paige's life."

"You're trying to save your own," I say, walking back to
the couch. His knees buckle.

"He's injured," Kyol says, lowering Lee to the floor. He pulls
up Lee's shirt, revealing his side. His black shirt and pants hid
just how badly he's hurt. There's so much blood, I can't even
see his injury. No wonder he's so pale.

"What happened to you?" I ask, my anger sizzling out as I
kneel beside the two men.

Lee's jaw tightens. "Glazunov got the gun out of my hand.
Grazed me with a shot."

"This is a graze?"

"It's just bleeding a lot," he says.

"You need to go to a hospital."

Kyol glances at me. I don't meet his eyes, but I know what he's thinking: I care too much. Here's a guy who broke into my apartment and threatened me with a gun, and I'm concerned about his well-being.

"Couldn't take Glaz with me," he says. He squeezes his eyes shut.

"Do you have bandages?" Kyol asks, sheathing his dagger.

"Yeah." Ten years of being around the fae has put me in the habit of having a fully stocked first-aid kit on hand. I walk to my tiny kitchen and grab the plastic Tupperware box from under the sink. I take it back to the living room, then hand Kyol a bottle of hydrogen peroxide. "This will disinfect the wound."

Kyol takes it without question, then pours the liquid over a two-inch gash that looks like it was made by a knife, not a gunshot. Lee's body jerks once, but that's the only indication of how badly the stuff burns.

"Can he help Paige?" Kyol sets the bottle aside. He knows how much I value my friendship with Paige. For the last ten years, she kept me sane. She never judged me, and I felt like a normal human around her. She's also saved my ass more than once. The first time was when we were roommates at Bedfont House, a mental institution we tried to sneak out of one night. She took the fall for that, letting me escape the place permanently while she had to stay and endure more counseling. Then, almost a month ago, when the remnants captured me, she gave me the key to my shackles. I wouldn't have been able to escape without her help.

Lee answers Kyol's question, giving him a quick summary of what he told me, saying again that Glazunov and Charles Bowman, the other vigilante he wants to abduct, will be able to find a cure.

"It's not guaranteed," I say when he finishes. "And why would they want to help you? They could stall and let you and Paige and anyone else who's been injected with the serum die. Or they might not even be able to find a solution. They've probably been trying to fix the serum since they learned it was fatal."

"We'll find a way to make them help," Lee says.

"You won't be able to trust anything they do."

"We'll have to!" Lee sits up straighter, his dark eyes flashing with anger. "I have to fix this. I won't let her die."

He's making this about Paige again. I don't know if he's doing that to get my support or if he really is more concerned about her life than his own. Maybe it's a little of both.

"I'll take the vigilante to Corrist," Kyol says, using the bandage I give him to wrap around Lee's ribs. The gauze and bandage aren't a permanent solution. Lee needs stitches. He needs a hospital.

"You won't bring the other vigilante here," Kyol continues. "You'll call McKenzie and arrange a place to meet."

Lee's jaw clenches. He might not hate the fae, but he admitted he doesn't trust them. I don't know if he'll trust Kyol. Of course, he doesn't have much of a choice.

"Fine," he finally says, slouching as the fight whooshes out of him.

I try to talk him into going to the hospital. He says he'll be okay—he just needs to rest—but I'm half-afraid he won't wake up if he goes to sleep. He's lost so much blood, and he seems to be sweating more now. His wound might be infected, or maybe since he's injured and weak, the serum will take his life early.

After Lee ignores my last plea and drags himself to my couch, Kyol touches my shoulder. "I'm going to the Realm. I won't be gone long."

He disappears into his fissure, and immediately I feel like I can breathe again. I didn't realize how claustrophobic I felt with him in this world. It was like I was trying to contain all of my emotions in a bottle not big enough to hold an ounce of water.

Now that he's gone, and now that Lee is passed out on my couch, I realize just how tired I am. I need to get some rest. How that's going to happen, though, I don't know. I have a vigilante in my bed and a half-dead man sleeping on my couch. Sosch, who's become accustomed to snoring on my feet at night, doesn't look too pleased with the arrangements either. He's on the breakfast table glowering at me.

"Looks like we're both sleeping on the floor," I tell him.

I need to shower and change clothes first, though, and that means I'm going to have to go into my bedroom. I really don't want to breathe the same air as the vigilante, but I walk to the door. As I'm turning the knob, I hear the sharp *shrrip* of a fissure opening behind me.

"That was quick," I say, turning to face . . . Aren.

The slash of light behind him winks out, leaving him framed in twisting shadows. For once, those shadows don't capture my attention. Our eyes meet, maybe for just one second, but in that single second, a million emotions crash through me. Even dressed in old, well-worn *jaedric*, Aren is gorgeous. On anyone else, the armor would look cheap and shoddy, but he makes it look durable and strong. I've always been physically attracted to him, a fact that infuriated me when we were enemies, but it's the deeper part of him that I fell in love with.

It's the deeper part of him I'm still in love with. I never doubted it these last three weeks, but the strength of that emotion makes me feel vulnerable. He could shatter my heart so easily.

The second of eye contact ends, and suddenly he's closed the distance between us. I expect some sort of greeting, an embrace, a kiss, a simple hello, but he lifts up my shirt with such urgency I stagger back. I grip his shoulders for balance as he runs his hands over my ribs. His touch isn't a caress.

"Aren," I say because I see the fear in his eyes. His right hand moves to my back, up to my shoulders. "Aren, I'm not hurt."

He's not listening. He continues searching for an injury I don't have.

I grab one of his hands. "I'm fine."

A chaos luster leaps from his skin to mine. The heat of our contact finally shows in his eyes. He meets my gaze again, and his pinched brow wrinkles even more.

"You're covered in blood," he says. He reaches up and drags his thumb across my cheek. Whether he's tracing the path of a chaos luster or touching a smear of dirt or blood, I don't know. All I know is I've missed his touch.

His gaze drops to my lips. He's breathing hard. I'm not breathing at all.

He swallows. "Taltrayn said you needed a healer."

"Hmm?"

"He said . . ." He fades off, and something more potent than worry is in his eyes. He closes his mouth, then opens it again as if he's determined to finish what he started to say, but no words come out.

His hand is still on my cheek. A flash of *edarratae* draws his gaze to it, then the lightning hits me, an erotic burst of pleasure that makes my entire body ache.

His muscles tense, and he's standing in front of me as rigid as iron when all I want to do is melt into his arms.

"Aren," I say, my voice uncharacteristically raspy.

"Sidhe," he curses. His stiffness disappears, and his mouth captures mine.

Instantly, I'm alight, burning from the inside out as if I've been scorched by lightning. The power, the need, the magical bite of his kiss seizes me. I dig my fingers into his shoulders, then slide one hand behind his neck pulling him closer, closer.

My lips part, inviting him to deepen the kiss. He does, and I moan, heat gathering under my skin. He tastes of the Realm, exotic and sweet and primal. I want more—the way his body shudders tells me he does, too—but he ends the kiss in a tender, exquisite pull that leaves my head spinning.

"Hi," I whisper when I can breathe again.

He gives a slow, almost imperceptible shake of his head before he responds, just as softly, "Hi."

We're still touching, still close enough that all I'd have to do to reignite the kiss is to press forward a fraction of an inch, but between two rapid beats of my heart, someone else's breaks.

I close my eyes, grimacing. There's no way I can hide this . . . this *need*. Even a world away, Kyol can feel it, and the tight ache in his chest makes me feel like absolute shit.

Aren's suddenly rigid again. He knows the reason why I grimaced, and in an instant, we're half a room apart. He runs a hand through his disheveled hair, an action that does nothing to quell my desire. I want my fingers there, wrapped in the sun-bleached strands.

"Why would Taltrayn tell me you need a healer?" he asks.

His voice isn't soft anymore. It's hard and emotionless. Somehow, I've managed to hurt him as deeply as I've hurt Kyol.

Fantastic job, McKenzie.

"I don't know," I answer because I need to say something to fill the silence. Plus, that's the truth. Kyol knew I wasn't hurt, so why would he . . . Oh.

"Lee," I say. Then, because I feel like I might explode if I don't move, I walk to the other side of the couch.

"He's the one who's hurt." I peer down at the passed-out human and concentrate on pulling air into my lungs one slow, steady breath at a time.

"Lee?" Aren walks to my side. When he sees the sleeping human, he asks, "Why is he here?"

"To tie a vigilante to my bed."

He's silent too long, and when I look at him again, his eyebrows are raised, waiting.

I give him a brief summary. He listens without comment, and that unnerves me. He's not acting like himself. He's usually relaxed and carefree, not quiet and tense.

"The blood on you is from him?" Aren asks, kneeling.

"No. Some of it's mine. Some of it is Kyol's." I wince when I say Kyol's name out loud. It feels like I'm driving a dagger into Aren's heart. He doesn't look up, doesn't give any indication that I'm hurting him now, but I feel like crap all the same. Kyol is the reason why Aren's stayed away from me these past three weeks. Aren was furious when he learned about our lifebond. The only reason he didn't strike Kyol down instantly was because he knew how much Kyol meant to me.

But, apparently, Aren doesn't know how much *he* means to me. I tried to tell him that I was his, that the life-bond didn't change anything, but he wouldn't listen. He was too hurt and angry to accept my words then. I think he might still be too hurt and angry to accept them now.

"Most of the blood is from the fae at the *tjandel*," I say past the lump in my throat.

Aren looks up. "The *tjandel*? You were in the Realm?"

"Yeah," I say. "Briefly."

His jaw clenches, and his silver eyes remain locked on

mine for a handful of heartbeats. I don't know what thoughts are in his head. He used to be open with me. He'd tell me what he was thinking and planning even when I didn't want to hear it. Now he just lowers his gaze back to Lee and asks in a completely neutral tone, "Why were you there?"

Because Kyol was hurt. But I won't say his name out loud again. Instead, I tell Aren, "The *elari* ambushed a group of swordsmen."

He unsheathes the dagger that's on his left hip.

"You know about the false-blood," he says as he carefully cuts off the bandage Kyol wrapped around Lee's ribs.

"Lena told me," I say, watching Aren place his hand over the gash in the human's side. Lee doesn't budge, not even when one of Aren's chaos lusters darts across his rib cage.

Oh, crap.

"Is he dead?" I ask, squatting next to the couch. "I'm going to kill him if he is. He's not, is he?"

"No," Aren says quietly. "He's not dead."

Is that a smile on Aren's lips? I stare at his mouth while he heals Lee, but the more I look for any slight bending of his lips, the more I doubt what I thought I saw.

He must feel me watching him. His head starts to turn my way, but then, he stiffens. His jaw clenches with what I'm certain is determination, and he locks his gaze back on Lee.

"Aren—"

"I'm finished," he says quickly, rising.

I stand, too. "Can we talk?"

"No."

His response is so terse, it feels like I've been punched. "No?"

"There's nothing . . ." His words fade when he looks at me again. He seems agitated, torn, and I hate that he's this distressed.

"This is about the life-bond?" I ask. He doesn't answer for a long time. He just stands there, staring at me with apprehension in his silver eyes.

"If it weren't for that . . ." He swallows. "If it weren't for that, I'd never leave your side."

I give a short, sharp laugh as my stomach does a somersault. "If you think I'll let you go after saying *that*, then the In-Between must have screwed with your head."

"I—" He snaps his mouth shut, shakes his head at himself. "Then I didn't mean it."

There's a slight smile on his lips, and *finally*, his eyes are lighter, less serious. I want to kiss him again. I want our arms wrapped around each other, our bodies pressed close, but when I take a step toward him, he takes a step back.

"McKenzie." He retreats another step. This time, an infuriated squeak cuts through the air.

Aren nearly falls onto the couch in his attempt to get off of Sosch's tail. The *kimki* squeaks again, then he darts out from underfoot, leaping straight from the floor to my chest.

"Sosch!" I yell, staggering under the weight of the fifteen-pound furball. "Sosch. Down!"

He moves to drape himself across my shoulders, his tiny claws pricking my skin.

"Sosch." Aren's mouth splits into a grin as he regains his balance. My balance is still off, though. I steady myself on the edge of my secondhand breakfast table, then bend down to Sosch's bowl of Goldfish.

"Here." I hold one up to his mouth. He devours it and the next two I give him. "Now down. Perch."

Sosch jumps off my shoulders, stops at my feet, then raises his front legs off the ground. Balanced on his hind legs, he stretches up just past my knees.

"Perch?" Aren asks, staring as the *kimki* eats two more crackers.

I nod. "It's different from 'sit.' I thought about using 'stand,' but 'perch' is cuter."

"Cuter?"

I frown at Aren, not getting the tone in his voice. He's not quite annoyed. It's more like he's . . . offended?

"Is something wrong?" I ask.

"You taught him . . . tricks?"

"To perch and sit and roll over, yeah."

He shakes his head. "You can't teach a *kimki* tricks."

"Obviously, you can."

"No, you . . . you just don't. They're *kimkis*, McKenzie. They're not"—he waves his hand as he searches for the right word—"pets." He almost chokes on that last word.

"It's not a big deal, and you do it all the time when you tell him to jump on your shoulders." I grab another Goldfish, then order, "Up."

Sosch leaps to my outstretched arm, then back to my shoulders.

"That's different. I wanted him to come with me, not to perform. This is . . . It's . . . It's . . ."

I've never seen Aren like this, so flabbergasted. It's funny, and I'm tempted to see if Sosch will start swinging his head back and forth when I say "dance," but he's still working on that trick, and so far, he's only done it when I play Matchbox Twenty.

But I *don't* tell Sosch to dance. Instead, I help Aren out. "It's sacrilege?"

"Yes!" Aren says, grabbing onto the word. "Sacrilege. *Kimkis* are endangered and wild. They do what they want, and sometimes their desires line up with yours, but . . ."

He fades off when Sosch nuzzles his furry head under my chin. Aren's eyes are still wide, still astounded, and I think maybe even a little . . .

I grin. "You're jealous."

Aren's gaze locks on my mouth. He's confessed to loving my smiles. He's told me he thinks they're rare, like a magic that went extinct during the *Duin Bregga*, but they were only scarce because we were enemies, and we were fighting a war.

"Jealous of a *kimki*?" The corner of his mouth tilts up. "Never."

"Of me," I say, stepping toward him. "I've stolen your pet."

"I told you"—he reaches up and glides his hand down Sosch's long back—"they're not pets, *nalkin-shom*."

Nalkin-shom. Shadow-witch. The title should infuriate me, but it doesn't, not when it comes from his lips, and especially not when his voice is deep and gently teasing.

"If I knew all it would take to get you here was Sosch," I say, "I would have sent a ransom note weeks ago."

His smile makes chaos lusters ricochet through my stomach. He's standing close, so he can pet Sosch, and his cedar-and-cinnamon scent makes warmth flood through me.

"I've missed you," I say.

His silver eyes meet mine. "You make me lose my focus."

"Good." I smile.

His head lowers toward mine, and his *jaedric* cuirass moves as his chest rises and falls beneath it.

My skin tingles. I tilt my head slightly as I lean toward Aren, not figuring out that the sensation is a warning until after a fissure cuts through the room. Kyol steps out of the slash of light with Naito, and the warmth that filled me half a second ago instantly chills.

And just like that, I've lost Aren. He moves away, and I swear even Sosch lets out a sad sigh.

SEVEN

◆·◆

"DID EVERYTHING GO okay?" Aren asks, turning his back on me. I focus on Naito, too, almost thankful for the distraction. *Almost.* I'd be more thankful if he and Kyol had waited at least a few more minutes before fissuring here.

"No losses," Naito answers, but his face is dark when his gaze locks on Lee, who's still asleep. Naito walks to the couch, then smacks his brother on the head. "Wake up."

Lee's body jerks, but he doesn't open his eyes.

Naito grabs a fistful of his bloodstained shirt and yanks him off the cushions. Lee moves again, this time more alert than before, but I don't think he realizes where he is or what's going on until Naito slams him against the wall. I wince when I hear something metallic jiggle in my neighbor's apartment.

"Is Caelar working with the false-blood?" Naito demands, inches from Lee's face.

"What?" Lee grabs at Naito's hands.

"Is Caelar working with the false-blood!"

"I don't know," Lee says, trying to shove his brother away. Naito has my complete attention now, too. If he's implying what I think he is, this could be majorly bad news.

"Why was he in Bardur?" He slams Lee against the wall again.

"I don't fucking know!" Lee yells. This time, he twists out of Naito's grasp.

"Hey!" I step between them before this fight gets louder. "If one of my neighbors calls the cops, I'm screwed." I nod toward Lee. "He says he hasn't talked to the remnants."

"And you suddenly believe everything he says?" Naito demands.

"Of course not," I say, but Naito still looks like he's about to kill his brother. I completely understand the sentiment, but I seriously do not need a dead body in here.

"What happened in Bardur?" Aren asks. He's leaning against my breakfast table now, looking relaxed and unruffled. Someone could tell him an army just fissured behind him, and he'd shrug it off and come up with a crazy plan to counter the hiccup.

"Nimael was there," Naito says, some of the tension finally draining from his muscles. "So was Caelar. They were meeting in a silver-protected warehouse in the middle of the city."

"Who's Nimael?" I ask.

"We think he's the false-blood's second-in-command," Aren tells me. I meet his eyes, uneasiness churning in my stomach. A month ago, Lena was worried about Caelar finding a Descendant who could rival her bloodline. If he presented an alternative ruler to the high nobles, they might have considered that fae over her. But Caelar never found someone willing to rule, and he lost so many fae in his last-ditch effort to retake the palace that he and the remnants aren't as much of a threat now as they were before.

But if he joins forces with a false-blood . . .

I glance at Kyol. He knows Caelar well. They were colleagues back when the king was alive, and Kyol respects him. He's always said Caelar wouldn't support a false-blood. Does he still believe that? Neither the life-bond nor Kyol's expression gives any indication of how he feels.

I turn back to Aren. "You think Nimael is the second-in-command or you know he is?"

Sosch hops up onto the breakfast table.

"If he's not his second," Aren says, sliding his hand over the *kimki*'s back, "he's close to it. He'll be able to give us in-

formation on the false-blood." He looks at Naito. "I take it you weren't able to capture him?"

Naito shakes his head. "He double fissured. I didn't pinpoint his location accurately enough."

The last part is said with more than a hint of aggravation in his voice. It's directed at himself, I think, but I can't help feeling responsible on some level. If I'd been there, chances are, Lena's fae would have caught Nimael before he was able to open a second fissure and escape. The maps I draw when I read the shadows are incredibly accurate. That's why Aren risked abducting me from my college campus a few months ago—the rebels almost never escaped when I was there to track them. Fae who are physically fit can fissure over and over again as long as they don't move more than twenty or thirty feet from their original location, but if they fissure farther away than that, it takes them almost a minute to recover enough to disappear into the In-Between again. That's plenty of time for the fae who see my maps to fissure to their location and capture or kill them.

"Nimael knows we're after him now." Kyol's level voice cuts into my thoughts.

"He'll go underground," Aren agrees. "Fortunately, that means we still have a chance." He hops off my table. "I'll find him again."

I'll read his shadows for you. I press my lips together to hold the words back. I'm not available to help. I have a job, and I'm supposed to *like* the normal life I'm building for myself. I don't need to screw it up further by shadow-reading again.

But then, I've never been able to turn my back on the people I care about either.

"It will probably take me a few days to learn anything," Aren says to Naito. "You should get some rest."

Naito nods, then turns to me, and asks, "Where's Glazunov?"

Glazunov. Right. One catastrophe at a time.

"My bedroom," I say, giving Lee one last pissed-off glare before I walk to the door and open it for Naito. He strides past me, straight to the bed, then draws a dagger from its sheath on his right hip. Glazunov is still awake and furious, but Naito

doesn't waste a second. He grips his dagger high up on the hilt then slams the pommel into Glazunov's temple. The vigilante head whips to the left, then he lies there, completely still.

I *really* need to learn the trick to knocking someone out like that.

"You have a car I can borrow?" Naito asks, using the dagger to cut through the duct tape binding the vigilante's wrists and ankles to my bed.

My jaw clenches. Naito needs to drive Glazunov to a gate so that the vigilante can survive fissuring to the Realm, but I don't want him in my car. If he wakes up and catches someone's attention, the license plate will lead back to me. Again, the last thing I need is cops knocking on my door.

"We can take my car," Lee offers from just behind me.

Naito slices through the last of the duct tape, then looks up. His nostrils flare slightly, and the grip he has on his dagger's hilt makes his knuckles turn white. The gate is only fifteen minutes from my apartment, but I'm not sure Naito and Lee can make it that far without someone ending up dead.

Naito shoves his dagger back into its sheath.

"Help me get him out of here," he says.

I let out a breath, then move out of Lee's way. When I do, a familiar, tingling sensation moves across my skin. I step back into the living room, but the fissure has already closed. It was Aren's fissure.

I bite the inside of my cheek while the shadows his fissure left behind twist through my vision. My hands itch to draw them out. If I had a pen and paper, I could pinpoint where he's gone. Without it, all I know is that he's in the Realm. I don't know whether to be hurt or pissed off. I know he has things to do back in Corrist, responsibilities that he can't put off, but he needs to . . . He needs to get over the life-bond and talk to me.

I wrench my gaze away from the shadows when Naito and Lee drag Glazunov out of my bedroom. The vigilante is slung between them, one of his arms thrown over each of their shoulders and his head lolling with each step they take. To me, he looks half-dead. To my neighbors, I hope he looks passed-out drunk.

I open the door, then follow them out. From the second-floor landing, I watch as they make their way down the stairs, gripping the rusty rails for balance. They manage to avoid the beer bottles and trash my lovely neighbors have left on the steps. I scan the parking lot, looking for anyone who might see them. It's dark and empty right now—the landlord seriously needs to fix the lights—but that doesn't mean someone isn't watching from a window. If they are, hopefully they'll believe Naito and Lee are just helping out a friend.

Of course, most drunk guys' friends don't stuff them into trunks.

"I don't like this place," Kyol says from behind me. He has his emotions locked down tight, but that doesn't mean I don't feel him. There's a steady pull, a constant awareness, of where he is.

"It's affordable," I say, watching as Lee pulls out of the parking spot. Truthfully, I don't like this place that much either. At least once a week, the police show up to settle some argument or domestic dispute, but this is the first home I've ever paid for on my own. Before Atroth was killed—and before I realized how violent he'd become and how much he had misled me—he paid for my college tuition and my apartment in Houston. That never sat well with me because the money wasn't exactly obtained legitimately, but I couldn't have survived without it. I can now, and if I keep my job and watch my finances, this apartment will be temporary.

When the taillights of Lee's car disappear around the corner, I head back inside. Kyol follows, closing the door behind him.

"I want you to move in with Naito," he says.

"What?" I ask, not bothering to hide my surprise as I turn to face him. "Naito's house is in Colorado."

"It would be safer for you," Kyol says.

"This place is safe." Safe-ish.

The protectiveness Kyol feels toward me leaks through his mental wall. He plugs the holes quickly, but that doesn't stop a warm, yearning feeling from swirling through my stomach. I draw in a slow breath, doing my best to quiet my emotions.

"Look, I'm okay here, Kyol," I tell him gently. "You'll fissure

Glazunov to the Realm, and the other vigilantes don't know where I live. Neither do the remnants."

"Or Lorn," Kyol says. "Or the false-blood. Many people want you dead, McKenzie."

"You're worried about Lorn?" I ask, trying to divert the conversation.

"He might not be entirely responsible for the war," Kyol says, "but he's not a good man, and he knows you had something to do with his imprisonment. He'll sell information on you to the false-blood if he has the opportunity."

I shake my head. "I have a job here." At least, I did this morning. "I can't move in with Naito."

He doesn't respond to that, he just stands there as grim-faced as usual. Or maybe, more grim-faced than usual. He's always been a solemn man, one with a million responsibilities on his shoulders, but the weight he carries seems heavier now.

"Then . . . be careful," he finally says. "Please."

I give him a little smile. "I promise I won't go fissuring around with a *tor'um* again."

Amusement leaks through the bond. It doesn't alter his expression, though. He's too much the perfect soldier. Always has been.

He says a silent good-bye with his nod, then steps away from me to open a fissure. When he does, Sosch *chirp-squeaks* from somewhere behind me. I turn, but the damn *kimki* scurries between my legs. I reach for the arm of the couch to catch my balance, and my hand knocks against the hilt of the unsheathed sword I leaned against it earlier. It starts to fall, and the image of a bleeding *kimki* flashes in my mind.

It's a ridiculous image—the worst Sosch might get is a nick—but I'm already moving. I catch the end of the blade on the top of my sneaker, flip it up. It arcs end over end in the air. Me around flying swords? Not a good combination. But my right hand darts out and wraps around the hilt as if I've done the move a thousand times before.

I stare wide-eyed at the blade as Sosch disappears into the fissure. Kyol's still standing here. His jaw clenches as he meets my gaze, and I know he's thinking exactly the same thing

I am: three weeks ago, there's no way I would have caught the sword.

I don't sleep in my bed. I don't sleep much at all. After I shower, I toss my dirty and bloodstained sheets into a laundry basket then curl up on the floor with a pillow that, fortunately, wasn't used by the vigilante. Not surprisingly, my dreams are unpleasant. My recurring nightmares about Thrain, the false-blood who dragged me into the Realm a decade ago, aren't the worst this time. The worst are the ones where my friends are dead. Lena's been made *tor'um*, I find Naito skinned alive and hanging from the rafters in the palace, and the head of Shane, the Sighted human I haven't seen since I lost him in London, is delivered to me in a box.

As for Kyol? I watch an executioner stab a sword through Kyol's chest over and over and over again, feeling every wound as if it's piercing my own heart. The high nobles are looking on, satisfied grins on all their faces because they're killing the fae who killed their king.

I can't wake from any of those visions. It's only my last nightmare that wrenches my soul so hard I lurch upright, sweat-soaked, wheezing, and with Aren's agonized scream echoing in my ears. He's locked in silver-plated shackles and forced to watch as I'm thrown onto a bed in a *tjandel*. We're both fighting, him trying to get to me and me trying to get away from the sick bastards who want to rape and skin me. The dream only ends when one of those assholes draws a dagger across my throat.

Wide-eyed, I stare at the foot of my bed from my pile of blankets on the floor, attempting to calm down my racing heartbeat. How much of my fear and horror Kyol felt, I don't know. He isn't in my world, but his wall is down. He's worried.

Just a dream, I think, reassuring both him and myself. *I'm okay.*

After a few deep breaths, I am for the most part all right. I've had nightmares my whole life. They've never predicted the future. There's no reason for them to become premonitions now.

I shove away the last traces of the dreams, then climb to my

feet. I'm lucky I woke when I did—it's later than I expected—and I have to throw on my work clothes and skip breakfast to make it to work on time. Judy's there and waiting. When she asks what happened yesterday, I tell her I had a seizure. It's clear she doesn't believe me, but she lets me stay on the condition that, if it happens again, I either need a note from my doctor or I'll be let go. Considering how I left and the fact that I practically kidnapped Kynlee, that's more than fair, so I thank her and park myself behind the reference desk.

I'm by myself for the first hour, so I go through my normal routine. I check my e-mail, hoping that I finally have some news on Shane. Not only have I contacted all the London hospitals, but I've talked to the police and even the U.S. embassy. None of them have seen or heard from him, and they're sick of my calls. It doesn't help that he didn't enter the country legally.

Paige swears the remnants didn't take him. She doesn't have a reason to lie.

But *someone* had to take him. If she's not lying, then . . .

Then I don't know what the hell happened to him.

I click off my e-mail—the three new messages I received were all spam—and scan the library. There's no sign of Kynlee. That's not unusual given that it's a Saturday morning, and she's usually only here after school. I totally abuse my position and access the library's patron records. Her last name is Walker, her dad's name is Nick, and apparently, they've lived here for at least the last six years. He's only checked out a few books over the years, nothing interesting. Even with a fae as a daughter, he's doing a much better job at living a normal human life than I ever did.

"Excuse me."

I tear my gaze away from the screen. A woman is standing at the desk.

"Sorry," I say, clicking off Nick's account information. "Can I help you?"

Hers isn't the last question I answer. We get busier during lunch, so I don't get a chance to call Paige until my break. I need to tell her about my conversation with Lee, but mostly, I want to ask her about Caelar. If he is working with the false-blood, Lena needs to know—and Paige needs to stay the hell

away from him and all the remnants. The false-blood is skinning humans. Paige chose her side, but she was my only human friend for almost a decade, and I'm the reason she's become entangled in the fae's world. She at least deserves a warning.

Paige doesn't answer my call, though. This is the longest we've gone without talking since I left the Realm. I'm sure she's probably okay—her cell phone might be dead or lost—but I can't completely shake off the feeling of dread that crawls across my shoulders.

I leave a voice mail telling her we need to talk.

A day passes. Then another and another. I should be relaxing into my normal, human life, but every morning, I wake up more tense and stressed out than the last one. Paige hasn't called me back. Neither has Lee, and the time I spend not working drags by almost as slowly as the time when I am. Hell, I even miss Sosch, who abandoned me when he leaped into Kyol's fissure.

I check the time on my computer screen—it's just after 3:00 P.M. A little less than an hour until I get off and go home to an empty apartment.

The thought has crossed my mind that today is a weekday, and if Kynlee sticks to her normal schedule, she should be here this afternoon. I have half a mind to make her take me to the Realm again. I won't. Not only is it dangerous for both of us, but her dad seems like a sling-a-shotgun-over-his-shoulder kind of man.

Still, my gaze keeps going to the Teen section. I'm curious about her, and I want to know if any other *tor'um* live in the area. Do they know any fae at all? Or is her dad keeping them one hundred percent isolated from her people?

"McKenzie?"

"Yes? Can I help—" I choke off my words when my gaze swings toward the voice. There, standing just in front of the reference desk, is Trev. I open my mouth to ask what's wrong, but close it quickly because I'm not on reference duty alone. A librarian named Rachel is here, and since she's not staring at Trev's *jaedric* armor or protesting the presence of the sword

belted around his waist, he has to be invisible. Fae almost always are when they're in my world.

Rachel's helping a patron, so I give Trev my best questioning look.

"We need you in Tholm," he says.

"Tholm?" I cover that question with a cough. Trev nods. Normally, I'd balk at fissuring to that city. Tholm isn't exactly in the middle of nowhere, but the nearest gate is in Corrist, a full day's walk away. That's fine if you're fae, but not if you're human. Twenty-something hours of nonstop walking pretty much sucks. It doesn't, however, suck as much as watching the clock in my world while wondering what's going on in the fae's.

And, fortunately, tomorrow's my day off.

I'm about to stand up when an older man approaches the desk. Trev steps out of the way at the last second.

"Can you help me find information on World War II?" the man asks.

"Um, yes," I say. My brain is so wrapped up in the Realm and the fae, it's hard to mentally shift gears, and his request is vague. I should ask him questions to narrow down exactly what he wants, but I just point to the Nonfiction section and say, "940s."

He thanks me and moves on, but there's a woman in line after him, and another man waiting. It figures that we'd be busy at the most inconvenient time.

"How can I help you?" I ask the woman.

"The computer won't let me sign in."

"I need an answer now," Trev says.

I throw Trev the tiniest glare, then say to the woman, "The pin number is the last four digits of your phone number."

Nine times out of ten, that solves the problem, but I use the excuse to leave the reference desk and follow the woman to her computer terminal.

"I won't wait any longer," Trev grates out.

Chill out, I want to say to him as the woman sits in her chair. There's only half an hour until I get off work. Rachel can handle the reference desk on her own. She might not even notice I'm gone. On the other hand, she might, and I'm already in

trouble with Judy. I could lose my job if I leave now, but if I'm needed in the Realm . . .

There's always a ticking clock when it comes to tracking the fae. We never know how long a target is going to stay put.

My choices are to wait half an hour and risk Trev leaving me behind or to leave, risking my job and the normal life I've always thought I wanted.

The seconds tick by as the woman types in her pin number. When the computer turns on, she thanks me. I nod, then look at Trev, whose expression is rigid and impatient.

After one last glance at the reference desk, I slide my keys out of my pocket. I can't abandon the fae.

EIGHT

❖

I DON'T KNOW if it's the cold punch of the In-Between, the icy bite of the driving rain, or the sudden surge of Kyol's emotions that makes my breath whoosh out of my lungs. Maybe it's the combination of all three that throws me off-balance. I slip on the cobblestones underfoot and land on one knee, stifling a curse when my pant leg gets soaked.

By the time I get back to my feet, Kyol's reined in his emotions. Obviously, he didn't know I was coming to the Realm.

I draw in a deep breath, willing myself to feel nothing, then I pull up the hood of the cloak Trev gave me. He gave me a sword and *jaedric* cuirass, too. The latter is cinched tight around my torso, and swung over my shoulder is my leather-strapped notebook. I haven't touched it since I moved from the hotel suite to my apartment—I almost forgot I'd stowed it under my driver's seat—but the familiarity of it pressing against my side is oddly comforting.

Trev squats down behind a low, stone wall. Reluctantly, I do as well. We're standing in almost an inch of cold rainwater. It seeps quickly over the top of my black dress shoes—fae always forget the shoes—instantly numbing my toes.

Lovely.

"This way," Trev says, leading the way alongside the wall. He stays crouched down low. I'm not sure why. It's night here,

and with the rain driving down so hard, no one will see us. I can barely see the *edarratae* on my own skin, and that's not an entirely good thing. If the weather doesn't change, I'm going to have to practically be on top of any fae I track. If Trev had commented on the weather when he asked me to come to Tholm, I might have gone straight back to my desk.

I'm not sure exactly where we are, but I remember the wall. It circles half the western portion of the city. Supposedly, sometime back before the *Duin Bregga*, it was topped by melted silver and contained all of Tholm, but five millennia of rain and erosion have nearly worn the silver away, and due to the fertile soil and its close proximity to the Imyth Sea, the city has long since overflowed the confines of the wall.

The rain increases as we climb a slope. I keep one hand on the wall in case I slip on the smooth cobblestones. It's odd being in such a heavy downpour with no lightning or thunder, just the torrential rain and a wind strong enough to twist my heavy cloak around my legs. Only the outer part of the cloak is drenched. The inside is lined with the soft, waterproof skin of a *sikki*, a sea animal that lives in the Realm's oceans. I wrap my hands into the wet folds of the material and try to keep it from tangling around my legs.

Trev doesn't seem to have any problems with the weather. He's sure-footed on the slippery stones. He has an advantage, though: his boots get far better traction than my dress shoes. The heels are the shortest I could—

Trev stops so suddenly, only a quick grab at the wall keeps me from falling on my ass. I grip the hilt of my sword, start to pull it out as I look for the threat, but then I see him—Aren—crouched down behind the wall.

He looks from Trev to me. It's dark, and with my hood up and the continued downpour, he can probably only see the flash of *edarratae* across my skin, not my actual face. He moves forward, then whips off my hood. His silver eyes meet mine for one heartbeat—for two—then he turns back to Trev.

"Where's Naito?"

"Derch," Trev answers. "It will take him six hours to reach the nearest gate."

Aren's hand is still fisted in my hood. It brushes across the

nape of my neck when he faces me again. The soft, brief contact is all that's needed for my *edarratae* to come alive. He feels the lightning's heat the same as I do, and he immediately drops his hand.

I clench my teeth together so hard my jaw aches. It's ironic, this reversal of roles. Two months ago, I was the one withdrawing from his touch and struggling with my attraction to him. Now, just because of a life-bond I had no control over forming, he doesn't want me anymore? I don't buy it. His behavior makes no sense, and it's pissing me off.

The life-bond and our relationship isn't something I can discuss in front of Trev, though, so I just meet Aren's gaze, making sure my expression is grim and determined. I'm here. He has to accept that.

He laughs. It's the last reaction I expected from him, and my anger dissipates a little.

"Okay," he says, a sideways grin stretching across his lips. "But there are conditions."

"Conditions?"

He nods, taking a step closer. I have to crane my neck to look up at him, and even in the pouring rain, I can smell him, all woodsy cedar with a mouthwatering hint of spice. I'm aching for the condition to be a kiss, but he only grips the front edges of my cloak.

"If I call it off," he says, his smile fading, "we walk away, no questions asked. If I tell you to run, you run." He takes my hand in his, then wraps it around the hilt of my sword. "If I tell you to kill, you don't hesitate."

It's that last condition that keeps me from responding immediately. The Realm is a violent world, and killing is a common thing. It's not common for a human like me, though, and in the last two months, I've killed more fae than I have in the last ten years. Even though every one of those lives was taken to defend myself or my friends, I wish I hadn't had to end them. I don't want to end any more. It's one of the reasons why living a normal life is so appealing. If I choose to remain involved with the fae, I'm accepting the fact that I may have to kill again.

I nod once, hoping that this shadow-reading will be simple.

Aren just shakes his head like he can't believe my response. Then he tucks a lock of my rain-drenched hair behind my ear, letting his fingers graze my cheek when he takes his hand away. It's a decidedly tender gesture, and I don't know what to make of it. The life-bond can't be the reason he's keeping his distance from me. I've come up with a few other theories—someone from his past is threatening to reveal some terrible secret about him, a high noble is blackmailing him into some shady dealings—but Aren's not one to let himself be manipulated. Something else is tearing him away from me.

I reach for his hand. "Aren—"

"Nimael is here," he says.

Nimael. The fae who slipped away from Naito and could be the false-blood's second-in-command.

"Is there any sign of Caelar or the remnants?" I ask, focusing on what we're here to do.

"No," Aren says. "But, technically, there's no sign of Nimael either. He's an illusionist. A powerful one if my information is good. Making himself and half a dozen other fae invisible is simple for him, even while fighting."

Damn, that's impressive. Illusion is a common magic, but most fae who are adept at it can only keep themselves unseen while they're fighting. Those who are stronger might be able to hide an additional fae or two, but concealing half a dozen fae who are all moving and fighting and lunging in different directions takes some serious magical skills.

Which makes our job anything but simple. I'll have to assume every fae with him is invisible.

"How do we know he's here then?" I ask.

"He's recruiting."

At my frown, Aren gives me his signature half smile then motions me to follow him over the low wall. I slide over the wind-worn stone and grimace when my feet squish into the ground. There are no cobblestones on this side of the wall. Or, if there are, they're underneath an inch-thick layer of mud. The city is built on a hillside, and we're standing in a shallow canal that cuts between tall, stone buildings.

Trev sinks into the muck beside me. Without a word, we both follow Aren. Since the fae are silent, I keep quiet, too, suppress-

ing a number of curses because it's hard as hell to keep my shoes on my feet. The mud keeps suctioning them off. It's slowing me down more than usual, so when Trev glares over his shoulder at me for the third time, I throw off the impractical dress shoes, hoping there's nothing in this sludge that will slice open my feet.

When I catch up with Aren and Trev again, I realize we're not alone in this canal. We're following a fae. I only see the back of his shaggy head, so I can't recognize him, but he's not dressed in any kind of armor. And, if I'm not mistaken, he looks young, too young to be one of Lena's swordsmen.

"He's *imithi*," Aren says, slowing his pace until I'm at his side.

Imithi? Curious, I squint through the darkness as the fae stops and faces us. Aren used to be one of them. They're orphans, fae who have no parents, no homes, and no roots linking them to anywhere in the Realm. They fissure from city to city, stealing, looting, and generally creating havoc wherever they go.

When we reach the *imithi*, the boy cocks his head at me, his silver-blue eyes openly taking me in from rain-drenched head to sludge-covered feet, which feel like blocks of ice now. I *think* he's young, but I've always had trouble guessing how old fae are. They age slower than humans do, except in their early years. From birth until the teens, we mature almost at the same rate. It's a good thing, too, because it would be freaking bizarre to talk to a twenty-year-old man who looks like a five-year-old boy. Still, it's difficult to figure out those later teenage years. The boy looks like he could be a high-school freshman, but he could just as well be the age of a college graduate.

"*She's the shadow-witch?*" he asks in Fae.

"*She is,*" Aren answers.

The boy makes a face. "*She doesn't look like she could slice a leaf.*"

Slice a leaf? I glance at Aren and see the corner of his mouth lift into a smile.

"*Careful,*" he says. "*She's stronger than she looks, and she has the willpower of a* kasnek."

I have no idea what a *kasnek* is, but Aren's words are clearly complimentary, and his tone is warm and affectionate. It makes me warm. And it makes me want to slide inside his embrace.

As soon as we have a moment alone together, he's going to tell me what's really making him put distance between us.

"Really?" the boy says. He shakes his head, flicking his wet, curly brown hair out of his eyes. *"Can I touch her?"*

"If you want to damage your magic, sure," Aren says with an it's-your-funeral kind of shrug.

I glare at Aren. It's human tech that damages fae magic, not humans, but most fae are so paranoid about their magic that they'll believe almost anything about us. It doesn't help that Aren's spread more rumors about the "shadow-witch" than I can count, turning me into some kind of mythological creature.

Aren just grins back at me. "This is Dicer."

It takes an effort to ignore the way that smile makes my stomach flip.

"You're letting the false-blood recruit him?" I ask, forcing my gaze back to the boy and remembering that Aren said recruitment was the reason Nimael was here.

"We're here to capture Nimael," Aren says, "so no one's going to be recruited. But, yes, that's the purpose of the meeting. I've been talking to Dicer and a few other *imithi* for the past few weeks, waiting for this to happen."

He says that as if he was all but certain the false-blood would eventually reach out to the *imithi*. But maybe he was sure of it. That's how Thrain found him. He was *imithi* until the false-blood decided to use him.

"How much farther?" Aren asks Dicer.

"It's just up here," the *imithi* says, walking a few more paces through the sludge, then stopping when he reaches the corner of the stone building that makes up part of the right wall of the canal. *"Straight ahead."*

Aren's gaze follows Dicer's pointing finger. He's just tall enough to see over the edge of the canal. I'm not. I move to the wall where a stone juts out from it, and use it as a foothold.

Aren steadies me with a hand—a subconscious touch, I think—then points to a detached home about thirty feet away. Two tall, short-needled plants sit in pots to either side of a dark door. Drapes cover the two windows I can see, making the interior look as black as the sky.

"Is it just us three?" I ask.

"No," he answers. "Jacia and Taber are paralleling us. They'll circle around to the back."

Automatically, I look to the left but only see the other wall of the canal. If the two fae are paralleling us, they're on street level. Which means they're not in this sludge. Lucky for them. Still, it's comforting to know they're here, even Jacia. Atroth wanted Kyol to form a life-bond with her. The king thought they were a good match, but Kyol refused the bond. I'm sure Jacia knows I was the reason for that rejection—anyone who wasn't blind realized it—but she's given no indication that she resents me for it. She's fully capable of annihilating a whole contingent of fae, and so is Taber, who's one of Kyol's top swordsmen. Aren doesn't have an army set to encircle Nimael, but he's brought powerful backup.

"Nimael is an older fae," Aren says, making me turn my attention back to the target house. "He's close to two centuries old and has streaks of gray in his hair. We need to capture him. The other *elari* in there won't be able to lead us to the false-blood. Tholm's silver wall will keep him from fissuring, so you shouldn't need to read his shadows, but you're all of our eyes. Make sure we know where he is."

I nod, then ask, "Are we going in or making them come out?"

"We'll see what happens when I knock on the door," he says.

My foot slips off the stone protruding from the canal's wall. "Knock on the door? That's your big plan to capture the false-blood's second-in-command?"

He gives me a devil-may-care grin. "You have no idea what I've accomplished by the simple act of knocking on a door. King Atroth was overthrown because I tapped on the right ones."

This is the Aren I fell in love with—confident, carefree, and sexy as hell. If he's still trying to push me away, he's doing a crappy job of it.

He reaches inside a draw-stringed purse that's attached to his weapons belt and takes out a coin. *Tinril*, the currency is called here. I have no idea what the different colors and sizes are worth, but Dicer catches the coin in the air.

"Now, run off," Aren says. *"Far off."*

"Of course." The boy grins in a way that makes me think he's not going to listen to Aren's instructions at all, and the way Aren watches him climb out the opposite side of the canal gives me the impression that his thoughts match mine. I'm betting *imithi* aren't so great at following orders.

There's nothing Aren can do about it, though.

"Are you two ready?" he asks, turning back to me and Trev. I nod, pull up my hood, then climb out of the canal behind the two fae. That's when I feel a flicker of anxiety from Kyol. He feels my focus, my slightly elevated heart rate, and he knows that I'm moving now.

Relax, I tell both him and myself. This should be simple. I don't even have to read the shadows; I just have to point out what I see.

We're halfway across the street. My focus is riveted to the narrow house's single window. Fae don't often use bows and arrows—their enemies rarely stay in one place and, many times, they're invisible—but we're in a part of the city that's protected by silver. If I were Nimael and thought there might be a chance someone was hunting me, I'd have at least one bow stashed somewhere inside.

But he has no reason to use it on us, I remind myself. He doesn't know we've found him. He's here to recruit *elari*, and we're just a few innocent, sludge-covered people crossing a street.

Suddenly, the front door opens. Three fae step out, and everything—the air, the rain, my heart—goes still.

"DON'T let them back in!" Aren yells. Before the last word leaves his lips, Trev's already acted, launching a ball of flames from his hand into the door behind the fae.

"Bring Taltrayn!" Aren grates out. The order is unnecessary. There's no stopping Kyol from coming. He felt the cold terror slide over me the second that door opened.

Aren grasps his sword in both hands and takes a step forward. "Where are they, McKenzie?"

"Shoulder to shoulder just outside the door."

"I can hide you," a voice pipes up just behind us. Dicer. No surprise there.

Aren doesn't hesitate. *"Do it,"* he says. To me, he adds, "Tell us when and where to swing."

I nod, then both he and Trev are rushing forward. Dicer must be a decently strong illusionist. I see the moment the *elari* lose sight of Aren and Trev. Two of the three fae take a half step backward as they bring their swords in front of them. They don't have humans to see through Dicer's illusion, and they can't fissure out of here. They're screwed.

But the fae in the center with gray-streaked hair doesn't look concerned. He doesn't even unsheathe his sword. With the door burning behind him, he—Nimael—takes a rustic red cylinder from his belt and untwists a cap. A thin, coiled rope falls to the ground, then, with a flick of his wrist, the rope snakes out in front of him.

Aren and Trev are almost on him.

"Jump! Jump!" I scream, but they don't understand, and with another flick of his wrist, Nimael's rope whips out. It's long enough to swing into both fae's legs. They crash to their knees, are up in an instant, but the damage is already done. Dicer's illusion breaks, revealing them both to the *elari*.

My sword is in my hands, and I'm rushing forward already, yelling for Aren to swing right and Trev to swing straight ahead. Both their blind attacks miss, and they roll, attempting to get out of the way.

Aren makes it, but Nimael's whip is wrapped around Trev's calf. It wraps around his knees during his roll. He curses, swings defensively once more, and his *elari* attacker hesitates the second I need to get there.

My blade cuts through the air, clashing against the *elari*'s with an impact that rattles me to the core. The *elari*'s invisibility breaks, and Trev's sword stabs upward, sinking home into the fae's gut.

I don't wait for his soul-shadow to appear. I whirl around to find both Nimael and the second *elari* closing in on Aren from both sides. Nimael has dropped his whip; I assume he's invisible again.

"Back, Aren!"

He misunderstands my order, twisting around to swing behind him. I won't get there in time, so I palm the pommel of my sword and thrust it into the air. It soars javelin-style and clips the *elari*'s side. Only strong enough to break the illusion, not to draw blood.

Dicer gives me a what-the-hell-was-that look, then the kid splits. Maybe he's decided we can handle this? It's two-on-two—three if you count me—and after a quick sidestep and an incredibly fast counterstrike, Aren sends the second *elari* to the ether.

"Where's Nimael?" he demands, rounding on me.

"There," I point, "to the left of the darker part of the street."

Nimael's nostrils flare. The glare he gives me reminds me of how cold the rain-drenched night is.

Aren grabs my arm. "The whole street's dark."

"The ground," I say. "The smudge on the ground that looks like a . . . a smiley face."

He pushes me back, then rushes forward, nowhere near where Nimael's standing.

Or was standing.

My cry of, "He's running!" is nearly drowned out by Jacia's, *"They're coming!"*

Five fae—all with the red-and-black-stoned name-cords that mark them as *elari*—burst out from the passageway between Nimael's building and the one next door.

"Nimael!" the dark-haired fae leading the way shouts, his gaze scanning the street for the fae. But Nimael is invisible behind his illusion, and speaking would give away his location, so with one last hate-filled glance at me, the older fae turns and runs.

"Aren, to the left. He's leaving!"

But Aren can't follow my directions. The dark-haired fae is on him. Their swords meet in a loud *clash, clash, clash.* Then the second fae is there, with Jacia right behind him.

We're outnumbered, even with Jacia's help. Taber was supposed to be with her. I don't know where he is, but it looks like none of these *elari* are illusionists. Aren doesn't need my

help, and Nimael is getting away, fleeing down a road that will take him to the eroded silver wall.

Half a second passes, then my decision is made. I scoop up my sword as I sprint past it, then run at top speed down a passageway that parallels Nimael's. If he's the false-blood's second-in-command, we need him captured and questioned, and since he's running roughly in the same direction Kyol's approaching from, we still have a chance to do both.

The storm and late hour have made Tholm more deserted than a ghost town. Not a soul hinders me, and the rain splattering onto the ground covers the sound of my footsteps. Buildings made of stone and stucco fly past me in a blur. I shrug out of my heavy cloak and keep running. I don't have to reach the silver wall the same second Nimael does; I just have to be near enough to read his shadows when he makes it to the other side and disappears.

I'm at an all-out sprint, practically flying over the wet pavement. The alley is clean, well maintained, but I'm heading up an incline, and the rain, the damnable downpour that let up for all of two minutes, has returned.

I reach a cross street, veer down it, and am spit out onto Nimael's road. He's there, so much closer than I expected but still running for the wall. He'll reach it soon.

I push on, funneling adrenaline into my legs. My lungs burn from the cold air, and my chest is tight, tight with Kyol's worry.

Intercept him! I try to translate those words into emotion, try to tell him I'm not running from someone, I'm running after him.

The ground rises steeply enough for stairs. I grab the two wooden handrails, use them to help propel me up steps.

"McKenzie!" Aren's voice is distant. It reaches me the same instant I see Kyol step into the street. His head whips to the left as Nimael sprints past him.

"It's Nimael!" I yell. "He's almost to the wall, dead center."

I don't think Kyol needs my directions. He's already moving, taking off after the *elari*.

It feels like it takes me hours to reach the wall, but really,

it takes no more than a handful of seconds. I unsling my notebook, open it on top of the low wall, and grab my pen. Nimael's
fissured out. Kyol's standing there, sword in hand just beside
the twisting shadows, waiting for me. Or rather, for my map.

Aren bellows my name again, closer this time, but I focus
on the shadows and, using my body to protect my notebook
from the rain, I begin to sketch what I see. A twist of shadow
in the upper left corner of my page, the tail of a river curving
down from a mountain, and a clearing. A valley maybe.

I flip to the next page of the book, watch the shadows con-
tort into more detail, a sharper image of Nimael's location.
Mountains to the east. Maybe to the north as well.

Brow furrowed, I squint at the shadows. Did he fissure into
the middle of a mountain range? Aside from the smooth curve
of a dark shadow, all the others are spiky and rugged and . . .
fading.

Damn it, I'm going to lose him.

Aren calls for me a third time. Kyol answers him, but I'm
still focused on the shadows. Where the hell did Nimael go?
I should be able to track him. I wasn't that far behind him.

Maybe the rain is obscuring my vision? I swipe a hand
over my face, slicking my drenched hair away from my eyes.
It's too late to start over. I try to modify what I've already
sketched out, find a detail that I've missed, or something that
jogs my memory. But there's nothing, and the last of the shadows wink out of existence.

NINE

"I LOST HIM," I say, meeting Kyol's gaze. He doesn't say a word. He doesn't have to. He knows as well as I do that I should have been able to pinpoint Nimael's location.

I break eye contact. Rain splatters on the low wall. This is the first time I've tried to read the shadows since the life-bond. I saw them clearly, but what if I've lost the ability to identify them? If I can't name the location, my maps are nothing, just scribbles on a page that no one can understand, and I'm . . . Well, I still have the Sight, so I'm not completely useless, but shadow-readers are rare. Lena only has two working for her: Naito and Evan. Evan and I have only met a few times. I helped him and Naito escape the palace eons ago when Atroth was still alive and king, but he's apparently terrible at reading the shadows, and Naito is already overworked. He can't continue to track Lena's enemies twenty-four/seven.

"McKenzie." Kyol's voice cuts through my thoughts the same instant I feel his focus sharpen. Goose bumps break out across my skin. No fissures have opened on the other side of the wall, but my sixth sense is screaming an alarm. We're not alone here. We're being watched.

"Back away from the wall," Kyol says quietly, calmly as he approaches me. I do as he says, tucking my sketchbook under my arm as I scan the darkened street. I take one step away from

the wall, two. The fae are standing so still, I don't see them at first. It's only after my gaze passes by them that my mind registers what I saw.

I look back at the main road, and this time, the six *elari* are clearly visible.

Kyol lets his mental wall slide away. If he was a man less in control of himself, I'd feel his worry, but all I feel is grim determination and a sense that he's not just focused ahead of us; he's attuned to something—or someone—behind us as well.

His sword is still drawn. Mine isn't. I slammed it back into its sheath when I took off after Nimael so I could run faster. I'm afraid to reach for it now. I don't want to trigger the fae surrounding us into attacking.

"Any chance they just want to chat?" I ask lightly, trying to reduce the tension that's building inside of me. Kyol doesn't answer. He doesn't even crack a smile.

I want to tell him he can go. We're outnumbered. There's no reason for us both to be killed. He can sprint back to the wall, leap over it, and fissure out before the *elari* reach us, but I know Kyol will never leave my side. He'll fight, and he'll die.

The fae begin to close in on us. Now would be the *perfect* time for Aren to make an appearance.

The distance between us shrinks. Twenty feet. Fifteen. Ten. To hell with triggering them, I drop my sketchbook and draw my sword. No way will I make this easy for them.

"*I'm Kyol, son of Taltrayn,*" Kyol speaks up suddenly. "*Lord General of the Queen's fae. I request—*"

"*There is no queen,*" the fae nearest us spits out. He's only a half dozen steps away now. I tighten my grip on my sword, say a quick prayer.

"*I request an audience with the* Taelith," Kyol says.

Five strides away.

"*Your request seems to be denied, Taltrayn.*"

I have no freaking idea where Aren's voice is coming from. Neither do the *elari*. They freeze. Then their gazes scan the street. Mine does, too. I look past the alley to my left, then to the wall behind us. Three fae stand in front of it. All *elari*. Where the hell is—

Kyol moves the same instant the six *elari* in front of us turn. It's only after one of them disappears into the ether that I see Aren. He cuts down a second fae before Kyol reaches the man nearest him.

Time slows as I spin back to face the fae at our backs. They move forward, and I swear I can see each droplet of water rise into the air as their boots splash across the wet street. Life only crawls this slowly when something terrible is about to happen, but I stand my ground and let Kyol's confidence sink into me. An instant before the first *elari* takes a swing at me, I sidestep to his right and bring my sword around in a wide arc.

I intend to take the fae's head off, but he intercepts my blade, easy. A part of my mind registers the fact that I'm screwed. The other part is still unnaturally confident I can kick the fae's ass.

My sword absorbs a blow from the *elari*. Then another and another, but there are two more fae trying to kill me, and I can't fight them all.

"Mind if I help?" Aren slides between me and two of the *elari*. The third *elari* turns his attention away from me when Aren kills one of the others. Dismissing the human. His mistake. My focus zeroes in on his right side, the vulnerable area where his *jaedric* is bound together with leather cords. Instinct tells me he's going to raise his right arm to take a swing, so I throw all my weight into a lunge forward, leading with the point of my sword.

It's a perfect strike, sliding beneath his rib cage and through his gut. He enters the ether the same moment Aren finishes off his opponents.

"I expected you to hesitate," Aren says, turning to me.

"What?" I ask, tearing my gaze away from the misty white soul-shadows. All but one of the other *elari* are dead. Trev is here, helping Kyol restrain him.

"You didn't hesitate," Aren says. He's not breathing hard; I can barely catch my breath. It takes a few seconds for my mind to remember the conditions he listed when I first arrived in Tholm, and suddenly, I have an almost overwhelming urge to throw my sword to the ground and step away from my crime. He's right. I didn't hesitate. I killed without a second thought.

A string of expletives comes from the last *elari*. Trev is trying to wrestle him to the ground, so Kyol can bind his hands.

"Nimael," Aren says. "You mapped his shadows."

He bends down and retrieves my sketchbook. He wipes beads of rain off the waterproof cover, then opens straight to my map. "What city?"

I bite the inside of my cheek. Looking at the mess of mountains and zigzagging lines again doesn't help me identify where Nimael went. I don't know, and that bothers me more than I ever would have guessed. I've *always* been able to read the shadows. Ten years ago, before I'd extensively studied maps of the Realm and of Earth, I wasn't very accurate, but within a few months, I started nailing down locations. Occasionally, I'd have to reference a real map to figure out where a fae went. I haven't had to do that in years, though, but maybe it might help me now? I'm certain Nimael stayed in the Realm.

At least, I think I'm certain he did.

"McKenzie?"

I shake my head.

"What's that mean?" Aren asks. "You're not going to tell me?"

"No."

"No?"

"No, not 'no,'" I say. "I just don't know. I couldn't track him."

That admission kills me. I take my sketchbook from Aren, slap it shut, then sling it over my shoulder.

"The map looked finished."

"It wasn't," I snap. I start to turn away, but Aren grabs my arm.

"Hey," he says. "What's wrong?"

"If you'd listened to me, he wouldn't have gotten away." I yank my arm free. "I told you where he was."

"You told me he was next to a smiley face. How am I supposed to know what that is?"

"It looks like a face that's smiling," I bite out.

"McKenzie." Aren says my name so softly, I'd have to be deaf not to hear how angry I sound in comparison. Not being

able to read Nimael's shadows unsettled me, but there's no reason to take it out on Aren.

"I'm sorry," I say, deflating. "It's just . . ." I close my eyes and draw in a breath before I reopen them. "I don't know where he went."

"Okay," he says, like it's no big deal. It is a big deal, though. A whole freaking province is opposing Lena because of the false-blood. She needs to be able to at least identify him to have any chance of disproving his claim. Nimael is the bread-crumb that could lead us to him. I doubt this other *elari* can help us.

I turn back toward that *elari*. His wrists are bound behind his back now, and Trev appears to have control of him. That isn't stopping the *elari* from letting him have it verbally. He's spitting out curses and slurs and angry words too quickly for me to translate. He's filled with blind rage, and in my experi-ence, people who are like him—people who can't control their anger—are rarely trusted with important information. He won't lead us to Nimael or the false-blood.

"We'll question him in Corrist," Kyol says. Trev nods, ac-knowledging Kyol's words, then he begins to half walk, half drag the *elari* toward the wall. That brings him closer to Aren and me. The *elari* looks at me, spits on the ground, then contin-ues his diatribe.

I'm pretty much tuning out everything he says, but as Trev wrestles him over the low wall, one of his accusations slowly translates itself in my mind. He's accusing Lena of building an army of Sighted humans. It's an outrageous accusation, especially considering that Lena is losing Sighted humans, not gaining them. I would entirely dismiss his words except for one thing: he used the word *kannes*. That can be translated into serum. Sight serum.

"Wait!" I say when Trev opens a fissure on the other side of the wall. "How does he know about the Sight serum?"

Trev frowns over his shoulder at me.

"He was talking about the Sight serum," I say. "No one should know about it."

Technically, that's not true. Lena and a handful of people she

trusts know about it. So do Caelar and a few of the remnants, but as far as I know, Caelar isn't fissuring around the Realm talking about it, and neither side is using it. It's fatal, and no one wants more humans than necessary to be aware of the fae's existence.

The *elari* is still spitting out curses. Aren vaults over the wall; then, without a pause, he slams his fist into the fae's jaw. That shuts him up long enough for Aren to ask what he knows about the serum.

The *elari* answers with the crap about Lena building an army again. He claims she's selling it to any human who can pay, which is just plain stupid because what is Lena going to do with money that's good only on Earth? It's worth nothing here. Besides, she could just have one of her fae fissure into a store or bank and steal it. That's what Atroth had his people do when he needed to pay the humans who worked for him. The *elari* has to be making crap up.

Still, when Aren nods, signaling to Trev that it's okay to go, an uneasy feeling lingers with me. It's too big a coincidence to ignore. If the *elari* said Lena was recruiting humans who already had the Sight or that Lena had found a fae with the magic to give the Sight to humans, that would be different. But he specifically said a serum gave humans the Sight. Somehow, he knows about the vigilantes' serum.

There's no way Lena would have let that information leak. The only way the *elari* could know about it is if Caelar told him, and why would Caelar tell him about the serum if they weren't working together?

"Caelar isn't working with the false-blood," Kyol says, standing a few paces to my right. His words sound firm, uncompromising, but the sense I get through the life-bond is that some of Kyol's conviction is missing. It's the same feeling I had a few days ago when it felt like Kyol's optimism about the Realm's future was diminished. I want to bring it back, to assure him that he's right, that Caelar is a fae who deserves Kyol's respect and that the Realm will be the world he thinks it can be, but I can't make those promises. He would feel my doubt if I did.

"I've told you before," Aren says, slamming his sword back into its scabbard. "You're wrong about Caelar."

"This isn't proof they're working together," I say. I realize a second later that I shouldn't have said anything. I spoke out of a need to reassure Kyol, but Aren's expression turns stony, and I can imagine what he's thinking: I'm not on his side. I'm on the side of my bond-mate.

"Aren—"

"I'll find out more in Corrist," he says. "I'll send back dry clothes and supplies."

"No," Kyol speaks up. "You'll stay with McKenzie."

Slowly, Aren's head turns toward Lena's lord general. Kyol's emotions are steady and calm now. Aren's aren't. The tension in his muscles is as clear as if *we* had a life-bond. Technically, Kyol outranks Aren, but I don't think he's been issuing many orders to him. I don't think they've been interacting much at all these last few weeks.

"I'll go," Aren says again. "You'll escort McKenzie to Corrist. It should be a safe enough journey."

It'll be a long journey, a full day's walk. A full day for me to learn what I can do to get Aren back.

"No," Kyol says. If Aren were anyone else, he would know there's no room for argument when Kyol uses that tone. Even the rain stops, almost as if it heeds the command in Kyol's voice.

But Aren is Aren, and even though he's now part of the Realm's legitimate government, in his heart, he's still a rebel.

"I'm fissuring out," he says. "If you choose to do so as well, then you're the one who'll be leaving her alone."

A slash of white light slices through the air beside him.

"Wait!" Kyol barks. "Just get her out of the city. I'll meet you within view of Tholm's westernmost building."

Then, before Aren can step into his fissure, Kyol opens one of his own and disappears.

Aren curses.

"I'm not that repulsive, am I?" I ask lightly.

Aren's gaze slides to me, and the way his silver eyes peer out beneath his dark lashes says my words are ridiculous.

I just give him a tiny shrug, wrap my arms around my now-shivering body, and start walking.

"Did you really need to get rid of your shoes and cloak?" Aren asks, falling into step beside me. He's looking at my bare feet. Throwing off my shoes wasn't a mistake—my toes were already numb, and I get better traction without them—but losing the cloak might have been.

I don't admit to it, though. Instead, I say, "You took off your cloak."

"It's easier to move without it."

"Exactly."

"Besides," he says, "I can keep warm."

"If you'd like to keep me warm, you can start any time."

Even in the darkness, there's a glimmer in his silver eyes when he looks at me. "You're determined to make this difficult, aren't you?"

We step onto a curved stone bridge. "If you're referring to you dumping me, then yes. I am."

"Did you make it this difficult for Taltrayn?"

"I—" The question surprises me, and I'm not sure how to answer. With Kyol, I knew the reason he kept his distance. I even respected it, and in the beginning, I believed that human culture was damaging the Realm. Over the years, I started to doubt that, but I never started to doubt Kyol. He was noble, a man of his word, and each time he told me we couldn't be together, I tried to move on.

I look at Aren as the bridge takes us across a canal. I have no desire to move on now.

"I didn't make it easy," I finally say, focusing on the long passageway in front of us. We're near the edge of the city. The homes are larger, the storefronts aren't smashed together quite as much, and even though dawn is still hours away, the shadows between the buildings don't seem as dark here.

It's still cold as hell, though, and Aren hasn't moved one inch closer to me.

I stop walking and turn toward him. "Will you just tell me what's wrong?"

He faces me and, almost reluctantly, meets my eyes.

"I don't understand why you're here," he says. "You have the normal life you always wanted."

Not breaking his gaze, I tilt my head to the side. "Don't you know? I could never be a normal human."

The smile that spreads across his face tells me he recognizes the words. He said them to me two months ago, right after the vigilantes attacked the inn in Germany. I was still fighting my attraction to him, still clinging to the hope that I was shadow-reading for a good and honest king.

"Look," I say. "You said I needed time to understand the life-bond. It's been almost a month. I get it. Kyol's in my head, but we're in the same world, and I'm not throwing myself into his arms."

"You're not," he says, "but you want to."

"God, just . . . just stop telling me what I want! And don't give up on us so easily."

"You think this is easy?" he says, agitation sliding into his voice. "Do you think I like knowing that *he* knows where you are every second of the day? That *he* knows when you're in trouble, when you're sad or scared?" He grabs my arms then gently pushes me back against a stone façade. "He knows when you're aroused, McKenzie." His head dips, bringing his lips closer to mine. "He knows when we touch, when we kiss. He'll know if we make love. Do you want that? Can you handle hurting him like that?"

"I can control it," I say, my gaze locked on his lips. "I'll find a way to control it."

He chuckles, low and sexy, as he eases closer to me, and whispers in my ear, "The last thing I want you to have when you're with me is control."

I'm not cold anymore. My body flushes with heat at his words. I turn my face toward him as he backs away. He's still holding on to me, but any second he could let go and leave.

"Your lips are blue," he says softly.

"There's a solution for that."

His gaze meets mine again, and my stomach flips. Even rain-drenched and in shadows, he's gorgeous. He's fully dressed, and the air is cold, but he looks like he's just stepped out of a steamy

shower. His hair is darker than normal, the wet locks curling slightly at the ends, making him look haphazard and sexy.

He swallows. "Please, McKenzie. I'm trying to do the right thing."

That's one of the reasons I love him. He's trying to undo a past that he regrets. He's trying to be a good man, and I think that might be why he's pushing me away. Fae respect the sanctity of a life-bond more than humans respect the sanctity of marriage, and in his mind, even touching me is a violation of the connection I have with Kyol.

But Naito and Kelia didn't care about that. Right now, I don't either. I grab the top of Aren's cuirass and pull him closer. "I am the right thing, Aren."

I thought my lips were numb. They aren't. They feel the firm, delicious pressure of Aren's mouth. The magic he's using to keep himself warm rushes into me, and chaos lusters fire across my skin, so sudden and hot, I lurch into him. I feel him shake, too, and he grips me tighter, one hand in my wet hair, the other moving down my back. His palm curves over my butt, pulling me firmly against him.

Jaedric protects both our torsos. I want so much to remove his, to run my hands over the hard planes of his chest and down the ridges of his stomach. I've seen him shirtless. I want to *feel* him shirtless. Naked and hot and lit by my chaos lusters.

He nips my lower lip, then sucks it between his teeth, but even as he does that, deepening the kiss in a way that draws a moan from me, I feel him holding back.

I reach up, intending to fist my hand in his hair, but he intercepts me, grabbing my wrist as he breaks the kiss.

"I can't," he whispers.

"We can, Aren. Please."

"No, it would be . . . I just can't. I'm sorry." He wraps his arms around me and rests his chin on my head, ending any opportunity for me to reinitiate the kiss. My cheek presses against his chest, and I listen to the steady thump of his heart.

"I'll find a way to sever the life-bond," I tell him.

"There's only one way for it to end, McKenzie," he says, and the pain in his voice is like a sword through the gut.

I close my eyes and bite my lower lip as I soak in his warmth. His words can't be true. I refuse to believe them because, if they are, then the only way to gain freedom from Kyol is for one of us to die.

TEN

•◆•

A REN AND I don't speak or touch the rest of the way through Tholm. Kyol fissures to the city when we reach the western edge of it. I don't know if that's a coincidence, or if he felt when I started searching for him. He's not alone. Trev and Nalst, a fae I've worked with before, are with him. The look Trev gives me says he's not here by choice, and I'm beginning to think his presence is a punishment from Lena. Whether she's punishing him or me, though, I don't know.

Kyol's mouth tightens when he sees me. He knew I was cold, but seeing me shoeless and soaked makes him angry. Without sparing Aren so much as a glance, he holds out a cloak. It's folded up into a square package that's fat enough to hold a pair of shoes and dry clothes.

I hold the wrapped-up cloak against my chest as I scan the area for someplace to change. It's not quite dawn yet, but the sky has a lighter hue to it. We're within view of the city and several of the outlying buildings, so I'm not exactly comfortable with stripping naked out here. I'm not about to wait to change clothes, though. I need to get warm now.

"I can hold the cloak around you," Kyol says, sensing my hesitation.

I make the mistake of looking at Aren. His gaze rakes down the length of my body, and the hunger in his eyes makes

my stomach tighten. His expression goes neutral the instant he notices me watching him. Then, after a quick, curt nod, he opens a fissure and disappears.

No good-bye. No promise to see me again. My emotions are so tangled, I honestly don't know if I'm more hurt or angry. It doesn't help that, for Kyol's sake, I'm trying not to feel anything at all.

I focus on the cloak in my arms and unhook the belt that's holding it tight around the boots and clothing Kyol brought. If my clothes were dry, I could put the cloak on and figure out a way to wiggle out of them, but since they're wet and sticking to my skin, Kyol's option is the best.

"Okay," I say, and he steps forward, taking the ends of the cloak and encircling me with them. His arms are around me, sort of. Not touching, but it feels intimate. He's averting his eyes, though. I try not to focus or think of him at all as I loosen the laces on my cuirass. My numb fingers have trouble with them, but I'm not about to ask for help. I undo them as much as I can, then lift the armor over my head.

I shed all my clothes as quickly as possible then pull on a pair of dark gray pants and a double-layered black shirt with straps that cinch tight over my chest. Socks and knee-high boots are last.

"I'm done," I say, taking the cloak from Kyol. I'm more comfortable, but I'm far from warm.

"Your hands," Kyol says, reaching for them. He massages my fingers and palms, sending a magically charged heat into them. "I didn't think to bring gloves, but it will be warmer when the sun rises."

"I'll be fine," I assure him, and we start the long journey to Corrist. Nalst leads the way, and Trev brings up the rear, walking a few paces behind us.

By the time the sun touches the horizon, hovering beneath a few gray clouds, I'm thoroughly defrosted. An hour later, I'm actually hot. I strip off my cloak and start to fold it over my arm but Kyol takes it from me.

"Nalst," he says. He instructs him to take the cloak to Corrist and to bring back a few things.

After Nalst fissures out, we sit down to rest and eat. It's

breakfast for the fae and dinner for me: warm bread encircling a layer of meat and an assortment of fruits from the bag Kyol's carrying. I lean my back against a fallen tree and stare out at the sea below us. We've walked along the edge of a forest for most of the way, with the Imyth Sea to our left. We're a good thirty feet above it. Our path has gradually risen, and the forest has thinned. Another hour, and it'll be all open plain between us and Corrist.

Kyol stands when Nalst rejoins us. I do so as well, eyeing the two red-hilted swords Nalst hands the lord general. When Kyol then hands one of them to me, I frown down at the blade. The metal is cloudy, not bright like most fae's swords, and the edge looks dull. The sword in the scabbard on my left hip is much better than this one.

"Hold it like this," Kyol says, wrapping both my hands around the red hilt. "Hold it tight, but loose."

"Tight but loose?" I echo. "What is this, Kyol?"

"'This' is something I should have done a long time ago." His silver gaze locks on me, and I forget what I was going to say. Maybe the emotion betrayed in his eyes is just evidence of how determined he is to do this, but it could just as easily be passion, especially when my chaos lusters leap to his skin. They're enticing, and something deep and familiar clenches low in my stomach.

I swallow. "Kyol—"

"When the fae attacked you in the *tjandel*," he interrupts gently, "it terrified me. I was afraid again when Lee startled you at your apartment and earlier when you went after the *elari*. I need you to be able to defend yourself."

Tenderness and affection leak through his mental wall. I'm not prepared for those emotions. My defenses aren't up, so an echoing warmth spreads through my chest, and his feelings become my feelings. It doesn't help that this is the way I felt about him for ten years. Standing here in front of him now, I want nothing more than to step into his embrace. He would wrap his arms around me and hold me like he used to. Like he wants to.

My chest rises and falls, and my entire body aches with a tangible need to move forward.

No, that isn't right. This isn't a tangible need; it's a magical one.

I keep hold of the sword hilt but pull my hands free from his, biting my lower lip to extinguish the desire running through me.

"This isn't going to help," I manage to say. "You and half the Realm have trained with swords since birth. I can't win a sword fight against any of you."

"More than half the Realm, McKenzie." Neither his tone nor his eyes betray any emotion, and now he has the leaks in his mental wall sealed up tight. "But you're human, and you're . . ." His gaze darts to Trev and Nalst, who don't know about our life-bond. "You're quick. Fae will underestimate you. They'll be overly confident and careless. They'll make mistakes. You need to be able to take advantage of those mistakes."

I want to ask him if he's attempting this because he saw how I caught the sword a few days ago at my apartment. The move felt like an instinct, and if I want to be honest, when I swung my sword at the *elari* back in Tholm, that, too, felt natural. I still doubt that I'll ever be good enough to fight a fae one-on-one, but I'd love to be proven wrong.

"You're the best swordsman in the Realm," I tell him, a small smile on my lips. "Let's see how good a teacher you are."

"Basics first," he says, then, as we continue on toward Corrist, he shows me how to protect myself and how to kill.

KYOL'S not a teacher, he's a tyrant. A heartless, unrelenting, and unforgiving tyrant. The training goes well for the first few hours. He drills me on the forms in a cool, emotionless voice, and I put up with it until fatigue settles into my shoulders and biceps. And my back. I didn't realize holding and swinging a sword used so many muscles.

I don't complain, though. I keep practicing the forms, defending when Kyol orders me to defend. I'm waiting for him to call a stop for the day—he knows how tired I am—but he doesn't show any signs of ending the training. When sweat begins to sting my eyes and blisters start to form on my palms and fingers, I lower my sword.

"I need to rest."

"Pitch right," he says, telling me how to defend his attack.

"Really, I'm done—ow!" He jabs the point of his practice sword into my rib cage.

"We're continuing," he says in the same level tone he's used all morning.

I hold my side, glaring at him. That one almost drew blood. It's definitely going to leave a bruise. It's not the first one, though, and it won't be the last, especially if we keep going. I'm moving twice as slowly as I was an hour ago, my hands hurt like hell, and pausing to fight so often is making the trip to Corrist take twice as long as it otherwise would.

"For how much longer?" I ask, trying to be patient. I *want* to learn how to defend myself, but I also want to be able to crawl out of bed in the morning.

Kyol calls out another strike. I barely knock his sword out of the way in time.

"Until you don't forget the forms or until we reach Corrist," he says.

I bite my lower lip. I didn't forget the form that time. I just made a mess of it.

An hour later, we're still going, and I'm seething with rage. I don't try to hold back the feeling. I do my best to throw it in Kyol's face because I've tried to stop twice now, and twice, he's slammed his sword into my back, all without a trickle of remorse or concern passing through our bond. I've been awake for more than twenty-four hours now, but even if I were well rested and hadn't been walking for half the day, I still deserve a break. Kyol was Atroth's damn sword-master. He's Lena's damn lord general. He's not attacking me with his full strength—not even half his strength, I'm sure—but he's not slowing his movements either.

He swings again, his practice sword cutting through the air. I raise my blade and manage to throw his attack off enough to not get hit, but I lose my grip on my sword. When it lands in the thick grass, I glare down at the red hilt. I know why it's that color now. The blisters on my hands broke a long time ago. They're bleeding, but you can't tell by looking at the sword.

Before Kyol orders me to pick it up, I grab it. Then I throw

it at his head. Miraculously, he doesn't get his sword up in time to knock it away. The flat side of the blade thumps into his temple.

Trev laughs at Kyol's wince. I feel only slightly satisfied.

"I'm done," I tell him. "I'm tired, I'm hurt, and I'm not touching that sword again."

"Very well," Kyol says, picking up the practice weapon. "I'll meet you in Corrist."

"What?" I demand, facing him fully. "Well isn't that convenient for you."

"Do you want me to stay?" he asks levelly.

"I want you to—" I strangle off my words when his mental wall cracks. He wants me to say yes. God, he wants it so badly my heart breaks. I want to tell him what he wants to hear. I want to say stay. I might be mad at him for . . . for treating me like I'm just one of his swordsmen, but I've liked being with him. This day feels like our days together before I met Aren, and suddenly I realize that I've missed this. I've missed spending time with Kyol.

And he's missed spending time with me.

My throat feels raw when I swallow. I shouldn't have come back to the Realm. This isn't fair to him. And it's too confusing to me.

"Go," I say before I give in to the part of me that wants him to stay. With a curt nod, he opens a fissure and disappears.

ELEVEN

•◆•

A KNOCK STARTLES me awake. I sit up and let out a string of curses. Holy hell, my body hurts. And not just from swinging a sword hour after hour. Apparently, I got out of shape in the few weeks that I was away from the Realm. My feet hurt from a full day's walk, and the muscles in my legs are so tight, I'm not sure I can straighten them.

Another knock, louder this time, shakes my door. Groaning, I force myself out of bed. I barely remember walking through Corrist yesterday. I didn't even attempt to have someone take me through the gate. I just stumbled into the palace and came to the room Lena's kept waiting for me.

And speaking of Lena, she's standing in the corridor when I open the door.

"You look terrible," she says, her gaze taking in my dirty clothes and knotted hair.

"Thanks," I say, "but you could have waited until the morning to tell me that."

"It is the morning," she says. She grabs my right wrist then turns my hand over to inspect my blisters. "Taltrayn made them out to be worse."

I pull back my hand. "It hurts worse than it looks."

She grabs it again, this time pressing her palm against mine. "I want you to speak to the vigilante."

"Glazunov?" I ask, the sudden request throwing me off. "About what?"

"About the Sight serum, of course," she says, releasing my right hand to grab my left. It's not nearly as blistered as the other. "He won't speak to fae."

"You've heard the rumors then?" Of course she's heard them. I'm sure she demanded a full report from both Aren and Kyol.

"I'd be concerned even if the false-blood wasn't accusing me of using it," she says. "The serum gives humans the Sight. I'd like to keep our existence a secret if possible, and I'm sure you'd rather humans not die."

"My life would be easier if humans knew about you," I mutter.

She scowls at me.

"It's true," I say, even though I recognize the ramifications if my world learned about the fae. Most humans wouldn't be content to let them fissure to and from Earth. They'd want a way to do the same, and they'd try to take control of everything—the fae's magic, their resources, their whole world, really—in the interest of making humankind safe.

Lena just lets out what sounds like a disappointed sigh as she turns and walks down the corridor. I close my door, then fall into step beside her.

"What?" I ask. Her face is smooth, unreadable except for her silver eyes. I was wrong about the sigh. It wasn't disappointed. It was annoyed.

"You need to make a decision," she says, her tone clipped. "Are you with us or are you not?"

"With you?" I ask. "With the rebels, you mean? Of course—"

"We're no longer rebels, McKenzie. I'm the only Descendant with a strong bloodline who's claimed the right to rule the Realm, and if I'm claiming the right to rule it, then I have the obligation to protect it. I need to know if you'll help me protect it from the false-blood."

"Why do you think I was in Tholm?" I ask.

She stops to face me. "You're not listening. You're still trying to lead dual lives. It's not possible. I need to be able to rely on you when I need you, not when it's convenient."

"It's never convenient to be here," I snap. "But I'm doing what I can. I'm trying to keep a job and my apartment and a glimmer of a real life because I need to stay sane."

"Naito is sane. He doesn't try to be someone he isn't."

"I'm not trying to be someone I'm not. I'm just trying to be halfway normal."

A level gaze and her silence are her only responses to my statement, and I can practically hear her thoughts. I'm not normal, not even halfway.

Frustrated, I turn away, continuing down the corridor before she sees that I get her point. In fact, I made the same argument to Aren yesterday.

"You think you're more a part of your world than ours," she continues, walking beside me. "You're wrong. You're one of us more than you'll ever be one of them, especially now. You're tied to Kyol, to us, for the rest of your life. Ignoring the Realm isn't an option anymore."

My jaw is tight. Lena's always been brutally blunt, but with her bluntness comes truth. She's right. But why is she right? A normal life is what I've wanted for the last ten years. Why am I okay with giving it up now?

It's not the life-bond. That makes me want to run as far away as I can.

I glance at Lena. Is it her and the fact that she sees me as one of them? Atroth and his Court fae always treated me as something *other*. Even Kyol treated me that way when we weren't alone. I wanted a future with him, but I could never picture it because he swore it would never be allowed. It's allowed now, and . . .

He's not pushing me away anymore. He wants me to be safe, yes, but he accepts me being here. Lena and all the rebels do. They would let me call the Realm home.

"Thank you," I say softly.

Lena's brow wrinkles, not understanding my response. "You're with us?"

I nod. "I'm with you."

After a few more paces, she says, "Good."

"I need a favor," I say, keeping my voice low as we make our way down a set of stairs.

She glances my way, her expression hardening as if she expects me to ask something impossible of her. And maybe I am.

"I need to find a way to sever the life-bond."

Her mouth tightens. Before she says she can't help me, I say, "I have to at least learn how to block my thoughts from Kyol. I'm hurting him."

"Your relationship with Aren would hurt him anyway," she says. "You're just aware of it now."

"I have no relationship with Aren right now. He won't get past the bond."

A single, concerned wrinkle forms between her eyes. "Aren hasn't been acting like himself since you left. He's . . . I don't know how to describe him. It's like he feels trapped. I think the palace suffocates him. He's not used to being restrained behind silver walls."

Aren grew up as an *imithi*, fissuring from province to province without ever having a real home. It makes sense that he wouldn't like staying in one place, and I know he's more comfortable designing attacks rather than defending against them, but that doesn't explain why he's not willing to attempt to get over the life-bond. He breaks rules and traditions; he doesn't abide by them.

"He's been speaking with Lord Hison a lot lately," Lena says.

I feel myself scowl at the name. Hison is the high noble of Jutur, but from what I've heard, he's just barely in charge of the province now. A month ago, the fae in his home city were rioting. He blames that on Lena and me, since I happened to be there when things got really bad. Personally, I think they're rioting because he's a crappy leader. Of course, my opinion might be biased because he's not exactly pro-human.

"Any idea what they're talking about?" I ask. The suspicion that someone might be blackmailing Aren circulates through my mind again. If Hison has anything on Aren, he's the type of man who wouldn't hesitate to use it to get what he wants.

Lena shrugs. "Aren's been talking to all the high nobles who haven't promised to confirm me as queen."

My eyes widen. I'm pretty sure my mouth is hanging open. "You haven't been *confirmed* yet? Are you kidding?"

She stiffens. "Transitions take time."

"You've held the palace for two months!"

"*I* didn't intend to hold it at all," she fires back. "The few high nobles who supported my brother have had to be reconvinced that the Zarrak bloodline is strong enough to sit on the throne. Those who do still believe it worry that the Realm will grow angry if we break with tradition and allow a woman to rule, and now I have a false-blood to deal with. I would have been confirmed if Lord Ralsech hadn't declared his support for the *Taelith*."

Lord Ralsech. He's the high noble of Derrdyn Province, someone I've always steered clear of because of his hatred of all things human.

"Are you ever going to be confirmed?" I ask. Her eyes narrow. I'm getting under her skin. I don't care. I assumed she'd been named queen despite the false-blood's appearance. She hasn't, and it seems like the political situation here is worse than it was when I left. Lena's been running in place this whole time, and it pisses me off. I didn't join the rebels to fight for the status quo. I joined them because the Realm needed to change.

"Atroth was king for fifteen years," she says. "That's considered a short reign. Even in your world, these things take time."

"Will they *ever* confirm you?" I demand.

The set of her jaw tells me she very much does not want to answer the question, but finally, she says, "Not until the false-blood reveals his ancestry."

"Why hasn't he?"

"Because he's a false-blood," she says, practically spitting the words out. "He can't prove he's a Descendant of the *Tar Sidhe*."

"Then why would Lord Ralsech support him?"

"The *Taelith* caters to his hatred of humans," she says. "He's telling people what they want to hear." Her hand reaches toward her face—I think to rub her eyes—but she stops herself and lowers the hand back to her side. "I need a majority of the provinces to vote in my favor. I'm four votes short."

"What about the dissolved provinces?" I ask. "You said you would reinstate them. Surely, their high nobles support you."

"They do," she says, "but I'm still short. The nobles in charge of the provinces that lost territory with the reinstatements were not fond of that decision."

I roll my eyes. "I hate politics."

She lets out a bitter laugh. "So do I."

"This can't go on," I tell her. "You can't stay in limbo."

"I know, McKenzie. I'm working on it. The high nobles—"

"I'm sick of hearing about the nobles," I interrupt. "Maybe you should stop trying to convince them that you should be queen and start trying to convince the rest of the Realm."

"It's not that simple."

"Lena," a voice calls out from behind us. The fae approaching us is wearing a fitted blue jacket with a gold design sewn into the wide cuffs of his sleeve. I'm pretty sure the loops and crossed threads mark him as an aide.

"Lords Hison and Kaeth request an audience with you," the fae says. *"They're waiting in your anteroom."*

Lena's face remains smooth. Her eyes, though, betray her irritation. Hison is one of the sharpest thorns in her side.

"I'll be there soon," she finally says.

The aide's mouth thins. *"They've been waiting for quite some time."*

"Then they can wait for more."

He stiffens. Then, after a brief hesitation, he nods and turns to leave. Lena scowls at his retreating back.

"Plotting an unfortunate accident?" I ask her.

Her gaze slips my way, and I shrug. She just shakes her head.

"Come on," she says, continuing down the cold corridor. "Glazunov's guard won't let you see him without my permission."

When we reach the palace's prison, I look into the barred windows of the doors we pass. I'm looking for the *elari* Trev captured in Tholm. His claim that Lena is selling the Sight serum still bothers me. I don't see him, though. He's either

out of sight in one of the cells we pass or he's being held elsewhere.

"He hasn't eaten or drank anything since he's been here," Lena says, directing my attention to a cell at the end of the hall.

My stomach sinks. "You're not feeding him?"

She turns to look at me. "He hasn't *accepted* anything we've offered him. I need you to find out what you can about the Sight serum. I want to make sure it's destroyed and that it's not being given to anyone anymore. If more people can see us, more people *will* see us."

"What are the chances of that actually happening, though? I didn't see a fae until I was sixteen. It's not like they're walking around in shopping malls."

"A number of *tor'um* have chosen to migrate to Earth, especially in the last decade," she says. "Atroth shunned them, but I don't, and I won't. They're still fae. I'll do what I can to protect them."

We reach the door at the end of the corridor. The guard opens it at Lena's request, revealing a small room with a cot against the right wall and a pot in a corner. Glazunov sits against the left wall, a tray of food and water untouched at his feet. He looks awful, pale and gaunt, with dark circles under his eyes and dry, cracked lips. His clothes—the same ones he was wearing when he was tied to my bed—hang off his slumped shoulders, looking like they're a size too big now. It's a huge change, especially considering he's only been here about three days, Earth time.

"I'll leave you with him," Lena says. "The guard is trustworthy, and he doesn't understand English. You can talk about the serum freely. When you're finished here, I'd like to speak with you again."

I nod without looking at her. Glazunov has gathered up what strength he has left and is giving me a murderous glare. It's not intimidating at all, though. He might be able to stand, but I doubt he's able to do so quickly.

Entering the cell, I sit cross-legged a few feet away from him. The tray of food and water is between us.

"Do you not trust what they're offering you to eat?" I ask.

"I have no intention of staying here forever," he says.

It takes me a second to understand his response. I'm so used to the fae, to their customs and traditions, that I never relate them to my world's folklore. So little of the reality made it into our literature that, in my mind, they're not even close to being the same.

"It's safe to eat," I say, demonstrating by grabbing a wedge of cheese and popping it into my mouth. "I'm free to leave whenever I want. I even have an apartment and a job back home." A job I'm probably going to be fired from and an apartment I'll be kicked out of, but he doesn't need the details.

"They've seduced you," Glazunov says. He's breathing hard, as if talking is difficult for him. He's in a lot worse shape than I expected.

"Will you drink something, at least?" I ask, holding out the wooden cup filled with water. I genuinely feel bad for him. I know it isn't reasonable, that I'm not responsible for the state he's in and that, if he's anything like Naito and Lee's father, he's a hate-filled man who can't be reasoned with, but I can't help it. This has always been my problem—I care too much.

Glazunov licks his cracked lips, then, to my surprise, he leans forward and accepts the cup. He stares at its rippling surface for a handful of seconds—

—then launches the cup at my head.

It thumps against my temple. A weak throw, but the water soaks into my shirt, and it's freaking cold.

I blow out a breath between my teeth. "Okay. I should have seen that coming."

He reaches for the tray. I lean forward, slapping my hand down on it before he can flip it into my lap. He uses my close proximity against me, grabbing a fistful of my hair. Damn!

I swing the tray into his side. He lets out a curse, but doesn't let go of my hair.

I'm not afraid. I'm pissed—mainly at myself for getting too close to him—so I swing a blind punch at his face. Another into his gut, but the damn vigilante won't let go.

"If you want your hand to remain attached to your arm, you'll release her."

Aren's voice is calm and close. He's standing just to my

left, I think. I'm able to turn my head enough that I can peer up at him sideways, my hair half-covering my face. I blow out a breath, moving a few locks aside for a better view.

His expression is as calm as his voice despite the fact that he has a dagger pressed against Glazunov's wrist.

Glazunov's fingers finally loosen. I pull my hair free, then slide back a couple of feet.

"Perhaps another scoot," Aren suggests, looking down at me, his eyebrows slightly raised.

I feel myself blush. I should have known better than to get too close to the vigilante. The fact that Aren saw my, um, predicament, is downright embarrassing.

"What would I do without you?" I mutter as I get to my feet with some semblance of dignity.

He chuckles.

I glare at Aren before turning my attention back to Glazunov. He's backed himself against the wall again and is dragging air into his lungs. He overexerted himself. I would have gotten free from him on my own eventually. I might have lost some hair in the process, but I didn't *need* saving.

"I see you've made a lot of progress with him," Aren teases.

I ignore him as I squat down a safe distance from the vigilante and meet his eyes. "Lee said you're in charge of the vigilantes now and that you helped create the Sight serum."

"And he and his little friend, Paige, are going to die," Glazunov says. Apparently, he has enough strength to sneer. "Yes. What a pity."

I do my best not to let his words affect me. Aren never lets his enemies affect him. He makes it look easy to shrug off their hate-filled words. It's not.

"You've given the serum to other humans. To vigilantes," I say. "You want them to survive, don't you?"

I'm watching his face carefully, looking for some sign of compassion or remorse, but he just stares at me as if he's imagining strangling me. Gentle questions aren't going to get answers from him. He was Nakano's second-in-command. You don't rise to the top of an organization like his by com-

promising on your beliefs. Glazunov hates the fae and any human who associates with them.

"We have ways of making you cooperate," Aren says. His arms are loosely crossed, and he's standing beside me all cool and relaxed. It's a calculated indifference, though. His posture is saying he's in control and that Glazunov is so insignificant he could squash him with his thumb.

My heart thumps in my chest, and my need for information wars with my conscience. Firmer methods of persuasion are common in the Realm. I don't like that fact, but I like the idea of the serum killing Paige, Lee, and other humans even less.

"Look," I say. "Lee is talking to the person who created the serum." *Talking to* is a stretch—I imagine he's abducting Charles Bowman the same as he did Glazunov—but I'm trying to find a painless way to get the information out of Glazunov. "We'll find a way to fix it, but we need to know who's taken it. We need to know if you're still giving it to people."

"We have magics that can make you talk," Aren says, taking a too-casual step forward. "You won't like my methods. I suggest you not make me use them. It would be . . . uncomfortable for you, and the outcome will be the same either way."

"I won't tell you anything," Glazunov says, but he doesn't look as certain as he did before. He's pressing his back against the wall, putting as much space as possible between him and Aren.

"You'll tell us everything," Aren says in a level, confident voice. "You'll tell us how you developed the serum. You'll tell us who knows about it and who's taken it. You'll tell us what makes it fatal and how to cure the humans who've already injected it."

"And you'll tell us if you're selling it," I put in.

Glazunov's gaze locks on me, surprised, I think. But I have a sinking suspicion I know the answer to that last question. The *elari* in Tholm said the serum was being sold. Maybe there was a tiny bit of truth in that accusation. The serum is being sold, but not by Lena. It's being sold by the freaking vigilantes.

"You can go roast in hell," Glazunov says.

Aren steps forward, then crouches down a couple of feet in front of Glazunov. "You're going to start answering our questions now."

The vigilante's nostrils flare. "You're going to have to kill me."

Aren's cold laugh raises goose bumps on my skin. "No, we won't do that. After all, you don't kill the fae you manage to capture." A pause. "Yes, we know what you do to them. Your experiments. We want to learn more about you, as well, and we're always looking for a disposable human to dissect."

I bite my tongue to keep from calling bullshit right there. The fae always go out of their way to protect humans. Well, most of the fae do. Aren's bluffing.

"Tell us how the Sight serum kills," I say, putting a gentle plea into my voice. The look I give Glazunov says that he can trust me. I'm with him and want to help him.

Glazunov shakes his head. No loud, profanity-laced outburst. I think he might be breaking.

"This is Jorreb," I say, indicating Aren. "He has an . . . interesting magical ability. He can pry the information we want from your mind. I don't want him to have to do that. It will hurt. You may not survive it."

Those are the words Aren said to me the first time I met Lorn. They nearly broke me. Never mind that it turned out that Lorn's mind-reading magic doesn't work on humans, no one knew it at the time. I believed the rebels would get the information they wanted out of me one way or the other. Glazunov looks like he believes it, too. His gaze flickers to Aren.

This is going to work. If I didn't know Aren, I'd be terrified of him.

"My patience is running thin," Aren says.

"You have to talk if you want me to help you," I say.

Glazunov stubbornly clenches his teeth together, but sweat glistens on his forehead.

Quicker than I can follow, Aren grabs the vigilante's forearm. Glazunov squirms and the first signs of true terror shine in his eyes as he stares at the lightning on his skin, lightning he can suddenly feel.

"What's wrong with the serum?" I ask.

Panic crawls across the human. He tries to pry Aren's hand off his arm, and he starts shaking and scratching as if cockroaches are crawling over his skin.

I frown. I'm almost certain Aren's not using any magic. Tiny *edarratae* would be flickering across his hand if he was, but there's only an occasional flash of light when one of Glazunov's . . . Oh.

I almost laugh. It's Aren's touch, the enticing, delicious heat of it, that's freaking the vigilante out.

"Let go!" Glazunov screams.

"It'll get worse the longer he touches you," I tell him calmly. "What's killing the humans? How do we cure them?"

Glazunov's body lurches and a sob escapes him. "Please!"

A bright bolt of lightning strikes up Aren's arm.

"How do we cure them?" I demand.

"You can't cure them!" Glazunov screams. His shoes slide across the smooth ground as he tries to embed himself in the stone wall.

"That's the wrong answer," Aren says, grabbing the vigilante's other arm.

"No. Listen. You can't fix it because it is fixed," he wails. "The serum is already fixed!"

TWELVE

.-.-.

AREN RELEASES THE vigilante's arm. I'm not sure if he's just ready to stop touching Glazunov or if he believes him. I'm not sure if *I* believe him. It's too easy an answer to a life-or-death problem.

"You're sure?" I ask, making my voice icy.

Glazunov curls into a ball, his left cheek pressed against the stone wall. "We changed the formula three months ago."

The knots in my stomach loosen a fraction. Paige has had the Sight for around two months. I'm not sure when Lee injected the serum, but I think it was relatively recent as well. They might both be okay.

"So, if someone injected the serum in the last couple of months, they're going to live?"

Glazunov's gaze flickers my direction. There's the slightest hesitation before he answers, "Right."

Aren hears the pause, too. He leans forward, staring into Glazunov's eyes. "I don't believe you."

A muscle in Glazunov's cheek twitches.

"Tell us the truth," Aren says, reaching toward the vigilante's neck.

"I am telling the truth," Glazunov says too quickly.

Instead of strangling the vigilante, Aren merely draws his finger down the side of Glazunov's neck. It's not anything

close to a caress or gentle touch, but Glazunov throws himself on the floor, trying to get away from him. Aren grabs his arm, flipping him to his back.

"Okay. Okay, okay, okay!" Glazunov shouts, fists swinging wildly. When Aren merely stands over him, Glazunov splutters out, "We still have the old formula. *Had* the formula."

"Keep talking," Aren says.

"Some of the vials are missing." He sucks in a shallow breath. "We don't know where they went or who injected them. Only a few of us knew of the serum's side effect."

"Death is a side effect?" Angry, I step to Aren's side.

Glazunov looks at me. "They took a pledge to eradicate the fae. They've lost people they love to the heathens. They all knew this wouldn't be an easy or bloodless fight. You know it, too. Think about what you've lost. Your family, your future, your freedom. You're their slave, but you could be free again. We can help you."

What the hell?

Aren looks at me, a small smile playing across his lips. "I think he's trying to recruit you, *nalkin-shom*."

I roll my eyes at him.

"Their magics have erased your good judgment," Glazunov continues. "We can restore it. We can cleanse you."

That sounds entirely unpleasant.

"The serum," I say, returning the conversation to where it's supposed to be. "Is there a way to tell which one someone injected?"

Cautiously, Glazunov sits up. "I don't know."

"Does anyone else know?" I ask. I haven't checked my e-mail or voice mails in more than a day, but maybe Lee's found Bowman or another vigilante and is trying to get in touch with me now.

"Maybe," Glazunov says. "You'll have to talk to them."

"Next question," Aren says. "Who is selling the serum?"

I glance at Aren, but he keeps his eyes locked on Glazunov. I keep quiet and look at the vigilante, too, holding my breath as I wait for his response. In terms of the fight against the false-blood and his *elari*, the answer doesn't matter. They already believe Lena has something to do with the serum. But

in terms of the fae's status on Earth? If the vigilantes are selling the serum to any random human who will pay . . . That could be a problem.

Glazunov's expression darkens. "With Nakano dead, we were running out of cash. Selling the serum was discussed as a new revenue channel."

"Discussed?" I ask.

"I told them we weren't going to sell it," Glazunov says. "That should have been the end of the conversation."

"But it wasn't?"

He shakes his head. Lena is going to be so pissed.

"Who decided to sell it anyway?"

Glazunov shrugs. "Any of them. All of them. I don't know."

I believe him. He doesn't know, and he's pissed about that fact. He was Nakano's second-in-command. He's supposed to be in charge now, but he can't keep his people in line.

Aren and I ask him a few more questions—where can we find the person selling the serum, how much was produced, where is the research stored and backed up—but his responses aren't very useful. There's a reason Lee decided to go after another vigilante: Glazunov is a dead end.

When we run out of questions, we start to leave, but Aren stops beside the open door, turning back to look at Glazunov.

"One last thing," he says. "You're going to start eating. If you don't, I'll come back and spoon-feed you myself. Do you understand?"

Glazunov doesn't answer, but he goes still, indicating he does understand.

Aren steps out of the cell and closes the door. He stands there looking at me as the guard locks it. He's tense—I'm not sure he knows what to say—and that's when I suddenly become aware I haven't showered in almost two days, and I'm wearing the same clothes I walked across the Realm in.

Well, isn't this an awesome way to show him what he's trying to push away.

He comes to some decision, and tension whooshes out of him in an almost visible cloud.

"That ended up being a surprisingly effective coercion technique," he says.

His tone is light, and his movement as we walk down the row of cells is easy, languid. He's always hid his troubles behind his devil-may-care smiles and his nonchalance, but I know him well enough to see through the façade now. He's uncomfortable around me.

I tilt my head to the side. "You are very good at seducing people to your way of thinking."

He laughs. "Too bad it doesn't work on high nobles and *elari*."

"You didn't get anything else out of the fae captured in Tholm?"

"No," he says. When his smile fades, I hate myself for asking the question. "We've captured other *elari* in the past few weeks. The false-blood doesn't trust easily. None of them have known his name let alone his location." A guard opens the door at the end of the corridor, and we leave the quiet cells behind us. "What made you think the vigilantes were selling the serum?"

"Nothing really," I say. "It just bothered me that the *elari* knew a serum existed. I couldn't get it off my mind and . . . Well, this doesn't exactly disprove that Caelar is working with the false-blood, but the *elari* could have stumbled across the information somewhere else. Lorn, maybe."

"Hmm," Aren says. I've never heard a *hmm* so devoid of inflection.

"What?"

"Nothing."

I step in front of him, blocking his path. He manages to stop before he touches me. He even takes a step back, putting more distance between us so that we don't accidentally come in contact.

"Lena sent you down here, didn't she?" I ask. Then, realizing how stupid the question is, I say, "Don't answer that. Of course she did. You wouldn't have come knowing I was there unless you were forced to."

"I passed her in the hall," he says, confirming my words. "Hison wanted to meet with her."

"Hison." His name puts a bad taste in my mouth. "You're running errands for him now?"

Aren stiffens. "No."

"What's going on with him?" I ask.

"It's nothing." He steps around me.

"Then why are you talking to him so much?" I demand, turning. "Is he blackmailing you?"

"I said it's nothing," he fires over his shoulder.

"That's bullshit, Aren." I grab his arm, and he spins so quickly I stagger back a half step.

"Here." He slaps something into my palm. "I came to give you that."

I look down. And stop breathing. It's Kyol's name-cord. He gave it to me years ago. I kept it in a jewelry box in my old apartment, and the last time I was there, I slid it into my pocket, intending to give it back to him. But the remnants came after me. We were trying to figure out who they were and what had happened to Paige, then I fell through the ice in Rhigh, trying to get to the city's gate. That's the last time I had the name-cord. Aren saved me. He brought me back to the palace.

And stripped me out of my wet clothes. He must have found it then.

"You've had it all this time?" I look up, suddenly angry. "Were you waiting for the right moment to throw it in my face?"

"If I wasn't here, you'd be with him," he says. The words sound more like a question than an accusation, but I take them as the latter.

"No, I wouldn't," I say, taking a step toward him. "If you weren't here, I'd be dead. If you weren't here, I'd still be blind and working for a king who cared only about staying in power. Years would pass, and Kyol would keep pushing me aside anytime our 'relationship' became too real for him."

"But if I died—"

"I *still*"—I emphasize the word with a fist to his chest—"wouldn't be with him. I can't. I would always wonder if the life-bond manipulated my feelings for him."

He catches my hand against his chest. Kyol's name-cord digs into my palm.

"But if you weren't so stubborn," he says softly, "you could make it work. Even with the life-bond."

"I want to make it work with you," I tell him. "Even with the life-bond."

"McKenzie." The word sounds more like a sigh than my name. I lift my free hand to the side of his face.

"I love *you*," I say. Then I slide my hand behind his neck and feel his resistance melt away.

He initiates the kiss, bending down to slant his mouth across mine. I'm addicted to his scent and his touch, to the way his arms encircle me, pulling me against him, but mostly, I'm just addicted to *him*. He's a light in all this darkness. He's strong and caring, and he's sacrificed so much for Lena and the Realm. He makes me happy, and I want so much to make him happy, too.

His tongue flicks across mine, and I draw him closer.

"McKenzie," he murmurs as he trails kisses along my jaw. When he nips my ear, lightning explodes through me, sending tendrils of pleasure through my scalp and down my neck. I stuff the name-cord into my pocket, then trail my hands up his chest. He's not wearing *jaedric*. His muscles are firm and chiseled beneath my palms.

"I want you," I whisper, and he murmurs something indecipherable into my ear.

Chaos lusters flash across my skin. They're becoming so frenzied, they're skipping to his mouth and hands, anywhere and everywhere our bodies touch.

I tug on Aren's arm to pull him . . . I don't know where. I draw in a breath, trying to figure out where we are, trying to think. Trying not to think. The corridor we're in is empty. It might not stay that way for long. Someone could interrupt us any second.

"Aren." I tug again.

He's not budging. His hands are locked on my arms, holding me in place as he takes my mouth again, and that's when I realize something's . . . not wrong, exactly. It's just not completely right.

It takes another long, languorous kiss to identify the

problem. Aren's not completely into this. Oh, he's kissing me. He's kissing me, and I'm kissing him, and it's hot and delicious, but he's holding back, not willing to cross the line with me.

I want to eradicate that line. I want to obliterate it, rip it into pieces, then burn all the frayed ends to ash. This is the same damn line I've treaded for a decade.

My hands move back to Aren's chest, not to admire his body, but to push him away. When I manage to get a few inches of space between us, I say, "I don't want your half-assed kisses."

He looks completely disoriented for a moment. He leans back toward me, almost as if he's starved for me, but then, after a slow, deep breath, he seems to pull himself together again.

"Half-assed?" he asks, the corner of his mouth quirking up. "I promise those were some of my very best kisses."

He's dismissing my words with a quip and hiding his feelings behind that relaxed, cocky smile. I know why he's doing it—it's his way of protecting himself—but it still hurts. And it still pisses me off.

"Three days, Aren," I say.

He lifts an eyebrow. "Three days?"

"Yes," I force myself to say. "That's how long you have to pull your head out of your ass. Then we really are over."

Part of me can't believe I'm saying this. I can't believe I'm giving someone I love so much so little time to choose me, but I won't wait for him like I waited for Kyol. I'm stronger now than I was then.

An eternity passes in the span of a heartbeat. Then Aren lets the few inches between us grow to a foot, to two feet.

"Good," he says finally. He gives me a nod, then shoves his hands into his pockets and leaves.

GOOD.

Good?

I repeat the word over and over as I climb the staircase to the ground floor of the palace. Aren is *glad* I'm giving him an ultimatum. And, of course, he is. If three days pass, and I'm strong enough to stay away from him, then he doesn't have to

be strong enough to stay away from me. He's already proven he's weak on that front. Nearly every time we've been together, his will has broken. He's taken me into his arms.

I could ignore my own ultimatum. I could pressure him more, attempt some sort of seduction, but throwing myself at him is too sad and pathetic. I'm not one of those girls who can't live without the guy she's in love with. Even when I wanted Kyol, I tried to have a life separate from him. I went to college, Paige set me up on a few dates, and every once in a while, I went out to the movies, the mall, and sometimes to a bar. I was okay without him, and I know I can survive a heartbreak now; I just don't want to have to.

Good? God, Aren is such a coward, either for not trying to work through the life-bond issue or for not telling me the truth about what's going on. I'm not going to wait around for him to grow a backbone. I'll find answers myself, and I know exactly where to start asking questions.

Lena's apartments are on the third floor. Hison is a long-winded fae, and I have no doubt he'll still be there meeting with her, so I walk quickly through the governing wing of the palace and enter an ornate corridor. Magically lit orbs are set into silver sconces, and the blue-white light they cast highlight the carvings on the walls and ceiling. I receive a few questioning glances from the fae I pass—mostly aides to the high nobles, whose offices are also here—but no one asks where I'm heading. I might have disappeared for three weeks, but my reputation didn't diminish at all. They know who I am, and they know I'm Lena's ally.

The guards let me into her greeting chamber, a large, comfortable room with silver carpets and waves of blue silk on the ceiling. Plush couches are arranged in an inviting setup to my left, and to my right is a long desk made from a dark wood. Lena's symbol—an *abira* tree with seventeen branches—is carved into its front, and rising from a chair behind it is Andur, a rebel I remember seeing with Sethan on more than one occasion. He acts as one of Lena's advisors now.

"Lena's meeting with Lords Hison and Kaeth," he says in thickly accented English.

"I know." I eye the door to his right, the one that leads into

a small meeting room. When I start that way, Andur moves out from behind the desk.

"I'm sure she wouldn't mind being interrupted," I say before he can emit a protest.

"I'm sure she wouldn't," he says, trying but failing to hide a smile. He doesn't move out of my way, though. No doubt, he knows Hison will be pissed if I walk in.

While he's weighing the pros and cons of taking on Hison's wrath, I pick up part of the muffled conversation behind the door. Or rather, the argument if I'm hearing the rise and fall of the voices correctly. I take a step closer to the door, then another when Andur doesn't stop me. It's not until I'm reaching for the handle that he says, "I'm strongly advising you not to enter."

I freeze, expecting him to knock my hand away from the handle, but when I glance his way, he's returning to the chair behind the desk. I start to give him a grateful smile, but then I hear a word that sends goose bumps prickling across my arms.

Garistyn. They're talking about the kingkiller.

Forgetting caution, I turn the handle. I haven't forgotten the problem of the *garistyn*, but I have conveniently shoved it to the bottom of my list of crises to take care of, mainly because I didn't think it would be an issue anymore. The high nobles were using the *garistyn* as an excuse to delay confirming Lena as queen, but I'd assumed they'd confirmed her anyway while I was gone. She *said* they would.

The door swings open silently. My gaze finds Lena first. She's standing rigidly in the center of the room, facing Hison and Kaeth. Her expression is neutral, but I swear her face is a half shade redder than normal. She might sound and appear calm, but she's not. I know her that well now.

"*I want their names,*" Hison is saying. "*I want their locations.*"

"*I can't help you,*" Lena tells him. "*I wasn't there.*"

"*We will learn the truth despite your interference.*" Hison's dark blue cape billows out behind him when he takes a step toward her. "*One of the witnesses is a very strong ward maker. The ledgers will lead me to him eventually.*"

Witnesses? Who is he talking about? Someone who knows something about the *garistyn*? Only Kyol, Aren, and I know who slid the sword into Atroth's back. The king had guards in his hall, but as far as I know, they're all dead. Hison would have questioned them long before now if they weren't.

Maybe that's it, though. Maybe he and Lord Kaeth just now found out someone else survived.

"The ledgers?" Lena says, ice in her whisper. *"You mean the books that Atroth forced every fae to record their magics in? The ones that are* completely *accurate because everyone was anxious to confess their abilities so that Atroth could conscript them into his service? I wish you the best of luck with that."*

Sarcasm. Rumor has it those ledgers are mostly false. Every fae was required to fissure to Corrist to write down their abilities in Atroth's books. I knew about the ledgers when I shadow-read for the king, but I didn't know how much the fae resented being documented or that the trip was forced upon them. Very few told the truth when they signed their names. *If* Hison has discovered there's a witness to the king's murder, it's unlikely the ledger will lead the high noble to him. I hope.

"King Atroth saw the importance of knowing the magics criminals and false-bloods could throw at us," Hison says coldly, arrogantly. *"Maybe one day, you'll learn so as well. Confirm the identity of the kingkiller, Lena."*

"You want to execute Jorreb," Lena says. *"That's the only reason you're insisting upon this."*

"This is about justice," Lord Hison says. *"If Jorreb didn't kill King Atroth, you or he would tell me who did. You're protecting him."* His gaze swivels to me, standing here in the doorway. *"Or you're protecting her. Lord Kaeth."*

Kaeth moves before my mind finishes translating Hison's words. He's on me in an instant, grabbing my shoulders and slamming me against the wall beside the door.

"Lord Kaeth!" Lena yells. *"Release her!"*

Kaeth ignores her, he ignores the bolt of white lightning that leaps from my skin to his, then he leans in close, and demands, *"Did you murder King Atroth?"*

"What are you, Hison's lackey?" I demand, but my voice

quivers. A potent, debilitating fear rushes over me. I feel an echoing terror move through Kyol.

"Tell me who murdered the king." Kaeth's voice slithers under my skin.

Kyol's name is on the tip of my tongue. If I want to live, I have to say it. I have to tell Lord Kaeth what he wants to know.

"It's magic, McKenzie," Lena snaps. "Don't say a word."

Magic? My whole body trembles, filled with fear. Kyol's sprinting this way now, and I can barely think with his terror mixing with mine. He doesn't know why I'm afraid.

Hold on a second.

I don't know why I'm afraid.

My gaze locks on Lord Kaeth's sharp silver eyes.

"Answer me, human," he hisses.

Oh, son of a—

I get my right arm free, then slam the heel of my hand into Kaeth's nose. Bones crunch, and he staggers back, eyes wide. I don't know if he's more hurt or surprised that I, a mere human, struck him.

Kyol was right about fae underestimating me.

I twist the wrist he's still holding as I jerk it back. As soon as he loses his grip, the artificial fear whooshes out of me. Lena steps between us before he recovers. Her hand is locked around the hilt of the sword sheathed at her hip, and the tension is almost tangible in the air. I'm not focused on it, though. I'm focused on the tension in Kyol and the fact that he's heading this way.

I shut down my emotions as completely as possible, letting only a sense of calm assurance leak through our bond. I don't want him anywhere near Hison and Kaeth. If the high nobles pressure him, if they threaten me or Lena and demand to know the identity of the *garistyn*, I'm afraid he'll answer them. He'll tell them the truth because he regrets killing Atroth, his king and his friend.

"Get out," Lena orders. *"Now."*

Unperturbed, Hison eyes her. *"Afraid the* nalkin-shom *will answer Kaeth's questions? That would be difficult since she isn't supposed to speak our language."*

Lena's mouth tightens, and I suppress a curse and another

wave of emotions. It's forbidden for humans to learn Fae. The law has been around for decades, and Atroth enforced it just as religiously as the previous kings, but the rebels didn't. They taught me their language. We've kept my knowledge of it under wraps because it's just one more transgression the high nobles will hold against Lena.

Lena keeps her eyes locked on Hison's. *"You have ten seconds to leave my apartments. If you don't, you'll learn my sword isn't just an ornament."*

Hison laughs. *"You won't harm us. The high nobles would never give you power if you did."*

I'm not as confident about that as he is, the Lena-not-harming-him part. The Lena I know, or the one I knew back before she became interim queen, wasn't just some figurehead leader. She knew how to fight, how to kill and maim. The role she's found herself in doesn't fit comfortably. All she might need is an excuse to be who she was before.

"I want the name of the kingkiller or the names of the witnesses by sunset," Hison says. *"If I have to hunt the witnesses down myself, I'll have your lord general and your sword-master arrested and you confined to your apartments. And in the end, I'll still learn the kingkiller's identity."*

With that, Hison departs, Kaeth following a step behind.

"Can he do that?" I ask when the doors close behind them. My voice is overly monotone because I'm still trying to quash my emotions. Kyol knows I'm not in danger now, but he wants to know what was wrong. He's still heading this way, and I'm afraid he'll cross paths with Hison and Kaeth.

"What?" Lena snaps.

"Can Hison arrest Aren and Kyol and keep you locked in here?"

She draws in a deep breath, calming herself, then moves to the window and peers out.

"Probably," she says. "Maybe. I don't really know. I don't have enough support to oppose him."

"Support from the high nobles?"

"From them," she says, nodding out the window. "From the people. From everyone."

"What happens if you never get their support?"

"What happens if I fail?" Her eyes look glassy when she meets my gaze. "Then my brother's death meant nothing, and the fae who have fought and died for him and who now fight and die for me . . . it all means nothing." She turns back to the window. "Atroth catered to the high nobles. They're used to his favors. They hate me because I won't make one group of people suffer just so they can prosper. They know I'll lower and equalize the gate taxes as soon as I have the authority to do so. And they know that, once I have access to the treasury, I won't use the *tinril* as bribes. I'll use it to help the *tor'um*, the *imithi*. All the fae whom they've shoved aside and ignored."

She looks at me over her shoulder. "Did you know there are fae living in the Barren?"

"I know fae shun the Barren," I say. I crossed that strip of land not too long ago. Thrain collapsed the gate in Krytta ten years ago, killing thousands of fae and making it impossible to fissure in a third of Sarna Province.

"We think they're *tor'um*," Lena says. "We don't know for sure, but they've been raiding stack houses that are near the Barren, stealing whatever is stored there before the merchants have a chance to load it onto their carts and take it to the nearest gate. Atroth had plans to send his swordsmen to Krytta to annihilate anyone they found there."

I bite the inside of my cheek. I gave ten years of my life to that king. He never struck me as someone who was capable of mass murder, not even in the end, and every time I hear about something he did or planned to do, I feel like a fool for not seeing what he'd become.

"It was Lord General Radath's plan," Lena says, as if she sees the regret written on my face. "Taltrayn spoke out against it. Perhaps Atroth would have listened to him."

And perhaps not. But she doesn't have to convince me that she's better for the Realm than Atroth was. She just has to convince everyone else.

"So you're no closer to being confirmed as queen," I say. "What are the high nobles' alternatives? The false-blood?"

She shakes her head. "The false-blood would have to take over by force. The high nobles may not like me, but they

won't confirm a fae who won't tell them his ancestry. No, they'll rule by council until they find a weak-blooded Descendant who'll agree to sit on the throne. It will be someone they can manipulate. Someone *Hison* can manipulate," she amends bitterly. "He might have a candidate already. He'll tell the others I can't unify the Realm, but his puppet can."

She looks so heavy-hearted. I want to rest my hand on her shoulder, assure her that everything will work out in the end, but I can't promise her that. There's too much uncertainty in the Realm right now. Besides, Lena isn't the type of person to accept that kind of comfort.

"Thanks for stepping in when Kaeth grabbed me," I tell her instead. "We've come a long way since you tried to kill me."

She still has a death grip on her sword. When I eye it pointedly, she drops her hand to her side as if she's been caught stealing. Heaven forbid she admit she was prepared to defend me.

"I never tried to kill you." A small smile bends a corner of her mouth. "I tried to have others do it for me."

That pulls a laugh from my chest, and it feels good, releasing a little tension.

Sobering up, I ask, "They're going to find out about Kyol, aren't they?"

Lena's mouth flattens out again. "Two of Atroth's guards survived our invasion. They laid down their weapons, and Taltrayn vouched for them. He wouldn't let me kill them." Her gaze slides to me. "Don't get that disapproving look, McKenzie. They were my enemies. I had the right to give them a good, clean death."

"I didn't say anything," I protest.

"It's the way things are done here," she continues, her voice firm. "But I took the advice of my lord general. I accepted their oaths of allegiance, then I sent them away. It was a temporary solution to buy me time. I've been trying to find ways to persuade the high nobles to approve me without giving them the *garistyn*, but I've run out of time. If word gets out that my lord general and sword-master have been arrested, and that I'm confined here, I'll lose the little amount of support that I have."

"You need to find a way to get more support now," I say.

She rolls her eyes, probably because I've stated the obvious. I'm about to cut off whatever smart remark she's going to say by pointing out how *human* her eye rolling is, but her mouth snaps shut. She stares at me silently. I frown as the seconds tick by, then raise an eyebrow.

"Are you okay?"

"Come with me," she says. Then, without explanation, she walks out of the room.

THIRTEEN

⬥•⬥

ANDUR RISES FROM the desk as Lena strides through the antechamber.

"Stay here," she barks at him.

He sends me a questioning look as I hurry after her, but I just shrug in response. I have no freaking idea what she's doing.

"Where are you going?" I ask, when we step into the corridor outside Lena's apartments. The guards standing to either side of the double-doored entrance straighten when they see her.

"Do you need assistance?" the taller fae on the left asks.

She doesn't answer either of us. She just turns to the right and keeps walking. I alternate between a jog and a fast walk.

"Lena—"

"You said I should get more support," she cuts me off. "That's what I'm doing." She doesn't even glance over her shoulder when she speaks. She moves down the wide corridor in long, confident strides.

Confusion travels along my life-bond with Kyol. I don't know if I'm projecting the emotion or if he is, but I can't do anything to clear it up. Lena isn't slowing down, and I don't know where she's going.

No, I *do* know where she's going. A short staircase takes

us to the entrance to the palace archives. Lena and her guard enter without hesitating, but I linger in the doorway. I knew the palace archivist. He was one of the few fae I considered a friend when I worked for the king. Trusting Kavok ended up being a mistake, though. When the rebels captured Tylan, a high-ranking remnant, Kavok betrayed us, freeing the fae and escaping with Paige and Lee.

Bracing myself, I cross the threshold. Then pause. The atmosphere inside the archives feels the same as the corridor. There's no change in humidity or air pressure like there was the one time I entered before. But then, of course there's not. Kavok was the one who magically regulated all of that. Since he's gone, the archives aren't being maintained the way they should. If she doesn't want to lose all the history documented here, Lena needs to find a replacement for him, someone who can control the environment and keep the papers from deteriorating.

Lena stops at a large glass display set against the wall at the back of the room. She tries lifting the top, but it doesn't budge. That doesn't stop her, though. Without hesitating, she lifts her hand then makes a slamming motion. I feel the atmosphere shift as she harnesses the air, then the glass shatters without Lena's hand coming close to touching it.

Heedless of the sharp glass, she grabs a heavy tome, then places it in my arms.

Reflexively, I keep hold of it though I nearly fall forward at the unexpected weight of the book. It's oversized and leather-bound, but I can't read any of the Fae written on its cover.

"What is this?" I ask. Similar books are hidden beneath the black bottom of the display case. Lena takes two of them out, then adds them to my arms. After she does, she tosses a pen to the floor. It's black and carved with symbols.

I realize what these books *must* be, so I amend my question. "What are you going to do with them?"

She meets my gaze. "I'm losing it."

"Your mind?" I ask, surprised she's admitting to it.

Her eyes narrow. "The Realm, McKenzie. I'm losing the Realm. But I refuse to hand it over to the high nobles without a fight. These books will be my first true swing."

She drops two more heavy tomes into my arms, then carries

the last one herself, leaving the archives as quickly as she entered them. Curiosity drives me to follow her. The books we're holding are the ledgers Hison mentioned, the ones Atroth required every fae to sign. Their magics—at least, the magics the fae decided to admit to—are listed inside of them.

The top ledger on my stack nearly slides off when I trot down the steps leading into the sculpture garden. It's almost noon here, so the open-aired courtyard is crowded with Court advisors and the high nobles' assistants. I recognize Lord Raen, Kelia's father and the high noble of Tayshken Province. I've barely spoken to him since Kelia was killed. He hasn't taken her death well. They were estranged, and he didn't have time to make amends.

"Lena?" Trev's voice cuts through the air. He turns away from the fae he was talking to, his gaze tracking Lena as she crosses the white-tiled floor.

"Not now," she says without so much as a hitch in her stride.

Trev's gaze shifts to me.

"I don't know," I tell him, "but you might want to"—I run a few steps to keep up with Lena—"to come with us."

He mutters something to the fae standing beside him, then jogs to catch up with me.

"What are those?" he asks, when the top book almost slides off my stack again. Instead of shifting it back into place, I shove the heavy tome into Trev's chest. His breath whooshes out of his lungs in an *oomph*.

"These are the magic ledgers," I say. "I don't know what she's doing with them."

By the look on Trev's face, he doesn't know either.

"Lena," he calls after her. She leaves the sculpture garden, heading into the southern wing of the palace. When she takes a straight path to the huge, double doors that mark the main entrance, knots form in my gut. *Now* I know what she's going to do, and it's either a brilliant idea or a foolish one.

"Open the doors," Lena orders as the guards double tap the pommels of their sheathed swords in a salute. There's a smaller, more practical door to the right she could leave through, but if my hunch is right, Lena intends to make a scene.

"A crowd is gathered on the plaza—"

"Good," she interrupts the guard. He glances uncertainly at the other fae standing sentry.

"Lena," Trev tries again, this time jogging to get in front of her. "You can't leave the palace like this. It's dangerous."

"No one's expecting me," she says, sidestepping him.

Trev places a hand on her shoulder. "You need more guards."

She freezes, and an icy silver gaze locks on the hand that's touching her. Trev goes still as well, looking at his hand as if he's not sure how it got there.

He snatches the hand away, and there's a flash of something in his eyes. Fear? No, that doesn't make sense. Lena isn't the type of person who's going to say "off with his head" for a mere touch. Maybe it was a flash of disbelief? Not just for going against her wishes and touching her in public, though. If that was it, he would have apologized immediately. He doesn't apologize at all.

Lena steps around him. When she passes, he runs his hand over his face. It's definitely the gesture of someone who can't believe what he's just done, but there's more to it than that. If I had to guess, I'd say he can't believe what he almost just revealed.

Trev cares about Lena.

Aren cares about her, too, I tell myself. That doesn't mean he's into her. They're friends. Trev's probably her friend, too.

Probably.

Trev looks at me. My expression must betray my suspicion because his face darkens. "Say a word, and I'll kill you."

Holy hell, I'm right. He *is* into her. No wonder he puts up with her giving him crappy assignments like chauffeuring me to and from the Realm and babysitting Kynlee. He does anything she asks.

"I mean it, McKenzie," he says.

I try *really* hard not to grin. That becomes a whole lot easier when I see the huge, double doors start to swing open. Lena's serious about going out there.

Still holding my two huge ledgers, I bump into Trev, urging him to turn. He curses when he sees her step to the threshold.

"Find Jorreb and Taltrayn," he barks at the nearest guard. *"Bring them here. Now!"*

"Taltrayn's already on his way," I say before I think better of it.

Trev scowls at me. "What?"

"I sent for him before I saw you," I improvise. Kyol's on his way, but he's not hurrying, probably because my emotions are confusing the hell out of him. Between questioning the vigilante, the make-out session with Aren, and the rush of fear Lord Kaeth injected into me, he has no idea what's going on with me. I totally have to apologize to him later.

Lena waits until the doors are completely open and she's lit by a stream of golden sunlight before she steps outside. The plaza is crowded, and not just by fae going about their normal business. I can't even see the kiosks that are typically set up around the perimeter. People clothed in blues and grays are gathered in groups throughout the open area, and there's a buzz in the air, an energy that's just barely on this side of chaos. One wrong move, and I have the feeling this crowd won't be civil for long.

Being here is a really bad idea.

Trev issues more orders, calling for swordsmen to follow us.

"Stay with Lena," he says to me. "Watch for illusions and . . ." His gaze dips to my waist. He mutters something under his breath, motions to a swordsman, then plops the ledger I gave him back onto my stack.

"Trev," I grate out, because it's not like these books are light. Then I feel him fastening a belt around my waist. A sword slaps against my left leg.

He looks me in the eye as he makes the buckle a notch too tight. "If anything happens to her, I'll kill you."

"You're just throwing around the death threats today, aren't you?" My scowl is mostly fake, partly because I'm ridiculously happy that I have something on Trev and partly because I have no intention of letting anything happen to Lena.

Still carrying all three tomes, I run to take up a position to Lena's left. Before she's taken a dozen steps out of the palace, the swordsmen Trev called on for help create a semicircle around us.

Several hundred fae are gathered here. I finally catch a

glimpse of a few of the kiosks on the perimeter, see their colorful canopies, which are designed to attract attention and keep off the sun. Their owners sell everything from fruits, grains, and meats to silver dust and anchor-stones, and they're usually the reason fae come to this plaza. Not today, though. They're here now to make their complaints known.

Lena's guards effectively keep the crowd away, but they look uneasy. Understandably so. With this many people out, it'll be difficult to protect her from an attack. The silver wall surrounding the Inner City prevents fae from fissuring, but it doesn't prevent them from using magic, throwing a dagger, or aiming an arrow her way.

A cool, gentle breeze moves through the plaza, but when Lena reaches the center of the cobblestoned area, the wind picks up. It's unnaturally strong, circling through the crowd and making cloaks and capes whip around their legs. Two giant blue flags, both sewn with Lena's symbol, come to life as well. Their poles are set to either side of the doors we just exited, and each time they snap in the wind, it sounds like a firecracker's exploding behind my ear.

This is a powerful display of Lena's magic, and it captures the attention of the fae gathered in the plaza. They frown up at the clear blue sky. These kind of gales only come when there's a strong storm rolling in . . . or when an incredibly strong air-weaver is present.

One by one, everyone's gazes lock on Lena. Trev and I and the rest of her guards are standing a few paces away from her, so it's easy for the nearest fae to spot her. The buzz of conversation abates, then dissolves completely.

A few seconds later, the wind disappears as well. There's not even a breeze in the plaza anymore. Everything and everyone is seemingly frozen.

Except Lena. She tosses the book she's carrying to the ground in front of her.

"King Atroth's ledgers," she calls out, making the air carry her voice across the entire plaza.

"I promised you changes," she continues. *"The high nobles are promising you the status quo. The last signature was*

written over two months ago. Who here would like to record your magics? Your children's magics?"

Silence greets her words. I scan the faces of the fae. Some of them are shifting awkwardly, some of them are staring at me. If this is her idea of a motivational speech, she's not off to an awesome start.

"I promised you changes," Lena calls out again. She turns to me, grabs the top book off my stack. She opens it, then she places her palm on the center of one of the pages. She's not adept enough at fire to throw it, but she has no trouble making tiny flames lick over her fingers.

"Here's your first change."

I watch the page ignite, and despite knowing how much the fae hate the ledgers, horror creeps over me. I mean, the book is a *book*. It's huge and heavy, but it's carefully bound, and the cover is etched with an ornate design in silver. Each ledger looks like . . . Well, they look like the types of books you'd keep protected in a glass case. Plus, I am—or rather, I *was*—an English major. Everything in me objects to the burning of books.

"Lena," I whisper.

She grabs the other two ledgers out of my arms, then throws them on the pile at her feet. She must do something to encourage the flames because they crackle and leap into the air, almost waist high.

The only sounds in the plaza are the *snaps* and *pops* of the burning pages. No one has moved. I'm not even sure they're breathing. I watch as the pages crinkle, turning brown, then black, and all I can think is that I'm going to English-major hell for being a part of this.

"Cadig!" A single male voice calls out the fae equivalent of huzzah. A shiver runs up my spine because I don't know if it's a pro-Lena yell or a . . .

Others take up the call, one at a time, starting from whoever first said it and moving through the crowd to the left and to the right, and soon, everyone's yelling it. They're yelling other things I can't translate, too. Their words become a chant—a passionate chant—and I take an uneasy step forward, moving closer to Lena's side.

Lena doesn't budge; she remains standing in the sunlight, her expression grim and determined.

I glance at the crowd again. It's moving, but not aggressively. Are they celebrating?

The "*cadigs*" and chants escalate. Swords are drawn, but they're raised in the air, pointed at the clear blue sky. Yes, they're celebrating. They're elated to see the ledgers burn.

Lena waves her hand, and the small bonfire at her feet shoots higher. The crowd cheers, and someone slips through the guards' perimeter. Trev moves between the fae and Lena, but the man just throws what looks like an empty crate—maybe from one of the merchant's kiosks?—into the fire before he retreats, sword stabbing victoriously into the air.

Another fae makes it past the guards, then another. They each add to the bonfire, throwing more crates—some that aren't quite empty—and cloaks and papers and anything they can get their hands on. Lena maintains her position as the flames grow; so do I despite the heat coming from the burning pyre, and a tingle runs through me when I realize I'm watching history. I've only seen scenes like these on television: the celebration in Baghdad when Saddam's statue was toppled, the open elation in Egypt when Mubarak stepped down as president.

A flash in my peripheral vision makes my head snap to the left. A ball of flame, bright even in the full daylight, shoots into the air. It dissipates a couple of hundred feet up, but on the other side of the plaza, a second fireball is launched. Fire-wielders are in the crowd, ones who are at least as strong as Trev.

Lena's guards are having trouble holding back the fae. Some of them are chanting Lena's name now. A few call out *nalkin-shom*, too. That's when I realize what we must look like from the crowd's point of view: Lena, dressed in tight-fitting black pants and a silky blue shirt that swoops over both her shoulders to cross in the middle of her chest, and me, a human covered in blue lightning standing with her behind a gathering mountain of flames with the silver palace as a backdrop. Lena might need to work on her speech-giving skills, but she's a pro at making a scene.

The crowd shifts again as fae jostle each other, everyone trying to get a better view and to get closer. A few more

people slip past Lena's guards. Most of them retreat back to their places but not all of them do.

"Lena," Trev says, yelling to be heard over the crowd and the flames. *"You must go back inside now."*

I agree with him. She's made her point, and this could all get out of hand in a matter of seconds.

The fire crackles and licks at the air; and then, finally, she nods once. As I turn to follow her back to the palace, a blur of red and black moves through my vision. My brain recognizes the pattern a second later, and a warning bell goes off in my mind. I turn back to find it.

There. A name-cord. It's braided into the hair of a fae who is *not* celebrating. He's loud, and he's angry. He grabs the arms of the people nearest him, yelling in their ears, pushing and pulling them. Then his gaze cuts across the plaza to another mass of people. I focus on them and spot the red-and-black name-cord worn by another fae.

Elari. More than just a few. They're strategically placed in the crowd, and they're inciting the fae around them.

While I'm watching, one of them motions to another, then jabs his fist forward, toward the great doors, which are still open and waiting for our return.

Oh, shit.

"Trev!" I shout, trying to get his attention, trying to warn him. He doesn't hear me, but I'm not the only one who realizes the risk of those open doors. Kyol is there. His gaze sweeps across the plaza as a dozen swordsmen emerge from the palace behind him, forming a line.

The giant doors slowly start to close, but before they've moved more than a foot, someone nearby, undoubtedly an *elari*, shouts out a call to storm the palace.

FOURTEEN

-•-

"LENA!" KYOL BELLOWS the same instant I do. I grab her arm.

She jerks away with a glare.

"*Elari,*" I snap. "They're mixed in with the crowd."

The glare remains as she scans the fae around us—fae who are much too close now. The south doors won't shut in time to keep them all out. Dozens of people have heeded the *elari's* call to storm the palace. Kyol's swordsmen are trying to hold them back. They're outnumbered, though, and the crowd surges forward.

Mob mentality. The fae were on the verge of getting out of control *before* Lena appeared. Now, with a few not-so-subtle suggestions from *elari,* they've tipped over the edge, their celebrations turning into mindless violence and destruction.

"We have to get in another way," I yell into Lena's ear. Either that, or we have to get out of here. Find some place in the city to hide until the fae disperse.

"We'll go to the eastern entrance," Lena says. She grabs my arm like it was her plan to go there from the beginning, then directs me through the crowd. Her sword is still in its scabbard—mine is, too—but the air vibrates with the fae's chants and shouts and stomping feet. We're going to have to fight our way back into the palace, I'm sure of it.

The gaps in the crowd around us shrink, then disappear. Lena shoves her shoulder into them, creating a few inches of space at a time, but our progress is slow. Too slow. An *elari* sees us. A woman. She's moving through the crowd, dagger in her hand and hate in her eyes.

The weapons belt Trev fastened around my waist only has a sword. The people around me are pressed too close for me to draw it. I try digging my elbow into the nearest fae's stomach, try shoving him away and turning for more space. I get the sword halfway out, but someone shoves it back into its scabbard.

I look for Trev, then for Kyol, who feels like he's only a few feet away, but all the faces around me belong to strangers.

All of them.

I whip around, searching for Lena. She was right beside me. How could I have lost her?

I duck beneath a swinging elbow, then shove my way forward half a foot. There's so little space to move. The familiarity of the situation settles over me, the press of the crowd, the panicked shouts that begin to rise all around me. My chest constricts, remembering how close I came to being crushed to death at the concert in London. Several humans died that night. Fae might die here today.

I won't, though, and neither will Lena as long as I can find her.

Someone runs into me. I throw my weight back into them then slip through a narrow gap I opened. I'm looking everywhere for Lena, but all I see is a mob that's becoming increasingly angry.

A hand locks on my shoulder. I grab the fae's wrist and twist. Or try to. The arm doesn't budge. I follow the arm to the fae's shoulder then to his face.

Aren, and beside him, hidden beneath the hood of a dark gray cloak, is Lena.

"Thank, God," I mutter out loud.

Aren shoves away a fae who slams into me, then he holds up a cloak that's the same dark gray as Lena's.

"For you, *nalkin-shom*," he says, his silver eyes practically sparkling.

I want to ask him why the hell he's happy, but I just grab

the cloak and slip into it. Aren tries to pull my hood up, but I stop him, turning and waiting for . . .

Kyol. He and two of his men carve a path through the crowd. Most of the fae scramble out of their way when they see the lord general and his men, or rather, when they see their swinging swords, but a few of them don't back off. Their swords meet Kyol's in attacks that are halfhearted. They're just causing trouble and are caught up in the moment. They're not *elari*.

Kyol shoves one last fae away, then grabs my arm.

"Where's Lena?" he demands. I nod toward my right. Lena's stony silver eyes meet his unflinchingly.

"Go," Kyol says, fury riding on his order. Pain pulses behind my cycs. It feels like someone's taking a jackhammer to my brain. I reach for Kyol's hand, intending to calm him, but he pulls back. His eyes lock on me, and he grates out, "Move."

What the hell did I do?

No time to verbalize that question. Aren and Kyol and his men create an opening in the crowd. They're effective, splitting the masses like a sea, and the farther we get away from the southern doors, the thinner that mass becomes. We don't escape unnoticed by any means, though. A few fae figure out that only someone who's important would be hidden beneath a cloak and escorted by a lord general and a sword-master. They trail us, some of them shouting profanities, others begging for help. I scan the faces of the followers, searching for the red-and-black name-cords of the *elari* or anyone else who looks threatening, but Lena's guards keep everyone away.

We make it to the eastern entrance relatively easily and, quite surprisingly, unscathed. I think I might have one bruise on my back from an errant elbow, but other than that, there's just a stitch in my side from running to keep up with Lena and the others' quick pace.

The guards close the doors behind us, sealing us inside the palace. Inside where it's safe.

Supposedly safe.

My heart rate doesn't slow down. With the number of *elari* I saw in the crowd—at least five of them—I can't escape the feeling that we made it out of there far too easily.

* * *

HALF an hour later, when I'm waiting in the private chamber at the back of the King's Hall, I'm still uneasy. It looks like I'm the only one, though. Aren's sitting on the edge of a table against the far wall, grinning and demanding Trev give him details about what Lena said and did, and how the fae on the plaza reacted. He's positively giddy, high from the energy of the crowd and the scuffles we had to get through to escape it.

Lena's here, too, but she doesn't interject any insight. She's staring at a collage of drawings and writings on the back wall. The drawings are penciled sketches of the high nobles of the Realm's seventeen provinces, four of which were recently appointed by Lena. They're split into three groups. I recognize Kelia's father, Lord Raen, in the smallest group, and I assume he and the other four high nobles there with him are the ones Lena is certain will approve her. The sketches in the second and, by far, the largest group have writing under their names. I can't read Fae, but my guess is that she's listed details about the high nobles and possibly ideas for how she might go about persuading them to vote for her.

The last group is a group of one. Lord Ralsech, the high noble who's declared his support for the false-blood.

I'm not sure if Lena is really looking at the collage, though, or if she's staring through it to the tunnel on the other side. Her arms are folded across her chest, and her face is hard and smooth. She wants to be visible, on the ramparts of the palace or at least seeing the nobles and merchants and endless number of other fae who want an audience with her, but Kyol insisted we hole up down here. That tunnel, hidden behind a foot-thick slab of rock, is the palace's only emergency exit. Only a few fae know about it. In fact, aside from Kyol and perhaps Naito, I'm not sure if anyone outside this room knows of its existence.

"Where is he?" Lena demands. I know she's talking to me even though she doesn't turn. She's asked me this question a dozen times now, and finally, I can give her a different answer.

"He's on his way," I say.

Not for the first time, Trev gives me an odd look. He knows we're talking about Kyol. I don't think he's figured out we have a life-bond yet, but he will soon if Lena doesn't watch what she says. I'm not sure she cares if he knows, though. That either shows how much she trusts him—or it shows that she's not aware of his existence.

When the door to the chamber opens, Lena turns. Kyol descends the narrow staircase that leads up to the King's Hall. When the blue-white light from the magically lit orbs illuminates his face, his expression is as calm and stoic as ever. But I know how furious he is, and not just because I can feel his rage vibrating across the bond. It's his eyes. The edges of his irises are so dark, they're almost black, and they're a shade of silver that reminds me of a hurricane coming to shore.

My headache—the one that's been lingering since Kyol learned about Lena's ledger burning—increases tenfold when he looks at her now.

"What were you thinking?" He doesn't raise his voice, but his words cut through the air, echoing in the small chamber. I have to give Lena props. She doesn't so much as flinch when his gaze bores into her.

"I was thinking," she says, emphasizing the last word, "that I needed to gain the people's support."

I shift uncomfortably. That's kind of close to what I told her to do earlier, but I absolutely did not suggest the ledger burning.

"The people's support will come when the high nobles approve your reign."

"Which will never happen if I don't act," she bites out. "I'm not sure if you've noticed, Taltrayn, but they aren't exactly rallying behind me."

"They can't rally behind you if you're dead."

"Your concern is touching, but it's unneeded."

"Lena," Kyol grates out. His hand tightens on the hilt of his sword, and I realize his patience is running thin. That's impressive considering he's the most calm and tolerant man I know. "Your actions started a riot."

She crosses her arms. "My actions started a celebration."

"They've lost their minds out there. People will be hurt. There are fires to put out."

"And those fires will be put out."

"It's not that simple," he says.

Lena turns to Aren, who's silently watching the exchange the same as Trev and I are.

"You approve," she says.

A crooked, haphazard smile leaps to his lips. "You know I do."

"See," Lena says to Kyol, and a mix of emotions twists through him: anger, annoyance, and a good dose of protectiveness, too. That last one surprises me. It hasn't passed through our bond in that quantity except when it was focused on me, and I think some part of him might . . . *admire* Lena for what she's done. He doesn't exactly approve, of course, but she took action. She did something for the people, for the Realm.

"You have to consult us before you do something like this," Kyol says.

"I consulted McKenzie."

When Kyol slowly levels his gaze on me, my eyes widen. I shake my head. "I just helped her carry the ledgers."

"Ease up, Taltrayn," Aren says, sliding off the table. "The people are happy, and Lena is safe and unscathed."

When Kyol looks at Aren, the tension in the chamber doubles. I doubt the two men have spoken more than a dozen words to each other since Kyol formed the life-bond with me. They were enemies for years, and I'm fairly certain any respect they feel for each other now is begrudging at best. Neither man would be upset if the other happened to die and enter the ether.

Something tickles in the back of my mind. The two guards who survived Atroth's death. How did Lord Hison find out about them?

I shut that line of thought down quickly, ashamed it ever entered my head in the first place. Aren wouldn't let that information slip out just to off his competition. I've told him a million times that he doesn't have to worry about Kyol.

On the other hand, death is the only way to sever a life-bond.

"Not unscathed," Kyol says quietly, concern moving through him once again.

"Not unscathed?" Aren repeats, tilting his head to study Lena.

Lena's gaze remains icy as she stares at Kyol.

"You're not putting your full weight on your left leg," he says. "And you haven't removed your cloak. A knife wound, I presume."

I frown down at Lena's leg. It's mostly hidden beneath her cloak. How he can tell she's not putting weight on it, I don't know.

"Lena," Aren scolds as he crosses the room.

"It's barely a scratch."

"A scratch deep enough that you feel the need to hide it," Kyol says.

Aren takes her cloak off. Her left hip is stained red, and when he lifts the bottom of her shirt, the cut he reveals is definitely not just a scratch. It's a gash that runs from just above her hip bone to her lower back. Her *very* low back.

Aren shakes his head. "Why didn't you say something?"

"She didn't want you touching her ass," I mumble under my breath.

Under my breath is, apparently, loud and clear enough for the fae to understand. Their heads whip my way. Lena looks annoyed, Aren lets out a laugh, and even Trev has a small smile on his face.

Not Kyol, though. His expression is still stony, but the tension I feel in him abates some.

"It's not life-threatening," Lena says, giving me a glare before she turns her attention back to Aren. "Someone else's injury might be, and you're exhausting yourself."

"My magic is fine," he says.

"*You're* not fine," she counters. "When was the last time you slept?"

His expression hardens. "When was the last time you did?"

Her silence makes his point for him. No one's getting enough rest. Well, except me. I had three weeks to recover from the invasion of the palace and the fight to retain it.

Aren moves closer to press his palm against her hip. She

stares over his shoulder as he heals her. Looking at Trev maybe? He's leaning against the wall with his arms crossed. He lifts an eyebrow, but I'm not sure she's really seeing him.

Aren slides his hand under the waistband of her pants, all but cupping her ass. Am I jealous of her injury when he does that? Yep. Maybe I should have let myself get pushed around more.

"Trev," Lena says. His other eyebrow goes up. "I want you to speak to the commanders of each of the wall watches. They're to reassign three swordsmen from each rotation to you. I'm placing you in charge of guarding the provincial gates. They need to be regulated again. Now. You'll have those swordsmen and half my guard under your command."

Aren's gaze locks on her as he slides his hand out of her pants. I look at Kyol, whose fury has suddenly and explosively rekindled. He's staring at Lena and standing so rigidly still, I'm afraid he might shatter if someone so much as sneezes.

Even Trev looks surprised at her command, but he nods in acknowledgment and starts for the staircase.

"Disregard that order," Kyol says.

Lena stiffens. She focuses on her lord general, her chin jutting out half a millimeter, and says, "Go now, Trev."

"No." The word rumbles out of Kyol.

Trev's boot is on the first step that leads out of the room. He looks at me as if I can give him guidance. Guidance on whose order to follow or guidance on whether or not he should be worried about Kyol killing her, I don't know. I can't help him anyway, so I just shrug.

Aren steps to Lena's side. He seems relaxed, but his hand is resting a little too casually on his sword hilt. He's not exactly happy about Lena's plan, but he'll back her up on it.

"You're exhausted," Kyol says. "Jorreb is exhausted. Every fae who serves under you is exhausted, and yet, you want to further thin our forces in Corrist? Are you determined to lose the palace, my queen?"

"I'm determined to officially become 'your queen,'" she says. "And I'm determined to reinstate order. The merchants have been begging me to send swordsmen to the provincial gates. They'll support me in this decision."

"It can't be done. Not now."

"It will be done, now," she says.

Kyol paces away from her, his hand rising to rub his forehead. His control on his emotions is slipping. That almost never happens. Even if we didn't have a life-bond, I wouldn't want to be nearby when he goes off. With the life-bond . . . My headache is going to get so much worse.

Kyol drops his hand as he turns back to Lena. "Do you have any idea what the palace guard is doing now? They're searching every corner, corridor, and closet looking for anyone who's not supposed to be here. The southern doors were open six minutes, Lena. *Six minutes.* My men fought off the crowd while we tried to get those doors shut. Some fae made it inside, and while my men *think* we found them all, they're not certain. So they search. They search when they could be resting, and you want me to tell them they must work longer hours now? That they must command and control the same amount of ground with fewer swords at their sides?"

"You will make this work, Taltrayn," she says, and in that moment, I want to tell her to back off. She's giving Kyol an impossible task, and he already has so much responsibility on his shoulders. But I can feel his resistance bending.

"Go on, Trev," Aren says quietly.

"You support this decision?" Kyol's voice is tightly controlled, but his words sound more like an accusation than a question.

"I support her completely," he says with a cavalier shrug. He's relaxed and confident, standing there by Lena's side. The consummate rebel.

Kyol's hands tighten into fists. One second passes. Then another. Finally, he gives Lena a single nod.

When he turns to leave, I close my eyes. He's going to take on this responsibility for her. She knew he would. I guess I did, too. I just hope this decision of hers doesn't cost him his life. I hope it doesn't cost all our lives.

FIFTEEN

◆—◆

WITHIN THE HOUR, I conscript a fae to fissure me back to Vegas. I need to get in touch with Lee and Paige. It's been almost five days since I heard from Lee, and I left Paige a dozen messages a little over forty-eight hours ago. Surely, one of them has called me back by now.

But that's not the only reason I leave the Realm. I *have* to go. Kyol is so exhausted and frustrated, he's not able to keep his mental wall in place. I'm trying to keep my emotions from him, too, and the constant concentration is wearing me down. My head is absolutely killing me.

The throbbing abates as soon as I return to my world.

"Thank you!" I practically yell to the night sky. My fae escort's eyes widen as he slowly nods. He murmurs a "you're welcome" before he disappears.

My reaction might have been a little much, but it's a relief, being able to think again.

Sliding my keys out of my pocket, I walk to my car. A TOW AWAY sticker has been slapped on my driver's side window. My car has been parked on the side of the road near the gate for two days. I'm actually surprised it hasn't been towed yet. I tear the sticker off, then grab my cell phone out of the central console as I slide behind the wheel.

The phone is dead, so I don't get a *ding* telling me I have

messages until after I start the car and the phone has charged for a few minutes. I put it on speaker and hit PLAY.

The first eight voice mails are from Paige. She's just returning my call at first, but she sounds more and more agitated with each message. By the time I reach message number seven, she's moved past being annoyed and is verging on worried. I'm pulling into my apartment when I get to Paige's last message. Her voice takes on a completely different tone. She tells me we need to talk in person, and it's about Caelar and the false-blood.

The voice mail ends abruptly, and I slam on my brakes, barely stopping before I hit the bumper of the car parked in the spot in front of me.

Shit, shit, shit.

I feel Kyol focus on me, but I can't help my reaction. This is so *not* what I wanted to hear. If "Caelar" and "false-blood" are used in the same sentence, I want it to be because Caelar has killed or captured the other fae. Or because he's discovered the false-blood's identity. Or his hideout. Or *something* that will help us get rid of him.

But no, I'm jumping to conclusions again. Paige didn't say they were working together. Maybe Caelar does just have information on the false-blood. Maybe he wants to sell it. Why he'd want to sell it to *us*, though, I have no idea.

I dial Paige as I get out of the car and walk to my apartment. Predictably, I get her voice mail. I leave a message telling her to call me back. I should be around for the next day or so.

After I lock my front door, I head to my bathroom and turn on the shower. I strip, then step beneath the water, not waiting for it to get warm. The icy stream pelts my face and shoulders, but I grit my teeth and watch the plastic floor turn brown as dirt and grime wash down my skin. I'm hoping the cold shower erases my mind for a few minutes. I'm tired of Kyol knowing how I feel, and I'm sick of worrying about losing Aren.

But when I block both of them from my mind, my other concerns crowd in on me. Like the fact that all my voice mails

were from Paige. None from Lee. None from Shane. The latter bothers me more than not hearing from Lee. If Shane was alive, there would have been some sign of him by now. But it's so hard for me to convince myself that he's dead. I need proof. I need to know that he's not being held hostage by the remnants.

Or by Lorn or the false-blood.

By the time the shower heats to something warmer than tepid, the water is almost clear. I pull my towel off the metal hanger. I don't have a bath mat, so I step onto my jeans so I don't slip on the wet linoleum. Something digs into my heel. I look down.

And see Kyol's name-cord half-hanging out of my pocket.

I draw in a breath, reach down, and pick it up. It's made of onyx and *audrin*, a pale stone native to the Realm. I've never seen Kyol wear it, but I had every intention of returning it to him when I took it from my apartment in Houston. I'm glad I can still give it back to him, but the way Aren slapped it into my palm . . .

I throw my towel against the wall, wishing it were heavy enough to slam or break something. It's not. It falls so quietly to the floor it might as well flutter.

I kick it into the corner, where my soiled clothes are. Three days until I lose Aren. I'm beginning to think that he might really let that time go by. That hurts. And it makes me feel like I'm a fool.

Swallowing back my emotions, I jerk on clean undies, a pair of cargo pants, and a black T-shirt. I stuff the name-cord in a pocket, swearing an oath to myself that I *will* return it to Kyol the next time I see him, then I grab a comb and pull it through my wet hair. I'm conquering the tangles one by one when tension explodes through my life-bond. I grab the edge of the sink, bracing for whatever is coming next, but Kyol gets control of his emotions and the situation he's in. He's not safe, and he's worried. Cautious. He's trying to settle down the celebrating mob, most likely. Has it grown more violent? Has it turned against—

Pound.

I spin toward my bedroom, ripping the comb free to clutch it in front of me like a dagger. The sound came from my front door. Or maybe it was a neighbor's door? Someone could have dropped something on the floor above me.

Pound!

That definitely came from my door. It's not exactly a knock, but it's not quite hard enough to say that someone's trying to break in.

Eyeing the peephole, I cautiously take a step forward.

"McKenzie."

I freeze. The voice is muffled through the door, but it sounds strained. And it sounds familiar.

I peek through the peephole. No one's out there. At least, no one's standing directly in front of the door.

Pound. Pound.

"McKenzie."

I back up, frowning. Surely, that's not who it sounds like.

I unlock the door, turn the knob, then pull it open. Lorn falls inside.

My hands slip under his arms just before his knees hit the floor.

"Jesus, Lorn." He's freaking heavy, and he's . . . wet?

I move him away from me, leaning his back against the doorframe. My breath catches in my lungs. Lorn's badly hurt. His face is a mask of red, and one bloodied hand is holding his stomach. I can't see how bad that wound is—I'm pretty sure I don't want to see it—but his clothes are shredded, his knuckles and hands cut, and his *edarratae* don't look healthy.

"What happened?" I ask, standing to flick off my light switch. I start to pull him inside my apartment—all I need is a neighbor seeing me crouched down and talking to my doorframe—but he grabs my arm.

"No—" He chokes on the word, and his lungs rattle. "No. I didn't quite outlast the interrogation."

A chill sweeps over my skin. "Interrogation?"

"We need to leave," he says.

Kyol's thoughts have turned toward me. I don't want to distract him, so I fight to keep my emotions stable. That's not

easy, considering this is the fae I accused of intensifying the war between the rebels and Atroth's fae so that he could make a profit. He was imprisoned because of me. He has every reason to want to cause me trouble.

But he's sitting here half-dead on my doorstep. I can't just turn him away.

"Why do we need to leave, Lorn?"

"The false-blood found me," he says, his eyes closing in a grimace. "The meeting didn't go exactly as I'd planned."

"The false-blood? You met him? You know who he is?"

"He is the *Taelith*." Lorn opens his eyes. "That's all I know."

"And now he knows where I live," I say. I bite my lower lip, start to shake my head, but then stop and glare at Lorn. "How the hell do *you* know where I live?"

He doesn't answer that. He just lifts one bloodied eyebrow, and his lips curve into a faint smile. Yeah, it was a stupid question. Lorn never reveals his information sources.

"How long do I have?" I ask.

"Minutes. Seconds. I'm surprised he's not here already."

I stare at Lorn. He managed to make his words so casual, I don't know if he's joking.

Crap. I don't think he is. I think he's serious.

My heart thumps against my chest. I draw in a deep breath, trying to slow it down and to ward off the adrenaline that's threatening to jet through my bloodstream. I don't need Kyol to fissure to my rescue. I need a break from his emotions, and he needs to concentrate on what he's doing so he doesn't get himself killed.

"You can't fissure?" I ask Lorn.

"Not sure if I can walk at the moment."

Fabulous. I can't run off and leave him behind.

I grab my keys off the counter, then sidle up next to Lorn to put his arm over my shoulder. "You ready?"

Lorn nods. I count to three, then push up to my feet.

He weighs so much more than I thought he would, and he's not even wearing *jaedric* or carrying a sword or dagger or anything. My quads are just barely strong enough to lift him. I so need to join a gym.

I shut my door, then we stagger to the staircase. He grips the rail, uses it as a crutch to help him down the first steps. It doesn't help, though. We're moving way too slow.

"You can't even fissure to the parking lot?" I ask.

He looks down and to the right, where cars are crammed between the narrow lines.

"I'll try," he says, letting his arm fall from my shoulder. God, he's really bad off. No smile, no arrogant reply, just a short, pained statement.

He clutches the rail with both hands. His magic has been weak since Kelia died. Add to that the fact that he fissured from his world to mine half-dead, and it's obvious how much of a struggle it is to open a path to the In-Between. He manages it, though, and after the strip of white light appears on the step below him, he falls into it.

I half expect to see him rolling down the stairs, but the In-Between catches him. My gaze goes to the parking lot just as the light spits him out, face-first, on the cement. He doesn't move.

"Shit," I mutter.

I take the steps two at a time, beeping my car unlocked as I run to Lorn.

"Are you alive?" I ask, putting my hand on his back.

"Mostly," he says, and I relax some. That note of amusement in his voice was more like the old Lorn.

"At least you landed next to my car," I tell him. I focus on Kyol's emotions as I open the passenger door. I'm going to have to give in and get him to fissure here. He's the only way I'm able to communicate with the Realm. He'll want to question Lorn, and Lorn will need a healer.

But I shove Lorn into the passenger seat without letting loose my emotions. Kyol is filled with the cold, calculating emotions that tell me he's still in the midst of a fight. Plus, I don't want him to fissure here if the false-blood might show up.

I turn on the car's engine, put my hand on the back of Lorn's seat so I can back out. He's slumped against the window, his eyes closed. I can't tell if he's breathing.

"Don't you die in my car, Lorn," I say.

A smile slips through his busted lip.

"Exactly how badly are you hurt?" I ask, backing out of the parking space.

"I would very much appreciate a healer."

"I know. I'm working on it." I brake, then shift into drive.

And a sword slams into the hood of my car. My brain registers the three slashes of white light a second later, but the other two fae have already swung their weapons.

A blade shatters my window, tearing through the back of my seat.

I hear a scream, think that it's mine until I realize I've slammed the pedal against the floor. My tires are squealing, my car lurching forward quick enough to save our lives until I ram into a parked truck.

I just barely keep my face from slamming into the steering wheel. Lorn's too out of it to brace for the minor crash. He hits the dash the same instant the fae outside my window stabs his blade forward.

Throwing myself over the central console, I manage to shift into reverse while hitting the gas pedal. The fae—the damned *elari*—loses his grip on his sword when the window frame catches his arm. The blade barely misses me as it flies into the backseat.

My neck pops when I slam into a vehicle behind us. Quickly, I shift gears again. One of the *elari* is standing three feet away in the beams from my headlights. I stare down the fae as he stares down me. It's Nimael, the fae who slipped away from us in Tholm, and the *elari* who might be the false-blood's second-in-command. A gut instinct tells me he's responsible for the slaughter of the women in the *tjandel*, and most likely the Sighted humans in London as well.

I want him dead. I want it so badly I can taste blood on my tongue.

With my left foot on the brake, I press the gas pedal with my right, revving the engine. Pure theatrics. I know Nimael will fissure out of the way before I can run him over.

My heart bangs in my chest. I need to get out of here before people leave their apartments to check on the noise, and definitely before the cops arrive, but I don't know what

the *elari* will do when I go. Will they try to follow me? Will they kill any humans they find? Will they—

Shit. Will they stay long enough for Kyol to fissure here? I have his complete attention now, and I've shattered his control so much that I can feel every ounce of his worry.

Stay away! I try to scream at him. Then I draw in as deep and calming a breath as I can manage and slam down the gas pedal.

Nimael fissures out of the way, no problem.

I check my rearview mirror. The three *elari* are there. They're not pursuing us, though. They're watching me drive away.

Beside me, Lorn murmurs something in Fae. He's awkwardly wedged between the dash and the passenger seat. He needs help. He needs a healer. My thoughts turn back to Kyol. He must be in the Inner City. If he weren't, he would have fissured to my apartment already.

But he's moving. He's trying to get outside the silver walls.

Think happy thoughts, McKenzie, I order myself. Rainbows. Ponies. *Kimkis.* I don't want him to fissure to my apartment just yet. In ten minutes, maybe. Surely the *elari* won't hang around that long.

I look again at Lorn. He's hurt and bleeding and saying things I don't understand in a feverish murmur. His chaos lusters are crawling across his skin. That's not normal. They should be quick and frenzied from being in my car.

My apartment complex vanishes from my rearview mirror when I take a left at the first intersection. I have no idea where I'm going. I can't take Lorn to a hospital, not even to a clinic or doctor's office. I don't know anyone in the city, and . . .

No, that's not entirely true. I do know someone in the city, someone who's familiar with fae.

SIXTEEN

◆

I SLAM ON my brakes outside Kynlee's house. Kyol's at my apartment. I hold my breath, willing him to be careful and praying that Nimael and the other two *elari* have already left.

Beside me, Lorn shifts. His eyes are shut, and he's still awkwardly sitting on the floor, not in the passenger seat.

"Lena." His voice is so weak, I barely make out the name.

"I'll get her here as quickly as I can," I tell him. Then, under my breath, I murmur, "Get away from my apartment, Kyol."

The *elari* must not have hung around, though. His heart isn't pounding like he's fighting for his life, but he's moving, following the pull of the life-bond in my direction. It took me fifteen minutes to drive here. He might make the trip in half an hour.

I turn off the car then look at Lorn, at his bruised and swollen face and his blood-soaked clothing. He's not going to be able to walk up the sidewalk on his own, but I don't want to leave him in the car. His *edarratae* are worrying me. He needs to get away from the tech *now*. Besides, if I somehow manage to drag him to the front porch, the presence of a half-dead fae might make it harder for Kynlee's dad to slam the door in my face.

I climb out of the car, then open the passenger-side door.

"Come on, Lorn."

His head turns toward my voice, and he lifts an arm, but that's all the help I get. I'm not strong enough to lift his limp body over my shoulder, so I pull him out of the car and onto the pavement. Hooking my arms under his, I back up one step at a time, dragging him across the cement.

I'm sweating by the time I prop Lorn against the porch wall, and I lean against it for a moment, too, catching my breath and looking back down the sidewalk. Lorn's left a line of blood all the way from my car. A normal human won't see the crimson trail, but one who has the Sight will. Kynlee and her dad will.

Nothing I can do about it now.

I ring the bell and pound on the door. Wait half a minute then knock and ring the bell again.

Still nothing, not even when I bang on the window to the right of the door. Both Kynlee and her dad must sleep like the dead. I'm considering the possibility that I might have to break in when the door finally opens.

I expect Kynlee's dad to be pissed; I don't expect him to shove the barrel of a shotgun into my chest.

"What the fuck are you doing at my house?" he demands.

I retreat a step. He presses forward.

"He needs help," I say, heart pounding as I hold my hands out to my sides. I remember reading his profile in the library database. His name is Nick. "Please, Ni—"

"Get out of here!" he yells. "I'll call the cops. I'll have you arrested for harassment, or so help me I'll kill you."

"Dad?"

Nick stiffens, and I say a quick, silent prayer of thanks. No way in hell is he going to shoot me in front of his daughter.

"Holy shit, Dad!" Kynlee squats in front of Lorn. "What happened?"

Nick curses quietly, then lowers the shotgun.

"Go back to bed," he says, propping the gun behind the door.

"But, Dad—"

"Go!"

Damn. So much for Kynlee softening her dad up. She retreats to a hallway.

Nick's gaze returns to me. "You're not welcome here. Drag him back to your car and leave."

I draw in a breath, bracing myself. "I can't. I don't have anywhere else I can take him."

"I don't give a goddamn—"

"Look," I cut him off. "Just let us in. Someone will be here to help him soon. After he's recovered, we'll leave. I'll leave Vegas even."

Nick's chest expands with each angry breath he takes. He's shirtless, wearing only a pair of jeans that he hasn't taken the time to button. I've offered him a decent deal, though. He wants me to stay away from his daughter. I'll stay away from the whole city if he'll help us now.

But my offer must not be tempting enough. He starts to shake his head.

Quickly, I nod toward Lorn, trying another tactic before Nick slams the door in my face. "He's visible." I'm pretty sure that's a lie, but a Sighted human has no way of knowing that without paying attention to the reactions of normal humans. "Are your neighbors nosy?"

"I told you—"

"He needs help," I say. "And we're not leaving your front porch until you let us in."

"He'll leave if he enters the ether," Nick threatens. He reaches for the shotgun again.

I pretend not to care, stand my ground, and meet his glare. His jaw works, clenching and relaxing, then clenching again.

Finally, he curses. He looks down at Lorn then says, "One hour. Then you're gone."

Thank God.

"Just help me get him inside," I say.

I slip under Lorn's right arm while Nick mutters something under his breath and slips under his left. Lorn's head lolls to the side, but he's semiconscious. His feet move, though not very usefully.

Nick kicks the front door shut as soon as we're over the threshold. The *bam* echoes in the high-ceilinged entryway.

"Go to the garage," Nick barks. "Turn off the breakers."

At first, I think he's talking to me. Then I see Kynlee peek-

ing around the corner. She looks chagrined for only the briefest moment before she nods and rushes off. We continue half
carrying, half dragging Lorn into the house. Nick grumbles
about the carpet as we make our way through the living room,
leaving a trail of Lorn's blood behind us.

"In here," Nick says gruffly, leading the way into a sunroom
at the back of the house. The full moon shines across the wooden
floors and a wicker sofa with white cushions. I start to lower
Lorn onto the sofa, but he slips from my grasp when Nick all but
throws him to the floor.

Lorn rolls to his back. Groans. From somewhere above us,
there's a click. I feel the air-conditioning unit shut down, and
Lorn's chaos lusters lose a little of their jaggedness. They're
still sluggish, though. Being in my world as weak as he is isn't
good for him.

I press my hand to his forehead, checking for a fever.

Stupidly checking for a fever. Fae are always hot when I
touch them. His chaos lusters heat my skin, and I pull my
hand back. I think he does have a fever, though. Sweat mixes
with the blood caking his temple, and, even in the moonlight,
his pale face looks flushed.

"Will this help?" Kynlee's voice comes from behind me.

I look over my shoulder. She's standing in the sunroom's
doorway, holding something that looks like a glass of milk.

"Yeah," Nick says. He rises to take the glass from her, then
he hands it to me. "She drinks it when she gets migraines.
Prop his head up."

He throws a decorative pillow on the floor. I pick it up,
then slide it under Lorn's head. Before I give him the drink, I
sniff it. Um, definitely not milk.

"Hey," I say, gently. "I need you to drink this."

I place the brim of the glass on his busted bottom lip and
tilt it back. Pretty much all the liquid trickles down his chin.

"You need to drink," I tell him. This time, he murmurs
something—Lena's name again?—and I use the opportunity
to pour the liquid into his mouth. He chokes on it, coughing
and wincing and, eventually, opening his eyes to glare at me.

"Poison?" he asks.

Smiling, I say, "I hope not. Here."

I make him drink more. After a few sips, he shoves my hand away. I take that as a good sign. A few minutes ago, I don't think he had the strength to lift a finger.

He closes his eyes in a wince as a wave of pain passes over him. "Should have gone straight to Lena."

"I'm surprised you didn't," I say.

"If the false-blood killed you, I wouldn't get my revenge."

"He sounds like he's worth saving," Nick mutters, grabbing Lorn's wrist to lift his hand away from his stomach wound.

Lorn hisses in a breath and starts to curl to the side, but I hold his shoulder down, keeping him in place.

"What else can I do?" Kynlee asks from the doorway.

"Scissors. Towels," her dad says.

Kynlee nods, starts to leave.

"The whole medicine cabinet."

She stops, frowns. "Really? Everything?"

Nick's jaw tightens. "Just the hydrogen peroxide and any gauze or bandages we might have."

"Need a healer," Lorn says. "Not human medicine." His voice is raspy, like he has liquid in his lungs, but he's alive. I think he'd be dead by now if some really crucial organ were injured. It's him bleeding to death we need to worry about.

"Stop talking, Lorn."

Suddenly, Nick's gaze snaps to me. "Lorn? As in . . . *the* Lorn?"

I think I see a tiny smile bend one corner of Lorn's mouth. If Nick hasn't been to the Realm since Kynlee was a baby, Lorn's been around a long time.

"That's his name," is all I say.

Nick drops Lorn's hand.

"How, exactly, did you come in possession of a *tor'um*?" Lorn asks. I'm surprised he's cognizant enough to ask the question.

Nick goes still, then, after a handful of heartbeats, he presses the heel of his hand into the fae's wound. Lorn cries out.

"Hey!" I say, trying to shove Nick away.

"She's my daughter, asshole," Nick says, leaning toward

Lorn's face. "Not a possession or something for you to condescend to."

"Nick, stop!" He's not listening. I ram my shoulder into him and manage to knock him off Lorn. He falls onto his back, but he looks ready to kill.

"I have the stuff," Kynlee says. Perfect timing.

Nick doesn't acknowledge her, so I do, motioning her in. She drops her armful of towels down beside me. The small pile is topped by a pair of scissors, hydrogen peroxide, and . . . a box of Disney Princess Band-Aids.

I pick up the latter, raise an eyebrow.

"It was all I could find," she says.

Yeah, so not going to help.

I set the Band-Aids aside and grab a towel. I use it to wipe some of the blood off Lorn's face. Most of it is from a cut on his forehead, but his cheekbone is swollen to twice its normal size, and his lip is bleeding from more than one cut.

"Is he dead?" Kynlee asks. Lorn hasn't moved since I shoved Nick off him.

"No," I say, finally getting Lorn to uncurl from his fetal position. "Fae disappear when they die."

"Disappear?"

The mix of fear and curiosity in Kynlee's voice makes me look up.

"We'll talk later, Kynlee," Nick says gruffly. "Go to bed now."

"We learned first aid in my health class," she says. "I can help."

"Go," he repeats.

A chaos luster jumps across Lorn's face. Weakly, he says, "You haven't taught her anything, have you—"

"Lorn, let's not antagonize our host."

"—Nick Johnson?"

Nick Johnson? I frown at Nick. His last name is supposed to be Walker, but the way Lorn meets his gaze makes it clear he knows the human.

Nick is as still as glass.

"I've kept her safe," Nick finally says in a cold whisper.

"Lorn," I say, not taking my eyes off Nick. "Just in case

you die"—or Nick kills him—"why don't you tell me what you know about the false-blood?"

Lorn's gaze swivels to me. "You're becoming quite mercenary, McKenzie. Good for—" His last words are lost in a cough that makes him grow pale.

I take Lorn's hand—the one not holding his stomach—and squeeze it. Despite my misgivings about his character and his involvement in this war, I have a soft spot for Lorn. I *want* him to be a good person. I definitely don't want to see him in this much pain.

"Kyol is almost here," I tell him.

"Kyol, the son of Taltrayn?" Nick asks.

When I say yes, Nick shoots to his feet.

"He knows you're here?" he demands. "Who else knows?"

"No one," I say.

"If Taltrayn knows, the king knows."

"No one knows," I say quickly. Then, when he takes a step toward the living room, I add, "The king is dead."

He stops, looks over his shoulder. "Dead?"

I nod.

"And Taltrayn's alive?"

I nod again.

"And Taltrayn hasn't told anyone else where I live? That's bullshit."

"Oh, no," Lorn says, a smile in his voice. "Not bullshit at all. I imagine it's quite an interesting story, actually."

I slap a damp cloth hard against the cut on Lorn's forehead. When Nick looks at me, I just say, "It's complicated."

Lorn's chuckle turns into a cough. Serves him right. He makes himself extremely difficult to like sometimes.

I wait on the Walkers'—or the *Johnsons'*—front porch for Kyol. It doesn't take him long to find me. He does it in close to the same amount of time as it took me to drive here. Since he can fissure within line of sight, he can travel incredibly fast, faster than I was able to find him in Corrist. But the pull of the life-bond is the same, basically shining a beacon of light down on my location.

When he fissures one last time, exiting the In-Between a few feet in front of me, I say, "I'm sorry. I didn't want to pull you away from what you were doing."

"What's happened?" he asks.

"It's Lorn," I say, my gaze scanning the street for any other slashes of light or sparks of blue chaos lusters darting across someone's skin. "He gave my location to the false-blood."

Kyol stiffens. "He did what?"

I wince at the iciness in his voice. Most people describe anger as being hot, but it's not. Not with Kyol, at least. His anger is so cold I shiver.

"It's okay. Well, it's not okay, but he didn't give the *elari* my location willingly. He's hurt."

"He's inside?"

"Yes, but he needs—"

Kyol slams open the door.

Damn it. I hurry after him, but catch up only when he suddenly stops at the entrance to the sunroom. He's not staring at Lorn, though. He's staring at Nick, who slowly, silently rises to his feet.

If it wasn't for the life-bond, I'd have no idea how surprised Kyol is. His face is a mask of stoic calmness. There's no sign he's startled or confused.

"Nick," is all he says.

The human clenches his jaw. "Taltrayn."

"I see you two remember each other," Lorn says. Finally, Kyol's gaze swings to the injured fae.

"He needs a healer," I finish what I tried to tell him on the porch.

"Please," Lorn adds.

Kyol angles his body slightly to look at me. "I left you only a few hours ago, and you've managed to find Lorn and Nick Johnson."

"He's Kynlee's dad," I say, nodding toward Nick Johnson or Walker or whoever he is. "And I didn't find Lorn. He found me." All I wanted to do when I got home was curl up under the blankets and sleep.

Kyol's expression softens. He releases his grip on his sword hilt and places his hand on my shoulder, squeezing it gently.

"It's okay, *kaesha*," he says. I stiffen, expecting to feel some wave of regret for calling me *kaesha*, but there isn't any. Roughly, the word translates into *loved one*, only, it's so much more than that. For the last decade, it's been Kyol's way of telling me that he loves me. He used it rarely since we weren't supposed to be together, but that only made it more special. It's still special now.

He senses my confusion, my unease, and drops his hand.

"You're safe here?" he asks. In other words, the false-blood doesn't know I'm here.

"Yeah," I say. He takes another look at Lorn, then at Nick. He must trust the human because he tells me he'll bring back help before he walks out the back door to open his fissure. Even though a pane of glass separates us, I get caught up in his shadows and the warm mix of emotions tumbling through my stomach. I can't tell if they're mine or his. Both, most likely.

A headache starts hammering behind my eyes. My personal life is one big fucking mess. The guy I wanted for a decade would finally and fully return that love now, but I've fallen for someone else, someone who wants nothing to do with me.

And I hate this. I hate hurting someone I care so much about.

I ignore the look I get from Nick as I pull a burgundy throw off a nearby chair and drape it over Lorn.

We wait. I watch Lorn breathe. He answers a few simple questions with grunts, but his sarcastic humor is gone. I'm worried about him. I don't know how long it will take Kyol to bring back help. Most fae know basic first aid, quite a few are the equivalent of techless doctors, but a healer is the only thing that can save Lorn's life now.

He falls into a restless sleep.

Sometime later, two fissures split through the night air. Kyol and Lena. They both look regal, standing next to each other in Nick's backyard.

Backyard? Why not fissure directly into the house?

I look at Nick. "You have silver here?"

He nods stiffly. "In the insulation."

Kyol opens the back door for Lena. She enters, her gaze locked on Nick as she walks to Lorn's side.

"You're alive," she says as she kneels.

Nick doesn't respond. He just rises and leaves the room.

"You know him?" I ask when he's gone.

Lena removes the throw and the bloodied towel that's been doing a poor job of staunching Lorn's bleeding. She looks at his side wound, then places her hand over it.

"He gave the throne to Atroth," she says.

I glance at Kyol.

"What do you mean?" I ask when she doesn't go on and he doesn't add anything. A human can't just give a throne to someone.

"He slept with fae. Many and often until he had sex with the wrong woman, Casye, the daughter of the former high noble of Ristin Province."

Ristin is one of the four provinces Lena reinstated. Tholm is on its western border. A small line marks the division between it and Corrand Province, just above the Imyth Sea, on the old maps of the Realm.

"Her father slaughtered all the *tor'um* in Ristin because of that," Nick says from the threshold of the sunroom. "Because of me. Killing and banning humans from his province didn't satisfy him."

He takes a sip of the drink he's poured himself, and it's like he's downing a shot of regret.

Kynlee. Nick must have saved her from the slaughter. But who is she? She can't be the result of his affair with Casye—or any other fae for that matter. Fae and human can't reproduce. Plus, fae aren't born *tor'um* because of something the parents did or didn't do. It's a completely random occurrence.

"Atroth stopped it," Kyol says.

Nick looks at him. "What?"

"Atroth stopped the cleansing. A few *tor'um* were killed, but not all of them. Not most of them. Atroth had Lord Kelyon arrested and executed for what he did."

"And he dissolved Ristin Province instead of allowing another fae to rise to the position of high noble," Lena adds bitterly. "That laid the groundwork for him to dissolve the

other provinces. Without that precedent, he wouldn't have been able to remap the Realm and strengthen his position as king."

The others included Adaris, her home province.

No wonder Nick hasn't been back to the Realm. Anyone in those dissolved provinces along with anyone else who opposed Atroth would blame him for what happened, and in a world as violent as the Realm, they'd kill him.

"Kynlee's from Ristin Province then?" I ask.

Nick's jaw tightens. He takes another sip of his drink and doesn't answer.

Lena shifts her weight. A bead of sweat breaks out on her brow, but for the first time in half an hour, Lorn opens his eyes.

"Lena," he murmurs. *"Lena, you came."* He's regressed to Fae again.

"Quiet, Lorn," she says. Surprisingly, her tone is gentle, not impatient or scolding. Lorn's so out of it, he just murmurs nonsense before he turns his head to the side and goes silent.

I sit beside Kyol on the wicker sofa. Nick leans in the doorway, finishing his drink. Five minutes pass. Ten. Lena's still healing Lorn.

Kyol stands.

"I'll return soon," he says. Then he walks outside to fissure out. I'm staring at his shadows, itching to draw them, when I see Nick's hand twitch in my peripheral vision. He's staring at the shadows, too, and I'd bet a million dollars he's not just a Sighted human. He's a shadow-reader, too.

I hug my legs to my chest, then rest my chin on my knee.

"Do you know what happened to him?" Kynlee asks, breaking the silence. I'm not sure when she returned. She was supposed to be in bed.

"I imagine he miscalculated," Lena answers, finally removing her hands from Lorn. She's sweating profusely now, and her *edarratae* are agitated. It's not easy healing someone on the brink of death.

"Kynlee," Nick says. "It's almost six. Get ready for school."

"School? But—"

"Now." His tone leaves no room for argument. Grumbling, she does as he asks.

When she's gone, Lena says, "Taltrayn mentioned the false-blood had something to do with this."

"I don't know details," I answer, "but Lorn said the false-blood interrogated him. He ended up giving him my location."

"That's all he gave?"

"I don't know," I say. "We didn't exactly have time for a lengthy chat. Nimael and two other *elari* showed up as I was driving out of the parking lot. If Lorn had gotten there a minute later"—or if he hadn't shown up at all—"I'd be dead."

I look at Lorn. Why did he warn me? Since it's looking more and more like I falsely accused him, I owe him, not the other way around.

Lena wipes the back of her hand across her brow. "I'll talk to him in the morning. He needs to rest for now." She looks at Nick. "Do you want him to remain on your floor?"

Nick clenches his teeth. The one-hour limit he gave me when he let us in has passed. He has every right to kick us out. Hell, he had every right not to let us in in the first place.

"There's a guest bedroom down the hall," he finally says. "He can stay until he wakes up." A pause. "Are you all staying?"

"Just McKenzie," Lena says.

Nick is silent for a moment. Then he says, "We have a media room upstairs. You can sleep on the couch."

SEVENTEEN

◆—◆

AFTER MY SECOND shower of the night, I pull on a pair of cotton shorts and a T-shirt Kynlee loaned me, then find the stairs. They lead directly into the media room, the only room on the small second floor. With the electricity still off, it's nearly pitch-black up here. The walls are painted a dark blue and are bare save for a large screen at the front of the room and a window with heavy drapes on the opposite wall. I pull those aside to let in some of the early-morning light.

Yawning, I turn around. Several large speakers and what I'm guessing is a subwoofer are set up in the corners of the room. A single leather couch is near the back wall. I head for it before I notice the closed laptop sitting on top of a side table. A thick cord leads into the wall. I'm guessing it connects to the projector in the ceiling. I'm about to ignore it and crash on the couch, but a flickering blue light catches my attention. The laptop's battery is powering it. On a whim, I open the computer.

It's not password protected. The home screen blinks on, and within a couple of clicks, I'm able to connect to the Internet. That surprises me considering Nick hasn't turned the breakers back on, but I take advantage of the convenience and access my e-mail. Nothing from Paige. Nothing from Lee or Shane. There is, however, a notice from my employer saying

that I'm being terminated. Despite the fact that I knew this was coming—my actions made it inevitable—it hurts a little. I'm a failure. I can't even keep a simple, minimum-wage job. I'm going to lose my apartment, my car, and my chance at . . .

No. Shut up, McKenzie. You chose a different life.

I click out of my e-mail, annoyed at myself. I should collapse on the couch now, get what little sleep I can, but there's something else I want to do. I've wanted to do it since I left Tholm.

I open a new Web browser, then Google "Sight serum."

This isn't the first time I've entered this search phrase. I've done it at least four times before and have always received pure junk in return. I get the same list of makeup miracles and other random, unrelated hits, but this time, there's one important difference: the top hit is a link to a Web site with a sales page.

Crap.

It's a simple Web site, not much more than an information and contact page, but it claims that a single injection of their serum will give people the ability to see fae.

"This can't be legal," I mutter. People can't be falling for this. The price tag is outrageous—$12,500 plus a required, in-person interview—and why would any sane person believe that the serum would work? Why would any sane person believe that fae exist? I denied it for a long time, believing I was seeing things that weren't really there. Surely, the vigilantes haven't actually sold anything.

But they might have.

I rub at the headache pounding behind my eyes. It's there despite the fact that Kyol has fissured back to the Realm. I need to sleep it off, but before I lie down on the couch, I do one more thing. I set up a new e-mail account, then send a quick message to the seller telling him I'm interested in his product.

SOMETIME after noon, I stagger down the stairs, feeling only slightly more rested than I did when I fell asleep. Dreams take their toll, and even though mine were, for once, pleasant, they

were stressful. Aren and Kyol filled them—thank God, not at the same time—and I woke bathed in the memories of their kisses more than once. The dreams with Aren were intense—cosmic, even—but they were tinged with fear. If I don't find a way to get through to him in the next two days, I'll lose him.

Kyol's dreams . . . Each kiss we shared made me miss him, and each kiss made my heart break a little. It wasn't real, but it felt like I was cheating on Aren. I shouldn't have two men on my mind. It's not right, and it's not fair to them. It's especially not fair to Kyol, who's able to feel what I'm feeling. He knows I'm in love with Aren, but he knows my stomach still flips when I think of him.

Guilt-ridden and feeling a little sick, I make my way through the living room, following the scent of coffee toward the kitchen. Kyol's back. He's sitting on one of three barstools that are lined up in front of the island. His back is to me. So is Nick's. The human is standing by the coffeepot, waiting for it to finish brewing, I presume. He must have turned the breakers on. The air-conditioning is running now, too.

Nick grabs a couple of mugs out of the cabinet. "I thought . . ." His shoulders rise as he draws in a breath. "I thought the cleansing would spill across the borders. Atroth always catered to the conservative fae, and they saw the *tor'um* as a corruption, the result of too much human influence."

"You didn't have to run," Kyol tells him. "We would have protected you despite your transgressions."

I stop at the edge of the carpet, not stepping onto the earth-toned tile in the kitchen. The guilt I felt a minute ago disappears. Kyol thinks sleeping with a human is a "transgression." That's it. That's why I chose to walk away from him. One of the reasons, at least. He'll always see his love for me as a weakness.

"I didn't know that," Nick says, pouring coffee into the mugs. "Atroth was secretive. You all were. But if I'd known *you'd* eventually transgress, maybe I would have stayed."

Kyol stiffens. I clear my throat, letting Nick know that I'm here. He glances over his shoulder, sees me, and looks only slightly chagrined by his words.

"Coffee?" he asks.

"Please," I say, stepping onto the tile, then taking a seat on the barstool to Kyol's right. When Nick sets a coffee mug in front of each of us, he says to Kyol, "I didn't steal Kynlee. Her brother came to me. He begged me to take her out of Ristin, and I agreed. I took her as far away as possible and changed my last name so no one could find us."

"Her brother will want to see her," Kyol says. "He's Ristin's high noble now."

Nick thumps down a third coffee mug a little too hard. "She's not going back to the Realm."

"He could visit her here."

"No." He thumps the mug down again. "She's safe here. She won't have a chance in the Realm. She'll be shunned. She won't be able to find work. No one will want to touch her, let alone marry her. She's staying with me."

I'm surprised he mentions the touching and marrying. He hits me as the type of dad who would sit on the front porch cleaning that shotgun of his anytime a boy showed up to take Kynlee out.

"She should know where she's from," Kyol tells him.

"She's from here, now."

"Kyol," I interject gently, my tone saying to drop the subject. He does, but he seems agitated. I don't think that's just because he thinks Nick is wrong. Something's on his mind.

"Lorn's still asleep?" I ask.

He nods. "For a few more hours, at least."

I look at Nick to see if he's going to protest our staying here longer. He's already been more accommodating than I expected, especially considering the fact that he's worried someone might try to take Kynlee away from him.

Stone-faced, he tosses his empty mug into the sink.

"I have to go to work for a while," he says. "I'll be back before Kynlee gets home from school. Make sure you're gone by then."

He grabs his keys off a hook by a door on the other side of the kitchen. After he disappears through it, I hear the grinding rumble of a garage door opening.

I take a sip of my coffee as silence descends between Kyol and me. I want to tell him about Paige's message and the Web

site I found, but he feels so . . . I'm not sure how to describe him. Exhausted, yes, but it's more than that. Soul-weary maybe. I don't want to burden him with more bad news.

On the other hand, we already suspected the vigilantes were selling the Sight serum. This just confirms Glazunov's words. And as for Paige's message . . . It's still possible Caelar isn't working with the false-blood.

"Tell me," Kyol says, staring down at the granite countertop.

I grimace. Of course he'd feel my turmoil. Proximity makes it difficult to hide our emotions from each other. That's why I'm aware of his mood even though his wall is in place.

"You first," I say.

His silver eyes meet mine, and it takes everything in me to not react to his familiar, stormy gaze. It feels like a cord is pulling on my heart.

Kyol draws in a slow breath as he looks away.

"It's nothing," he says.

"Nothing?" I ask, that heart-cord snapping in annoyance. "Well, then. Nothing is on my mind either."

"McKenzie—"

"Are you trying to protect me from something?"

"No."

"Because I can handle it, Kyol. I've always been able to handle it."

He swivels on his barstool, facing me fully.

"There is nothing specifically wrong," he says. "I swear it."

"Then what's wrong generally?" I ask, not dropping the subject.

His jaw clenches. So does mine. I'm pissed at Aren for this same reason. Something is wrong with him, but he doesn't trust me enough to tell me what. It's ridiculous for me to have this problem with Kyol, too. There's no reason to withhold information from me after everything we've been through.

I slide off my barstool, start to leave, but Kyol grabs my arm.

"I'm worried about you, McKenzie."

I look down as lightning circles my elbow. I'm mad enough that the lick of heat doesn't make me want to move closer to him.

"That's it?" I ask, letting doubt slide into my voice.

He releases my arm, then reaches for something beside the counter. When he turns back to me, he's holding two dull swords with familiar red handles.

I barely suppress a sigh. Maybe I am what's bothering him. God knows I'm not as good at hiding my emotions as he is, and he's never had a life-bond before either. This is as new to him as it is to me. I'm probably stressing him out with my chaotic mood swings.

"Please," he says, holding one of the practice swords out for me to take.

Even though my anger is quickly disappearing, I cross my arms over my chest. "Are you going to be an ass when I get tired?"

After a brief pause, he says, "You learn more quickly when I'm an ass."

I can't help the smile that spreads across my face.

A few minutes later, we're in Nick's backyard. I insist Kyol be visible in case one of the neighbors gets nosy, so he takes off his *jaedric* armor. He wears it so often, always prepared for an attack, that I'm sure he feels naked holding a sword without it, but his black pants and shirt can pass as human made.

"And if someone sees the swords?" Kyol asks, raising his blade between us.

"We'll tell them we're with the SCA."

He lifts an eyebrow.

"Society of Creative"—I fake a direct attack, swing down toward his left leg—"Anachronism."

He blocks my wild move with ease and counters with an unnecessarily hard hit to my ribs. "Practice the forms. No wild swings."

Wild swings are for the untrained. He told me that at least a dozen times between Tholm and Corrist. Wild swings rely on luck not expertise, but isn't that the whole point of my training? I need to be good enough to be lucky because, God knows, if I end up in a sword fight with a fae, I'm going to need a huge dose of luck to survive it.

Besides, Aren gets away with wild, messy swings when he

fights. It's not that he isn't trained, but sometimes, being unpredictable can create an advantage.

"Your focus is elsewhere." Kyol hits my practice blade so hard, I nearly drop it.

I grit my teeth and tighten my grip on the red hilt. Right. Focus. I can do that.

Within minutes, my skin glistens with sweat. It's frustrating considering Kyol isn't even breathing hard.

"You need to leave Vegas," Kyol says, swinging at my left thigh.

"Aren't I supposed to be focusing?" I ask, blocking his attack. But I knew he'd bring this conversation up.

"You can't return to your apartment."

"I—" His blade arcs toward my head. I fall on my ass, avoiding a concussion. "Jesus, Kyol."

He squats in front of me. "Good. Next time, roll away from your opponent. Roll to your feet."

He offers me his hand. Is this his attempt to not be an ass? Or is it a trap?

My eyes narrow, and just in case, I get to my feet on my own.

"You're doing well, McKenzie."

I keep my guard up, still suspicious. "Are you patronizing me?"

"No," he says, stabbing toward my stomach. I block his attack and turn sideways, making myself a smaller target.

"It takes fae years of training to develop muscle memory," he continues, launching another attack, this time a low one aimed at my knees. "You're developing it within hours. And you're quick." A jab toward my left shoulder. "Quicker than you used to be."

I get what he's saying, and even though this can be seen as a positive thing, the implication makes me uncomfortable. What else has the life-bond changed? And are all the changes for the better?

Kyol senses the dark path my thoughts are taking, so I give him a small smile, and say, "Good thing I'm bonded to the Realm's best swordsman."

The corner of his mouth quirks up ever so slightly.

"Is that a smile, Lord General?" I tease. "While you're in the midst of a fight? Sloppy."

I feign an attack at his midsection, but dodge around his block, balling my off hand into a fist, which I aim at his jaw. The move is smooth and natural, and the blow would probably hit if Kyol *weren't* the best swordsman in the Realm. But he knocks my fist with his elbow and somehow manages to clip my chin in the process.

Ow.

I step away from him, reach up to rub my jaw. I yelp instead, seeing his sword arcing toward my calves. No time to block it so I try to leap over it and—

Fail. His blade hits so hard, he knocks my legs out from under me. I land on my right shoulder, my sword pinned beneath my body.

A twinge of guilt moves through the life-bond, but Kyol extinguishes it quickly.

"You were supposed to block that," he says, kneeling in front of me.

"Yeah," I snap. "I kind of figured that out."

I sit up, then pull up my pants leg to look at the injury. Our swords are dull, but I expect to see a gash in my leg anyway. There's not one. Just an angry red line that's beginning to turn purple.

"Is it broken?" Kyol sets down his sword, then runs his hand over my calf.

"I'm not that brittle," I say. I mean the words to be angry— an accusation of sorts—but his hand is warm, and a bright blue bolt of lightning skips to my skin.

Touching opens our bond completely, and Kyol's lust rushes into me. I rock back, dizzy with the intensity of it, and my body flushes with heat.

It's just magic, I tell myself. This feeling isn't real. It isn't. It isn't. It isn't.

Kyol meets my gaze. His hand is still on my calf, desire is still rocking through him.

I want another chance.

He doesn't say those words out loud, but his emotions are screaming them.

I pull my leg away from him, and some emotion akin to hurt moves through the bond. It's barely noticeable beneath the want, but it makes my throat burn. I can't do this. I can't keep hurting him.

"Kyol—"

"Again," he says, grabbing his sword as he stands. A thick wall drops between us, silencing his emotions.

Swallowing, I get to my feet. I try to build my own wall. I try not to let him feel my frustration and angst, my regret that I can't say the words he wants to hear. I focus completely on the moves he teaches me. My muscles remember them, even a few forms he hasn't taught me yet, like the slight twist to my wrist I need to slip through his overly slow defense. I let my mind go blank, focus only on the movements of my body and his. I watch his eyes, the set of his shoulders. My peripheral vision is attuned to his sword. I block a third of his attacks, which is a huge improvement from the last time. His blows hurt when they hit home, but it's a dull pain that I can shove to the back of my mind.

Circle and attack. Follow up. Parry.

I'm drenched in sweat, but I keep going, keep concentrating on the rote movement of my body and the soreness in my muscles.

Dodge a high swing. Counter with a low one.

My worries fall away, and I let my subconscious take over until Kyol lowers his sword, his eyes closing.

"There," he says, tension pouring out of him.

I'm so, so tempted to attack while he's vulnerable, but I haven't felt him this relaxed since he formed the life-bond with me.

"There?"

He opens his eyes. "That's how I keep my emotions from you."

I frown. "How?"

"If I concentrate on the forms, on mine and my opponents' movements, everything else falls away. That's what you've just done, and it's . . . peaceful."

"You block your emotions when you're not fighting, too."

"I have decades of practice," he says. "I'm able to re-create the emptiness. Most of the time."

I nod slowly. "I'll work on it." I'll work on it every second of my existence until I'm able to keep him out.

I raise my sword, ready to re-empty my mind.

"We're finished for today," he says.

"I have a few more minutes left in me."

Before I have time to even blink, he disarms me. My sword flips once in the air and lands in his left hand.

"We're finished for today," he says again, this time looking pointedly at my hands.

I glare down at them, too, angry that they didn't hold on to the sword. Then I see the blisters. Apparently, my emotions weren't the only thing that I faded out. I blocked out the pain, but now that I see how red and agitated they are, they hurt. So does every part of me that Kyol hit, which is basically everywhere.

"I didn't know you were available for lessons, Lord General."

I turn toward the back porch. Lorn is there, leaning against a column. I wouldn't say he looks great, but he doesn't look half-dead anymore.

"I have a few fae who could use your expertise," he says, when we approach.

Kyol doesn't bother answering. He turns to me, tells me he'll be back soon, then he fissures out.

My gaze locks on his shadows, and I itch to draw them out. I haven't attempted to shadow-read since Tholm. The earlier worry I had about the bond bringing negative changes circles through my mind again. I wasn't able to identify Nimael's location, and I should have been able to. I need to sketch out a map again.

But Kyol's heading back to Corrist. I don't need a map to tell me that. As soon as the shadows completely disappear, I head inside.

Lorn tsks as he follows me in. "No thanks for saving your life?"

If I thank him, it'll imply I owe him a debt, so I follow Kyol's example and ignore him. I walk to the kitchen and turn on the faucet to wash my hands. Holy crap! The blisters burn.

"You at least owe me an apology, don't you think?" Lorn says, hovering behind me.

At least he's back to his usual, haughty self. And he's found clothes. I don't know how Nick is going to feel about Lorn raiding his closet, but the black slacks and white button-up shirt fit Lorn's personality. The shirt is wrinkle-free and crisp, the cuffs buttoned.

"Lena's the one who arrested you," I say. "I just told her my suspicions."

"Lena is a beautiful, vindictive *chessra*."

I don't know what that word means. Something not flattering, I'm sure. And I don't see how she's vindictive. She and Lorn worked together against the Court. They're basically partners. On the other hand, Lorn isn't the most altruistic person in the world. I'm sure he's done something to piss her off.

I shut off the faucet, grab a towel, and carefully pat dry my hands. "The fae you had me track in Nashville—Aylen. She fissured to Eksan. That's where I tracked a remnant to a day later. It was too big a coincidence to ignore."

He scowls. "Lena arrested me based on *that*?"

"Not just that," I say. "You gave her the tip about Paige being in London, didn't you?"

"Of course, I did. That was our deal. I found her for you. You're welcome, by the way."

"How did you know she was there?" I ask.

His expression doesn't change, but something about him gives me the impression that he's feeling a little less jovial than a moment before.

"My sources told me," he says.

"Your 'sources'?" When he doesn't respond, I say, "The Sighted humans who worked for Atroth were there. They were dead. And the remnants received an anonymous tip saying that I'd be there. It was a setup."

He presses his lips together, then says, "That is a little incriminating, isn't it?"

I raise my hand in a there-you-have-it motion.

"So, do you want to tell me who Aylen is? Why you needed me to read her shadows?"

"In a moment," he says, turning to look out the window as three fissures rip through the backyard.

EIGHTEEN

•◆•

W E TAKE OVER the living room, Lena sitting on the edge of a sofa chair while Lorn lounges back in another one with a glass of *cabus* in his hand. Without so much as a hello to me, Aren drags in a chair from the kitchen. That gets on my nerves. He could at least acknowledge my existence, but he straddles the chair and drapes his arms over the back, all carefree and relaxed.

"Are the breakers in the garage?" Naito asks me, as I take a seat on the couch. He fissured in with Kyol, Lena, and Aren.

"I think so," I tell him, and he leaves to go find them. Lorn's *edarratae* are still slow and erratic, and Lena's and Aren's look slightly agitated, too. Kyol's are steady, though, flashing only occasionally across his face and forearms. He sits at the opposite end of the couch, his mental wall holding back his emotions.

I make an effort to establish my wall, but it doesn't work very well. I keep looking at Aren. He never looks at me.

The electricity clicks off. I stare down at my hands, which rest gingerly on my knees. Hison has to be blackmailing Aren. I have to find out what he's holding over his head. I don't know how I'm going to do that, though. It's not like Hison will just hand over the information.

My gaze locks on Lorn, a connoisseur of information. If

he doesn't already know what Hison has on Aren, he could find out, I'm sure of it. I just have to find the right price to buy it from him.

"Well," Lorn says lightly, when Naito rejoins us. "This is a familiar gathering. Are we making plans to lay siege to a high noble's manor?"

"The false-blood," Lena says, obviously not entertained by Lorn's cavalier tone. "You met him. Tell us what you know about him."

"I know that I want him dead."

"My patience is thin, Lorn. Give me details."

"Patience?" He smiles. "My dear, you've never had anything of the sort."

I think he's trying to get under her skin. Why, I don't know. She saved his life. He owes her. There's no need to antagonize her, especially now. Healing him wore her out. The circles under her eyes are darker than they were a day ago. She deserves a break.

"You were going to tell me about Aylen," I say, before Lena snaps.

Lorn looks at me. He raises his glass of *cabus* in a small salute, as if he knows exactly why I've spoken up. "Yes, Aylen. I had you read her shadows because I believed she was selling information to my competitors."

"Was she?" I ask.

"She *was*," he says, drawing out the last word in a way that makes it clear she's no longer capable of doing so. Sent to the ether, I imagine. Lorn didn't become lord of the Realm's underworld by letting people cross him.

"You could have just told me that," I say. "Or told Lena when she questioned you."

"I never had the chance to question him," Lena says. "The high nobles forced me to release him within a day of his arrest."

"The false-blood," Kyol says. The hilt of his sword—his real sword, not the practice one—is clasped between his hands. "You gave McKenzie's location to him. You spoke with him."

"I wouldn't call it a conversation," Lorn says. "But, yes,

I've met him and his *elari*. Aylen wasn't selling information *only* to my competitors. She sold it to the *Taelith* as well."

"The *Taelith*," Lena says, her lips twisting as if the title puts a bad taste in her mouth. "Who is he?"

Lorn sets his glass of *cabus* down on the side table and leans forward. "He is our nemesis, my dear."

Lena stiffens. I'm not sure why. If Lorn sees the false-blood as his nemesis as well as ours, it's a good thing. It means there's a better chance he'll help us.

"I need a name," Lena says.

"I didn't learn a name."

"Then tell me how you met him. Tell me something, Lorn."

"Even my patience is growing thin." That's from Aren, who's been silent until this moment. He's still sitting backward in his chair, arms draped across it in a way that makes him look sexy and rebellious. He still won't look at me.

Lorn leans back in his sofa chair and drags a finger around the rim of his glass. "I'm afraid I may have been inadvertently providing the false-blood with information. And supplying him with silver. And weapons. And—"

"*Sidhe*, Lorn!" Lena explodes to her feet. "Have you abandoned all reason and become an *elari*?"

Lorn sets down his glass as he stands, too, albeit much more slowly than she does. Kyol rises as a precaution. And a threat. Lorn's gaze slides to him. He looks more annoyed than worried, though.

"I've always worked with false-bloods," Lorn says. "It's easy money, and they've always been ripped apart by the Court. They never had a chance of success, so why should I not profit from them? If I hadn't provided aid to Sethan, your rebellion would have died within months of its inception."

"My brother was not a false-blood," Lena snarls. "I'm not one either. You've always known that. You shouldn't be supplying *anything* to my enemies."

"I should change my lifestyle and business practices to suit you?"

"Yes!" she hisses.

"I—" Lorn cuts himself off, shutting his mouth with a sharp click of his teeth. Seconds tick by. Neither of them backs down or looks away.

"Sit down," Aren finally orders. He's still relaxed, but his expression is much more somber than it was a minute ago.

Lorn gives in first, plopping into his chair and reaching for his *cabus*. Lena and Kyol sit next. Lena still looks tired and pissed.

Lorn takes a sip of his *cabus* and clears his throat. "As I said, the information I supplied was inadvertent. The majority of the *Taelith*'s *elari* come from Lyechaban. He's taken advantage of their hatred of everything human and has made promises to cleanse the Realm."

"Cleanse?" I ask. That word has been tossed around a lot all of a sudden.

"Cleanse it of everything that might weaken the Realm's magic. That includes *tor'um*, human tech and culture, and, especially, humans. He's particularly interested in capturing the *nalkin-shom*." He looks at me. "You have a reputation. He wants you as an example. He's promised his *elari* that he'll skin and hang the shadow-witch."

My gaze slides to Aren. For the first time, he looks at me.

"Maybe I've exaggerated your reputation a little too much," he says.

"You think?"

Aren gives me a sheepish grin that makes me roll my eyes. It also makes my stomach do a flip.

He turns back to Lorn. "How many followers does the false-blood have?"

"More than he should," Lorn says, "And they're quite passionate in their support for him."

"Why?" Lena demands.

"I imagine it has something to do with his magic. He's a *cacer*. He has the ability to put people to sleep with a touch."

My eyebrows go up. That's an extinct magic. It hasn't been around since the *Duin Bregga*.

"And he isn't claiming to be a Descendant," Lorn continues. "He's claiming to be *Tar Sidhe*."

Tar Sidhe? That's ridiculous. The fae's Ancestors lived centuries ago. The Realm's been ruled by half-blooded Descendants ever since then.

I sit back, waiting for someone to laugh. When no one does, I look around the room. No one is moving. No one is making a sound.

Dread slides over me. It feels like someone's punched me in the chest. Or rather, they've punched Kyol in the chest. It's hard to breathe, and I wish Naito hadn't turned off the breakers. I need the air conditioner—or at the very least a fan—to circulate the air.

"That can't be true," Lena finally says, either fear or exhaustion making her voice break. "The *Tar Sidhe* entered the ether thousands of years ago."

"Or they created the ether thousands of years ago," Lorn says with a shrug. "It all depends on which legends you believe."

"But either way, they're all dead," I find myself saying. The *Duin Bregga*, the war that erased most of the fae's history, was fought about five thousand years ago. That's when the *Tar Sidhe* disappeared, and that's when many of the fae's magics became extinct or endangered. Other than that, my knowledge of the Realm's ancient history is sketchy at best.

"Yes, they're dead," Lena snaps. "Fae don't live five hundred years, let alone five thousand."

"Of course they don't, my dear," Lorn says. "But if the *Tar Sidhe* created the ether, they have control of the ether. One might also think they have control over who enters and exits it."

I'm suddenly aware of Naito sitting next to me. A month ago, the palace archivist convinced him he knew someone who could bring Kelia back from the ether. Naito wanted her back so badly, he believed the fae and agreed to help him escape the palace with Caelar's brother, Tylan. It's cruel for Lorn to bring up the possibility of fae returning from the ether again. He knows how much Naito loved Kelia.

"If that was possible," Lena says, her voice flat, "all the *Tar Sidhe* would be here."

"Would they? Or would they turn their backs on a world that's become polluted with violence and human technology?"

"He's not *Tar Sidhe*, Lorn," Lena says.

He holds up his hands in a gesture of mock self-defense. "I agree. I'm only playing demon's advocate."

"Devil's," I murmur.

"I'm only telling you what the *Taelith* is telling his followers," Lorn continues. "The *elari* believe he is *Tar Sidhe*. He's not telling anyone his ancestry because, supposedly, he doesn't have one."

"He has to be related to someone," Lena says. "He didn't raise himself."

"What if he grew up *imithi*?" I ask.

Lena looks at Aren.

"I would know about him," he tells her. "We may not have family, but we band together for survival."

"Maybe he was a loner," I say.

Aren shakes his head. "If he didn't have someone he trusted watching his back, he would have been killed. He has ties to someone. The problem is finding out who those ties are to when he may have murdered anyone who had knowledge of his past."

"So, basically, you're saying it's going to be impossible to prove he's not *Tar Sidhe*."

"It's going to be difficult," Aren says. "Not impossible."

It might as well be. It's not like the *Taelith*—or any fae for that matter—is going to submit to a DNA test.

"We need to find him so we can question him," Lena says. "So far, Nimael is the only fae we know who might be in direct contact with the *Taelith*."

"Are you so sure about that?" Lorn asks.

She gives him a cold glare. "And you, but for some reason I doubt you'd be willing to reconnect with him."

"He's always found me. I've never found him," Lorn says. He sounds a little bitter about that fact. I'm sure it doesn't make him happy that his network of spies can't gather the information he needs. "I was referring to someone else who's spoken directly to the false-blood."

Lena's brow wrinkles slightly. She doesn't know who he's talking about, but I do.

I let out a sigh, then say, "Paige left me a message. She wanted to talk about Caelar and the false-blood."

Lena closes her eyes in a long blink. When she reopens them, she stares at Kyol. "We have to assume the rumors are true. They're allies."

The life-bond passes along his disbelief—no, his refusal to believe—that Caelar would join forces with the false-blood.

"I didn't say they are working together," Lorn chimes in. "I merely suggested that they've been in contact. You should talk to him."

"I've made numerous offers to speak with Caelar," Lena says. "He hasn't responded. We've tried tracking him down with no luck."

Lorn empties his glass of *cabus*, then sets it aside. "Perhaps he doesn't want to meet with you because you're still sending swordsmen out to kill him and the few supporters he has left."

"If I don't send fae after him, he'll come after me again."

"Will he?" Lorn asks. "Perhaps he's just trying to survive now? Or, perhaps all he wants is Aren's head?"

Lena's gaze moves to Aren. Mine doesn't. A decade ago, just after King Atroth took power, Aren exposed the fae Caelar was in love with to tech. Brene was in a position to become Atroth's sword-master, but she succumbed to the tech, losing her mind when her magic broke. Caelar won't forgive Aren for that. He's a conservative fae, but if not for Aren's involvement in the rebellion, I think he would at least be more open to a discussion with Lena. He's angry King Atroth was killed, but he wants a lawful Descendant to be placed on the throne.

"Making Aren your sword-master might not have been your wisest decision," Lorn says. "Your fragile position as would-be queen would be going better if he were out of the equation." He looks at Aren. "No offense intended, of course."

"None taken," Aren says, deadpan. His gaze is on me. I can't decipher his expression. It almost feels as if he's trying to figure me out. But I already know about his past, and I've forgiven him.

"I need you to call Paige, McKenzie," Lena says.

"She's already tried to get him to talk to you," I tell her.

"Make her try again," she says. "I need to meet face-to-face with Caelar. Paige is the only human who's allied with him.

He needs her Sight to see illusioned fae, and that gives her some influence. She needs to convince him to meet with me. It can be in public. It can be here in this world."

"Lena—"

"Make it happen, McKenzie."

Her tone of command makes me swallow down my protest. If Caelar's working with the false-blood, any meeting with him could be a trap, but Lena isn't going to take no for an answer. A day ago, she asked if I was committed to her cause. I told her yes, and I meant it, so I just give her a curt nod as I stand.

And stifle a litany of curses. Holy hell, I *hurt*. In the short time I sat on the couch, my muscles locked up. They're bruised and sore from sparring with Kyol. For no reason other than pride, I do my best not to let it show as I walk across the living room. I didn't grab my cell phone when I fled my apartment with Lorn, so I have to use Nick's landline.

I check my voice mail first. There's one new message. From Lee. Just a "call me" and a click. Since the conversation with Paige is likely to be longer than the one with Lee, I dial him first. He answers on the first ring.

"It's McKenzie," I say.

"He committed suicide."

"What?" My last conversation with Lee feels like it was ages ago. He left Glazunov with me because he wanted to talk to—I assume he really meant kidnap—the vigilante who was primarily responsible for developing the serum.

"He gave the serum to his son six months ago."

Oh. Six months ago. That's long before the serum was supposedly fixed. I don't have to guess what happened to the son. He died, and apparently, his father couldn't forgive himself for not being able to save him.

"I talked to Glazunov," I say, then I give Lee a quick rundown of what the vigilante said, telling him the serum might not be fatal anymore and ending with the information that the vigilantes are now selling it.

"Christ, they're selling it? It damn well better be fixed. How long ago did Glaz say they changed the formula?"

"Three months," I tell him. "You injected Paige two months ago, right? When did you inject it?"

A pause. There's road noise in the background, maybe the clicking of a blinker.

"Three months ago," he says finally. "If I can get a vial of the old serum and one of the new, I can do some tests to see what changes it makes to our blood."

"I might be able to help you with that. I sent an e-mail to the Web site. I'll let you know if I get a response."

"I'll be at your apartment in an hour," Lee says.

"Okay— No, wait. Not my apartment. It's not safe there."

"Where then?"

"Um." It can't be here. Not only is Nick likely to kick us out the second he gets home, but I don't want Lee to know about Kynlee. Once we're out of here, she and her father should get back to their normal lives.

There's a tap on my shoulder. I turn, see Naito holding out his hand for the phone. I give it to him.

"Hey," Naito says. "No . . . No . . . Hotel. No."

He hangs up the phone. I watch him return to the living room, and that's when I notice the others are staring at me.

"You contacted the vigilantes?" Aren asks.

I nod. "I found their Web site, so I sent them an e-mail."

"Were you going to tell us about this?" Lena demands.

"I just found out this morning," I tell her. "I set up a fake e-mail, used a fake name. I don't even know if they'll respond."

"If they do, you have to meet with them," she says. "We need to find out where they're keeping the serum and—"

She breaks off. A second later, I hear what she does: the garage door grinding open. Nick's home. He was gone for more than a few hours.

Our conversation stops there. When the door to the garage swings open, Kynlee comes in first. She looks at me, then her gaze goes to the living room. She grins like she's happy to see the fae. When Nick steps into the kitchen behind her, he glowers like he's not.

"You all can stay the night," Kynlee says, all but bouncing on her toes. "I can go to the Realm Saturday."

I meet Nick's eyes. He just shakes his head like he's lost a fight, tosses his keys on the counter, then walks through the living room without one word to Lena and the others.

"You guys hungry? I'll order pizza." Kynlee grabs the phone, completely oblivious to the worry she's causing her dad.

NINETEEN

•◆•

DURING DINNER, KYNLEE interrogates the fae. She directs her questions to Lena at first, probably figuring a woman will be more likely to give her the answers she's looking for, but Lena's responses are dry and short. It's Aren who gives Kynlee the information she wants, and he's up-front with her, telling her exactly how *tor'um* are treated in the Realm—and how Lena plans to change that.

Lena plans to change a lot of things, and as Aren describes fae society and how it's become more and more segregated over the years, with the upper classes collecting privileges and favors while *tor'um*, *imithi*, and the weak are pushed to the side, I once again see the lighthearted but rebellious and cunning Aren, who draws people to him with his reckless smiles and crazy, convoluted schemes. It's easy to see why the rebels were able to stir up such a strong opposition to the old Court.

In the decade I worked for King Atroth, no one, not even Thrain, gathered as much support as the rebels did. They made Atroth tighten his fist over the Realm, raiding people's homes without cause and interrogating individuals who had no knowledge of the rebels' plans. Atroth's actions actually strengthened the Zarraks' case for a change of regime. But even if they hadn't, the rebels would have still been a thorn in

the king's side. Sethan was a diplomat. He gathered support with honesty and reason while Aren recruited fae using pure charisma. He makes people *want* to be on his side.

Kynlee giggles at something Aren says, and he smiles at her. It's a genuine smile. He seems to like talking to the girl. His tone is teasing and protective, like he's talking to a kid sister, but I think Kynlee might be developing a crush. I can't blame her at all.

A little pang settles in my chest. We've passed the halfway point of my ultimatum. Aren has less than thirty-six hours to choose to be with me. I'm aware of each minute that ticks by; he doesn't seem to be aware of any of them.

I turn away so I don't have to see him laugh, and my gaze settles on Nick. He's listening to Aren and Kynlee's conversation from a barstool in the kitchen. The fact that he hasn't interrupted Aren or sent Kynlee off to bed makes me think he appreciates Aren's honesty. Aren hasn't sugarcoated anything.

A warm movement of air tickles the back of my neck. I reach up to rub away the sensation, but my hand encounters something cool, wet, and whiskery.

I look over my shoulder, expecting to see a cat, but instead of a fluffy feline, a silver-furred *kimki* stares back at me. My mood cranks up a notch when he drags himself over my shoulder. I reach up to scratch behind his ears, then I stand, keeping him balanced where he is. The last time I saw Sosch, he leaped into Kyol's fissure at my apartment. I've missed the furball, and I'm grateful he's here now. He always seems to know when I need cheering up.

My muscles are still sore, so I pull him off my shoulder and into my arms as I leave the living room. I need a few minutes alone, so I head to the darkened sunroom. It's not until I enter the room that I notice Lorn is here. He's sitting in a wicker chair in the corner.

"Finally coming to apologize?" he asks. Blue bolts of lightning dart across his small, smug smile.

If I weren't already sinking down onto the sofa, I'd leave. But my sore and bruised body won't let me stop my descent, so I press my lips together to keep myself from saying something I'll regret. The truth is, I don't really feel like I owe him

an apology. I accused him of prolonging and profiting from the war. He's admitted to the latter, and while he might not have been the fae who slaughtered the Sighted humans in London, he certainly hasn't been forthcoming about his role in the war. Hell, the false-blood had to almost kill him for Lorn to even admit that he's talked to him.

But I swallow back all the words I want to say and force out an apology. "I'm sorry, Lorn."

His smile widens. "Ah, so the shadow-witch *does* want something from me. How intriguing."

"I was just apolo—"

"No need to deny it, my dear," he interrupts. "Everyone wants something. Perhaps I can provide it."

I glance away, shaking my head out of disbelief more than denial. Lorn can't help being a jerk sometimes.

After a quick look back into the living room to see that Aren's still talking to Kynlee, I turn back to Lorn. There are several questions I want to ask him, like how to block out a fae on the other end of a life-bond, but I definitely don't want Lorn learning I'm linked to Kyol. So I settle on my other question.

"I need to know if Lord Hison or anyone else is blackmailing Aren."

Lorn laughs way too loudly. "I'll answer that one for free: no."

"No?" I echo. "Are you sure?"

"Very sure," he says. "He can't be blackmailed. Trust me, I tried. Don't look so surprised, McKenzie. How do you think he became known as the Butcher of Brykeld so quickly? His only fault in that massacre was ordering the wrong person to create a distraction while he attacked his real target. I'd already made threats to hurt the rebels' cause by marring his name if he didn't do a few favors for me, so when he continued to refuse"—Lorn lifts his hand in a what-was-I-to-do gesture—"I had no choice but to stretch the truth a little."

"And you wonder why we questioned your role in the war? I still don't know if we can trust you."

"Oh, you most assuredly can now," Lorn says. "I want the false-blood dead. I want his head in a bag and his body rotting in the sun."

The casual delivery of that last part makes my skin crawl. Lorn isn't joking, and he's not being unusually cruel. Severing a fae's head is the only way to prevent the body and soul from entering the ether. It's a cruel punishment, but without seeing a corpse, the only way to tell if a fae has truly died is by finding a fae who can sense the other side. That magic is extremely rare, though, and the fae has to have personal contact with the person who's passed on.

"You helped him in the past, though," I say to Lorn. "The only reason you're here now is because he learned you could find me."

His eyebrows go up in feigned offense. "And people accuse me of being egocentric. He didn't turn on me because of you. He turned on me because I refused to kill my cows."

What? I give him a skeptical look.

"I told you many of the *Taelith*'s *elari* are from Lyechaban," he says. "He has to appease them, give them a good show so they think he hates humans as much as they do. But when he ordered me to destroy everything Earth-made that I've brought to the Realm, I very politely told him he could go rot in the Barren. Apparently, he took offense at that."

"How surprising," Lena's flat voice comes from behind me. Sosch hops off my lap when I turn and see her standing just inside the sunroom.

"I assure you," Lorn says, "I was quite surprised. If I'd known he planned to—"

"You would have still made a deal with him," Lena cuts him off. "I've known you a long time, Lorn. Your insistence on putting a price on everything is the reason you're here. You strike bargains with everyone you meet, manipulating as much of an advantage as you can from them. You gamble on every rumor, every shred of information you learn, and it has caught up with you."

In short, his shady dealings have finally bit him in the ass.

"My dear," Lorn says, lounging back in his wicker chair. "I don't know what you're talking about."

"Let's see if this fits." She strides into the room. "You met the false-blood months, perhaps even years, ago. You pro-

vided him weapons and silver and information. He provided you with *tinril*. Everything went smoothly for a time, then the *Taelith* returned, this time asking you for something you weren't willing to give."

"Your cows," I put in.

"You weren't able to charm your way out of business with him, and since you weren't cooperative, he tried to send you to the ether."

All signs of amusement have disappeared from Lorn's face, so I'm guessing Lena's summary is close to the truth.

She faces me, almost completely turning her back on Lorn. "Paige?"

"I called her a little while ago," I say. "She didn't answer. I left her a message to have her phone in her hand at noon tomorrow. I'll try her again then."

She looks annoyed by the delay, but she doesn't voice her thoughts out loud. She turns back to Lorn, then she demands he tell her every detail of every meeting he's ever had with Caelar and the false-blood. She's confident I can get Paige to make a meeting between her and Caelar happen. I'm less so, but she calls in Aren and Kyol, insisting we come up with a strategy for gaining his allegiance, whether he's now allied with the false-blood or not. By the time we call it a night, my muscles have almost completely locked up on me, and I'm agitated by everything. I head to the media room, taking with me the sleepshirt, pillow, and blanket Kynlee left out for me.

I'm dead tired, so I strip to my undies, then, groaning when I force my stiff arm muscles to move, I slip Kynlee's sleepshirt on over my head. She's smaller than I am —it barely covers my ass—but I'm anxious to get out of my bloodstained cargo pants and T-shirt. I'm going to have to arrange some kind of clothing allowance; I think I've ruined half my wardrobe in the week since I returned to the Realm.

I toss the pillow Kynlee gave me onto the end of the couch, then pick up the blanket.

"I've been ordered to heal you."

Aren's voice startles me. I look over my shoulder and see him standing in the doorway, his *edarratae* bright and

captivating in the dim lighting. Haphazard and sexy, that's how I'd describe him, and I want so badly for him to be here because he *chooses* to see me, not because he's been ordered to.

"I'm fine," I say, turning back to the couch and unfurling the blanket.

"Taltrayn mentioned blisters and bruises."

"You don't want to be here, Aren."

"He outranks me," he says. "And he'll know if I don't heal you."

"He'll get over it." I start to sit on the couch, but Aren crosses the room and grabs an end of the blanket. I try to jerk it free, but he doesn't release it, and that makes the material slide across my sensitive palms. I hiss as I let the blanket go.

"Just give me your hands." He grabs them, turning my palms up, and when he presses his fingers against the raw skin, my mind flashes back to two months ago. I'd just slid down a rope made from sheets, and he insisted on healing my damaged skin. I resented his touch then, the hot lick of his chaos lusters that made me want to lean into him. I resent it now, too. If he doesn't want me as much as I want him, then I don't want to feel this way. I don't want to think of the warmth of his mouth, the kiss of his *edarratae*, or the subtle but drugging scent of cedar and cinnamon that makes me want to melt in his arms.

I clench my teeth together and stare at his chest because I refuse to get lost in his eyes.

My palms mend quickly, but Aren doesn't move away. He slides both his hands up my arms, finds the bruises on my right wrist and the ugly one just hidden under my left sleeve. A pleasant burn runs through me.

God, I want him.

I thought Aren's chest would be a safe place to stare. It isn't. It's rising and falling with his breaths, and all I want to do is slide my hands up his body. I want to kiss his neck and linger until his chaos lusters pool beneath my lips.

He drags himself back a step, and, finally, I look up. He quickly looks down, tilting his head slightly then—

"*Sidhe*, McKenzie." He drops to his knees in front of me, his palm pressing against my right calf.

"Ow!" I say, kicking his hand away.

He grabs my leg again, this time flaring his magic. "He's supposed to protect you, not injure you."

"He's teaching me to protect myself."

"Which will be hard to do if you can't walk or hold a sword."

"Careful," I say. "You almost sound like you care."

He peers up at me. "I never said I didn't care."

I cross my arms, look away, and stand rigidly, waiting while he heals me. When he's finished with my calf, he starts to rise, but then he spots another injury: the deep bruise on my upper, outer thigh. Slowly, he slides his hand up my leg. The lower hem of my sleepshirt lifts slightly as he places his hand over the bruise. His palm is hot. I'm hot.

"Please tell me this is the last one," he murmurs, his hand easing upward a fraction of an inch.

"There's another," I say quietly. "It's higher on my left side."

Slowly, he rises. He looks almost afraid when he meets my gaze. "How much higher?"

"Upper ribs."

He draws in a breath as if he's steeling himself, then he lifts my sleepshirt. It slowly, softly slides up over my hips and stomach. His hands are level with my breasts. He should be able to see the bruise now, but his silver eyes never leave mine.

A heartbeat passes. Two. Then three. He lifts the sleepshirt over my head, then his hungry gaze rakes over me. My body thrums as if it's wrapped in *edarratae*.

"*Sidhe,*" he breathes out. "You're . . ."

He closes his eyes, shaking his head as if he can get the image of me out of his mind. That's the last thing I want.

I grab his hand, slide it down my body until it rests over the deep bruise on my side.

His eyes open. He nods as if I've asked him a question, then he pulls his hand free from mine.

He drops to a knee again then focuses intently on my injury. He places his palm against it. Then I feel him shake.

Before I can ask him if he's okay, he slides his hand around to my back and presses his mouth against the bruise.

His magic flares and, holy hell, my legs nearly buckle. I have to lock my knees to stay upright.

He moves his lips, sending his healing magic into the upper part of my injury. I'm dying to fist my hands in his hair, but I settle for his shoulders, afraid of pushing him too far, too fast. I can feel how tightly he's coiled. He's holding himself back, giving himself the smallest taste of me.

His lips slide to my stomach. Another taste.

His mouth moves higher. A lick, just under my breast.

I'm trying to hold myself still—I don't want to pull him out of the moment; I don't want him to stop—but my body gives a tiny buck, and he freezes. His breath is warm on my breast, and I want him so badly, I ache. I bite my lower lip, silently pleading for him to continue.

Suddenly, his hands leave my body. He stands, taking a half step away from me.

Damn it, damn it, damn it.

I wrack my brain for something to say, some way to pull him back to me, but he just stands there staring at me as if he has no fucking idea what he's doing.

"Aren—"

He moves, his mouth taking mine in a brutal, bruising kiss.

Fire explodes through me, ricocheting in my stomach and sending a hot, molten heat downward. I grab his shoulders again because I'm not going to let him go. I dig my fingers into the muscles of his back and part my lips, inviting him to deepen the kiss.

He does, tasting me. I moan and press closer.

He grabs my hips as he pulls my lower lip between his teeth. His bite surprises me, sending a sharp jolt of pain or pleasure—I'm not sure which—through me.

I gasp a second later, not from Aren's nip but from the alarm vibrating through my life-bond. But I can't stifle the need building inside of me, and quickly, Kyol catches on. I feel him vanish from this world, feel a wall fall between us. I should be concerned about him, considerate of his feelings, but Aren's scent is intoxicating, and I can only think of him.

I fist my hand in his shirt, slide it up.

"I want this off you," I say. I slip my fingers under his weapons belt. "This, too."

"Yes." No hesitation. No protest. He's mine.

He loops his arm around my waist, swinging me around. The back of my legs hit the couch. Aren pulls off his shirt, drops his belt to the floor, then moves over me. My gaze is locked on his chest, then on a bright bolt of lightning that zigzags across his perfect abs. Perfect even with a deep scar cutting between the muscles. My fingers find a new one on his shoulder, then I slide my hands to his face, pull him closer.

I can't lose you, I want to say, but I kiss him instead, my hips rising to press against his.

He's still wearing his pants. I tug at them, kiss him harder.

He breaks the kiss, separating from me just enough to gaze into my eyes.

The light from his chaos lusters reflects off my skin, and my heart thunders in my chest. This is the brink, the one I've stood on too many times to count, and I can practically hear Aren's thoughts demanding for him to stop.

I jerk harder on the hem of his pants, rubbing against him.

He shudders. A moment later, his pants are gone. Then my underwear, too.

His body is hard, lean, exquisite. My hands explore him while his lips explore me, trailing hot shocks of lightning down my neck, my collarbone, lower. I lurch into him when he kisses the lower swell of my breast again, then drags his tongue upward. I didn't know I could want him more, but desire explodes through me, creating a hot ache between my legs. His hand is there the next second. Making the ache better or worse? I don't know.

He murmurs into my ear. Something in Fae. A question. My mind is too filled with him to do anything but nod yes. Yes to everything he wants.

He watches me as he repositions himself, something akin to wonder in his silver eyes. I feel exotic. I feel treasured. Then I feel him sliding into me.

No pain. Just heat and pleasure and *Aren.* He's experienced. I'm not, but my body reacts to his movements, matching his thrusts to bring him closer, deeper.

The ache between my legs intensifies, and I'm filled with an indescribable yearning. I wrap my legs around his hips, wanting more even though I can't possibly take more.

"Sidhe," Aren gasps, then, a heartbeat later, we both cry out when an incredibly hot and potent chaos luster strikes between our connected bodies.

My eyes spring open. I'm not sure when I closed them but the media room is bright with the lightning flashing across our skin.

Our skin. And, impossibly, it isn't just his blue *edarratae* causing the glow. My *edarratae*, which should only appear when I'm in the Realm, are white-hot and spiraling around us.

And spiraling within us. They're moving faster and faster, matching the intensity of the pleasure building between my legs. So hot. So heavenly. So *much*.

I dig my nails into his back. I need to be grounded, or the lightning will shatter me, I'm certain of it.

"Sidhe," Aren rasps out again. All his muscles are taut. He's at the edge of his control. I'm so far beyond mine.

The ecstasy builds, current by current, and the frenzied light flashing around our bodies is almost constant. I'm not sure anything but the *edarratae*'s heat is touching us now. The lightning shoots around us like starlight, lifted inches above our glistening skin.

"Aren," I gasp. "It's—"

"Hold on to me." His voice is strained. He's moving in and out of me, his pace as frenzied as the lightning's.

And then it happens. Our chaos lusters solidify into a disc of light that explodes outward when the rush of pleasure hits, and the release, the ecstasy. It's indescribable.

TWENTY

·◆·

"I TOLD YOU I was the right thing," I murmur later when I'm wrapped in Aren's arms. I love the way his chuckle rumbles against my back.

"You were right, of course." He presses his lips to the crook of my neck.

I close my eyes and smile, soaking in the warm simmer of his kiss. It took a few rounds, but our chaos lusters have finally settled. We can even touch, lingering in each other's embraces, without the lightning arousing us too much.

"This is nice," I say, the biggest understatement of the century. Lying here with him is pure bliss.

I feel him smile against my neck.

I pull the blanket up to my chest, wriggling to get just a tad more comfortable.

"Careful," Aren says, loosening his arms enough to let me move as much as I want.

"Sorry," I say, grinning as I turn my head to the side. He places a kiss on my cheek then rests his arm across my stomach, above the blanket. My finger slides over the hard muscle of his forearm, leaving a trail of tiny chaos lusters in its wake. Absently, I draw a random design, loops and lines that fade away after a few seconds.

"I was a fool to think I could stay away from you." His lips

dip to my neck again. This time, he slides them along the raised skin there. It's an inch-long scar he gave me when we were enemies, and I refused to read the shadows for him in Lyechaban. It's a small, minor blemish, but I can feel regret in the way his lips linger.

Regret is the last thing I want him to feel right now.

I press the tip of my finger into his forearm twice, then swoop a curved line under the two dots.

"Smiley face," I say, nodding toward the flickering sparks on his arm. He laughs, squeezing me tighter as the tiny lightning bolts fade.

A few minutes pass. I close my eyes, trying to keep my mind empty. I just want to relax in Aren's arms. I don't want to think of anything or anyone else.

"I want to stay here forever," I murmur.

After a long moment, he replies softly, "Me too."

I scowl at the unspoken "but" on the end of his sentence. "But we have a false-blood to hunt down," I say.

Another hesitation as he rests his cheek against mine. "And vigilantes to track down and question. Lena's going to want to find everyone who knows about the serum. She's going to want to make sure it's destroyed and that no one has the ability to replicate it."

The serum and the research *should* have been destroyed when we burned down the vigilantes' compound in Boulder. The lab was there. So was a network of computers. But, apparently, Nakano was smart enough to back up the research and store some of the serum off-site.

I run my hands over my face. A minute ago, I was blissfully relaxed in Aren's arms, but now, the stress and tension I've been living with for the past several months slowly seep back into my body.

"What time is it?" I ask reluctantly.

"A few hours from morning," he says with a shrug. That was a stupid question to ask him. The days and nights in the Realm and on Earth don't match up, so he can't tell me the exact time. Even in the Realm, fae usually speak in terms of hours or half hours before dawn, noon, dusk, and midnight—the real mid-

point of the night. Time isn't as important to them as it is to humans.

"I contacted the vigilantes yesterday around noon," I say, reaching for the laptop on the table beside the couch. "They might have replied."

It's a sign of how tired I am that I don't realize what I'm doing until I open the laptop and press the power button.

"Torture, *nalkin-shom*?" Aren asks at the same time that I say, "Shit. Sorry."

I start to get up, but he laughs and pulls me back against him. "It's fine."

"Are you sure?"

"Completely," he says. "Nick still has the power off, and you've chased away my headache." He slides his hand, the one that's under the blanket, over my hip, then down my leg.

"What does it say?" he whispers, letting his lips brush against my ear.

"Mmm." I move my finger across the laptop's touch pad, trying to concentrate on what I'm doing, not on what he's doing. "I, um, need to log in."

"Okay," he says, letting his fingers skim lightly up and down my inner thigh.

I manage to get into my e-mail. I read the one new message that downloads to my in-box.

"The seller's responded already," I say. "He wants to know how long it will take me to get to Boulder."

Aren's hand stops moving. "Boulder, again?"

"Apparently, the vigilantes didn't flee the city."

We were there just over a month ago. That's where Naito's father set up his compound inside a closed-down ski resort. Naito and I and a few rebels went there to destroy the Sight serum. Normally, fae go out of their way to avoid human deaths, but the vigilantes are ruthless and cruel, and they're a threat to the fae. We left the compound in ashes, and more than a dozen humans died. The Boulder police are calling it a cult suicide. The first part isn't far from the truth, but the second? Aren and the rebels—and probably the remnants who eventually showed up, too—killed the vigilantes, who

were waiting to spring a trap on us. Most of them were slain with swords, but Nakano wasn't. Naito shot him twice before Trev used his magic to burn down the compound. Since it's obvious the fae learned where the vigilantes' base of operations was, I'm surprised any of them decided to remain in the city.

I start typing a reply.

"What are you writing?" Aren asks.

"I'm telling him I live only a few hours away and can meet him at six tonight. You can fissure me there?"

He doesn't respond immediately. I click SEND, then look at him.

"Yeah," he says, a warm smile on his lips.

"What?" I ask.

"You didn't think twice about being the person who meets with them."

I set the laptop aside. "Who else would do it? They would recognize Naito and Lee, and you can't do it. They'd kill any fae who showed up."

"They'd *try* to kill any fae who showed up," he says. "My point is, you get hurt so often—"

"That's not my fault. People keep trying to kill me."

"I know," he says with a laugh. "I know, but any normal human would say they're done with this. They'd leave us to fight our own war. You don't. You always pick yourself up and put your life at risk again and again."

I tilt my head. "Are you calling me an adrenaline junky?"

His arms tighten around me. "I'm calling you brave."

I return his smile, shifting a little in his arms. Then I rest my cheek on his chest.

"McKenzie?"

"Hmm?" I respond. His heartbeat is comforting. It could lull me to sleep.

His hand moves along my inner thigh again. "I think my headache is coming back."

I open my eyes, grin up at him. "Is it?"

His chaos lusters, which have been on a pleasant, simmering after-buzz from our previous lovemaking, suddenly strike hotly across my skin.

"Oh, yes," he says, pulling me higher on top of him. "It's definitely back."

SEVERAL hours after the sun rises, Aren and I finally tear ourselves away from each other. We need to get to Boulder, so we make plans to meet at the Vegas gate. Naito and Lee will be coming with us as well. They'll recognize the vigilantes, and it doesn't hurt to have a little human backup.

The wind whistles through my broken window as I pull to a stop in front of a hotel on the outskirts of town. I vacuumed out the broken glass at a gas station, but I think I might have missed a few shards in the back. Lee curses as he climbs into the car.

"Sorry," I mutter when I look into the rearview mirror and see his reflection staring down at his palm. He plucks the glass from his hand without another word.

Naito doesn't say anything either. Not even a hello to his brother. He hasn't said much since we left Nick's, and as soon as I hit the road again, the silence stretches between us. He's not the same person he was before Kelia's death, and even though I know it's unreasonable, I can't help feeling a little guilty after last night. Aren and I had what he lost, and our human-fae relationship is a reminder of what he'll never have again. I don't know if he'll ever love someone like he loved Kelia.

Naito's the one who told me that once I'd been with a fae, I'd never want to be with a human again. After last night, I believe him. I don't have anything to compare it to, but being in Aren's arms, feeling him move against me, then feeling the lightning strike between us . . .

The memory brings a rush of heat to my cheeks. *That* was definitely worth waiting for. It felt earth-shattering. Literally. I'm surprised there weren't burn marks on the walls from the explosion of the *edarratae*. We reached the point where they coalesced into a disc of light four times during the night—a feat Aren insisted wouldn't have been possible if it weren't for me and my humanness—and I thought I saw a black scorch line on the walls long after the light disappeared.

I shake the images from my head, not just because Naito's sitting next to me, but because Kyol's picking up on my emotions. He's training with his swordsmen right now, trying to reinforce his mental walls. Problem is, those walls keep his feelings from me more than they keep mine from him, and last night, I was incapable of building a barrier between us.

I feel like I've stabbed Kyol in the back. But I wasn't naïve. I knew Kyol would know when Aren and I were together. I knew I'd have to deal with the pain of hurting him. I guess I just hoped I wouldn't hurt him so much.

I tighten my grip on the steering wheel. I need to focus on something besides Kyol and Aren.

"You going to tell him the plan?" I ask Naito.

He doesn't respond immediately, but after I turn onto the rural road that'll take us to the gate, he gives Lee a quick rundown of what we're going to do in Boulder. The vigilante who responded to my e-mails didn't give a name. I think whoever it is has watched a few too many espionage movies because he wants me to wear a red scarf and meet him at a bar.

As I pull to the side of the road, Lee says, "It's gotta be Harper. The guy's paranoid."

"You're all paranoid," Naito tells him as he gets out of the car.

I toss my keys into the glove box—they're useless in the Realm—and climb out just as Lee slams his door.

"*They're* all paranoid," he says.

Naito studies his brother over the hood of my car. After a handful of seconds, he nods once, then heads for the gate. Aren, Trev, and Nalst are there waiting for us.

"Lena wants to know if you've talked to Paige," Trev says when we reach them.

My jaw clenches, and I shake my head. I tried to get in touch with Paige before we left Nick's. Sure, my "noon" phone call might have been half an hour later than I said it would be, but it wouldn't have killed Paige to keep her phone on and in her hand for a little while longer.

Unless, of course, Paige is already dead. If Caelar and the false-blood are working together, the false-blood may have insisted upon it. He might have . . .

I bite my lip, forcing the image of the skinned humans in London and at the *tjandel* out of my head. I'm almost certain Caelar and Tylan wouldn't let that happen to her.

"I'll try to call her again when we're finished in Boulder," I say.

Trev doesn't look like he believes I tried at all. Whatever. He can get over it.

"Let's go," Aren says.

Trev and Nalst fissure out with Naito and Lee, leaving me alone with Aren. He gives me one of his sexy half grins as he reaches for me.

He leans me against a tree, kisses my neck, then says, "Naito and Lee can probably take care of the vigilante."

He kisses my collarbone. "The vigilante's expecting me."

"Mmm," he murmurs, sliding his hands under my shirt. My stomach tightens when a chaos luster skips across my ribs. "You're telling me no, then?"

"I'm telling you later." My voice is suddenly raspy. His hands have moved down to my waistband. His thumbs dip under it, and my legs turn molten when an unbelievably hot bolt of lightning shoots down low.

"What if the evil vigilante steals you away?" he asks, his lips brushing against my ear.

"Then you'll come find me." I dig my fingers into his shoulders. "Or I'll kick his ass. Whichever is easier."

Aren chuckles.

"I've missed you," he says, tucking a lock of my hair behind my ear.

"It's only been an hour."

"You didn't miss me then?" he asks, kissing the corner of my mouth.

"I've missed you for the last month," I tell him, and as soon as I say those words, I remember the other kisses we've shared over the last week. The reluctant kisses, the ones he tried so hard not to give me.

I take a half step away from him. His smile wavers. It's brief—no more than half a second passes before it returns—but it's telling.

"You haven't told me why you tried to push me away."

His chaos lusters are darting across my skin. It takes everything in me to stand there, not giving in to the desire to kiss him again.

His smile turns into a tantalizing half grin. "Would you believe it was because I was the Realm's biggest fool?"

"Yes." A particularly hot bolt of lightning makes my voice break over the word. "And no," I force myself to say. "I want to know the truth, Aren."

"I told you the truth."

"You told me you couldn't accept the life-bond."

He looks away from me, back toward the road. That's when I feel Kyol's apprehension. Thinking about the life-bond has made me more aware of him, and I'm all but certain he's braced for Aren and me to be together again.

"That's close to the truth," Aren says, his brow furrowing. "Life-bonds are sacred between fae."

"I'm not fae," I manage to get out. I'm trying so hard to build a mental wall.

Aren nods. Then his gaze settles on me again. "That makes it worse." He takes my hand. "Come on. Someone's just pulled over."

He presses an anchor-stone into my palm, then leads me to the edge of the river. Still trying to put up a wall, I look over my shoulder and see a police officer walking to my car. He's not looking in this direction, thank God, but I'm betting I'll have another TOW AWAY sticker slapped on my car when we get back.

Aren doesn't release my hand when he dips his into the river. His chaos lusters spiral up my arm. They're heating my skin, making me flush, and as the fissure *shrrips* open, I welcome the chill of the In-Between. It extinguishes my lust just enough that I'm able to build a fairly solid mental wall when we step out of the light in Boulder.

"It doesn't affect you much, does it?" Aren asks, pocketing the anchor-stone.

"What?" I hedge because I'm not sure how to answer. If I tell him the truth, that yes, knowing that Kyol feels how much I love and want Aren is wearing on me, Aren might think I regret last

night. He might try to put distance between us again, and I don't want that.

"You usually hold on to me more tightly when we step out of a fissure," Aren says. "You're not off-balance or shaky. The life-bond's made you more resilient."

Thank God I didn't answer. He wasn't asking if the life-bond affects me; he was asking if the In-Between does.

"Yeah," I say with a shrug. "It's had some interesting side effects. Kynlee was able to take me through a gate without—"

"Kynlee," he interrupts, his silver eyes widening.

"Yeah. She—"

"You fissured with Kynlee? With a *tor'um*?"

"I've already been informed how risky that was. I wasn't exactly thinking straight." I'm surprised he's just now learning about this.

"It wasn't risky, it was suicidal. *Sidhe*." He runs a hand through his already disheveled hair.

"Hey," Naito's voice comes from behind me. We've fissured to the edge of a wooded area. When I turn, Naito is stepping between the foliage. "Are you two coming, or do you need some time?"

"We're coming," I say.

We're just a handful of paces away from a parking lot that's crammed with cars. Lee's on the phone, arranging for a taxi to pick us up. When he sees me, he starts walking toward the entrance to a shopping mall. After a short debate on whether it's actually necessary for me to have on a red scarf—Naito thinks it is just in case we don't recognize the vigilante, but Lee's certain the vigilante will be Harper—I grab some cash from Lee, run inside, and buy a scarf that's more pink than red. It'll have to do.

Half an hour later, I'm sitting alone at the bar. It's ten minutes before six, so the place isn't crowded. That's kind of a problem. Lee's hunkered down in a corner booth. He's wearing a baseball cap that he picked up at the last minute from a street vendor, but if the vigilante *is* paranoid and looks closely, he'll see Lee's face. Plus, there's always the possibility that my contact isn't coming alone.

"What can I get you?" the bartender asks. She's skinny with a tattoo inked from her left wrist all the way up to her shoulder.

"Nothing right now," I say. "I'm waiting on someone."

"Are you waiting on him?" She nods toward a man sitting at the end of the bar. He's older, pushing sixty at least, with a deeply pockmarked face. A briefcase sits at his feet.

"If so, you're the third"—she eyes my pink scarf—"reddish-scarfed woman he's met here recently."

"That's probably him then. Thanks," I say, staring at the man. He's still not looking at me. And Lee isn't moving. He's here instead of Naito because, theoretically, he'll recognize more of the vigilantes since Naito hasn't been one of them for several years. Honestly, though, I'd rather have Naito here, or Aren or Trev, but they're all waiting outside in inconspicuous locations. The vigilante would either run or fight if he saw a fae, and we don't want to cause a scene.

If Briefcase Man *is* my contact, I could just walk out of here. We could follow him to see where he goes, or we could maneuver him into a dark alley and question him. Either way is simple and would work. Really, all I need to do is make sure he's who I think he is.

I'll give him until 6:05. Then I'll go talk to him.

When the clock behind the bar reads exactly 6:00 P.M., Briefcase Man picks up his briefcase, walks to me, then with a curt "Follow me," he heads for a narrow hall at the back of the bar. Presumably, it leads to the restrooms and rear exit.

As I stand, I glance at Lee. He won't see me if I go down that hall, and he's not looking my way now. He's staring out the window. I hesitate, waiting for him to check on me, but he seems riveted to something outside.

Crap. I can't call out his name without alerting the vigilante, and I can't wait for him to turn. I follow Briefcase Man, thinking. Aren, Trev, and Nalst should be watching the back exit. Naito's watching the front. Even without Lee following me, I'll be safe.

I step into the hallway, see the back exit then—

The vigilante turns, swinging his briefcase at my head while he kicks open a door.

I manage to duck beneath the briefcase, but he rams into me, making me fall into the side room. Instinctively, I roll to my back, intending to kick up and knock his head off, but someone's behind me. They grab the arms I brace against the floor, then drag me all the way inside.

TWENTY-ONE

●◆●

"DON'T MOVE. DON'T make a sound." The man holding me presses a gun into my ribs.

In front of me, Briefcase Man closes and locks the door. We're in a restroom. The men's restroom. Three urinals are on the wall to my right. Gross. I want to peek under the two stalls to see if anyone is in them, but I'm sure I already know the answer. They're empty, and no one in the bar had a view of the hallway or my abduction.

I draw in a deep breath—through my mouth, not my nose—and do my best to keep my heart rate steady. I'm going to get through this without Kyol fissuring to my rescue. Hell, after last night, he might not come to my rescue at all.

"We knew we'd get their attention sometime," Briefcase Man says to me.

I reestablish my mental wall as well as I can under the circumstances, then decide to play dumb. "Whose attention? Who are you? What do you want?"

The gun digs deeper between my ribs.

"You're here with Lee," the man behind me hisses into my ear. "He hasn't reported in to us in over a month. He's been turned."

"Into a vampire?" I say, eyes wide and innocent. Is this

guy really prepared to fire his gun? Everyone in the bar would hear it go off.

The vigilante grabs the scarf around my neck and pulls it tight.

"There's fae with you," he says. "Where are they?"

I choke, then cough until he loosens the damn scarf. Kyol's thoughts are focused on me. He's not alarmed yet. I concentrate on my breathing, forcing myself to stay calm.

"Okay," I say, scrambling for some plausible explanation. "Okay. Yes, a fae fissured me here. I'm supposed to meet him tomorrow morning so he can fissure me back home. But I'm not here because of them. I'm here because of the Sight serum."

"You already have the Sight," Briefcase Man snarls. He sets that briefcase on the sink and opens it.

"Yeah, but Lee didn't," I say, still trying to buy time. "We heard it's lethal, and we're here to find out if that's true."

The scarf tightens again. "Tell us where you're supposed to meet the fae. Tell us what type of magics he has."

I cough again, more to buy time to think than because the scarf is too tight. Surely, Lee's noticed me missing by now. I've been gone at least two minutes.

"You need to start talking," Briefcase Man says. He's holding a vial of pale, yellow liquid in one hand and a needle and syringe in the other.

Oh, this is great.

"The Sight serum," I say, eyeing the vial as he fills the syringe.

"The Sight serum," he acknowledges. "Some of it kills." He pushes the plunger until a tiny droplet of the yellow liquid comes out. "Some of it doesn't. I'll let you guess which batch this is from."

My heart pumps a little harder. I might already have the Sight, but I have no doubt that the wrong batch of the serum will kill me just as it killed the others who injected it.

Briefcase Man takes a step toward me. I could use some help right now, or even a good distraction. How is it possible that we're in a bar, and no one's so much as knocked on the restroom door?

He takes another step. I'm going to have to risk it. Here's

to hoping the man behind me doesn't really want to fire his gun.

I slam my head back and drop my hand to the gun as I turn in my captor's arms.

There's a loud *crack*—his nose breaking, not the gun firing—but the weapon won't budge from his hand.

I aim the barrel away from me, knee the guy in the groin then blindly swing a backhand behind me, expecting Briefcase Man to come for me.

He's there. My fist catches his neck instead of his face, but that works to my advantage. He chokes, giving me the second I need to lurch past him.

He grabs my ankles before I reach the door. I catch the handle, manage to get it unlocked. Before I crash to the floor, I shove it open and yell.

Briefcase Man yanks my leg. I twist to my back, see him lifting the syringe.

Crap!

I jerk out of the way just in time. The needle breaks against the floor, and I slam my heel into the asshole's face. I get my ankle free, then scurry to my feet and out the door.

The back exit's the closest. Someone from the other direction asks if I'm okay. I'm about to scream, "He has a gun!" when I spot Aren behind the concerned human.

I can't see into the restroom from where I'm standing, which means the vigilantes can't see me, so I force myself to laugh, then say to the human, "I went in the wrong restroom."

He gives me a slow nod, his expression saying I'm crazy for yelling and dashing out like I did. It's a look I've grown used to in the last ten years.

Aren presses his back against the wall and slides along it toward the open restroom door. I'm on the other side of the opening.

"Two of them. One gun," I say, just loud enough for him to hear.

He nods once then, dagger in hand, he opens a fissure in front of the doorway and disappears.

Silence. That's weird. Inside the restroom is the only place he would have fissured.

Cautiously, I peek in. Aren's there, staring down at the two vigilantes who are still on the floor. Briefcase Man is clutching his bleeding nose. The other man—his nose looks broken, too—is clutching his privates.

Aren looks up at me, surprise and appreciation and maybe a little something else in his silver eyes.

My stomach does a flip.

"The bond has a couple of other side effects," I say, stepping inside the restroom and picking the vigilante's gun off the floor before he recovers.

Aren gives me a grin, then he looks down at the vigilantes again. "On your feet. Both of you. You're going to walk out the back door without a word to anyone."

The gun's safety is on. I leave it that way, then motion for the two humans to get up. Briefcase Man does; the other vigilante is still holding his privates. Surely, I didn't knee him *that* hard.

Aren grabs a handful of his shirt and forcibly pulls him to his feet. "Move."

I slip the gun into my waistband and cover it with my shirt. Then, after picking up the syringe and broken needle, I throw them into the briefcase, close it, and follow the others out.

Trev, Lee, and Naito are in the back alley. So is another man. A human. Lee has the guy's arm twisted behind his back. When he sees the vigilante who grabbed my arms in the bathroom, he gives a little snort.

"Told you Harper was involved."

Naito glares briefly at his brother, then says, "Their car is parked a block away. Let's get them out of here."

I hand the vigilante's gun over to Naito, and we maneuver them down the alley. They walk without a word and without one ounce of resistance until we hit the main street. Harper glances at Briefcase Man, then, simultaneously, they run opposite directions.

Running from the fae never works out well. Aren and Trev both fissure directly in their paths, taking them down to the ground and ending their escape attempt three seconds after they sprung it.

"You're going to go to your vehicle," Aren says, loud enough

for both vigilantes to hear him. "You can go there conscious or unconscious. It's up to you."

Both decide to remain conscious. A few minutes later, Naito uses Harper's keys to beep a black van unlocked. Lee searches it and, conveniently, he finds rope and a few pairs of handcuffs.

Silver-plated handcuffs.

I remember the question Harper asked earlier. He didn't just want to know where to find my fae escort; he wanted to know what types of magic he could wield as well. At the time, I assumed they wanted to know how to defend against any attack the fae could throw at them. Now, I think I was wrong.

I look at Harper. "You wanted to capture the fae."

He gives me a murderous look as Naito shoves him into the backseat. Naito uses a pair of handcuffs on the vigilante, slipping them behind something under the seat before hooking them to both of Harper's wrists. Harper has to sit bent over and with his head practically in his lap. Not the most comfortable of positions, but he's not going anywhere.

"A few vigilantes want to use their magics," Lee says, taking the briefcase from me.

I watch him open it on the hood of the van. "Use them?"

He nods. "You know how much money con artists make from supposedly healing the sick?" He glances at Aren. "Imagine what someone could make if they could really heal people."

"Except healers can't heal diseases or genetic conditions," I say. If they could, Lee and Paige wouldn't have to worry about the Sight serum being lethal. Aren could heal the problem away.

He shrugs and sorts through the briefcase. It's filled with papers and several small, black cases. He opens one up while Naito handcuffs the other two vigilantes inside the van.

Aren places his hand on the small of my back. "Trev and I are going to go back to Corrist."

Since the nearest gate is over an hour away by car, it makes sense.

"Are we taking the vigilantes there?" I ask, turning toward him.

"The high nobles are already complaining about the other one," Trev says before Aren can answer. "Lena won't be happy to have to make excuses for three more suddenly appearing."

The "other one" is Glazunov. We're going to have to do something with him. We can't just leave him in the Realm forever.

"We can take them to my place," Naito says, sliding the van's door shut. "It's a longer drive, but there's a gate within walking distance. We can decide what to do with them and the serum when we get there."

"Vials from both batches are here," Lee says, closing the black case. "There's also a barbiturate that can knock a human out in a few minutes or a fae in thirty seconds or less if it's injected."

Naito looks at his brother. "You spent a lot of time with Dad."

Lee's mouth tightens. He closes the briefcase without a word.

Aren's hand is on my hip. He slides his thumb over it, back and forth in an absent caress.

"See you at Naito's then?" I say.

He looks down at me, smiles, then nods. "Tonight."

I love hearing the promise that rides on his words.

BECAUSE of a wreck on the highway, it takes two hours to get to Naito's house on the south side of Denver. Trev's waiting for us. Aren needed to talk to Lena before he fissured back here, so he sent Trev to help us get the vigilantes inside. As soon as we secure them in the basement, Trev collapses on the couch.

I don't think he intends to go to sleep, but within two minutes, he's out cold and snoring.

An unexpected tendril of sympathy twists its way through me. While Naito and Lee hole up in Naito's study, I grab a blanket out of a closet and lay it over the sleeping fae. I know he's not the only one of Lena's people who is tired—they all are—and I wish there was something I could do to help them get rest soon. But all I am is a reliable set of eyes and a shadow-reader. A shadow-reader who might have lost some of her skills.

Quietly, I leave Trev and head to the kitchen. I haven't eaten anything since we left Nick's, and I'm sure Naito and Lee are hungry, too. I check the pantry for options, then the fridge. Apparently, Naito hasn't been here in months. The milk is way past expired, and the leftovers in a plastic container are fuzzy and unidentifiable.

I toss both into the trash and am about to open the freezer when tension spikes through Kyol. I pause with my hand on the door, tilting my head as if I can hear his thoughts, but he slams his mental walls into place, making himself the hard, unemotional soldier again.

I open the freezer, look inside, but my thoughts are completely centered on Kyol. He feels . . . strange. I don't understand what's going on. He's not fighting—I'm certain of that—so why is there a strand of horror woven into his emotions?

My brain registers a frozen pizza in the freezer. I pull it out as I try to draw Kyol's emotions across the life-bond. They're faint behind his wall. I wouldn't feel them at all if I weren't concentrating on him.

Another surge of emotion pounds through him. He shuts it down before I can identify it, but screw that. I won't stay here wondering what the hell's going on there.

"Trev," I call out, throwing the pizza back into the freezer.

He doesn't respond, and when I get to the living room, he's still lying unmoving on the couch.

"Trev," I say again, stopping less than a foot away from his head. He turns his head to the side and lets out another snore.

Really? Fae have better hearing than humans, and they're supposed to be bad-ass fighters. You'd think they'd all be light sleepers, springing to their feet, ready to defend themselves at a moment's notice.

Maybe Trev is just that tired.

"Trev!" I say, shaking his shoulder.

Trev twists off the couch so quickly, he nearly barrels into me. He lets out a curse when he hits the ground, his nose inches away from the sword he left lying in its scabbard on the floor. He reaches for it, but I step on its hilt first.

"Relax, it's me," I tell him.

He looks up, still half-asleep, I swear. "McKenzie?"

"I need you to take me to the Realm."

"What's wrong?" he demands, waking all at once. He scans the living room as he jerks his sword out from beneath my shoe.

"I don't know," I tell him.

He rises, his gaze finishing its sweep of the room before resting on me. "You don't know?"

"I need to talk to Kyol."

Trev scowls. "It can wait until the morning."

"No, it can't. I need you to fissure me there now."

"I'm sure Taltrayn is busy." He sinks back down on the couch.

"Something's wrong, Trev," I say, and when he looks up at me now, something clicks. I see it in his eyes, the suspicion.

"How do you know?" he asks.

When I don't answer, he lets out a short, dry laugh. "The fae who were at the *veligh* when the remnants attacked said you'd died. I thought they were exaggerating your injuries and that the rumors of your resurrection were Aren's doing. I never thought . . ." He shakes his head. "You're sure something's wrong?"

I didn't die—the life-bond kept me alive—but all I do is nod.

Trev lets out a tired sigh, then rises. "Let's go."

TWENTY-TWO

◆—◆

W E'VE FISSURED INTO one of the safe houses Lena's set up just outside the silver wall. Trev opens the front door and leads the way out.

It's early morning in Corrist. The first rays of sunlight are just beginning to smear the lower portion of the sky. The street is uncharacteristically crowded for the early hour, though, and no one looks like they just woke up. They look like they've been up all night.

A shout rings out from down the street. The fae it came from has a sword in his hand. He raises it into the air and yells, *"Cadig!"* the same *huzzah* the fae were chanting after Lena burned the ledgers.

"Are they still celebrating?" I ask Trev.

"I'm not sure," Trev says hesitantly. His hand is on the hilt of his sword. The chanting fae down the street isn't the only one who has his blade out now. Others have joined him, yelling as they thrust their weapons toward the sky. "We need to get inside the wall."

I nod, already walking toward the wall of silver towering over the stretch of homes and shops in front of us. A narrow alley leads between an anchor-stone store and a cafe. We follow a trio of fae down the pathway and pass more than a few other people heading back our way. One of the latter locks his gaze on

me. My chaos lusters are bright in the still-dark morning, especially with us eclipsed in the shadows of the alley. I return the fae's stare, keep my shoulders straight and confident until the fae's gaze falters.

We emerge from the alley not far from the western entrance to the Inner City. Trev stays close by my side, so close, the lightning on my skin flashes erratically across my left elbow, threatening to leap into him at the slightest brush. But he's not going to step away anytime soon. He might not be my biggest fan, but he'll protect me with his life, and that's something he might very well have to do. Something isn't right in Corrist.

It's not unusual for the gates to the Inner City to be closed overnight, but it is unusual for so many people to be gathering in front of them this early in the morning. They should be opening soon, but I'm not even sure the fae want to go inside. The air buzzes with their shouts and chants and the low, constant murmur of a thousand conversations.

My brow furrows as Trev and I make our way through the crowd. It's too loud and discordant for me to decipher what they're saying. I ask Trev again if he knows what's going on. He shakes his head, presses me forward. Most of the fae who see the lightning flashing across my face and arms back away, but a few of them don't. They deliberately brush against me, agitating my *edarratae* and heating my skin. I grit my teeth and keep moving, trying to look as pissed and determined as possible to keep them from messing with me. And trying to figure out just what the hell everyone's doing out so early in the morning.

Before we reach the wall, a small, discreet door opens. The portcullis behind it is already lifted, and four armed fae step out. Trev and I reach the guards—who most likely spotted us the second we stepped out of the alley—and enter the Inner City without much trouble.

The guards follow us in, closing the door behind them, then lowering the portcullis.

Trev turns to the nearest fae. *"What are they celebrating?"*

"The kingkiller has stepped forward."

Every ounce of blood drains from my face. My mouth goes dry, my chest tightens, and I'm cold. Colder than I was in the In-Between.

"No," I say. I mentally focus on Kyol, trying to break my way through his mental wall. He pushes back, and I can't read him. I can't rant or scream or rage at him.

Not from this distance.

I don't remember the run through the Inner City. I only vaguely recall Trev shouting my name. My heart thunders against my chest, and the only thing I can focus on is stopping Kyol. I can't let him do this. King Atroth was his friend. Kyol killed him to save me. He wouldn't have done it otherwise.

The plaza outside the palace's main gate is just as packed as the area ringing the silver wall. When I reach the edge of the crowd, I falter for the first time. Yesterday, they were celebrating the burning of the ledgers. Today, they're celebrating the pending execution of one of the most respected fae in the Realm. The fae are a fickle, violent people. I've always known that, but I've never before loathed them so much for it.

The crowd parts in front of me. Not out of fear of a lightning-covered human but because I've picked up an escort along the way. Trev and half a dozen swordsmen make a path for me. I take it, striding through the mass of fae and reaching an open door just as the sun peaks above the eastern city.

No one says a word once I'm inside. I keep silent as well. I don't need them to tell me where Kyol is. He might be eclipsing his emotions, but he can't hide his location. He's in the northern wing of the palace. In Lena's apartments, most likely.

Less than ten minutes later, I'm stopped before I enter the queen's antechamber. I don't recognize the fae standing between me and the open double doorway, but my guess is they're fae who are loyal to Hison. The high noble is inside. He's speaking to Lena. Her back is to me, so I can't read her expression. She's rigid, though, and I'm hoping she's angry and resolute, that she's refusing to allow Hison to arrest and execute Kyol, who's somewhere in the room.

I try to push my way past the fae in front of me. One of them, a tall, thick-chested man with a green-and-white namecord braided into his hair, shoves me back.

I slam into Trev, who steadies me before he takes an aggressive step toward the other fae. All the fae guarding the

door must be on edge. They overreact, drawing their weapons and moving to intercept each one of my escorts.

"Kyol!" I yell, but I already feel him moving toward me, shoving aside Hison's men.

"Don't do this," I tell him as he pulls me into his arms.

"Quiet!" he orders.

I dig my fingers into the hard muscles of his forearms. Hison's ordering his men to arrest Kyol; Lena's ordering them to stand down. I won't let them take him away. I have to get through to Kyol, use everything in my arsenal to make him deny his involvement in the king's death.

"The life-bond—"

"Quiet!" Kyol says again, shaking me. We're touching. All my emotions jumble with his. I can't sort them out.

"Please, Kyol."

"Lord Hison, control your fae," Lena says. *"You've taken my sword-master. You cannot have my lord general as well."*

Hison issues an order to his people. They step back.

Kyol's jaw clenches. His silver eyes are dark and pain-laced as they stare into mine. "I'll fix this, McKenzie," he says. "I'll find a way to fix it."

"Fix it?" I echo. He never should have admitted to it in the first . . .

You've taken my sword-master. Lena's words ring in my head. The room seems to spin. This whole situation is wrong. If Hison knows Kyol is the *garistyn*, why is he letting him stand here armed and unshackled?

Realization slides over me.

"No." I back away. "No, Aren wouldn't . . ."

Kyol grabs my arm, pulls me close, then lowers his voice. "You must stay silent!"

It feels like a knife has lodged in my heart. My blood roars in my ears, so loud I barely hear Lena order Hison and his fae to leave.

"Where is he?" I ask as soon as the room is clear of everyone but me, Lena, and Kyol.

When Lena doesn't answer immediately, I face her fully. "Where is he?"

"I don't know," she bites out. "Hison doesn't trust me. His men took him away until the . . ." She presses her lips together, and when she speaks again, her voice is tight. "Until the execution."

"Why didn't you stop them?"

Lena grimaces, then turns slightly away from me, staring at the antechamber's closed doors.

"You didn't try," I whisper, interpreting her silence. "You sacrificed him."

Her shoulders quaver when she draws in a breath. She doesn't deny my accusations, though. She let them take him.

Horror twists through my gut. How could she do that? Aren fought for the throne for her. He fought for her family for years. He's the only reason she's alive, and she's turned her back on him.

A litany of curses and accusations scream through my mind. The only thing that keeps me from saying them out loud is the expression on her face. It's a mix of regret and self-loathing, maybe a touch of helplessness.

"Hison came to arrest us," Kyol says. "It would have crippled Lena. She'd have no hope of becoming queen."

"She's never going to become queen!" I yell.

"He told us not to fight."

"What?"

"He told us not to fight, McKenzie," Kyol says again.

I lower my voice, make it as hard as steel. "And you both just listened?"

In my peripheral vision, I see Lena's head lower. She says, very softly in Fae, *"I'm sorry."*

The apology infuriates me. I just barely manage not to explode. Instead, I lock eyes with Kyol and say, "We're freeing him."

"We don't know where Hison's holding him," he says.

"You can find out."

He doesn't respond to that, probably because we both know it's true. The fae respect him, especially the palace fae. Someone will have seen where Aren was taken. They'll tell Kyol. All he has to do is ask.

And he *will* ask.

* * *

I'M sitting on a bench in the palace's sculpture garden, staring at the ground. I hate this, the waiting. The doing nothing. I shouldn't be here, and Aren shouldn't be crowding my mind. I should be focused on other things, like the false-blood, the remnants, or the Sight serum. I should be concerned about Lena and her fragile Court. I shouldn't be worried about members of that Court executing an innocent man.

Aren shouldn't be facing down death. No one should.

A sudden tension runs through Kyol. I tilt my head slightly, as if that will make me more in tune with him and his surroundings, but his emotions return to a warm, neutral simmer. He's still in the palace, but he's not moving anymore. Maybe he's found Aren?

Or maybe men loyal to Hison have found Kyol.

"I heard what happened."

Naito's voice startles me. I look up, notice that his shadow is falling over me. "How long have you been standing here?"

"Not that long," he says, then he sits next to me on the bench. An anchor-stone is in his hand. He runs his thumb over its surface. It's smooth there, like he's rubbed that same place over and over again. "What are you planning?"

"The assassination of a high noble," I say, not surprised by his question. He wouldn't expect me to sit back and do nothing any more than I'd expect him to if someone he loved was in trouble.

He meets my gaze, scrutinizing me as if he's trying to figure out if I'm joking or not. "Are you sure that's a good idea? It might be . . . difficult."

"I'm being trained by the best swordsman in the Realm. Of course it's a great idea."

At that, he chuckles.

"Aren is more of a brother to me than Lee has ever been." His thumb slides over the anchor-stone again. "I'll do what I can to help you get him out, but we might want to start with something a little more achievable."

"Kyol's trying to find him."

"Is he trying to free him?" Naito asks the question way too casually.

"If he has the opportunity, yes," I say, lowering my voice. No one's near us, but the fae have excellent hearing. I don't want to take the chance that one of them can understand English. "I don't think he'll be able to, though. He can't let Hison or anyone else know he's involved with Aren's escape. Once we find out where he is . . ."

I fade off, trying to identify the emotion that spikes through my life-bond. Kyol tames it within seconds, but I swear his heart rate is escalated. He hasn't moved from where he was a few minutes ago. God, please don't let him be in trouble. I can't save both of them.

"McKenzie?"

I focus again on Naito. "Sorry. I'm distracted."

He stares at the anchor-stone. "Kelia always said Lorn's emotions were muted when they were in different worlds." A small, nostalgic grin touches his lips. "So she preferred to be in the Realm when we made love. It was her revenge."

I smile, too. You can't force a life-bond on someone. Both parties have to want it. On some level, I must have wanted it when Kyol made the connection with me, and Kelia must have wanted it with Lorn. I'm not sure what he did to deserve her vengeance, but knowing Lorn, I'm sure it was something.

"There's really no way to break it?" I ask.

"There were rumors," he says, turning the stone in his hand, "but I promise you, we tried all of them. We tried hunting down fae who supposedly could sever the bond. They were all dead ends. Then Kelia attempted to form a new bond with someone she hated less. When that didn't work, she tried exhausting her magic to the point I made her stop because I was afraid she'd turn *tor'um*. Death is the only cure."

I bite my lower lip, refusing to cry. I don't want Kyol to die, but I don't want Aren to, either. And why would he do this? Why would he sacrifice himself to save Kyol when he hates him? He can't be doing this just because he knows how much it will hurt me if Kyol dies.

My throat burns when I swallow. Kyol's moving now, making his way back in this direction. Maybe he'll have answers.

"What are you doing here?" I ask Naito. "I thought you were helping Lee test the serums."

"Trev came back for us. He mentioned what happened." He pockets the anchor-stone. "We're finished for now, anyway. We have to wait a few hours, then see what the serum does to the blood samples. Theoretically, we'll be able to match the changes in the test tubes to the changes that have already happened in Lee. Something like that, at least. He acts like he knows what he's doing."

"You'll need Paige's blood, too?"

"To make sure she injected the nonlethal serum, yeah. You still haven't talked to her?"

"No." I rub at the headache forming between my eyes. I must be a terrible person because Paige's situation—the possibility that she might be dead or dying—is the furthest thing from my mind.

"Kyol's heading back," I say, standing. "I need to talk to him."

Naito nods. "I'll help any way I can."

I give him a troubled smile, then head off to intercept Kyol, praying he has a plan to rescue Aren.

I don't need the life-bond to know that Kyol isn't bringing good news. He meets my gaze as he strides toward me. There's no hesitation in his steps, no flicker of emotion in his silver eyes. He's only this rigid and controlled when things aren't going well.

My stomach tightens into knots. I brace myself for the worst, then ask, "How is he?"

"Not here," he says. He passes by, leaving me no choice but to follow. The corridor we're in is empty, but apparently not empty enough for him. He leads me to the palace's residential wing, then to my room. Closing the door behind us, he says, "I talked to Jorreb. He refused to take back his words. He said it wouldn't matter now if he tried. In the high nobles' minds, he's been guilty since they learned of Atroth's death."

My eyes sting, and nausea churns in my stomach. I believe the last part, that the high nobles think he killed the king. Even though Aren never intended to take the throne himself, he led the fight against Atroth's Court fae. His sword killed the king's soldiers, soldiers who came from each of the Realm's provinces.

The high nobles won't let that go. But I don't believe this is just about bringing the kingkiller to justice; this is about revenge. The high nobles thirst for it.

"The high nobles can go to hell," I say. "I won't let them kill Aren. How do we free him?"

I keep my eyes locked on Kyol's, waiting for his answer. The seconds tick by. His expression doesn't change, but I feel a dozen emotions tumble through him. His walls are fragile right now.

"Kyol?" I press.

He draws in a breath. His shoulders hunch slightly, then he says, "He asked me to let this happen, McKenzie."

"Let what happen?" I ask, refusing to understand him.

"The execution."

Those two words knock the air from my lungs.

"He wants us to let Hison kill him?" It doesn't make sense at all. Aren isn't suicidal.

"It's the best thing for Lena and the Realm," Kyol says. "It's the best thing for you."

My mind locks on the words *It's the best thing for you*, and the fear and frustration I'm trying so hard to hold to a simmer explode into a full-out boil.

"You want him to die!" I yell.

"No—"

"If he's dead, you think you'll have another chance with me."

He reaches for my arm. "McKenzie—"

"You won't!" I jab my finger at his chest. "I gave you ten years of chances, and you turned them all down."

My heart shatters when I feel his break, but I hold the pieces of mine together with sheer willpower.

"This isn't about me, McKenzie. This is what Jorreb wants."

"I'm sure you tried to talk him out of it," I say with a bitter laugh.

"I did," Kyol says. "I swear to you, I did."

"Bullshit!"

My words make him flinch, and he retreats a step. I pursue him, my rage increasing, not decreasing. "Everything I feel

for you now is manipulated by magic. I won't give in to it. Even if Aren dies."

My voice cracks over the last word.

"I know," Kyol says. "I know!"

"I'll talk to Hison. I'll tell him . . ." I can't tell Hison the truth. As angry as I am at Kyol, I won't let him die either.

Kyol grabs both my wrists, backs me up against the wall. "I'm sorry, McKenzie. *Sidhe*, I'm sorry." He drops his gaze to the floor, shakes his head slowly. "I'd tell the high nobles the truth if it wouldn't kill you."

My chaos lusters leap from my skin to his. We're touching, so they're hot and potent, but my eyes pool with tears.

"It *would* kill you," he says softly. Then he swallows and meets my gaze. "The other human-fae life-bonds . . . They all ended the same. When either person died, so did the other. That's why he's doing this, McKenzie. He's sacrificing himself to save you, not me."

It takes several heartbeats for his words to sink in, but I shake my head in disbelief. That can't be true. Lorn survived Kelia's death. I've seen other fae survive the deaths of their bond-mates as well. I've never heard of both dying.

But, God, what if it is true? Lena told me life-bonds between human and fae always ended badly, and when Aren learned about our connection, he said the only reason he didn't kill Kyol on the spot was because it would kill me. I thought he meant that figuratively.

"If I die, McKenzie," Kyol continues, "you die. And if you die, I will. I'm sorry. I'm deeply sorry for every time I've hurt you."

"You're hurting me now," I say. The words are true on so many levels. He's touching me, so his emotions, his pain and angst, move freely into me. So does his resolve. I can feel it solidifying in him. I can feel Aren slipping further and further away.

"I know." He closes his eyes and swallows. He wants so much to pull me into his arms and comfort me.

"You're not going to help me save him," I whisper because I need to hear him say it out loud.

"No," he says. "And I'm to tell you that, if you try to free

him on your own, he won't go. He's doing what he thinks is the right thing for you. You never should have been caught up in this war."

I don't know if those last words are his or Aren's. It doesn't matter. Fury builds under my skin, threatening to kindle the breath I draw in. Kyol knows how close to exploding I am. I feel his misery, but nothing I say or do will change his mind because he thinks Aren's doing the right thing, and he thinks it's his duty to make sure it happens.

I bite my lower lip and taste blood. Screw them both. They're not making this decision for me. Aren's an idiot to think I'll let us end like this. We won't. I'll free him myself if I have to.

"I'll stop you," Kyol says softly.

I meet his gaze, see the regret in his stormy eyes. I've never felt so betrayed.

TWENTY-THREE

❖

I WATCH LEE drop three white tablets into a bottle of *cabus*. After they disappear into the crimson liquid, Lee stuffs the cork back into the top, then shakes the bottle to dissolve the pills.

"Are you sure it won't hurt him?" I ask.

"I'm sure," Lee says. "Dad used them all the time on fae. They were fine."

I glance at Naito, who's sitting on a padded bench. He gives me a curt nod.

"It'll take ten to twenty minutes to work, depending on how much he drinks, but it'll knock him out for around six hours," Lee says, handing me the bottle. I nearly drop it.

"Six hours? I don't need more than one or two."

Lee shrugs. "You're the one who wanted to drug him."

His nonchalance annoys me. I'm furious at Kyol, but I don't want to harm him. Lee, though? He doesn't care about him at all. He doesn't care about any of the fae. Both he and Naito were raised to hate them, and while Naito's completely shaken off that brainwashing, his brother hasn't. He still doesn't trust the fae.

Lee lets out a sigh. "I promise he'll be fine."

I have to accept him at his word.

I turn to Naito. "I can't give this to Kyol. He'll know I've done something to it."

"You should be able to hide your emotions better," Naito says, standing. "I'll make sure he gets it. Here, you'll need this." He takes the bottle, then places a gun in my hand. It's not as heavy as the firearms I've held before, but a similar feeling of discomfort moves through me when I tighten my hand around the metal grip. The barrel of the gun looks odd, most likely because bullets aren't fired from it. Specially made darts are.

"How does it work?" I ask.

"You pull the trigger," Lee says.

I roll my eyes at him. "How does the tranquilizer work? Will the fae go down immediately?"

"They'll be disoriented immediately. Most lose consciousness within twenty seconds."

"And if they don't?"

"Shoot them again," he says. "Then give them one of these if you want them to live."

He hands me a thin black case. Inside are twelve syringes prefilled with a pale yellow liquid.

"What does this do?" I ask.

"It's adrenaline and some other drugs. It acts like an antidote. The tranquilizer will screw with their circulatory system. If they don't get this, they'll go into cardiac arrest."

Fantastic.

"What about Kyol?"

Lee shakes his head. "We're giving him a sedative. It takes longer to work, but it doesn't have the same side effect."

"I'll be with you most of the time," Naito says. "I'll make sure they're okay."

I just nod and slip the gun into my backpack with my other supplies. Tranquilizing the fae is the best option we have. As much as I dislike Hison, he's not exactly an enemy. Neither are the people who work for him. I don't want to hurt or kill them, but I won't let them hurt or kill Aren either. I'm going to get him out of the palace, make sure he makes it to the other side of the silver wall, then he's going to fissure back to my world.

After that, Lena will hunt him down. She doesn't know

this yet—Naito and I haven't told her our plan—but we have to make sure she isn't blamed for this. We'll fake Aren's death, then, after a few months, he can return to the Realm. Not to Corrist, of course, but there are plenty of places to go where people won't recognize his face.

Half an hour later, the wooziness hits Kyol. I lean against the wall, focusing on a crack in the mortar between two gray bricks to make sure my world stays steady. Kyol's up and moving still, and he's pissed. I can feel his focus shift to me—there's no doubt in his mind I'm behind this—then his emotions dim suddenly. I can picture him hitting his knees, see him brace a hand against the floor, struggling to stay awake, to fight the drugs running through his system. Within minutes, he's unconscious.

I clench my teeth together, refusing to feel guilty for something I've been forced to do.

Dragging my backpack across the table, I sit in a chair to wait. Lena is supposed to be meeting with the high nobles in a couple of hours. Naito's going to keep an eye out for Hison, and when he arrives, Naito will meet me in the servants' corridor that leads to the high nobles' offices. I'm certain that's where I felt Kyol stop earlier when he talked to Aren. Since we're within Corrist's silver walls, all the nobles have only minimal security here. We expect Hison will have more because of his prisoner, but Naito and I should be able to take care of all of them with our tranq guns.

Lee loaned me his cell phone, and Naito has his. They obviously don't get reception here, but they keep track of Earth's time, which is what we're going by. I wait impatiently for the hours to pass, and try to picture this plan working, not failing. But I'm sick with worry, and every time I close my eyes, I see Aren's execution. The fae behead kingkillers. It's considered a cruel and dishonorable death because it's the only way to prevent the fae from crossing to the ether, the fae equivalent of heaven. I can't let Aren die, especially not like that.

When the two hours pass, I throw on a cloak, grab my backpack, then make a beeline for the servants' corridor. My adrenaline is pumping when I slip into the darkened space. I lean against the wall, feel my tranq gun press against the small of my back. The case of syringes is tucked inside my

backpack. Just so I'm ready, I take two of those syringes out, keeping them more accessible.

My heart thumps in my chest. It's so hard to keep still. I *need* Naito to get his ass here. The servants access this corridor mostly during the early mornings and late evenings, but it's not entirely unlikely that someone will pass through here in the middle of the day.

Finally, I hear footsteps. It's the first set I've heard in what feels like a millennium, so I'm not surprised when they come into my darkened corridor without hesitation. I am surprised, however, when the face I recognize belongs to Lorn, not Naito.

"McKenzie," Lorn says, his eyes ridiculously wide. "Why in the name of the *Sidhe* are you here?"

My nostrils flare. He knows exactly why I'm here.

"Where's Naito?" I demand.

"He's with a few of my associates. He regrets that he won't be able to aid you in this"—he waves a hand in the air as if he's grasping for the right word—"this little quest of yours."

"You're here to stop me," I say, my voice flat.

"I'm here because I made a promise."

"A promise to whom?" I demand, taking a step toward him.

"A promise to myself, of course," he says, as if I shouldn't expect him to give his word to anyone else. "I intend for Naito to have a long and prosperous life. This desperate and doomed jailbreak would likely prevent that."

"God," I say, more loudly than I should.

"God?"

"You're all the same."

An eyebrow lifts.

"You all look down on us. On humans. You think we're weak just because we weren't born with swords in our hands and because we can't fissure without a fae. You treat us like *tor'um*. Those of you who don't shun us think we need to be taken care of. We don't. We can make our own decisions, and I'm sick of you trying to take them away from us."

"Impressive speech, McKenzie, but Lena's meeting with the high nobles has already adjourned. Hison will be back with his guards any minute now. You won't have Naito's help on this."

My chest tightens painfully, and the fear I've been holding back threatens to take over. My hands shake.

"You're going to help me." I intend the words to be an order, but my voice cracks, and it sounds more like a plea.

Lorn sighs. "No, McKenzie. I'm going to stop you. Aren is going to die. You're going to live, and you're going to move on. You, too, will have a long and prosperous life. That's another promise I've made."

All I can do is stare at Lorn. He didn't listen to a word I said. He's deliberately and consciously taking this decision away from me.

I explode.

"What is this, Lorn? Your fucking revenge?"

"He asked me for a favor."

"He made it worth your while!" I shove my hands into his chest. He stumbles back a step.

"McKenzie—"

"What did he offer you?" I demand.

"I'm sorry?"

"What did Kyol offer you? I'll make you a better offer."

"Kyol didn't offer me a thing."

"You're lying."

"Calm down, McKenzie. Yelling will only draw attention, and I suspect you don't want to be caught with the contents of that bag." He nods toward the backpack I dropped. "The high nobles will hold it against Lena if you're found with tech."

"They won't find me." If I do this right, they won't see me. I'm dressed entirely in black and wearing gloves and a tight, hooded jacket. The tranq gun is an issue, but I intend to shoot Aren's guards long before they have a chance to see it.

Lorn lets out a long sigh. "You're risking yourself for nothing, McKenzie. I spoke with Aren just over an hour ago. I offered him employment, and he refused me. He asked me to keep you away from him. You think he's going to change his mind for you?"

"Third time's a charm," I say with a confidence I don't feel. That's the biggest flaw in my plan. What will I do if Aren refuses to be rescued?

Lorn's lips thin into a tight smile. "I promised him I'd keep you safe. I can't let you do this. I am truly sorry, McKenzie."

"So am I," I say, then I tranq his ass.

NOT his ass, precisely. I aimed for Lorn's left arm. The dart juts out from his bicep. He yanks it free then his gaze moves back and forth between the dart and the tiny drop of red that's staining his impeccably clean white shirt.

He looks at me.

"What iss thiss?" His words slur. He stumbles.

I leap forward, grabbing his arm so he doesn't fall back into the main hall.

"It's a tranquilizer," I say, half-carrying him into the darkness of the servants' corridor. He teeters too far forward for me to keep him balanced. I shoulder him into the wall, and he slides down it.

I lower him to his back. There's just enough light for me to see his silver eyes blink up at me. He tries to say something, but it's just a jumble of syllables. His eyes close, then his body goes slack.

Reaching blindly behind me, I grab a syringe from my pocket. I have half a mind not to give Lorn the antidote. He had no right to interfere, and he's at least partly to blame for our problems with the remnants and the false-blood. But I don't want to kill anyone, and he did save my life, so I take off the syringe's protective plastic cover, then jab the needle into his arm.

Seconds later, I've recovered the needle, shoved the emptied syringe into my backpack, and reloaded the dart gun. Lorn said the meeting with the high nobles has ended. Hison could be on his way back, or he could linger, talking to the others. If I'm really lucky, he'll head home to his estate, but I can't count on that. I might have only minutes to find and free Aren.

My gut knows it's not enough time, but I won't give up. I can't. If I don't get Aren out of here now, he's dead.

I pull up my hood, then peek out into the main hall. It's clear except for one guard standing in front of the closed door to Hison's reception room. None of the other high nobles had guards on their doors. Aren has to still be here.

From the cover of the servants' corridor, I take aim. I'm much farther away from the guard than I was from Lorn, and I have zero experience shooting at a target that's more than ten feet from me, but I line up the sight of the gun and the end of the barrel with a spot on the fae's neck—the easiest area to hit that's not protected by *jaedric*—and squeeze the trigger.

The dart hits low, and the fae reacts so quickly, reaching up to slap at his neck, that I don't know if the needle actually sunk in.

Shit.

I take out another dart from the inside pocket of my cloak and reload as the fae stares down at the one in his hand.

I raise my gun, but he moves, taking a step away from the door. Damn it, my aim isn't good enough to hit a moving target.

I'm already running, sprinting up the hallway toward the fae. He sees me immediately, tosses the dart aside to grab his sword. He doesn't get it halfway out before his knees buckle.

Thank God.

He face plants before I reach him. I don't stop to watch him pass out; I throw open the door behind him and burst inside with my gun held up and ready in front of me.

There's movement in my peripheral vision. I swing the barrel that direction. The fae has her sword out. She moves forward. I wait half a second until I'm sure I won't miss, then I fire.

The dart sinks in just above her collarbone. It doesn't slow her down. Reloading my gun, I backpedal. Just as the dart slides into place, she grabs my left wrist.

"Who are you?" she demands in Fae.

I keep my head tilted down so she can't see under my hood, then I raise my right hand, the hand holding my dart gun and fire it not at her, but at a second fae who's rising from behind a desk to my right.

"Drop that!" the woman who's bruising my wrist orders. Why the hell isn't she unconscious? I try jerking my arm free, but her grip doesn't loosen.

She brings her sword around and stops with the edge of the blade just touching the black sleeve covering my wrist. Her sword is sharp—she could easily sever my hand—but, *finally,*

her eyes glaze, and she lurches forward. I pull my arm free, but not before the weight of her sword causes it to cut through my sleeve and into my skin.

I bite out a curse. The cut isn't deep—it's more like an extreme paper cut—but it stings like hell.

I shake it off, confirm that the fae behind the desk is going down, too, then go back to the hallway and drag in the first guard. Not an easy task. He's freaking heavy, but I get him inside, then close and lock the door. For good measure, I drag the desk in front of the door, then lean against it.

My breaths come out quick and shallow, as if I've just gone through half a day of training with Kyol even though I didn't even lift a sword. I force myself to slow down my breathing, then I take the antidote case out of my backpack and inject the three unconscious fae. Eight syringes left, one still in my pants pocket.

The woman saw my tranq gun. The fae behind the desk might have as well, but Lee told me there's a chance they won't remember what happened a few seconds before they lost consciousness. I hope like hell he's right.

The door the woman stood in front of isn't locked. It opens into a short hallway with four closed doors, two on each side. With my reloaded dart gun held ready, I try the first one on the right.

The knob turns. The room is dark and silent as the door swings inward, and I'm about to move on when I hear a familiar *chirp-squeak*.

I push the door all the way open and step inside. Sitting in the back corner of the room, hands bound to a pipe behind him, is Aren. Sosch is there, snuggled up in Aren's lap. His blue eyes are bright in the darkness. His whiskers twitch as he chirps again. This time, the sound seems sad, as if the *kimki* knows something bad is about to happen.

My gaze rises to Aren's face as I take another step inside. His eyes are shut, his head is tilted to the side and leaning against the pipe he's bound to. I set my backpack on the ground as I go to my knees in front of him.

"Aren," I whisper just before I press my lips against his.

His body jerks as he wakes up. I grab the back of his head and deepen the kiss. He gives a little grunt, then leans into me. The knots in my chest unwind as lightning brightens my skin. The *edarratae* make my mouth tingle, and when Aren nips at my lower lip, I moan. I feel alive again, electric. Now that I've had Aren, my body is attuned to him. It responds to him, and all I want is to be with him again. To be with him forever.

Only the fear of that forever being cut short makes me ease away from him.

"We don't have much time," I whisper.

His forehead creases. Then he looks around the room. When his eyes once again settle on me, he curses.

"This isn't a dream," he says.

"No, it's not." My mouth tilts into a smile as I unzip the big pocket of my backpack.

"*Sidhe*, McKenzie." His shackles clatter against the metal pipe when he tries to move. "Where's Taltrayn?"

"He's unconscious," I say as I take out a pair of bolt cutters that just barely fit in the bag. Lee knows how to prepare for a jailbreak, I have to give him that.

"Unconscious?" Aren echoes. Then his gaze locks on the bolt cutters. "McKenzie."

I ignore him, open the bolt cutters, and close them over the thick, silver chain. Not pure silver. It's friggin' hard to break. I put all my muscle into squeezing the twin handles together. Finally, the chain snaps, falling to the floor.

"Come on," I say, holding out my hand to help him up. *Edarratae* leap down my wrist when he wraps his hand around mine, but he doesn't stand. He pulls me down, slamming my mouth into his.

This time, Sosch protests my presence, probably because I half fall on top of him. He scurries out of Aren's lap, and I drop the bolt cutters to run the fingers of my free hand into Aren's disheveled hair. He drinks in the lightning my body freely offers. I feel it building under my skin, and I shiver as the memory of our bodies wrapped in our chaos lusters strikes through me.

He ends the kiss, tilting his head down slightly so only our foreheads touch.

"Taltrayn was supposed to keep you away," he says.

"No, he was supposed to free you."

"McKenzie—"

"You're an idiot if you thought I'd just sit back and let you die."

I shove the bolt cutters into my backpack and stand. This time, Aren stands, too.

"We have to hurry. Hison might be on his way back."

Aren doesn't budge.

"We have to go *now*," I tell him. I'm trying to be patient, trying not to get pissed off because we don't have time to fight right now.

"You haven't thought this through."

"I've thought it through to the point where you're *executed*, Aren."

He shakes his head. "No, listen." He grabs my hand. "Lena is just a few votes short of becoming the permanent queen. Hison hates me—that's why he won't vote for her—but when I'm gone, he will. Others will follow his lead."

"You don't know that."

"I do," he says. "He gave me his oath. We signed an agreement. Kelia's father, Lord Raen, witnessed it. My written confession and cooperation will clear her way to the throne. But it's not just that. I've done . . ." He drops my hand to run his fingers through his hair. "You know I've done things I'm not proud of. I'm the reason Caelar is still fighting. He'll stop when I'm dead."

"Oh, God, Aren. Caelar is weak."

"He's working with the false-blood."

"You don't know that!" I scream the words this time. I have to do something to get through to him.

He doesn't retreat. He steps closer, glaring down at me. "If you don't care about the Realm or Lena's future, then think about yourself. Think about yourself for once!"

"I'm thinking about all of us! Lena knows nothing of this plan. Once we get out of here, you'll disappear for a while. We'll find—"

"Hison won't believe she had nothing to do with this."

"We'll find a good illusionist," I continue through gritted teeth. "We'll fake your death. Hison will be happy then."

"It won't work, McKenzie."

"It *will*," I say. It has to.

"*Sidhe*, you're . . . you." He grabs my shoulders. "McKenzie, I love you. I love you more than I ever thought it was possible to love. I *want* to go with you. I want to spend the rest of our lives together, but my death will solve so many problems and . . . And Taltrayn loves you. You can be happy." His Adam's apple bobs when he swallows, then he turns his back on me.

I'm going to kill him. I'm going to fucking kill him. "I chose *you*, Aren. I chose you because I love you, and I have *never* regretted that decision. I've *never* wavered. You're the one who keeps . . ."

He keeps pushing me away. My heart drops out of my chest.

"This is why you've kept your distance from me. You . . . You planned to sacrifice yourself from the beginning." My laugh borders on hysteria. "So what was last night? You sleep with me, then decide you have to run off and kill yourself?"

"No." He turns back toward me, shaking his head. "No, McKenzie. I didn't plan this." He closes his eyes briefly. "I mean, this was my backup plan. I've been trying to find a way to break your life-bond. I've read every word written about them, I've chased every hint of a rumor across the Realm, and I . . . I haven't found a way, and I ran out of time. Hison was going to arrest Lena. I couldn't let that happen."

"I can't let this happen," I tell him.

He takes my hand, pulling me closer to him. "Please." His voice cracks, and he lowers his head until his forehead is pressed against mine again. I don't know what to do. He's angry and desperate and hurting, but so am I, and I refuse to lose him.

"McKenzie, please let me do this."

"Please let you commit suicide?" I swipe the back of my hand across my face, smearing tears I didn't know I cried. "No."

"Suicide." He lets out a bitter laugh. "You're well acquainted with that, aren't you?"

"What?"

"I heard what happened at the *veligh*. You put yourself between the fire-wielder and Taltrayn. You claim you chose me? You chose him when you sacrificed yourself."

"I was saving the palace! I was saving you and Lena and the whole fucking Realm!"

"And I'm saving you and Taltrayn and Lena's whole fucking Court, but my actions make me suicidal while yours make you a martyr."

"It's completely different!"

"It's not!" he roars.

I flinch back, and I can't scrape up any more words. It's strange how emotional distress can cause physical pain. My stomach hurts as if someone's twisting a knife in my gut. If I look down, I'm almost certain I'll see my shirt stained red. This feels like a betrayal. Aren isn't fighting for me like he promised; he's giving up.

"This is why I didn't want to see you," Aren says, and another knife pierces my stomach. "I don't want our last words to be angry."

"Me neither," I say. My voice sounds hollow. I feel empty. If Kyol was conscious, he wouldn't sense a thing from me.

Aren's arms encircle my waist. I'm stiff when he pulls me against his chest. I don't want to make this easy for him. I want him to realize how much he's hurting me and just how big a fool he is. I want him to know—

"Nalkin-shom," he whispers in my ear. "Please."

I break. The stiffness whooshes out of me all at once, and I'm malleable as potters clay. My body fits inside the shelter of his arms just the way it should, and when he tilts my chin up for a last kiss, I can't refuse him. I can only close my eyes and hold him tight as my lightning sears his lips. He trembles, and my heart shatters, not just because he's set on leaving me but because there's a trace of fear in his kiss. He's scheduled to *die* in a few hours. He's been sitting here thinking about that, about the end of his life and his body rotting in the sun. Beneath his strong veneer, he's afraid.

I reach up and clench my fingers into his mussed-up hair, pulling him closer and making the kiss fierce. Bruising. My

body flushes with the heat of passion instead of anger, and there's an audible *crackle* when lightning skips from me to him. Aren groans, dropping his hands to my hips. He moves forward, and I stumble back until I hit the wall, then his hands are under my shirt. His palms leave a trail of delicious heat as they skate over my ribs.

Taking my lips off his is like ripping the *edarratae* from my skin, but I put my hands on his chest, fisting his shirt as I put half an inch of space between us. He cradles my face between his palms. His chest rises and falls over and over again in quick succession as my chaos lusters flash across his hands and up his arms. I sense the electricity moving through him. It's building in his blood. He needs to funnel it somewhere as much as I do, but just before I'm certain he's going to brand me with something too powerful to be called a kiss, he backs away, clenching his fists by his sides.

"You have a plan to get out of here?" he asks softly.

I swallow down a sob.

"The window," I say, my voice tight. Hison's office backs up directly to the rocky foothills of the Corrist Mountains.

Aren's laugh is short and quiet, and it makes the pieces of my heart fall into my stomach. My words haven't swayed him. He's choosing to stay here.

He picks up my backpack and hands it to me, then he clucks to Sosch. The *kimki* jumps onto his shoulder without further prompting.

"Come on." He places his palm on the small of my back and guides me out of the storage room. When we reach the main reception area, he stops suddenly. His gaze takes in the three unconscious fae lying on the floor.

"This was all you?" he asks.

Clenching my teeth, I nod. Then I unzip the big pocket of my backpack.

Aren grins. "I'm impressed."

I love his smile, the sexy, sideways tilt of it.

"You have a rope?" he asks as he goes to the window, unlatching and swinging it open.

I pull it out of the backpack, hand it to him, then reach for my dart gun. My hand clenches around it as he ties the rope

off to a second desk in the room. This is my Plan B, but it isn't any plan at all. I can't carry Aren unconscious to the gate. I'll be lucky if I can lower him safely to the ground.

But I haven't given up this fight yet.

I aim the gun at Aren's back just as a yell erupts from outside the room.

TWENTY-FOUR

❖

SOSCH LEAPS OFF Aren's shoulders as he and I both spin toward the door. The handle jiggles.

"Unlock it!" Hison orders from the other side. His men will have a key. Shit. I have no time.

I click off the safety on my dart gun and reaim at Aren, but he's already moving, dodging left and grabbing my wrist.

"McKenzie," he grates out, jerking the gun out of my hand. His eyes search mine, undoubtedly trying to see if I was going to tranq him. My glare tells him hell yes I was.

Aren curses, shoving the dart gun into my backpack.

"Hison can't see you with this." He throws the backpack out the window just as the door unlocks. More shouts come from the hallway as the fae try to shove their way in.

I face Aren down. "I'm not leaving!"

"You are!" he yells. Then he grabs my elbow. "Listen, I'm—"

The desk flies across the floor, hitting one of the unconscious guards, as the door slams open. Magically shoved, I'm sure.

Aren grabs my arms as I grab his, determined to get him out of here. But he's stronger and faster than I am. As Hison and his cohorts surge into the room, Aren all but flings me out the window. He slaps the rope into my hands as he turns, and I have no choice but to hold on or fall fifty feet to the rocky ground.

"Jorreb!" Hison yells.

The rope slips through my hands. I wrap my left arm around it, manage to stop my descent. I grunt as the weight of my body tightens it, cutting off my circulation. My feet scrape against the side of the palace, trying to find a ledge.

"Aren!" I growl through clenched teeth. It's not a plea for help—it's a pissed-off promise that I'm going to kick his ass.

I'm a good six feet below the window. I hear scuffling, shouting, and a *bam!* that sounds like someone's hitting a wall or door.

"Shit," I hiss out. I look down, not at the rocky death trap below but at the rope hanging between my legs. If this were *Mission: Impossible*, Tom Cruise would be wrapping a leg around it. I try that, and lo and behold, it helps. It doesn't exactly solve the problem of me hanging out a window, though.

I curse again, then I funnel all my strength into my upper body. My left hand grabs the rope just above my right, and I pull myself up half a foot. Hison hasn't hauled Aren back to the closet yet—I can hear them both in the reception room. They're having a whole freaking conversation with me dangling out the window.

I pull myself up another half foot, then another. Something's still slamming against the wall up there. I have no clue what it is. And there are other noises, like muffled clanks and grunts, that don't make sense.

My biceps tremble, and I'm only rising inches at a time now. Damn it, I'm almost there. If I can hold on with one hand, I'm almost certain I can reach up and touch the window's edge.

Ignoring the angry red marks already on my left arm, I wrap it in the rope again, grit my teeth, and strain, trying to stretch my right hand up toward the building.

"McKenzie!" Aren suddenly pops out of the window. I slip a few inches.

"Aren," I grind out.

His eyes lock on me and he laughs. The bastard actually laughs.

"*Sidhe*, I love you." He reaches down, grabs my arm, and pulls me up as if I don't weigh 130 pounds. But my next protest

dies on my lips when he crushes them beneath his. He, quite literally, kisses my breath away. That's not completely due to his skills, though the way he pulls my lower lip between his teeth does send a bolt of lightning through me, but I just climbed my way up the side of the palace. I need a second to catch my—

Aren's tongue brushes against mine, and anything else I might need vanishes from my mind.

"Jorreb!" Hison barks.

With a grin, Aren peels himself away from me. I frown past him, taking in the high noble, his guards, and the fact that the main desk is in front of the reception room door again. A fae is there, one hand on the desktop and one on the door, magically holding it shut, I presume.

"What's going on?" I ask.

"Your oath," Aren says to Hison. *"Now. Or I cut the rope and trap us all here."*

"You have it, tchatalun-min!*"* He hisses what I'm sure is an unflattering term.

"Aren?"

He faces me fully and takes both of my hands in his. "We have a chance, McKenzie. If we survive this, we have a chance."

He gives me another brief but powerful kiss, then he accepts the sword Lord Hison hands him.

"Go," Aren orders, and Hison is the first out the window.

"What the hell is happening?" I demand, the knots in my stomach twisting and untwisting. I don't know whether to be relieved or terrified or both.

"The false-blood is here," he says. "He's invaded the palace, fissured into the King's Hall with a dozen men. Lena wasn't there. She'd be dead if she was."

"I'm letting it go," Hison's last fae says from the door. He must be the one who used his magic to blast it open, too. He's keeping it shut now despite the fae ramming it from the other side.

Aren nods, acknowledging his words without taking his gaze away from me. "I have to find Lena. I want you to go with Hison, make sure no illusionists get close to him."

"Go with Hison?" My mind reels. A minute ago, Aren tossed

me away because he was set on sacrificing himself. He expected me to accept his decision and move on, and now, he wants to make another decision for me? He wants me to, again, leave him here to die?

"It'll be safer for you," he says, as Hison's last fae runs past us. "You know what the false-blood and his *elari* will do if they catch you."

"God, Aren, you . . ." I snap my jaw shut as the door cracks and splinters, then I hurry to the nearest unconscious fae and confiscate her sword and dagger. "I'm staying with you. I care more about Lena than I do about saving Hison's ass."

And I'm furious enough to kill anyone in my path.

"I thought you'd say that." Aren gives me a small smile.

The *elari* shove the desk aside and rush in. There are two of them. They go directly for Aren. He blocks and sidesteps the first fae's swing, pivoting around him to engage the second one, too. The first turns his back on me to attack Aren, giving me time and opportunity to swing my sword in a wide arc.

The blade cleaves deep into his side. His knees buckle, and his body makes a wet, sucking sound as I yank my sword free.

Aren spins toward me. He's already dispatched the second fae—I see his soul-shadow dissipating into nothing—and he lifts his sword to strike the one I injured, the one who's dropped to all fours.

Aren finishes the job I started, and I watch the fae's body disappear. I refuse to feel remorse. I refuse to feel nausea. I refuse to feel . . .

Oh, God. "Kyol."

I don't feel anything, not even his mental wall, because I had him drugged. He's lying unconscious and defenseless in his room.

"McKenzie, don't," Aren says, but I'm already running for the door. He grabs my arm before I make it to the hall.

"McKenzie," he says, turning me toward him. His eyes are worried but determined. "I *have* to find Lena."

"I . . ." I want to scream. Lena's more important than Kyol. In my head, I know that. In my heart . . . Kyol's a part of my history, but he's also a part of *me*. How can I abandon him?

"God." I press the heel of my free hand against my temple. I'm so sick of having no choices.

"Okay," I say, hating myself. "Okay. We'll find Lena." And maybe Kyol will be safer in his room.

Aren lets out a breath, then he steps into the hallway. It's not empty. Lena's fae are at both ends, fighting off the false-blood's people. If Aren and I join the fight, we'll even out the numbers, but I'm not anxious to go blade to blade with the *elari*.

"It sure would be nice if I had my tranq gun," I mutter.

Aren, who decided it would be a great idea to throw my backpack out the window, gives me an apologetic smile. "Didn't think we'd need it. Anyone heading our way?"

I focus on the *elari* again. One of them has crept past the swinging blades.

"Left wall, ten paces," I tell Aren, shutting out everything to do my job. He continues forward so casually I'm not sure he heard me, but just when I'm about to shout a warning, he surges forward, closing the distance between him and the fae.

The *elari* intercepts Aren's attack with ease, but he's visible now.

And now, he's dead.

"Beside me, McKenzie," Aren says. I run to catch up with him, and he takes me into the servants' corridor. The same corridor I hid in earlier and where I—

"Lorn?" Aren says before I can warn him. He crouches beside the fae, who's sitting up. The antidote neutralized the tranquilizer quicker than I thought it would. "What happened?"

"He tried to stop me," I say before Lorn can answer. I fully expect to get an earful anyway, but Lorn accepts the help Aren offers him, and they both rise.

A scream rings out from the main hallway. Lorn frowns in that direction.

"What's happening?" he asks.

"The *elari*," Aren says. "They've invaded."

Lorn's eyes widen. He's definitely not himself yet, though. His pupils are unnaturally large.

"Lena," he says, swaying. "Is she okay?"

"We don't know. We're looking for her." Aren's head

whips left as a second scream erupts from farther down our narrow corridor. "McKenzie?"

I move past him, my gaze searching the darkness. "I don't see anyone."

"Can you walk?" Aren asks Lorn.

"Barely," he says acidly, looking at me. I hold his gaze for half a second before I start down the corridor.

"If you could watch our backs," Aren says, "I'd appreciate it."

"Lena should be in the Mirrored Hall," I tell Aren when he catches up with me.

"Yes," he answers, though I wasn't asking a question. The Mirrored Hall was where Lena met with the high nobles. If she's still there or has fled this way, we should come across her. If we don't . . . If we don't, it won't be a good sign.

We're only a few steps down the corridor when my spine tingles. I feel someone following us, someone besides Lorn. Tightening my grip on my sword, I turn.

Ah, hell.

"No, Sosch," I say, kneeling down as the *kimki* scurries into my arms. "No. You can't follow us."

"Scratching behind his ears isn't going to get rid of him," Aren says behind me.

I don't answer him; I just push Sosch away and tell him, "Go."

He rolls to his back, belly up.

"Nom Sidhe," Lorn curses. "Just get rid of the animal."

Sosch looks at Lorn, and I swear his next *chirp-squeak* sounds more like a *chirp-hiss*.

I stand, then, more firmly, I say, "Go."

When he rolls onto my foot, I give him the gentlest shove with my shoe. His whiskers twitch as if I've just attempted a field-goal kick with his head.

"Come on," Aren says, taking my arm, pulling me down the corridor. When Sosch follows us again, Aren turns and, in Fae, growls out, *"No! Go find a fissure!"*

The damn *kimki* listens to him, of course. He curls into a ball and blows air out of his mouth, wiggling his whiskers in discontent.

We don't stumble across any more of the *elari*, but when

we step out of the corridor and into the Mirrored Hall, evidence of their presence paints the floor and furniture. Blood streaks across the long wood table like spilled wine, and more than half the chairs are overturned. My foot hits a sword that's lying in a pool of crimson, and the smell . . . It's acrid and metallic.

I breathe through my mouth and try not to gag. I try to ignore the scene entirely. I can't let the violence touch me.

"How do we know if she's alive?" I ask quietly. The wide, double doors to this room aren't completely shut. My gaze swings between them and the almost hidden servants' corridor we exited. It unnerves me that no one is here. Where are the *elari*? Where is the false-blood?

Where the hell is Lena?

Aren doesn't answer my question. He walks slowly alongside the table, taking care not to step in the blood. Finally, he says, "The false-blood shouldn't be capable of this. We have guards on the *Sidhe Tol*—all four of them."

"He wouldn't have to use a *Sidhe Tol*."

I glance over my shoulder as Lorn makes his way toward us, using a chair for balance. Even with its aid, he looks like a sailor who hasn't gained his sea legs yet.

Or, he looks like a man who was knocked out with a tranq gun.

"Do you know something we don't?" I ask. It's actually a stupid question. Of course Lorn knows something we don't. That's his joy in life. Hell, he probably knows the location of all the *Sidhe Tol*, the extremely rare, special gates that allow fae to fissure to places protected by silver.

"A slaughter like this would be easy to accomplish if your enemies trust the fae they're fighting with."

Aren's jaw clenches. Lorn notices it, and says, "I decouraged Lena's recruitment drive."

Discouraged. I don't know if the tranq is causing him to trip up on his words or if it was just a mistake, but I get what he's saying.

"We screened the new recruits."

"You didn't screen them well," Lorn says. "You've added several of my fae to your lists."

Aren gives Lorn a tight smile. "We know."

"Do you?" Lorn asks. "Or do you know only the fae that I want you to?"

I roll my eyes. "This isn't accomplishing anything. We need to know if Lena's alive."

"You moved too quickly taking over the palace," Lorn says. His words sound like an accusation, like he's blaming Aren for this invasion.

"The opportunity was there," Aren fires back. "We had no choice but to take it."

"That's exactly what the false-blood wanted. You weakened the king, the king's remnants weakened you. Makes it simple for the *Taelith* and his *elari* to take over now."

"It would have been helpful if you'd given us that information months ago." He turns his back on Lorn, nods to me, then makes his way toward the double doors.

To the double doors that are silently swinging open.

Terror moves through me as a fae comes into view. It's him, the false-blood. I know it the instant I see him. There's something different about him. His face is slender, with hollow cheekbones and a high hairline. His hair is black and . . . and something about him is familiar. His eyes? They're bright, with more color than a normal fae's, and they're ringed in a dark band of silver. They're wicked and calculating, and they're locked on me.

TWENTY-FIVE

•◆•

GOOSE BUMPS PRICKLE across my arms. Lorn said the false-blood was interested in finding me. He wanted to use me as an example. The way the false-blood tilts his head to the side and gives me a cruel, teeth-filled smile, tells me that's still true.

He takes an easy, almost lazy step inside the Mirrored Hall.

"Nom Sidhe," Aren whispers. Then, "Lorn. Get McKenzie out of here."

Lorn's hands are clenched on the back of a chair—he needs my help more than I need his—but I've already taken a step back. When I realize I'm retreating, I make myself stand my ground. It takes a conscious effort to do so, but I'm not leaving Aren to fight on his own. He might be able to take on the false-blood by himself, but it would be stupid to leave when I can tilt the odds in his favor.

I tighten my grip on the hilt of my sword and stride forward.

"McKenzie," Lorn calls after me. I intend to ignore him—I won't let him talk me into abandoning Aren—but then he adds, "You might consider turning around."

The hair on the back of my neck prickles. I spin in time to see an *elari* emerge from the servants' corridor.

Lorn lets go of the chair and takes a wobbly step toward

the fae. His sword is held ready, but it's blatantly obvious he's in no condition to fight.

The fae's gaze moves from Lorn to me, then back, as if he's considering which of us is the bigger threat: the noble who can barely stand or the human who can barely hold a sword.

At least, it *appears* that I can barely hold it. I take a step forward, volunteering as a target, and when I swing my blade, I hope the fae sees how awkward the movement is.

He does. He focuses on me, looking extremely unimpressed with my skills. Good.

I deliberately do everything wrong when I swing for his head: I stare at where I'm aiming and I prep the attack by hunching my shoulders.

He deflects my blade with ease as Lorn sweeps forward, attacking from the left. The *elari* blocks that, too, then he follows up with a powerful slash at Lorn's midsection.

Lorn's blade catches the blow, but the weapon flies from his hand. That's all the diversion I need. The *elari*'s momentum carries his blade just a fraction too far to the left, allowing me to plunge my sword into the small area under his arm that's not protected by *jaedric*.

It isn't the easiest place to embed a blade, but I put all my weight behind the move and plunge deep enough to nick his heart. His body disappears an instant later, and my gaze locks on his soul-shadow, a white mist that twists as it rises.

"McKenzie!" Lorn shouts out a warning just as something dark parts the mist.

I lunge awkwardly for the new *elari*, stabbing forward and praying I can kill him before he can kill me.

I don't know what happens next. Maybe he sidesteps, maybe I stumble, but somehow, he's close enough to backhand me across the cheek.

I hit the ground, roll to my back, then swing my sword out in a protective arc of defense.

He's out of range. He flips his sword in his hands, pointing the blade down and raising his arms above his head.

In the corner of my vision, I see Lorn grab his dropped sword. He's too slow, too far away.

The fae's muscles tighten, readying for the downward

thrust, but then, a spasm wrenches through his body. A second later, I notice the blade protruding through his stomach.

The fae's jaw goes slack. He drops to his knees, revealing his killer behind him.

Trev tugs his sword free of the body a second before the *elari* disappears.

"Thank God," I say, climbing to my feet.

Trev wipes the back of his arm across his forehead. He's sweating and breathing hard. Getting to us couldn't have been easy.

"Lena?" he asks.

"We don't know," I tell him. "Aren's—" I break off as I turn toward the front of the Mirrored Hall. He's not here. My breath freezes in my lungs.

"He didn't like the scenery," Lorn says, wheezing. "He stepped outside with the false-blood."

I start for the doors.

"No," Lorn says, catching my arm. "You're leaving with me. You think far too much of your skills."

"I think far too much of yours." I try to shake him off. He tightens his grip.

"I need her eyes," Trev says, attempting to step between us.

"The King's Hall," I say. "If Lena's alive, the false-blood would have taken her there." That's complete speculation on my part—wishful thinking, even—but that chamber in the back of the King's Hall is our best chance to get out of here.

A handful of seconds tick by. Lorn looks resolute, but finally, he sighs and releases my arm. "Very well."

We leave the Mirrored Hall, stepping out onto a balcony that overlooks a marble floor. Trev and Lorn come to a sudden stop. So do I. They're just as stunned as I am by what we see. Or rather, by what we don't see.

There's no blood below. No signs of violence.

No sign of Aren.

My heart hammers in my chest. Aren's not here, but neither is the false-blood. If one or both of them died, there would be a sign of the struggle. There would be at least one drop of blood spilled, and the fae below us wouldn't be standing there with their weapons safely sheathed in their scabbards.

Three of those fae are *elari*. They're speaking to the high nobles—Lord Raen, Lord Kaeth, and Lord Brigo. The nobles shift their weight from foot to foot, but the *elari*—even after they glance up at us—all look unconcerned.

"The King's Hall looks rather welcoming," Lorn says.

It does. The doors are wide open and unguarded.

"I think it would be wise to take that as a sign to run," Lorn adds.

"Can't," Trev says. "The *elari* blocked off the exits."

My hands are shaking from too much adrenaline and fear. I try to make them stop as I follow Trev along the balcony. I try to concentrate on my breathing, and I make my mind picture us escaping through the hidden tunnel.

Better yet, if we can kill the false-blood, we won't need to escape at all.

A cry from below makes us stop and turn. It's Lord Raen. One of the *elari* pulls his sword free from the high noble's shoulder.

"Are there any other opinions?" the fae asks.

Kelia's father hits his knees. His right hand clutches his shoulder and the first drops of blood splatter onto the marble floor.

Trev's eyes burn with fury. Even Lorn looks more steady, more ready to kill.

"The false-blood," I remind them. "We have to kill the false-blood."

Grim, Trev nods. Then he moves to my right side. Lorn falls into step on my left, and I lead the way to the open doors, keeping my shoulders back, my stride confident, and my sword held ready. My pace doesn't falter until I step over the threshold. It's not due entirely to what I see, though the bloodshed here makes the long, large room look like a slaughterhouse. Smears of red mar the white-stoned floor, and the blue carpet that leads down the center is wet enough to glisten in the light streaming in from the hall's tall windows.

But my steps faltered before my mind completely registered the violence. Kyol is stirring. He's not completely awake, but his emotions begin to travel over the bond. It's only been a few hours since Naito gave him the drugged drink. He's moving

much sooner than he's supposed to. Because of my adrenaline? I can feel a faint echo of it pumping through him.

Once again, I wish I could communicate with Kyol. I wish I could tell him to get the hell out of Corrist, but the best I can do is let him feel what I feel: fear and foreboding mixed with grim determination. And a little hope. Lena's standing at the foot of the dais.

She's not alone. I stride down the blue carpet, ignoring the way my shoes squish into its blood-soaked fibers. I have to assume Lena's guards are all dead. The only people in here are Lena, the *elari*, and the false-blood himself. He's waiting for us at the foot of the silver dais.

Again, I'm hit with the feeling that we've met before. That has to be impossible, though. I'd remember those eyes and that cruel . . .

That cruel smile. That's what's familiar. I've seen it on someone else's face before. Whose?

I scan the other fae, hoping inspiration will hit me. There are nearly a dozen of them, all unfamiliar and all wearing the red-and-black name-cords that mark them as *elari*.

Twelve against four. These are the crappiest odds ever. Where the hell is Aren? He wouldn't have fled, leaving Lena and me behind, and I refuse to believe the false-blood killed him.

Four of the *elari* move toward us. We can flee back out the doors, or we can continue down the carpet. Outnumbered like we are, we won't be able to fight our way out of here.

God, we need a plan.

No, we need a freaking miracle.

We stop half a dozen feet away from the silver dais, and still, there's no sign of Aren.

"Lorn," the false-blood says.

"Taelith." I have to give Lorn credit. He greets the false-blood like this whole situation bores him. He knows we're screwed, just like I do, but he's putting on a good show, acting like he's unafraid of the fae who beat the shit out of him just a few days ago.

"I allowed you to live," the false-blood says. *"And you used the life I gave you to warn the shadow-witch that I was coming for her. I am not pleased."*

Lorn sighs. *"I admit that it wasn't the wisest decision I've ever made."*

I glance at Lena. She's standing tall and regal at the foot of the dais despite a blackened eye and a deep gash over her right forearm. Her right side is stained red. I'm not sure if that's from the arm injury or some other wound I can't see beneath her clothes.

The false-blood turns his attention to me. *"Shadow-witch, I have a present for you."*

Every ounce of blood drains from my face. I stop breathing, terrified his present will be a half-dead Aren.

Kyol latches onto my horror. He's moving more quickly now, his veins filling with his own adrenaline, but he'll never reach me. He's too weak, and there are too many *elari* between us. If he tries, he'll die.

We'll die.

I force myself to breathe, to draw air into my lungs and let it out through my nose. I can't worry about that right now. I have to worry about the false-blood, the so-called *Taelith*. He's . . .

Oh, God.

My hand trembles on the hilt of my sword. I know who he is. Or rather, who he's related to. I recognize the demonic spark in his silver eyes.

I try to keep my mind grounded in the present, but my vision narrows as if I'm in a tunnel, and all I can see is the image of the false-blood who first pulled me into this world. I've had enough nightmares about Thrain to know every feature on his face. There's no mistaking the resemblance between him and the *Taelith*. They're brothers. Or, perhaps, father or son. I have no idea how old Thrain was when we killed him, and I have no idea how old this fae is. All I know is he's full of shit. He's not *Tar Sidhe*. He's a con man.

My mouth has gone dry. I swallow, trying to loosen my throat, when something moves in my peripheral vision. I turn my head, see two *elari* dragging a limp and bleeding body between them.

My heart stops beating. The world seems to go still as a fae yanks back the injured person's head.

A chaos luster flashes across the man's face. It's not Aren. It's . . .

It's Shane.

I'm not sure when I moved, but Trev and I attack the *Taelith* simultaneously, Trev swinging high, me swinging low. Neither of us hits our target. The *Taelith* moves back with the uncanny speed of a fae. I hear his *elari* move forward, hear Lena yelling and Lorn cursing, but I'm already following up my attack with a lunge forward and another swipe at the false-blood's legs. It's a move I perfected when training with Kyol, but it's a move Kyol always easily blocked. The false-blood blocks it aside as well, his sword suddenly appearing in his hand. And that's when I slide into the secondary form Kyol taught me, the one I almost broke through his defenses with. I feint right, lift my left shoulder in a blatant tell, only I don't swing my sword in a wide arc. I let it intercept the false-blood's blade even as I spin to the left, letting go of the hilt of my sword with one hand so I can strike the false-blood in the jaw.

It's a powerful hit, one that sends a sharp twinge through my elbow. I ignore it, try to slash my sword across his body, but his armor protects him. He grabs my wrist and twists.

My sword lands on the ground with a loud clatter, and it's only when the echoes fade that I hear the struggle behind me. I yank my wrist free of the fae's grip, then turn in time to see an *elari* carve a strip of flesh from Shane's left arm.

He's not unconscious. He screams. The two fae holding him keep him on his feet but immobile. Blood pours down his arm to the floor. The cut is so deep, it might as well be a canyon.

"Shane!" I yell, forgetting my fight with the false-blood to try to help him.

I don't make it two steps before something slams into the back of my head. Then I'm being held facedown on the floor, black splotches swimming through my vision.

"You can't help him," Lorn says quietly. "Stay down. Stay still . . . Oh, damn."

A shadow falls over me before Lorn's weight suddenly vanishes. I turn my head in time to see him land hard on his back, then an *elari* fists a hand in my hair and lifts me to my

feet. I try to free myself, try to elbow, kick, and head-butt the *elari* away, but he doesn't let go.

I grab the *elari*'s wrist, struggling to get loose, when I see Lena pick up my dropped sword. She stalks toward an unworried false-blood, unworried because an *elari* raises his sword behind her.

I shout out a warning, but Trev's thrown a fistful of fire. The *elari*'s scream pierces the air.

The *elari* holding me slams a fist into my face. Adrenaline blocks out the pain. I ram my knee into his stomach, then aim for his groin, but the bastard won't let go of my hair.

Another fae charges Trev. Then another. Trev's sword meets the first one's attack, fire meets the second's. Even to my eye, the flames are weaker this time. Trev's too exhausted to wield his magic anymore.

But Lena's not. She sweeps her hand through the air, and a blast of wind hits the false-blood. He staggers backward, and Lena's on him the next instant, her sword slashing and stabbing and nearly breaking through his defenses.

For the first time, the *elari* are alarmed. They move to aid their *Taelith*. I use the opportunity to grab the arm of the fae holding me, putting my weight behind me and pulling him around as hard as I can.

My hair rips out, but he stumbles over the leg I kick out, and I throw him to the ground. Lena has my sword, but I still have my dagger. It's in my hand then, sinking down through the *elari*'s exposed neck, quick as any fae could do it.

The *elari* dissolves into mist, and I look up. My gaze finds Lena. She's fighting three *elari*, her back turned to the false-blood. Trev's by her side, Lorn's slowly getting to his feet, and Shane . . . He's trying to lift himself off the floor. His hand slips in his own blood, and he collapses.

I scurry to my feet, grabbing a sword on the way to help Lena. She has to survive this. I have to get her out of here. I need to—

The false-blood steps behind her and lifts not his sword, but his hand. He rests it on her exposed shoulder, and she goes limp, collapsing to the floor.

"No!" Trev screams. He slays one of his opponents, hits the next one so hard the *elari* stumbles back under the blow, then he's swinging at the false-blood, trying to get to Lena.

I'm yelling a warning and trying to get to him. Another *elari* steps behind him, sword raised and arcing through the air.

It keeps arcing, severing Trev's head from his shoulders as if it's cutting through air.

His body drops to the ground, pouring blood across the white tiles, and his head rolls until it hits the dais.

My body lurches as one painful, grief-filled sob bursts from my chest.

Lorn blocks my path with his arm. "We must buy time."

My heart slams against my chest and my breaths come quick and shallow, but I nod, acknowledging Lorn's words. Time. Time for Kyol to get here. Time for Lena to wake up and escape. Time for Aren to . . .

I close my eyes, draw in a slow breath so that I don't fall apart. My mind knows that Aren's dead, but my heart is clinging to the hope that he isn't.

Drawing upon the strength and steadiness Kyol's offering me through the life-bond, I open my eyes. The so-called *Taelith* stands in front of me, that cruel, Thrain-esque smile plastered on his face.

"I know who you are," I say in Fae. My voice doesn't sound like my own. It doesn't crack or shake, but it feels hollow. Foreign.

"I'm Tar Sidhe," the false-blood says. *"Everyone shall know who I am soon."*

"Oh, that's absolutely ridiculous," Lorn says suddenly at my side.

The *Taelith*'s gaze shifts from me to the fae. *"Tread carefully, Lorn. You're alive only because I may find you useful."*

"You'll find me quite useful," he says, pulling on the cuffs of his no longer white sleeves. *"But this fiction you've created and all the unnecessary violence"*—he waves his hand in Shane's direction—*"is the reason why I couldn't become one of your followers. You're only antihuman when you have an audience."*

The *Taelith* lets out a single snort of laughter. *"Any fae can see that the Realm's magic has weakened over the centuries. It's due to the humans' influence. They taint our world, and they will be eradicated."*

"Thrain," I say loudly. *"You're related to Thrain."*

The false-blood's grin falters, and I know I'm right. Making the accusation out loud, though, might have been a mistake. When he plasters his smile back on his face, it takes on a more twisted edge. If this fae is anything like Thrain, he has a fiery temper. Thrain could go from calm and reasonable to violent and irate in under a second, and his fists were like steel. I had more than one broken bone when Kyol discovered me.

"Thrain?"

In my peripheral vision, I see Lorn tilt his head to the side. Studying the false-blood, perhaps? I can't be sure without taking my eyes off the *Taelith*, and I'm not about to do that. His eyes narrow, and he takes a step toward me.

I've lost my sword and my dagger, but I don't retreat. I can't. The *elari* are behind me.

The false-blood stops a few feet away.

"You," he says in a whispered sneer. "You have changed."

It feels like a fist is squeezing my heart. He knows me? I've never seen him before; I only recognize Thrain's features in his face. But Thrain kept me in a windowless room. It was dark except for my chaos lusters. Fae checked on me from time to time, but Thrain was the only one who ever entered with an orb of light. Maybe the false-blood was one of those other fae. He could have been in Thrain's camp the whole time I was there. I don't know.

But Aren might.

I bite the inside of my cheek hard to keep my whole body from trembling.

"Where's Aren?" I ask. I wish my voice were strong and loud, but I'm terrified of the false-blood's answer. Just over twenty-four hours ago, Aren said it was likely the false-blood had killed anyone with knowledge of his past. That list would include Aren.

But Aren can fight, I tell myself. Kyol's the best swords-

man in the Realm, and even he would have trouble killing Aren.

But the false-blood dropped Lena with a touch. He could have done the same to Aren.

"I do believe I see the family resemblance," Lorn pipes up beside me.

I refocus on the *Taelith*, see his expression darken.

"Thrain was your brother," Lorn says, switching to Fae. *"That would make you . . . Cardak, I believe?"*

"I've only recently returned from the ether," the false-blood—Cardak—lies.

"You must have been busy these last ten years," Lorn continues without pause. *"King Atroth conveniently slaughtered most of your brother's followers, but you slipped through his fingers. Just like McKenzie slipped through Thrain's."*

None of the *elari* react to our accusation. I shouldn't be surprised. What was I expecting? They'd accept the word of a human and a fae on the false-blood's shit list and turn on their leader?

Cardak points a single finger toward Lena. Immediately, an *elari* puts a sword to her throat.

Lorn opens his mouth to speak. I hold my breath, worried he's going to say something to make Cardak order Lena's throat slit, but wisdom must enter Lorn's mind at the last second. He snaps his mouth shut.

The false-blood smiles. *"Good. Perhaps you and I can come to an arrangement where you are allowed to live."* He turns his attention back to me. *"You, however, must be destroyed."*

Something sharp presses into my back. I can feel the *elari* breathing on my neck. I don't have to see him to know he's anxious to make me bleed. They all are.

My gaze goes to Shane, who's lying on the floor. He's alive—I can see his chest moving—but I almost wish he weren't.

I almost wish I weren't. No one should have to endure that kind of torture. But if I fight, if I force the *elari* to kill me, Kyol will die. If I live, he has a chance to get out of Corrist.

The *elari* grabs my left arm and places his blade just under my elbow. I hold my breath, order my shaking body to stay

still, but the second the dagger sinks into my flesh, I break. I twist away from the fae as I grab for the dagger.

My hand wraps over his, preventing him from slicing my arm off, but I'm not strong enough to—

Something white streaks across the floor.

Sosch!

He leaps into the air just like he usually does to perch on my shoulders, only his aim is off. His sharp teeth latch onto the *elari*'s arm.

I wrench the dagger from the fae, then immediately plunge it into his gut. Sosch hisses, then leaps behind me.

I spin toward my new opponent the same instant Lorn decides to react. He uses the distraction to dodge around the nearest fae, disarming and slaying him. I evade an attack from the *elari* in front of me and order Sosch to get out of the way. The *kimki* doesn't listen, not even when the *elari* grabs him by the scruff of the neck. I can't get a clean kill.

Lorn kills a second *elari*. I have to turn my back on Sosch to defend myself against another attack. I fall back under it, barely managing to withstand the power behind the blows. I try to remember Kyol's training, try to draw upon the instinct the life-bond has given me, but this fae is fully trained, and he's furious.

With a viscous *chirp-hiss* Sosch finally releases the fae he latched onto. He comes to my rescue again, this time doing a double leap from the ground to the *elari*'s arm, then to his face. I ram my sword through the fae's side. When his body disappears into the ether, Sosch hits the ground with a squeak, his long body rolling until he scurries to his feet again.

The false-blood curses. He finally looks like he's going to join the fight.

The *kimki* readies himself to leap at another *elari*.

"Sosch! Goldfish!" I yell, faking a throw to the left. I can't let him get hurt.

His bright blue eyes follow my fake crackers, and I charge forward, catching the *elari*'s sword before it can sever the *kimki* in two.

I try to push his sword away. He's so much stronger than I am. My blade hits the ground, and he kicks it out of my reach. I back up, look for Lorn. He's fighting the *Taelith*. I don't

know how he's still on his feet. Half his face is bloodied and there's a deep gash on his upper left shoulder. He's killed more than a few *elari*, already. Only five are left standing. If he hurts or kills the false-blood . . .

Cardak sidesteps and extends his arm. His fingertips barely graze across Lorn's jaw, but Lorn collapses like a corpse.

"Tchatalun," the fae in front of me hisses. There's an echoing hiss at his feet. Before Sosch can leap up and attack, the *elari* launches a vicious kick at his head.

"Bastard!" I yell, as Sosch skids across the tile. He's on his four little feet a second later, but that's when Cardak grabs him behind the neck. He lifts the snarling and hissing *kimki*, places his other hand on his haunches, then twists.

There's an audible crack when Sosch's spine breaks, then the most horrific, despondent high-pitched squeak fills the air. It echoes through the chamber again and again.

I'm screaming, and Sosch is still squeaking when Cardak chucks him over his shoulder. He's still squeaking when he hits the floor beside Lena. His body twitches once, twice, three times.

Soft *chirps*, almost like hiccups, interrupt his squeaking as he tries to make his body work, to pull himself across the tile toward me.

He lets out one last, gut-wrenching *chirp-whimper*, then goes still.

Fury blinds me. I ignore the fae closing in on me and launch myself at the false-blood.

One of his *elari* clotheslines me. I barely register my head cracking against the floor. I'm back on my feet, still screaming, still trying to get at the bastard, but someone grabs my legs, pulls them out from under me.

I slam into the floor again. The false-blood stops in front of me. I want to keep screaming, I want to claw his fucking face off, but Kyol shoves his way into my mind.

Steady, his emotions tell me.

I don't want to be steady. I want to kill the son of a bitch crouching in front of me.

"The Realm will love watching you suffer," Cardak says.

Steady, Kyol urges again.

"I'm going to kill you," I whisper, as the *elari* pulls my arms behind my back.

Cardak smiles. *"Sure you will."*

He lifts his index finger, and with a wicked twist to his lip, he touches my forehead. A wave of dizziness passes over me, then . . . nothing.

TWENTY-SIX

·◆·

LITERALLY NOTHING. IT takes a whole half a second for me to realize Cardak's magic isn't working, then, after the briefest *oh hell* moment, I collapse to the floor, doing my best to fake unconsciousness.

It's one of the hardest things I've done in my life. Sosch is dead, but I can still hear his squeals in my mind. I can still see his body twitching, see it go still. I want to fight and scream and kill the bastard who broke his back, but I can't give up this one advantage. I'll lose my chance at revenge if I do.

So I lie still, ignoring every protest of my heart.

"Lock them in the back chamber," the false-blood says.

Someone grabs my right ankle. I'm facedown on the tile, and it takes everything in me to stay limp as I'm dragged across it. I screw up a few times, tensing when my face slides through something wet and again when my shoulder hits what I assume is the edge of the dais. If the fae paid close attention to me, if they had any idea there might be a chance that Cardak's magic hadn't worked on me, then they would have noticed.

My head bangs down the chamber's first step.

Stay limp! I silently scream.

Another step. My cheekbone cracks.

Stay limp! Stay limp! Stay limp!

The fae sits me up just enough to plant a foot on my chest and shove. I tumble backward, land hard on my spine, and slide the rest of the way down the stairs.

The chamber door slams shut, and I have to fight the instinct to curl into a ball. I'm alive. I'm awake. How is that possible? Surely, the false-blood tested his magic on other humans. On Shane even.

God, Shane. I left him behind in London. He's upstairs, cut up and half-dead.

I'm shaking with sadness and fury and . . . adrenaline. Kyol's fighting now. He's trying to get to the King's Hall. He'll never make it. He . . .

He has to be the reason I'm awake. This adrenaline I'm feeling—it's making my heart pump so much faster than it should be. It's keeping me conscious, just like my adrenaline helped Kyol regain consciousness.

I push up to all fours and lean my back against the wall, waiting for the dark room to stop spinning. Only a single orb lights the table, the chairs, Lena . . . and *Aren*.

He's on his back, unconscious and with blood pooling beneath him, but I can see his chest rise and fall. I crawl to him, gasping when a sharp lance of pain strikes down my back. I ignore it and only stop when I collapse between the two unconscious healers.

That's when I laugh. It's the laugh of someone who's lost it, someone who's seen too much and can't take anything more. Despite closing my eyes, tears leak out. I don't have time to cry. I have to pull myself together. I have to find a way to survive so that Kyol will survive, and I have to get us out of here.

I build a wall as thick and solid as Kyol's has ever been, and I make myself feel nothing. It's the only way I can function. I have to stay numb. I can't think about Sosch. I can't think about Kyol or Trev or Lorn or Naito and Lee, who are somewhere in the palace. I can't think about anything but getting out of here.

I open my eyes. My gaze goes to the back wall, the one covered with sketches of the high nobles. The exit tunnel is behind it. It would be convenient if the life-bond gave me at least a tiny amount of magic so that I could touch the trigger

that slides open the wall, but no such luck. I need a fae to open it. I need Aren or Lena conscious.

My hand goes to my pocket and wraps around the syringe I have there. It's filled with the tranq-dart antidote. Lee said it was a mixture of adrenaline and some other medications. Will it wake up the fae? They've been put to sleep by magic, not by drugs. What if the antidote does more harm than good?

The false-blood or his men could come back any second. I have no choice except to find out.

My gaze shifts between Aren and Lena. They're both hurt. Aren's bleeding from a deep gash in his left leg, and Lena isn't much better off. My heart drops when I realize I can't save both of them. I only have one syringe. I have to choose.

The wall I created thins. I drag in a ragged breath then I press my lips against Aren's, praying that he'll wake up. One of my chaos lusters strikes across his face, but this isn't how the fairy tale goes. The prince kisses his princess, not the other way around. Aren doesn't move.

We have a chance, he told me. If we both survived, we would be together. I'm still pissed at him for choosing to die, to stay behind when I had a plan to get him out of the palace, and I'm pissed that I'm in this situation, that once again, my choices have been taken away.

Slowly, the reality of my situation sinks in. There isn't a choice here. I know what I have to do. Aren's pale from blood loss. His leg might not support him.

Another strangled, almost maniacal laugh escapes me. I'm not much different from Aren or from Kyol. I'm making the only choice I can.

I take the protective plastic off the syringe, turn my back on the fae I love, then jab the needle into Lena's arm.

I pull it out and wait, but she doesn't move.

Shit.

I place two fingers on the side of her throat, hoping I haven't killed her. I feel a faint but even heartbeat.

Okay. She's still alive—that's a plus—but what do I do now? Slap her?

Before I take my hand away to do that, a chaos luster skips

to her cheek. It shatters into five thinner bolts of lightning, and her body jerks.

"Lena?" My voice is hoarse, scratchy from screaming and crying, and she doesn't open her eyes.

I grab her chin and shake it. "Lena."

Silver peeks between her dark lashes. Her pupils get slightly bigger, then smaller, then bigger again as she tries to focus.

"We don't have much time," I tell her. "I need you to open the tunnel. Do you understand?"

Her body jerks again. Her eyes widen, and she flails as if reaching for a weapon.

"Hey, shh." I grab her arms. "It's me. It's McKenzie. I gave you medicine to wake you up. We have to get out of here *right now*."

She still looks startled. She attempts to roll away from me, but I hold her down. The fact that I'm able to do that isn't a good sign. She should be able to fling me away with ease.

Our prolonged contact agitates my chaos lusters more. They strike down both my arms, and a hot, tingling sensation swirls in my palms before ricocheting into my chest. She feels it, too, and finally, recognition shines in her eyes.

"Let go of me," she orders.

Letting out a sigh of relief, I comply. "Can you open the tunnel?"

She nods as she slowly pushes herself into a sitting position. She sways. Her eyes close, and I grab her arm again to steady her. Damn it, we don't have time for her to be light-headed.

I draw in a breath, then, in one move, place her arm over my shoulder and surge to my feet. My back protests the movement, and the muscles in my legs just barely comply. Lena's too hurt and too off-balance to be much more than dead-weight.

We don't exactly walk to the wall—it's more of a badly controlled stumble—so when we actually reach it, I don't have the strength or the balance to stop us. Lena's face smacks into the stone.

She grunts.

"Sorry," I say, when she glares at me. "Consider it payback for breaking my arm in Germany."

A smile bends her busted lower lip. Good. I need her energized, her spirits high, and for her to have hope that we'll get out of this.

"Open the tunnel," I order.

She braces a hand against the wall, moves a half pace to the left, then reaches up to a stone set high above her head. When she flattens her palm against it, a blue glow flares out from her hand. Then, with what seems like a deafening rumble, the wall slides open.

The tunnel is pitch-black and narrow, barely wide enough for Lena and me to stand side by side in it.

"How long until he wakes up?" she asks. She's looking at Aren.

"I don't know," I tell her. "I injected you with something to wake you up."

The eyebrow she lifts is caked with dried blood. "With something?"

"Ask me about it later," I say. "We need to get out of here."

"We can't leave him." Her voice is weak, and the only reason she's still standing is because she's leaning against the wall. In her eyes, I see how much she wants to move away from it, how much she wants to go to him and drag him out of here.

I want so much to do the same.

"I can't carry both of you," I say. My voice doesn't tremble, but I feel my throat tightening. I feel my eyes burning and brimming with tears.

"You can't wake him up, too?"

"I only had one dose." And I *had* to use it on her, I tell myself. Aren's hurt. He couldn't carry Lena out of here any more than she could carry him.

Lena's eyes widen slightly when she realizes I chose her over Aren.

"We can't leave him," she says again.

"We have to," I whisper. "But we don't have to leave him here."

After I make sure she's steady, I walk to him and crouch behind his head. On the outside, I'm in control. I've accepted my decision. I'm doing the right thing. On the inside, though, I'm dying. I want to scream, *Move, damn you!* But I just hook my arms under his, then, with a grunt, I drag him into the tunnel.

Lena attempts to heal the gash on his leg. I stop her before she finishes. She looks like she's about to pass out. She protests but finally gives in. She closes the wall, then we begin our stumbling journey through the black tunnel.

Sometime later, I collapse. My lungs ache. My back and shoulders hurt from being knocked around and thrown down the stairs, and carrying Lena hasn't helped. She's barely able to support any of her weight. I didn't realize how badly she was injured until I put her arm over my shoulder. Her side pressed into my side, and my shirt is now wet with her blood.

I'm not a healer, and she can't heal herself. We have to find help quickly.

I put her arm over my shoulder again.

"McKenzie," she says.

"It can't be much farther." I just have to get her outside the silver wall.

She slides away from me. "You can't continue to carry me."

"Feel free to help me out," I say. Then I glance behind us again.

Maybe this is why my neck hurts. I've looked over my shoulder more than a dozen times since we started our escape. Lena's looked back more than a few times as well. It's not just because we're worried about the false-blood pursuing us. Every step I take away from Aren leaves a piece of my shattered heart behind. We're both hoping he'll catch up with us. We're both hoping he'll live.

Lena starts to push herself to her feet. She almost makes it, but she suddenly grabs her stomach. Her shoulders hunch, and I know what's going to happen next.

I pull her hair out of the way as she dry heaves. This is the fourth time she's done this—there's nothing left in her stomach anymore. The medicine I injected her with is wreaking havoc on her system.

"Better?" I ask when a handful of seconds passes without

her heaving again. Weakly, she nods. I put her arm over my shoulder, and we continue stumbling down the tunnel.

I keep my sleeves pushed up. My contact with Lena is making my chaos lusters go crazy. I don't want to touch her, but I don't have a choice. The white bolts of lightning provide the only light in the tunnel. It's not much—just enough to prevent me from cracking my head on low-hanging sections of rock.

More minutes pass. I don't know how many. We're both weak and covered in sweat, but the faint glow ahead makes me press on. It's a narrow exit. We have to squeeze through it one at a time. As soon as Lena's feet are clear, I crawl through the gap, my fingers finding tiny cracks in the rock to hold on to so I can pull myself across the hard surface.

Moonlight touches my face. Another pull, and I slide off a ledge, landing on my hip beside Lena. She's on her back, looking up at the stars. They're bright, even with the moon lighting the sky, and they're completely foreign to me. The constellations of another world.

I make myself sit up when all I want to do is lie down. After using a craggy boulder as a crutch, I peek over it at the Realm's capital city, which is below us now.

We're at the base of the Corrist Mountains. Not too far from the gate, thank God. This is where I planned to escape with Aren. This is where Hison should be, and for once, I want to see the high noble. We need help. I don't know how we'll get to the gate on our own. It looks like the *elari* are guarding it. Cardak most likely knows we're missing by now.

I scan once again for the high noble and his fae, but they're nowhere in sight. They might have been captured already. Hison might have been killed.

I look up into the mountains. Or, he might have escaped. It's possible.

It's possible for him. Not for us. I can't carry Lena any farther.

Exhausted, I turn my back to the boulder, then slide down until I'm sitting. Lena's still lying on her back. Her eyes are closed, and she seems . . . serene. Like lying beneath the stars in the open mountain air calms her.

Oh, hell. This would be a perfect, peaceful place to lie down and die.

"Just a little farther," I say, moving quickly to Lena's side. No rest for us. We're going to survive this.

I expect a protest, an order for me to sit down and rest, or at least a glare, but apparently, she doesn't have the energy even for that. I get her into a sitting position and stand.

Or I try to stand. It feels like her weight has doubled since she lay down.

"You're going to have to help me."

She nods. I get my arms under her again, lift . . .

And end up sprawled on top of her.

Three more times, I try to get her on her feet. I meet with less and less success. Finally, I sit and lean my back against the boulder, breathing hard and sweating despite the chilly air. It'll be sunrise soon. If the false-blood hasn't already ordered his followers to search the foothills, he will soon.

"We're outside the wall," I say softly to Lena. "You can fissure."

Her eyes open briefly. "You can't."

"I'll find someone else to fissure me."

She shakes her head. It's a small movement, a barely noticeable side-to-side twitch that I would miss if I weren't watching her closely.

"I won't leave you behind, McKenzie."

"Your life is more important than mine."

She lifts one shoulder in a tiny shrug. "I'm nothing without the people who support me. You might be my last living shadow-reader, and I need my lord general. He's obviously still alive." She pauses to take a few breaths. "Any chance he will be here soon?"

"He's having trouble getting out of the palace." I think that's what's happening. He was close to the King's Hall not too long ago. He's near the western entrance, now, but his frustration is growing. His desperation. He feels how weak I'm becoming.

Lena suddenly stiffens. One finger goes to her lips. Her opposite hand goes to her hip, where her sword would be if she had one. I hear voices a second later. Slowly, silently, I peek over the boulder again.

And duck back down after the briefest glance. *Elari*. At least six of them.

"*—will search every crevice. They still live. You will find them. The* Taelith *wishes it.*"

The speaker's voice is deep but monotone, and it's coming nearer.

I get my feet under me, ready to do . . . something. I have no weapon. I can't flee with Lena over my shoulder. I'm not even sure if I have enough strength to shove her back into the almost invisible crevice we emerged from.

"*We have all the exits covered. They couldn't have escaped—*"

"*They did,*" the fae in charge cuts off the other *elari*. "*And they must be recaptured* today. *They're here. They're nearby.*"

They're right under your goddamned feet.

I wipe a bead of sweat out of my eyes. I'm going to have to try to get Lena back into the tunnel. It's hard to see the entrance, and I think it might even be hidden by illusion. The only hope we have is for the *elari* to overlook us.

"*I'll send more followers to help you search.*"

I risk one last look over the boulder, praying the *elari* aren't moving their search this way.

They're facing away from me, but I can almost make out one of their profiles, the leader's, I think.

He turns another fraction of an inch.

I duck behind the boulder. It's Nimael, the false-blood's second-in-command and the fae who escaped us in Tholm. He's going to fissure out.

He's going to fissure out, and I'm close enough to read his shadows.

I bite my lower lip, staring at Lena. She manages to raise one eyebrow.

I shake my head, putting my finger to my lips as I move toward her and take the draw-stringed pouch that's tied to her belt. Quietly, I dump out the anchor-stones and spread open the cloth. It'll work for paper. I just need something to write with.

The crevice we climbed out of is covered with a thick, dark layer of dirt and dried mud. I drag my fingers through it,

then, just as my skin tingles to tell me a fissure has been opened, I turn back toward the *elari*.

Nimael is gone. His shadows twist in front of me. The other *elari* are turned away, moving their search westward, so I give in to the itch to draw them. They're familiar, but they're foreign. I drag my pointer finger across the material in front of me, leaving a dark streak behind. When I run out of dirt, I switch fingers and draw mountains to the north, to the south.

Mountains everywhere. It's the same place, the same damn place Nimael fissured to when he was in Tholm, and once again, I can't name the location. It's in the Realm, though. Why the hell can't I name it?

Then, just before the shadows vanish, they twist one last time. I stare, not trusting what I think I see.

"McKenzie?" Lena asks again.

I slide back down the boulder and place my makeshift map on the ground between us.

"I think it's the other side of the Jythkrila Mountains."

As soon as I say Jythkrila, Lena's eyes widen. I was right. The magic worked. She could fissure after Nimael now, probably right on top of him. I haven't lost my ability to read the shadows.

"There's nothing beyond the mountains," she says, but doubt fills her voice.

Folding the map up carefully, I tuck it into my back pocket, then get my feet underneath me. I'm about to reach for Lena so I can get her up to the crevice and the tunnel where she can hide, but loose pebbles skitter down the rock behind me.

I look up. An *elari* is standing on my boulder. His gaze is focused upward on the mountain, but all he has to do is look down. We're screwed.

We're screwed unless . . .

I look at Lena. She can't run. I can't carry her.

Fissure, I mouth.

Her eyes are locked on me. She shakes her head a fraction. No.

Yes! I order. I grab the first anchor-stone my fingers touch out of the pile at my feet then edge closer to her, holding it out in my hand, palm up.

She stares at it, then finally, she seems to understand what I'm planning. Again, she shakes her head. She doesn't think

I'll survive fissuring without a gate. I don't think I'll survive remaining behind, and I'd rather die in the In-Between than die at the hands of the false-blood.

She meets my eyes and mouths, *Kyol.*

That's low, using him against me. I know the consequences of my actions. The thing is, I think I *might* survive this.

A sound of alarm behind me signals the end of our time.

"Now!" I yell, grabbing her hand.

She curses.

The *elari* leaps off the boulder as Lena opens her fissure. I charge into it, using my momentum and my last ounce of strength to pull her up and into it after me.

I'm eclipsed in white light and ice and . . . pain.

So much pain.

Oh, God. I was wrong.

TWENTY-SEVEN

❖

*T*HUMP . . . *THUMP . . . TH-THUMP.*

It takes a millennium to recognize the sound as my heartbeat. I'm alive, but I feel like hell. So weak, and my skin feels like it's been frostbitten by the In-Between. I want to roll to my side and empty my stomach, but I don't have the strength to do that. I don't even have the strength to open my eyes.

How many times can a person almost die? If there's a limit, I'm pretty sure I've hit it. The In-Between completely kicked my butt.

My heart beats a little faster. The In-Between. I freaking survived it. I can travel without using a gate.

Not that I want a repeat experience anytime soon. Every muscle in my body hurts, and my head throbs. Then, oddly, it bobs. I force my eyes open and see the sole of a shoe. Or rather, a fae boot if I'm not mistaken. The shoe nudges my forehead again.

"You're kicking my head," I say. My voice is so scratchy I barely recognize it.

It taps me again.

I can't see Lena—just Lena's boot—so I roll to my stomach. Somehow, I rise to my hands and knees. Her foot is the only thing that's moving. It's absently twitching from side to

side. That might be all the movement she can manage. She looks exactly how I feel, like a zombie raised from a rotting grave.

My gaze moves past her, focusing on our surroundings. It's dark, and my vision is blurry. It takes me a while to recognize where we are, and I only do so after I see my car parked on the side of the road. We're at the Vegas gate.

It's not the best anchor-stone I could have chosen, but there are much worse places we could have ended up, and at least we have transportation.

If I can get Lena to my car.

"Think you can walk twenty paces?" I ask. She's still hasn't opened her eyes.

I crawl toward her head.

"Lena." I shake her arm. Her head rolls to the opposite side, and she mumbles something in Fae.

"Lena!" I try again. Still no response. Damn it.

I can't carry her to the car, so after finding the key in my glove box, I bring the car to her. She's heavy—deadweight, really—and her skin feels *tor'um* cold when I finally get her into the passenger seat.

The next twenty minutes are the longest of my life. Lena still hasn't said a word, and the tech surrounding her is agitating her chaos lusters. I don't know if this was the right decision, putting her in my car, but I couldn't leave her at the gate. She needs help, and she needs it quickly.

I need help. My vision is still blurred and I swear it goes completely dark at times. I don't *think* that's because I lose consciousness or close my eyes, but I shouldn't be driving.

When I finally pull into a driveway, a bright blue bolt of lightning lights up the interior of the car. Jesus, what if I've damaged Lena's magic permanently?

I shut off the engine, pocket the keys, then get her out of the car as quickly as I can. I'm not sure how I make it to Nick's front door, but I'm standing there knocking when it finally swings open.

"Hello . . ." Kynlee stares at Lena then back to me, then at Lena again.

"Dad!" she calls out.

Nick appears in the doorway.

"I don't know where else to take her," I tell him.

My arms are shaking, trying to keep Lena upright. Nick's jaw clenches. A few seconds later, he opens the door wider.

"Kill the breakers," he says to Kynlee, then he scoops Lena into his arms. When he turns and takes her inside, I stumble over the threshold. I only make it two more steps before my body decides it's had enough. Nick has Lena. I've done all I can.

My knees buckle. I collapse on the tiled-entryway floor and don't make any effort to pick myself back up.

I awake ages later on the couch in the media room. I don't move, I don't think, I don't feel. I just lie there, staring at nothing and knowing that if I attempt to do anything at all, I'll be filled with pain. Physical pain, yes, because I pushed my body far past its limit, but that's not what I fear the most. The emotional pain, the pain of loss . . . that's what will destroy me.

Don't think, McKenzie. Just sleep.

ANOTHER millennium passes. This time when I wake, I do feel something. I feel *someone.* Kyol's nearby. He made it out of the palace. He survived, which means I'll survive. I can't find the energy to feel relieved.

My back is to the door when it opens. I don't turn. I don't move at all.

"Kaesha," he says. He places a hand on my arm. The bond opens fully, pouring his fear and his worry, his strength and his love into me. I close my eyes tighter, wanting to feel none of it.

Normally, he would go away, leaving me alone and allowing me space to heal. But this time, my heartbreak is too much. He gently pulls me off the couch and into his arms. My muscles scream in protest, but I say nothing. I just sit there stiffly, refusing to be comforted.

"Please," is all Kyol says, tightening his embrace. My back

is against his chest. He presses his cheek against mine, then whispers again, "Please."

My resistance shatters. He needs this as much as I do.

The emotions rush through me. The devastation and the loss. Aren. Trev. Sosch—

Remembering the snap of the *kimki*'s spine and his terrible, dying *chirp-whimper* does me in. It's all too much. The tears come, and I can do nothing to stop them.

I cry myself to sleep. When I wake up, Kyol's still here, a strong, comforting presence at my back. His arms are still around me, but he's pulled the blanket off the couch, draping it over me and thus, shielding me from the touch of his *edarratae*.

He senses that I'm awake.

"I can't make this better," he says softly, and a soul-crushing sense of failure moves through him.

I shake my head, turn slightly in his arms. I hate how he carries the world on his shoulders. He shouldn't feel this way. He should be angry at the false-blood and at me for nearly getting him—us—killed. If he hadn't recovered so quickly from the drugs we gave him . . .

"I understand why you did what you did," he says. "I don't agree with the decision, but I understand it."

"Stop reading my mind," I tell him, attempting to make my tone light.

I feel him smile. "I can't do that, *kaesha*."

No, he can only read my emotions and draw upon our ten-year history together. It would be so easy to fall into that past. He wants it. I want it.

But everything has changed, and I want Aren back more.

"I couldn't save him," I choke out.

"Hison had half a dozen swordsmen guarding him. It was impossible—"

"No." I shake my head. "I made it to him. We got out of Hison's office, but the false-blood . . ." I swallow. "I left Aren behind." My chin quivers. "I couldn't carry him and Lena,

and I knew . . . I knew what I had to do, what you would do and . . . I left him."

I fight back tears again because my anguish is killing Kyol. He takes my face between his palms, holds firmly, and looks me in the eyes. "Never second-guess what you've done, McKenzie. Never."

His *edarratae* heat dual paths down my neck.

"I'm sorry," I say, closing my eyes briefly, trying to focus. "I'm sorry I was so angry before. I know you didn't want him to die, but I was just . . ." I draw in a breath. "I shouldn't have attacked you like I did. I shouldn't have drugged you. I respect you too much for that."

Those words hurt him more than they help. He wants more than my respect. He wants me.

"Kyol, I can't—"

"I understand, McKenzie," he says quickly, using his words as a shield. "You don't have to say anything. I understand. I lost any chance I might have had with you when I forced you into the life-bond."

No, he lost his chance with me when I fell in love with Aren. I don't correct him, though, because on some level, he's right. Even with Aren out of the picture, I can't be with Kyol. The life-bond changes everything. I don't know how much of what I feel for him is real and how much is based on magic.

"You didn't force me, Kyol. You saved my life, and"—I meet his eyes, don't attempt to hide my emotions—"and I never thanked you for it. God, I'm so selfish. Kyol—"

"Shh." He pulls me into his arms again, silencing me. I rest my head on his shoulder. I keep my eyes open because I'm afraid of what I'll see if I close them. So I stare at the wall. Then at what's resting at its base.

My bloodstained cargo pants and shirt are lying there. It seems like it was ages ago when I last slept here. I expected Nick to throw away or burn those clothes, but I'm glad he didn't. Pushing away from Kyol, I stretch out and grab the pants. Curiosity moves through him as I reach into the pocket.

And pull out his name-cord.

His lips part, releasing a stunned breath. "You still have it."

I nod, running my thumb across the smooth onyx stone

and the rougher *audrin*. "It's been through a lot these past few months." *Just like we have.*

He meets my eyes. The silver storms in his calm, and he nods as he reaches out to take it.

The string of stones slides from my hand.

"Thank you," he says softly, leaning back against the couch.

I fold my legs against my chest, rest my chin on my knee. I've described Kyol as feeling soul-weary before. That's how I feel now. Soul-weary and hopeless. Kyol isn't lending me strength anymore. The Realm—the world that he loves so much—is in the hands of a false-blood. He's fought for the Realm his whole life, given up everything for it, but the hope he has for its future is gone. He feels as defeated as I do right now.

I close my eyes as I draw in a breath, open them when I slowly let it out. We're still alive—so is Lena—and I'm not yet ready to give up this fight.

"The false-blood is Cardak," I say.

Kyol must be lost in his own thoughts. He blinks a few times before he focuses on me.

"He's Thrain's brother," I add.

His expression remains neutral, but a spike of surprise leaks through our life-bond.

"I recognized Thrain in him," I say, and I tell Kyol everything that happened. I manage to talk about Shane and Trev, about Sosch, Lorn, and Aren, all without crying. And I tell him how I overcame the false-blood's magic, thanks to our life-bond, and how Lena and I escaped through the tunnel. I'm finishing up my story, handing him the draw-stringed pouch that I drew Nimael's shadows on, when there's a light knock on the media room's door.

Kynlee peeks her head in. "My dad wanted you to know that Lena's waking up."

"WE lost the palace?" Lena asks a few minutes later. Her voice is weak and raspy, but I'm glad to hear her say something. She's pale, her face is still bruised and swollen, her lip still busted. The rest of her injuries are covered by a heavy

blanket, but I doubt she's able to rise yet. It still looks like her hold on life is tenuous.

Kyol's silver gaze doesn't waver. "Yes."

"But you made it out."

"Yes," he answers again. When he sits in a chair beside her bed, I lean against the guest room's dresser.

"Did others make it out?"

"Some did," he says in his deep monotone. "Most did not."

She stares up at the ceiling. A chaos luster creeps across her face. Nick's power is turned off, but she's so weak, the dead tech still affects her.

"My allies among the high nobles." She pauses, closing her eyes. "Did they survive?"

"I didn't see every death," Kyol says. "I heard rumors and the speculation of the *elari*."

She opens her eyes. "Did Lord Raen survive?"

"No," Kyol answers quietly.

Her lips thin. "Lord Brigo?"

"No."

She names two of her other strongest allies. Both, according to rumor, are dead.

"Nalst?" she asks.

"Most of your swordsmen were executed, Lena. Dishonorably executed."

Her face hardens. "Taber?"

Taber was Kyol's right-hand man, his friend, and one of his most trusted soldiers. He answers, "Dead," with the same emotionless monotone as he does the others.

"Brayan?" Lena asks.

"Dead," Kyol says.

"Andur," she names her advisor.

"Lena." Kyol's voice softens a fraction, and I feel his emotions gentling. This isn't achieving anything; it's only hurting her.

"Andur!" she demands.

Kyol lets out a sigh. "Dead as well."

She goes on, naming fae after fae. Some names, I recognize. Most of them, I don't. And most of them, I never will.

After a few minutes, a familiar sense of failure moves

through Kyol. The deaths don't just weigh heavily on Lena;
they weigh heavily on him as well, and I feel his guilt, his
remorse keenly. He couldn't save the palace for Lena. He
couldn't save the lives of her most loyal swordsmen.

"Trev?" Lena asks. For the first time, her gaze goes to me.
I swallow down the lump in my throat, whisper, "Dead."

She gives no reaction to my proclamation. I doubt she
knew the way he felt about her, why he did whatever she said
without protest or complaint.

"Lorn?" her eyes are still on me. I didn't *see* Lorn die. It's
possible he could have survived.

"The rumors say he's dead," Kyol answers.

I want to contradict what he says. I want to give Lena some
hope, tell her that I never saw Lorn cut down, but in the end,
my focus wasn't on him. It was on her and Sosch and the false-
blood.

Lena blinks. Her eyes become glassy. She looks back up at
the ceiling and draws in a slow breath. I'm surprised Lorn's
death affects her so much. More than once since I've known
her, she's wanted to kill him herself. But maybe she's just
bracing herself for the next name.

"Aren?" she finally asks. Her chest stops rising and falling,
waiting for the answer.

Kyol is silent.

"Aren," she says again, angry this time. She lost her
brother, Sethan, two months ago, her parents years before
that. Aren was the closest thing to family she had left. Kyol
knows his death will crush her. He knows it will crush me.

"I'm not certain he's dead," Kyol finally says. The life-
bond tells me those words are just short of a lie. He thinks
Aren's entered the ether.

Lena turns her head to look at him. "I want the truth, Taltrayn."

Apparently, I'm not the only one who can tell when he's
twisting facts. It's something he does so rarely, and only to
protect the people he cares about. Sometime in the last two
months, he's grown to care for Lena. I'm glad. I think it softens his guilt over killing the king.

"I saw no sign of him," Kyol says evenly. "And the rumors

I heard all came from unreliable sources, not from fae I would ever trust."

He's giving us hope. I'm not sure if that's a good or bad thing at this point.

"I need to get out of this bed," Lena says. She attempts to sit up on her own, but Kyol's there in an instant, taking one of her hands in his and placing his other behind the back of his would-be queen.

She closes her eyes when she's upright, swaying just a tiny bit. Kyol remains there, steady, until she nods once and releases his hand. He returns to his chair.

"Can you estimate how many *elari* the false-blood has?" Lena asks, her cool silver eyes locking on his.

"Fewer than two hundred have taken and are holding the palace," he says.

It sounds like such a small number. Lena's soldiers were overworked, but I'd guess she had close to five hundred swordsmen in the palace and guarding the silver wall. The *elari might* have killed and executed a number of our people, but they lost of number of theirs as well. Maybe our odds aren't as bad as I think?

Kyol's gaze doesn't waver from hers. "My opinion is we cannot retake the palace from the false-blood."

Lena's mouth tightens. She looks like she's about to ask Kyol to do the impossible, to find a way to retake the palace anyway, but instead, her eyes slide to me, and she asks, "Have you shown him the map?"

"Yes," he answers for me.

"It's the false-blood's camp," Lena says. "He's been hiding there, building an army and plotting to take the throne for a decade."

"We don't know it's his camp," Kyol says.

"I want it searched," she continues as if he didn't speak. "I want every piece of paper read, every anchor-stone's location determined, and I want arrests. I need his followers to deny him."

A few seconds pass, then Kyol says, "I'll do what I can."

Cardak's followers, at least the ones who are close to him,

are fanatics. I'm not sure they'd believe the truth even if they were buried in evidence of it.

I run my hands over my face, trying to ease the tension building behind my eyes. It doesn't help. I feel like I'm going to be tense and tired for the rest of my life.

TWENTY-EIGHT

·—•—·

"WHERE'D HE GO?"
Kynlee's question makes me wrench my gaze away from the backyard. It's ridiculous that I'm staring out there so often—the life-bond tells me Kyol's still in the Realm—but I'm more on edge than usual. I can't take any more losses. My heart's already in pieces. The only thing holding it together is Kyol.

Plus, there's the whole issue of our lives being linked.

"He fissured to Corrist," I say.

"The capital?" she asks. She's sitting cross-legged on the couch with her homework resting on her lap.

My gaze goes to the kitchen as I nod. Nick is there, the sleeves of his buttoned shirt pushed up to his elbows so he can wash the dishes. Kynlee knows some of what's happened in the Realm, but I'm not sure if Nick wants her to learn more. She lost her permission to visit the palace when Cardak took over.

"Do you think my brother is still alive?" she asks.

Nick shuts off the faucet.

"I haven't heard that he isn't," is all I say.

Kynlee throws a glare over her shoulder. It doesn't seem to have any effect on her dad.

"It's not going to kill me to know what's going on," she says, facing me again.

I agree—I'm always furious when people withhold information from me—but Nick is her dad, and he has the final say in how much his daughter should know. On the other hand, he's not telling me to keep my mouth shut.

"I think there's a good chance he's alive," I say. Her brother, Lord Garon, is the high noble of Ristin. He wasn't one of Lena's close allies, but he didn't oppose her, either. If he's smart, he's kept his mouth shut and hasn't opposed the false-blood either. "Kyol will be able to tell us more."

"When is he supposed to be back?" she asks, closing her notebook and setting it aside.

"Anytime now," I say with a shrug. I'm trying to appear less worried than I am, but I can't get a good sense of what Kyol's doing right now. His mental wall is in place, and he's a world away. He's not giving me the slightest hint as to whether he's found any of the high nobles or Lena's swordsmen alive.

Or someone more important than them.

My throat tightens, and that weak, shaky feeling that comes with crying begins to spread over me. I don't cry, though. Honestly, I don't think I have any tears left.

I need a distraction, so when Nick finishes in the kitchen and joins us in the living room, I ask him if there's any chance he'll use his Sight and shadow-reading skills to help Lena.

I expect an immediate no. Instead, he says, "She told me she wants to protect *tor'um*."

"Yeah. She wants . . . I guess you'd say she's fighting for the fae to all be equal, *tor'um* included. That's why it's been hard to get support from the high nobles. They don't want to lose their power and their privileges."

"Why does she care what they want?" Kynlee asks. "Wouldn't the majority like those changes?"

"It's not a democracy," I say. "It's . . . a different kind of society, based on bloodlines and magic."

"It's based on the whims of the ruler," Nick says.

"That's one of the things Lena wants to change."

He meets my gaze. "It'll be interesting to see if she actually makes any changes."

She will. I have every confidence of that now.

A flash of light draws my attention back to the window. An

instant later, Kyol's presence slams into me. I grip the arm of my chair, waiting for my equilibrium to level out. It does quickly—I'm getting used to being near him—but then I see a second slash of light wink out. He isn't alone.

The way I launch myself to my feet must startle Nick and Kynlee. They jump up, too, Nick reaching for the drawer in a side table.

"Wait," I say, waving him off. "I think it's okay."

"You think?" Nick asks, his voice rough. His hand is on the knob of the drawer.

"Lord Hison is with him," I say. I'm not sure if that's a good thing, but Kyol's emotions are steady. He isn't angry or alarmed.

The back door opens, and the two fae step inside.

Nick finally lets go of the drawer. Hison doesn't look like a threat. He looks incredibly uncertain and out of place. It's not just because of his embroidered black shirt, fae pants, and high boots. His shoulders are hunched, and his head is slightly bowed as if he's afraid some piece of tech—the fan, maybe—is going to drop from the ceiling. He's one of the most antihuman high nobles I've met, and I'm sure he's never been to Earth before.

He stops after just a couple steps inside the house. His face is twitching, probably because he catches an occasional glimpse of the *edarratae* flashing across his nose or cheekbones.

"What's he doing here?" Nick demands. I'm not sure if he's angry because he knows Hison or if he's simply mad because Kyol brought a high noble here without permission. He was supposed to tell Lena's remaining supporters to meet us in Adaris in a week. That's when we think Lena will be healthy enough to fissure between worlds.

"He's here to speak to Lena," Kyol says.

Nick's jaw clenches. "You planning on bringing every high noble here?"

"Most of the high nobles are dead." Lena's voice carries across the room.

I look over my shoulder, see her standing just outside the hallway with one hand braced against the wall. She shouldn't be out of bed—I have the feeling her knees could buckle any second—but she manages to make herself look tall and regal standing there, not pain-ridden and broken.

I swear the life-bond growls. I glance at Kyol, but his expression is as neutral as always.

"Sit." His order isn't directed at anyone in particular, but I catch a glimpse of relief on Lena's face. She makes it to the sofa chair—the nearest seat in the living room—without showing any other sign of weakness.

Kyol focuses on the high noble. *"Sit."*

Hison's nostrils flare, and the way he eyes the couch makes me want to laugh. Furniture in the Realm is handmade while ours is made mostly with machines, but it's completely harmless. Even the TV remote sitting on the side table is a miniscule amount of tech.

When Hison still doesn't budge, I roll my eyes, grab the remote, then elaborately motion for him to sit.

His expression hardens as he takes two stiff steps toward the couch, then, not taking his eyes off mine, he gingerly sits on its edge.

"Does he always act like he has a stick up his ass?" Kynlee asks.

"Kynlee," Nick snaps at the same time I answer, "Yes."

Hison doesn't understand English, but his scowl deepens.

Actually, Hison is stiffer than usual. That might have something to do with the fact that I tranqed three of his fae freeing Aren from his offices.

"He should lighten up," Kynlee says.

Hison's lip twitches when he looks at Kynlee. This is probably the closest he's been to a *tor'um* in decades, and he's not doing a thing to hide his distaste.

With all the aplomb of an American teenager, Kynlee folds her arms across her chest, cocks her hip, and meets his glare.

"Kynlee. Room. Now."

"But—"

"Now," Nick says.

She lets out a sigh as she turns and leaves the room.

I sit on the arm of the second sofa chair.

Lena levels her gaze on Hison. *"You better have a good reason for bringing him here, Taltrayn."*

"I can set up a meeting between you and Caelar," Hison says.

Lena studies the high noble, and I know what she's thinking. We're all but certain Caelar is working with Cardak. Is Hison working with him now, too? He looked terrified when he burst into his office, and he was desperate enough to make a deal to let Aren go free if we helped him escape. But maybe he didn't escape. The *elari* were searching the foothills of the Corrist Mountains for Lena and me. They could have found Lord Hison then.

"Why would I want to meet with Caelar?" Lena asks.

"You need him and his swordsmen to retake the palace."

"If I recall correctly, Lord Hison, you have never wanted me in the palace."

"I want the false-blood there even less!" he says between his teeth.

"False-blood?" Lena questions coolly. *"He told me he's Tar Sidhe, not one of their Descendants. I believe that makes him a completely different species of fae."*

"That's a ridiculous claim."

"Lord Ralsech believes it," Lena says, referring to the high noble of Derrdyn, the province that declared support for the false-blood. *"The* elari *do as well."*

"Ralsech is a fool," Hison says. *"If you believe the false-blood is Tar Sidhe, you are as well, and I'm wasting my time."* He stands, takes one step toward the back door.

"Sit!" Lena snaps.

He takes another step, but then Kyol is there, cutting off his retreat.

"Sit," Lena orders again.

Hison straightens. He looks like he's about to tell Kyol to get out of his way.

"You managed to escape the false-blood when many others did not," Lena says. *"And given our history, you'll have to forgive me if I'm skeptical about your newfound cooperation."*

It's not an apology, but it's enough of a peace offering for Hison to stiffly return to his seat.

"The false-blood," Lena says when he's settled. *"Do you have evidence he is not who he claims to be?"*

"If I did, I wouldn't be sitting here talking to you."

Lena's eyes narrow slightly. *"We believe his name is Cardak. He's the brother of Thrain."*

"Thrain," Hison says. *"He's dead. So are all of his supporters."*

"What are they saying?" Nick asks quietly. I didn't notice him approach.

"She's telling him we think the false-blood is related to Thrain."

Nick stiffens.

"You've heard of him?"

He nods. "He was giving King Atroth problems about the time that I left with Kynlee."

"He's the fae who found me when I was sixteen." I don't say more than that—Nick's expression indicates I don't need to. I turn back toward Lena and Hison and concentrate on their conversation again.

"The word of a human won't change anyone's mind," Hison is saying, his silver eyes darting to me briefly before returning to Lena. *"We must return to Corrist and kill him. That's the only way we'll convince his followers they've been lied to."*

"And I'm sure you would love to be there, fighting at our sides," Lena says.

I snort out a laugh.

Hison doesn't bother to look at me.

"You need Caelar's help," he says.

"Caelar refuses to speak to me."

He gives her a small smile. *"With the kingkiller dead, I believe I can convince him to meet with you."*

My muscles tense, ready to launch myself at him and wrap my hands around his throat, but Kyol drops his mental shield. Our link opens, and he sends steady, calming emotions my way. I glare at him, trying to shove those emotions back in his face. But I get the message: don't strangle a potential ally, even if that ally is a bastard.

"You've been speaking to Caelar for a while, haven't you?" Lena asks. Her voice sounds tighter now.

Hison gives her a single-shouldered shrug.

"I'll meet with Caelar," Lena says. *"But it must be in this world, somewhere public."*

She looks at me. The meeting is going to have to be close by. She's in no condition to fissure.

"Is there somewhere nearby they can meet?" I ask Nick.

"There's a coffee shop over there." He nods toward the back of his house. Beyond his fenced-in backyard is the shopping center I saw the first time I drove here. "It's not usually crowded, but there's enough traffic passing through to make everyone stay in line."

Lena looks at Kyol. "Do you have an anchor-stone you can imprint?"

He nods. "I'll be back in a moment."

When he leaves, Lena says, *"I assume I'll have your support once the false-blood is killed?"*

"You are the strongest-blooded Descendant," Hison says. *"And the kingkiller is dead. I won't oppose you anymore."*

"You don't need him," I say. "Cardak's killed most of the high nobles. You'll have to appoint new ones."

"And they'll vote for me," Lena agrees. "But I can't afford to make enemies right now."

"What is she saying?" Hison asks, staring at me.

Lena smiles. *"She's very happy for your support."* She braces a hand on the arm of her chair, then stands. She nods toward the fissure opening in the backyard. *"You'll give that anchor-stone to Caelar. He'll fissure directly to the coffee shop. You won't bring him here."*

Kyol opens the back door.

Hison nods. *"We'll meet you at noon."*

He accepts the anchor-stone Kyol's just imprinted with the cafe's location, then, as quickly as possible but while still maintaining some semblance of dignity, he flees Nick's house.

Lena remains standing until the high noble's fissure cuts through the air outside. As soon as he disappears into the slash of light, her knees buckle.

Kyol's arm snares her waist, keeping her on her feet. It kills Lena, having to accept help from anyone, but even if she could get to her room on her own, at this point, Kyol won't let her.

"You must rest," he tells her, his voice low and rough.

She nods, clutching his shoulder.

Without another word, Kyol scoops her into his arms and carries her back to the guest room.

I spend the rest of the day, the night, and the next morning alone. I don't sleep. I can't. Every time I close my eyes, I see Aren's face, and every time I see Aren's face, I grow angrier. I know it's irrational, that he didn't intend to let the false-blood kill him, but he intended to let the high nobles do it. He told me his reasons for that, and on some level I understand them, but I don't understand why he wouldn't escape with me. If he'd just left when I asked him to, if he hadn't argued and tried to talk me into leaving him behind, we would have been gone minutes before Hison pounded on that door.

And Lena would probably be dead.

I run a hand over my face, wishing I'd had two antidotes on me. I could have awakened them both. But, again, that's Aren's fault. He threw my damn backpack out the window. If I'd had that on me, I could have tranqed the false-blood without anyone needing to get close to him.

If, if, if.

I replay all the scenarios in my head, see so many different outcomes, so many ways I could have saved Aren and Sosch. By the time I stumble down the stairs a little before noon, I'm a wreck. I'm exhausted both from not sleeping and from grief, and I feel like I might throw up any second.

Lena's standing in the living room. Her back is to me, and she's staring out the window at Nick's backyard. Maybe she's replaying the false-blood's attack in her mind, too.

"McKenzie."

Kyol's deep voice makes me tense. He's standing behind me, but I don't turn. I owe him an apology for the chaos of my emotions, but telling him "I'm sorry" when they're still so out of control is pointless.

He places a hand on my shoulder. "You should eat something."

"I'm not hungry."

"You need to eat," he says gently.

I shake my head, take a step away from him, but he catches my arm and pulls me toward the kitchen. Reluctantly, I let him.

"This?" he asks me, holding up a container of bagels. My shrug is enough of an affirmative for him to take one out, set it on a plate, then grab a jar of jelly out of the semicool fridge. The electricity is back on, but it was off long enough to spoil everything left in the fridge. Nick or Kynlee must have made a run to the store, though, because there's a new, cold container of cream cheese sitting on a shelf. I exchange it for the jelly.

Kyol watches me eat without a word. I'm pretty sure he thinks if he weren't sitting here with me, I wouldn't take a bite. He's right, and in the end, I only manage to get down a little less than half the bagel.

At five minutes to noon, he's sitting beside me in the coffee shop. He and Lena are both invisible, so I pull out the chairs far enough for the fae to sit.

The coffee shop is longer than it is wide, and one of its walls is made up of floor-to-ceiling windows that look out onto a crowded parking lot. At exactly twelve o'clock, two fissures open on the sidewalk: Hison and Caelar. Paige isn't with them. I was hoping she would be. It would make sense. Caelar should want a set of human eyes to make sure Lena doesn't have anyone hiding behind an illusion.

We rise as the fae enter the shop. Hison looks even less comfortable than he did in Nick's house, and Caelar's expression is hard and angry, pretty much exactly the same as the last time I saw him, when he held me captive in the Corrist Mountains.

"Caelar," Kyol says in greeting.

Caelar's glare shifts from Lena to her lord general.

"Taltrayn," he says, and there's a note of begrudging respect in his voice. I forget how well they know each other. Caelar was one of King Atroth's top swordsmen, and the Court fae looked up to him almost as much as they looked up to Kyol. If Caelar hadn't been the one to rally the remnants together, Lena wouldn't have had nearly as much opposition to her reign.

Kyol sits when I do. Hison is next, followed by Caelar.

Lena is the last to take her seat. All are careful not to let the few humans in here see the chairs move.

Lena steeples her fingers together on top of the table. *"Thank you for meeting with me."*

Her words receive a single nod from Caelar. A bolt of blue lightning flashes across his stony face. He doesn't look like he wants to be here, and I get the impression that, if Lena says something wrong, he'll open a fissure and leave.

But leaving is better than an ambush or a fight. I let my gaze scan the coffee shop and parking lot again, but there are no other signs of fae. If Caelar was working with the false-blood, and this was a setup, the *elari* would be here by now.

Lena flattens her hands on the table. *"We can agree that the false-blood must not remain in the palace?"*

Another silent nod from Caelar.

"What can I say to make you support my petition to rule the Realm?" Lena asks.

The table remains quiet. Caelar's expression hasn't changed, and Hison is sitting beside him, more concerned about the espresso machine hissing across the shop. He tugs at his shirt collar.

Finally, Caelar says, *"Nothing."*

Lena's lips thin. She stares at Caelar for a long, drawn-out moment, then her gaze slides to Hison. *"Then it looks like we're finished here."*

Hison must be paying attention to the conversation as well as the tech. He stiffens, looks at Lena, then turns to Caelar. *"We don't have a Descendant to place on the throne."*

"Someone will step forward."

"Who?" Hison demands, keeping his voice low, as if he's afraid the cashier or one of the customers will overhear him. They can't unless they have the Sight.

"Someone," Caelar says, not taking his gaze away from Lena. *"The son of Hrenen. The son of Joest."*

"They can barely call themselves Descendants," Hison says. *"Both their bloodlines are diluted."*

"What, exactly, do you have against me, Caelar?" Lena asks.

"You think nothing of the Realm's traditions and magic."

"I care more for the Realm than Atroth did. The Realm would be nothing without the fae. Atroth might have claimed his policies were protecting our society and our magic, but they were only protecting himself and the nobles. He cared nothing about the rest of the Realm—the majority of the Realm. He made the strong stronger and the weak weaker. He turned his back on the tor'um, hid them away like they were plague-ridden. You had to beg him to release Brene to your care—"

Caelar rockets to his feet, sending his chair crashing to the floor.

"You have no right to speak her name," Caelar says.

I grimace, not just because more than one human is staring at me, but because that wasn't the wisest thing for Lena to say.

"I will offer her and others like her aid and protection," Lena says.

"Sorry," I tell the cashier, pushing my chair back. I circle the table, meet Caelar's furious silver gaze.

"Please, sit," I whisper as I right his chair. I don't stand there waiting for him to comply—the cashier is still watching me—I walk back to my seat.

"Where is Paige?" I ask quietly, because he's still standing.

Caelar's eyes narrow, but he sinks down into his chair, thankfully without moving it.

"She's with Tylan," he says.

"She's okay?"

He nods.

I rest my hand against my face, hiding my mouth from a human couple at a nearby table. *"She should be okay long-term. We don't think the serum Lee injected her with is fatal."*

"I'm glad to hear that."

"She left a message for McKenzie a few days ago," Lena says. *"She wanted to talk about you and the false-blood."*

Caelar shakes his head slowly. *"Tylan and I had an argument. The Taelith wanted to meet with me again."*

"Again?" Lena asks.

His jaw clenches. Lena's getting him to talk. I think he's just now remembering he's supposed to be pissed at her. He looks away from the table, as if he's still considering leaving.

"He gave me the location of the Sidhe Tol *my people used to fissure inside the palace,"* he says, turning back to Lena.

"That's how you found it?" Lena asks. *"What did you give him in return?"*

"Nothing."

"What did you give him in return, Caelar?" she demands again.

His expression darkens. *"If I choose to—"*

"We need to be sure we know what we're facing when we retake the palace," Kyol cuts in. *"Any information you can give us is appreciated. No one wants to leave a false-blood on the throne."*

"That's why we need to cooperate with her, Caelar," Hison says, leaning forward without touching the table. *"She is our best chance to kill the* Taelith.*"*

"I promised him nothing," Caelar says, turning a glare on the high noble. They might be working together, but I don't think they're the best of friends. *"I indicated I would be open to a future meeting, that is all."*

Lena's eyes narrow. *"You want me to believe he gave you a* Sidhe Tol—*a Sidhe Tol!—without making any request of you?"*

"It actually makes sense," I put in. A quick glance over my shoulder tells me the humans aren't paying attention to me anymore, so I explain. *"We're assuming Cardak has had his eyes on the throne ever since Thrain died, right? He learned from his brother's mistake and the mistakes of the false-bloods we've fought since then. He knew he couldn't go up against Atroth, so he let you"*—I look at Lena—*"the rebels, do it instead. But you were too strong."*

"Because of Taltrayn." She turns her attention to her lord general. *"Very few of the king's swordsmen would have joined me if not for you."*

"The false-blood used me to weaken you," Caelar says quietly. His gaze turns somber, introspective.

"You disagreed with some of Atroth's decisions as much as I did," Kyol says. *"There were other choices he almost made that you and the rest of the Realm never knew about. They . . ."* He pauses. *"He listened to my counsel on many of*

them, but in his last days, he chose to disregard all opinions except Radath's."

Caelar's eyes narrow at the mention of the former lord general's name.

"I would have preferred to arrest Atroth," Kyol continues, *"but I didn't have the authority, and he would not have allowed it."*

Caelar rests his hands on the table. His head is bowed slightly.

"Perhaps we can come to an agreement on a new Descendant," he says after a moment, wearing the weariness of someone who's found himself on the losing side of a war. *"Is there anyone you would su—"*

A flash of blue light in the parking lot makes him cut off his words. Everyone stands simultaneously. The fae reach for their swords, and I'm poised to reach for the dagger strapped to my leg beneath my jeans.

But only a single fae stands on the other side of the window. It takes me half a second to recognize the face staring back at me.

TWENTY-NINE

•—◆—•

"A REN," I WHISPER.

He fissures inside the building, relief shining in his silver eyes. I start to run for him, but Kyol's hand locks around my wrist just before Caelar's chair slams to the floor again.

"You said he was dead!" he snarls at Hison. His sword is out of its scabbard. He takes a step toward Lena, but she's staring at Aren as if she's seeing a ghost. We both are.

Aren finally wrests his gaze away from me. He looks at Lena, then at the other two fae. Something passes through his eyes, and I think he's just now realizing who Caelar is.

"I thought you were dead," Lena whispers.

Caelar rams his sword back into its scabbard. *"This meeting is over."*

"Wait," Lena says, pulling herself back together. *"Please, wait."*

Hison grabs Caelar's arm. *"Listen to what she has to say,"* he hisses. *"We need her help. We don't have a choice."*

Caelar jerks his arm away. *"There's always a choice."*

"I did not deceive you," Lena says. *"We all believed the false-blood killed him."* She pauses, draws in a breath. *"Since that is not true, you may kill him now."*

"What?" I blurt out. The human couple sitting near the

window frowns. They've been watching me since Caelar's chair hit the floor a second time.

"We will not interfere," Lena continues.

The hell we won't. I try to rip my wrist away from Kyol, but he only tightens his grip and pulls me into his chest.

"Not a word, McKenzie," he says. "She has to do this."

"Riquin?" Caelar asks.

Lena nods. *Riquin?* What does that mean? Is she suggesting a duel to the death? It's freaking ridiculous.

"His death must be at your hand and without Lord Hison's aid," Lena adds.

"I don't need help," Caelar says, drawing his sword.

"And I will handicap him with silver."

"Good, Lena." Kyol's whispered approval is barely loud enough for me to hear. If he wasn't holding me so tightly, I'd elbow him in the gut.

"No silver," Caelar says, his hate-filled eyes locked onto Aren.

"I don't agree with this," Aren says, keeping his hand away from his sword. *"I won't fight you."*

"You have no choice," Lena tells him.

"Is something wrong?" The question comes from the man sitting at the window. His wife or girlfriend is openly gaping at me.

"Seizures," I say. It's an excuse I've used many times before.

"Not in here," Lena says to Caelar. *"Outside."*

Caelar and Hison both open a fissure. Their exit fissures appear a half second later on the other side of the windows.

Aren's jaw clenches. He shakes his head. "He has a right to want me dead."

"You'll do this," Lena says.

"Lena—"

"It's an order, Aren," she cuts him off.

He glances outside. His face is stony, unhappy. He runs a hand through his already disheveled hair, then he looks at me. When his gaze shifts to Kyol, I'm suddenly aware of how close we're standing. My back is pressed against his chest, and his arm is wrapped around me. He's not holding me as

tightly as he was a moment ago, but our skin is touching, and Kyol's chaos lusters are zigzagging up my arm. My heart's beating so rapidly, I barely noticed them.

Aren swallows. I take a step toward him, but he turns away and fissures outside. My gaze goes to the parking lot in time for him to step out of the light.

Caelar's expression darkens. He raises his sword and swings it at Aren's torso.

No!

I sprint to the front of the coffee shop, shove open the door.

Aren's on the pavement. He must have turned his back to the blow because he's not bleeding; the *jaedric* he's wearing stopped Caelar's sword from delivering a mortal wound.

"Get up!" Caelar barks.

Aren complies. *"Brene had information I needed. You would have done the same."*

"I wouldn't have used tech!" His fist slams into Aren's jaw. Aren staggers back a step, nearly stepping off the curb and in front of a car that's circling the lot.

"You would have used fists and blades," Aren says. *"I couldn't risk killing her."*

"Draw your sword," Caelar says.

"No."

"Draw it!" Caelar swings his sword at Aren's midsection. Aren raises his arms above the blade's arc and leaps back a step, but the edge cuts a shallow groove in his armor.

Keeping his eyes on Caelar, he unbuckles his weapons belt. *"People I cared about died because I didn't press Brene for answers quickly enough."* He tosses the belt to Lena. *"They were her parents, and yet, she's willing to ally with you."*

"Quiet!" Caelar lunges forward, stabbing his sword into Aren's chest.

Or, into the air where Aren's chest was before he fissured out of the way.

God, that was way too close.

"Aren," I call out. "Please!"

A mom with her two kids frowns in my direction. I ignore her, take a step forward, but once again, Kyol grabs me.

"Wait," he orders.

I clench my teeth, then look back at the one-sided fight. Caelar swings at Aren again and again. Aren's favoring his left leg, the one Lena didn't have enough strength to heal, but he's able to dodge most of the attacks. I don't think Caelar is trying to kill him right now. It's dishonorable to fight an unarmed opponent.

"Fight!" Caelar yells. Aren isn't able to evade his next attack. Caelar's blade slices into his upper arm.

Aren curses as he twists away from Caelar. Blood flows from the wound, but he regains his balance, meets Caelar's gaze, and says, *"No."*

Enraged, Caelar sheathes his sword. Then he balls a hand into a fist and launches it at Aren's face. Aren stumbles backward and, this time, a car does hit him. There's a loud thump, then Aren's spinning. He slams into the passenger door, almost gets pulled under the car, but the tires screech to a stop.

My heart feels like it's splitting in two. What the hell is wrong with Aren? He's so set on wasting his life. I don't understand why.

"He knows what he's doing, *kaesha*," Kyol says. "Be patient."

The driver gets out of his car, looking for whatever he hit, but Aren's still invisible to normal humans. Aren gets back to his feet and faces Caelar again.

And Caelar hits him again.

And again.

And again.

I try not to watch—I try not to think or feel or do anything—but even when I close my eyes, I hear the thuds of Caelar's fists.

"Just a little longer," Kyol says, still holding me. "It will be okay."

I shake my head. His arm tightens around my waist.

"Let go," I say, trying to knock Kyol's hand away. He moves it from my hip to the curve of my jaw, makes me lift my chin to meet his eyes.

"Wait." Our bond opens fully, flooding me with his strength and confidence. He's certain Caelar will stop short of killing Aren.

I close my eyes and turn my head to the side, resting my cheek on Kyol's chest. Hison is standing in my line of sight.

He's watching Caelar beat the shit out of Aren with the most neutral expression I've ever seen the high noble wear.

Aren's grunts of pain grow farther apart. So do Caelar's blows. It probably hasn't been more than four or five minutes, but it seems like forever to me. I'm sure it seems like forever to Aren.

Finally, Caelar says, *"There's no honor in this."*

I'm afraid to turn away from Kyol, but I force myself to look. Aren's on the ground, bloodied and unmoving. He's collapsed out of the flow of both vehicles and people.

"You will not heal him," Caelar says to Lena. He's sweating and breathing so much harder than Aren is. It doesn't look like Aren's breathing at all.

"No," Lena answers coolly. *"It would be foolish to attack the false-blood without the aid of one of my best fighters. I will heal him, but I'll give you three days."*

Caelar's eyes narrow, but he says, *"He'll have no place on your Court."*

"Done," Lena agrees. *"I'll need a new sword-master, however."*

He tightens his hand into a fist then stretches his fingers out, easing tension from knuckles that are bloodied and swollen. Ten minutes ago, he clung to the chance that he might be able to find someone else who could rule the Realm. Now, he's changing his mind about Lena. Her offering of Aren as a sacrifice worked.

"I'll think about it," Caelar says.

"Thank you," Lena answers.

"Not all my people will join you, but I'll speak with them. I'll meet you here at nightfall."

Lena nods.

As soon as Caelar and Hison fissure out, Aren rolls to his back. God, he looks awful. His face is red and swollen, and he's holding his right side. Likely, he has broken ribs, probably other fractured bones as well, and that cut on his arm is bleeding badly.

I try to remove Kyol's hand from around my waist.

"There are too many humans watching," Kyol says.

I freeze. Then, for the first time, I look at my surroundings. There *are* people watching me. Most of them just glance my

way with you're-crazy expressions as they cross the parking lot, headed to the coffee shop or the electronics store next door, but a few people have stopped and are openly staring. Kyol's been holding me relatively still this whole time, but I've called Aren's name at least once.

"I'll release you," Kyol says, "but you mustn't draw any more attention to yourself."

Biting my lip, I nod.

It's hard not to rush to Aren's side the second Kyol lets me go. But Lena's already there. She doesn't have to worry about the humans.

She crouches next to him.

"Where have you been?" she demands. No *Hi*, *How are you*, or *Thank God you're alive*. I want to know the answer to the same question, though. I left him in the tunnel. All it would have taken was a half-hour jog to move beyond the silver wall, but it's been three days since we lost the palace. There's no way the false-blood's magic kept him passed out for that long.

Aren winces when he draws in a breath to speak. "I didn't know you were alive," he says, staring up at the sky. "Either of you, and there was . . ." He closes his eyes, reopens them. "The false-blood put a human on display. Skinned and unrecognizable. He told his people it was the shadow-witch and . . ." His silver gaze shifts from the sky to me. "I had to confirm it was you. I took an *elari*'s name-cord, pretended to be one of them so I could get close."

"It was Shane," Kyol says. He's standing beside me.

Aren gives a small nod.

"He's dead now," he says. "I kept looking for you, but I ended up finding Naito and Lee instead. They made it out of the palace and were hiding in the Inner City. I fissured them to Naito's house this morning. I didn't think to look for you at Nick's until an hour ago."

In my peripheral vision, I see a man light up a cigarette. He's strolling this way, so I quietly say, "We should get back to Nick's."

Really, I just want to get Aren someplace where I can wrap my arms around him.

Kyol takes a step forward, then offers his hand to Aren. "I will fissure you there."

Despite his injuries, Aren stiffens. I do, too, until I feel the reluctant respect that travels along the life-bond. This is the first time the three of us have been in the same place since Aren and I slept together. If Kyol were a lesser man, all he'd feel for Aren is resentment.

Aren closes his eyes. His bloodied forehead creases, and his jaw clenches. After an agonizingly long moment, he accepts Kyol's outstretched hand.

BY the time I walk across the shopping-center parking lot, cross the street, then make my way into Nick's neighborhood and to his front door, Aren's passed out in Lena's bed. Lena's in the living room with Kyol, discussing plans and strategies for dealing with Cardak. I leave them to it and quietly slip into the guest room.

Aren still looks like hell. A bandage is wrapped around his injured arm, but that's all that's been done for him. His face is still bloodied.

I'm afraid I'll wake him if I try to clean the cuts and bruises, so I just curl up in the bed beside him. He doesn't move. Keeping the sheet between us, I risk draping my arm over his body. He's hot, and despite the blood and sweat clinging to his skin, his cinnamon-and-cedar scent makes its way into my lungs. It should soothe me, but it doesn't. I'm terrified I'm going to wake up and find that this is a dream. I've been keeping my grief at a distance so that I can function, but now, it hits me again, so much more potent than it should be since I have Aren right here with me. He's not dead, and Naito and Lee survived. Others might have as well.

But not Sosch.

Not Trev.

Maybe not even Lorn.

I kiss the back of Aren's neck, only long enough to feel the heat of his *edarratae*. They reassure me that he's alive and here, and I let myself close my eyes.

A soft rap on the door wakes me. It feels like I've only

slept for minutes, but when I open my eyes, the room is dark.
No light is shining in through the window, so it has to be well
after nine.

I look to the door, see Kynlee peeking her head in.

"Lena's sending Kyol and Caelar to the false-blood's camp.
She said you need to name the nearest city?"

If Caelar's here, and they've already discussed a plan, I've
slept a hell of a lot longer than I thought.

Careful not to disturb Aren, I get out of bed and follow
Kynlee into the main part of the house. Lord Hison and Caelar are sitting at the kitchen table across from Lena and Kyol.
Nick is here, too. I slide into a chair beside him. My map,
messily drawn in dirt on the pouch that held Lena's anchor-
stones, is spread out on the table, along with other maps and
a few notebooks, which I'm guessing Nick loaned to the fae.

"*Jythkrila,*" I say, watching Caelar's and Hison's expressions. Recognition flashes in both of their eyes. They've never
been there before, but seeing my map and hearing the location is as good as if they fissured there on their own.

"*Do you know what we will find there?*" Caelar asks.

"*I'm hoping you'll find evidence that Cardak is not* Tar
Sidhe *as he claims to be,*" Lena answers. "*If we can link him
to Thrain, it will give people a reason to doubt him.*"

"*They need reason to doubt him?*" My voice is unexpect-
edly tight, and I'm surprised by the anger that's pumping
through my veins. I'm mad at the fae, I realize. I'm mad at
every single one of them who has so much as entertained the
idea that the false-blood could actually be *Tar Sidhe.* Wanting
to rid the Realm of human influences is one thing; torturing
humans and using the fae's hatred of them to further your
cause is something else entirely.

"*He has an extremely rare and powerful magic,*" Lord
Hison says. "*And he's presenting himself as a savior. Many
fae want that. That's why the* elari *are growing in number.*"
His expression sours, and he glances at Lena. "*That's why we
need you. We may have ignored certain parts of the popula-
tion for too long.*"

May have. Well, that's certainly an improvement in his
attitude. Hison hasn't mentioned his wish to see the kingkiller

brought to justice again. I don't know if that's because of the position he's found himself in, or if it's because he's honoring the pledge he made to Aren at the palace. If Aren and I hadn't stayed behind to face the *elari*, they would have captured or killed the high noble and his people.

"Taltrayn and Caelar are fissuring to the Jythkrila camp tonight," Lena says. *"Tomorrow, Caelar will agree to meet with the false-blood."*

Caelar raises an eyebrow. *"I will?"*

"When the false-blood allows you in the palace," Lena says, *"you'll have access to the surviving high nobles. You will make our case to those you believe will be amenable to ousting Cardak."*

It's a risky mission, as risky as any she's ever asked Kyol to accomplish, and Caelar stiffens at the command in her voice. His jaw clenches and unclenches, but after a handful of seconds, he nods exactly the same way Kyol would.

"Taltrayn," Lena says.

Kyol stands. When Caelar does as well, I rise, too, assuming they're going to fissure to the false-blood's camp now.

"You'll stay here, McKenzie," Lena says.

"If Nimael is there, they'll need a set of reliable eyes." The words are out of my mouth before I remember that's not necessarily true. Kyol can see through fae illusions now. Or, he can at least see shadows of invisible fae. We haven't tested his vision out to see how well it is.

"We don't know if there will be a gate nearby," Lena says. "Taltrayn and Caelar will make do. If they're seen and outnumbered, they'll fissure out immediately." She looks at the two men and emphasizes, "Immediately."

"Of course," Kyol says. Lena looks appeased by his words, but I'm not. His definition of "outnumbered" isn't the same as hers or mine.

THIRTY

•-•-

"**I**S HE OKAY?" Lena asks for the umpteenth time. She's not pacing back and forth in Nick's living room, but I'm sure she would be if she wasn't still recovering from her injuries. After Caelar's so-called fight with Aren, she fissured back to Nick's. It was a mistake. It drained her magic and has made her impatient and short-tempered.

"I'm still breathing," I tell her, trying to hold on to my patience. "So, obviously he is."

"But he's still there?" she asks.

I sigh. "Yes, he's still there."

Kyol and, I assume, Caelar are both in the Realm. I think they're both still in the false-blood's camp in the Jythkrila Mountains, but I can't be sure. His heart isn't pumping adrenaline through his veins, though, and he's not injured. Both are good signs.

"They're not fighting anyone," I tell Lena, hoping that will calm her.

"They're not supposed to be," she bites back.

Kynlee looks up from her homework, wide-eyed. Yeah, Lena is touchy. But she's worried, hurt, and generally exhausted and stressed out, so I'm trying to be understanding.

I just give Kynlee a shrug as Nick walks into the living

room. He's carrying a glass filled to the top with a white liquid that I'm guessing isn't milk. He holds it out to Lena.

"What is it?" she asks without taking the glass.

"It's something I mix up for Kynlee when she's not feeling well," he says.

"I call it a Happy Colada," Kynlee speaks up from the couch. "It has coconut in it."

"And some other things," Nick says with a nod.

"Lorn drank it," I tell Lena when she still doesn't accept the drink. Slowly, she reaches up to wrap her hands around the glass. Then she takes the tiniest sip.

And makes a face that's a lot like mine whenever I drink *cabus*.

"It's good," Kynlee insists, her brow furrowing.

Lena glares at her, then takes another sip. When she makes another sour face, I almost laugh.

"Thanks," I say to Nick, hoping the drink will help her. I haven't been able to convince Lena to rest. Her magic won't completely recover until her body does.

Nick just nods, then stands there with his hands at his sides, looking like he has something to say. It's probably something along the lines of "get the hell out of my house." I'm surprised he hasn't insisted on it yet, especially since we brought two new fae—Caelar and Lord Hison—here. But maybe he misses the Realm and the action more than he thought he would. He's asked me several questions about what's going on. He's also asked about a few fae he used to know, and a few cities he frequented. And more than once, when a fae has fissured out, I've seen his gaze go to the shadows, his fingers twitching as if he wanted to trace their peaks and valleys.

"Another day or two," I say, "and she and Aren can probably fissure to Naito's house." That's well over five hundred miles away, but I think they'll be able to make it. If not, Kyol can fissure them there, taking the drain of passing through the In-Between on himself.

"Good," Nick says.

"You should be resting." Lena sets her glass aside.

I frown until she slowly turns her head toward the hallway behind me. Looking over my shoulder, I see Aren.

"I did rest," he says. His gaze is locked on me, and my heart does a somersault in my chest. He's hurting, but his silver eyes are still intense, still mesmerizing.

"Can we talk?" he asks.

Something in his tone makes my breath catch, and not in a good way. But I want to talk to him. I want to hear his voice, his laugh, and I want to touch him and taste his lips, so I just nod, then follow him out the back door, hoping I shouldn't be bracing myself for bad news.

Nick's porch is covered. Aren steps off it and onto the lawn. When I do the same, he turns toward me. He's holding his side. He starts to lift his hand away, but then winces, returning it to his ribs. I hate seeing him this badly hurt. Caelar beat the hell out of him. The cut on his forehead needs stitches, and his right eye is so swollen, I'm certain he can't see out of it. I'm not so certain he doesn't have serious internal injuries. His breaths sound wet and raspy, like he has blood in his lungs, and there's blood at the left corner of his mouth that looks fresh.

Lena promised not to heal him until three days pass. He hasn't even made it through one yet.

He takes a step toward me. He tries to hide how much that hurts him, but the corner of his nonswollen eye crinkles, and the way he winces makes that cut on his forehead reopen. Blood begins to trickle down his temple. Oddly, that's when the tension whooshes out of me.

"You're such an idiot," I tell him. What is the deal with fae attempting to ignore their injuries?

He goes still. "Those aren't exactly the words I'd hoped to hear."

"Just sit down," I tell him. I ignore his sharp intake of breath when I grab his arm and maneuver him back onto the porch, where there are table and chairs. I pull one of the latter out and all but shove him into it. His body tightens up when he lands, and he closes his eyes, waiting for what has to be a wave of pain to subside.

I feel a little guilty about that.

"I'm not an idiot," he says when he can talk again. "I'm determined."

"Is that what you call this?" I ask. "Is that what you call your insistence on suicide?"

"I told you why I stepped forward as the *garistyn*," he says. "Hison arrested Lena. He was about to do the same to Taltrayn. I had to—"

"I gave you a way out, Aren." That's the part of the whole thing that I don't get. I understand why he stepped forward even though I don't completely agree with it, but he'd already taken the blame for killing Atroth. He could have escaped with me. Lena had an alibi. We would have faked his death, then lived happily ever after. "You should have taken the way out."

His forehead creases again. "I did take it."

"No, you didn't." I glare at the renewed trickle of blood from that head wound. It's driving me crazy. "You threw my backpack out the window and all but launched me out after it."

"I told you I was going with you."

My eyebrows go up. "No, you didn't."

"I did," he insists. Then he says, "I think I did. Or I was going to before the door flew open."

"Really?" I ask, letting doubt creep into my voice.

He gives me a small smile. "I swear it."

Damn, I've missed him. Even with his lip busted and swollen, I want to wrap my arms around him and kiss him until he feels nothing but chaos lusters on his skin.

"You should have told me why you were keeping your distance from me," I say. "I'm still pissed at you for that."

"I told you it was the life-bond."

"But neither of you told me our *lives* were linked."

"Would it have changed anything?" he asks. Before I can answer, he says, "It wouldn't have. It would have only made you worry more. And I was trying to find a way to end it without killing either of you."

"I could have helped—"

"That's another reason I didn't tell you," he says. "If you had started asking questions about life-bonds, you would have raised suspicions."

I sink back in my chair. "You still should have told me," I say, this time halfheartedly.

"I also wanted to be sure you couldn't work things out with Taltrayn." There's a question in his voice, and a note of foreboding, as well.

My attention turns inward, toward Kyol. He's still in the Realm and still okay. There's an occasional blip in the life-bond, a tiny leak of emotion that I equate with surprise, but I'm not worried about him. He's okay, and I'm hoping those blips are a result of finding incriminating information on the false-blood.

Kyol feels my attention, though, so I do my best to block him out and refocus on Aren. The small smile I give him is sad, regretful even, because I still hate hurting Kyol.

"Kyol and I worked things out," I tell him. "We—"

A slash of light splits through the air in the center of the backyard. A fae steps out of it. A fae I don't recognize.

Aren and I both leap to our feet. The fae's gaze locks on us the instant mine locks on the name-cord in his hair: red and black. He's *elari*.

He fissures out before my next breath, and Aren curses.

"Lena!" he yells, grabbing my arm as he reaches for the back door.

"I can map his shadows," I say.

"Did he go to the Realm?" Aren demands.

I look over my shoulder, see the shadows shift and twist. "Yes."

"Then I can't fissure after him yet." He slams open the door. "Come on."

Lena's on her feet.

"A scout," Aren says, cutting of her question. "Can you fissure?"

"Not far," she answers. "How did he find us?"

"I don't know."

"What's going on?" Nick asks.

"The *elari* know we're here," Aren says. He reaches down behind the back of the couch where his and Lena's weapons belts are lying. He tosses Lena's to her and fastens his around his waist, all without a grimace of pain.

Nick curses under his breath then, "Kynlee! Kynlee, in the truck. Now!"

"What?" she yells. She's not in the living room. Her voice comes from down the hall.

"Hison?" Lena asks, buckling her belt.

Aren shakes his head. "If Hison betrayed us, the *elari* would *know* we were here. They're guessing, testing out anchor-stone locations and rumors. McKenzie, you have a car?"

Anchor-stones.

"Shit," I say out loud. Lena meets my eyes. A second later, she gets it. I dumped her anchor-stones out so I could draw Nimael's shadows on the pouch that held them. The *elari* must have found them.

"Keys are in my room," I say, heading that way and running into Kynlee.

"What's happening?" she asks, as I steady her.

"Go with your father," Aren says. "The *elari* will follow us, not you, but you can't come back—"

The backyard erupts with light. It's like a flash bomb going off, there are so many *elari*. One, maybe two dozen.

"If we're separated, we meet at Naito's," Aren says, drawing his weapon as the *elari* burst inside.

They break through the windows and kick open the door.

"Kynlee!" Nick shouts.

"Oh, crap," his daughter says.

I grab her arm, pulling her out of the hall. The only reason we're not already dead is the silver Nick's hidden in the insulation. The *elari* can't fissure behind us.

But they can rush in and divide us: me, Kynlee, and Aren on one side, Nick and Lena on the other.

"Taltrayn?" Aren demands, standing between us and the approaching fae.

"On his way," I say. I've let him feel every ounce of my fear.

Aren nods. "Run. Get Kynlee out of here."

The first fae attacks him, then the second. I don't know how he's able to block their blows, but he does, his blade ringing off theirs and countering.

I chuck a lamp—the nearest object I can find—at a third

elari, keeping him away from Aren. I don't want to leave Aren and Lena, but I can't put Kynlee's life at risk either.

The third fae sneers at me, bypasses Aren, and hefts his sword.

Shit!

I shove Kynlee behind me as I back toward the front door. The fae doesn't charge forward—I think the silver and the tech is making him cautious—but even at his stalking pace, he's quicker than me.

I turn to reach for the doorknob. When I do, I see Nick's shotgun propped in the corner.

The *elari* attacks. I block his swing with the shotgun's barrel, cock it, then pull the trigger.

And it slams hard into my shoulder, knocking me into the wall.

"That's not how you hold it," Kynlee says, grabbing the weapon from my hand. She turns, presses it against her shoulder, aims, and fires.

Then she fires again.

And again.

Other shots ring out from the living room—Nick has a gun—and a surge of emotion tells me Kyol just entered this world. Better odds, but not great.

"I'm out," Kynlee says, lowering the shotgun.

I ignore the throb of pain in my shoulder, grab her arm. "Let's go."

We run out the front door. It's the middle of the day, but the street is empty save for my car parked on the curb. I don't have my keys. Nick's garage door is still down. We're going to have to—

An *elari* steps out of the house.

"Just run!" I yell. "Run!"

I shove Kynlee toward the side of the house, where we'll be out of the fae's line of sight, but we're only clear for half a second. He reappears before we reach the gate to the neighbor's backyard. When he opens a fissure again, I reach down, grab a shovel lying against the base of the house, and swing it as hard as I can as I turn.

The *elari* appears exactly where I thought he would, and the metal shovel slams into his head.

I swing again before he reorients himself. His head cracks. His face is bloody and cut.

A third swing, and he drops his sword. I grab it as he's scrambling toward his fissure. He disappears before I can drive the blade through his heart.

Kynlee's staring at me, wide-eyed.

"Come on." I run to the neighbor's fence and open the gate. The yard is an exact replica of Nick's. I can hear the fight continuing on the other side of the fence, but I don't hear a gun firing anymore. I hope that's not a bad sign.

"Now what?" Kynlee asks quietly.

I came this way to get out of sight, but we're far from safe. If someone sees us—

The gate creaks as it reopens. A shout of *"They're here!"* rings through the air.

I'm already shoving Kynlee toward the back fence. "Over it!"

Whether it's fear and adrenaline or just the fact that she's fae, Kynlee sprints to the wooden fence, leaps high enough to grab the top, then vaults herself over it.

My trip over it is a hell of a lot less graceful. I toss my sword over first, barely manage to hoist myself on top of it, then I fall to the other side, the wood raking across my skin before I hit the cement sidewalk.

I force myself to my feet, grab the sword, and sprint across the street. Kynlee runs with me, entering the shopping center's parking lot. It's filled with cars and witnesses, though I don't know if the fae will give a damn about the latter.

"They're following us!" Kynlee yells, the first note of panic entering her voice.

"Get down. Crawl," I say when we reach the first line of cars. I lead her on a zigzag through the parked vehicles. If the fae can't see us, they can't fissure on top of us.

I pause in between a sedan and an SUV. The taller profile of the latter casts a shadow over us but the cement is still scalding hot. It's been baking in the hot Vegas sun all day.

Kynlee looks at me. She's biting her lower lip and trying not to put her hands on the ground. Or her feet. I'm just now noticing she's not wearing shoes. Damn.

The SUV beeps.

Double damn. We don't have time to scurry to another hiding place, a woman with a shopping bag comes around the back of the vehicle, then freezes when she sees us.

I grimace when she drops the bag, then backs away, but what was I expecting? I have a sword in my hand, and I'm pretty sure my face is scratched up from my slide over the fence.

I curse again then pull Kynlee up.

"In the store! Hurry!" I yell, catching only the briefest glimpse of the *elari* as I turn and run.

We make it to the wide sidewalk, but the fae fissures in front of us, cutting off our path.

"Can you fissure inside?" I ask Kynlee, not taking my eyes off the *elari*.

"Maybe, but—"

"Do it." I bring my sword up as he rushes me.

He snarls *tchatalun* as he swings. I block his attack, but my angle of defense is wrong. His blade slides off mine, slashing down my left knee, which I've left too far forward.

He swings again. I backpedal under the blow, step off the curb, and lose my balance.

I land hard on my back, my head slamming into the concrete. I blink black splotches from my vision, look up, and see the *elari* sneering down at me.

He smiles. I do, too. Then, sweetly, I say, *"Go to hell,"* because I see Aren step behind him.

The *elari*'s sneer turns into a gasp of shock as Aren's blade slides through him. A second later, his body *poofs* into a soul-shadow.

Aren reaches through the white mist and lifts me to my feet.

"You okay?" he asks between quick, shallow breaths.

"Me?" I touch his face. "God, Aren, you were already hurt."

"I couldn't . . ." He fades off, maybe because he doesn't have enough air to speak, maybe because he doesn't have the words. Instead, he pulls me into his embrace.

I wrap my arms around him, hug him tight. Over his shoulder, a number of humans gape at me. Someone asks if this is a prank or a TV show. Fae are naturally invisible in my world unless they choose to be seen by un-Sighted humans. They didn't see me fighting the *elari*. They don't see Aren holding me now. They see a crazy woman with a sword. Right now, I don't give a damn.

Aren stiffens. I move back slightly, just enough to see his gaze is focused behind me.

"Inside," he says.

I keep hold of his arm as I turn. It's Nimael . . . and Cardak. The false-blood himself came to kill us.

"Come with me," I say, pulling Aren toward the entrance. He resists.

"You're hurt, Aren. They're not."

His jaw clenches, but he nods, lets me pull him inside the automatic doors, and into . . . the electronics store.

Crap. It's wall-to-wall tech: flat-screen TVs, sound systems, computers, laptops, even refrigerators and freezers. Aren sways under the bombardment of it all. Even Kynlee looks uncomfortable, standing in the middle of the aisle.

I look over my shoulder, praying Nimael and Cardak won't risk this much tech. They're standing just on the other side of the threshold.

"Hey, you can't bring that in here," a human, one of the store clerks, says, eyeing my sword. Most people in here are smart. They're backing away.

"Sorry," I say, keeping my arm relaxed at my side. I don't want to look threatening, but I'm not about to let it go, especially not when Cardak cautiously steps into the store.

"Damn it," I mutter. "Come on."

I pull Aren toward the back of the store. He's way off-balance. If Caelar hadn't beaten the hell out of him less than twenty-four hours ago, he wouldn't be affected quite this badly, but this isn't good for him. I need to get him and Kynlee out of here as soon as I can.

Kynlee glances behind us. "They're both coming!"

"In here." I lead us through swinging doors and into the store's back room. It's filled with boxed electronics, but there should be an exit somewhere.

A few TVs and computers are plugged in along the right wall, awaiting repairs it looks like. A workbench is behind them, and an employee drops his screwdriver as he leaps to his feet.

"Is there an exit this way?" I ask him. He nods, then he hurries back the way we came.

He passes Nimael and Cardak. My heart pounds, hoping they don't turn their swords on him.

They don't. Nimael opens a fissure. I hear the sharp *shrrip* of him reappearing behind us. We're sandwiched in.

Shit. Shit. Shit. Aren can't fight both of them. Neither can I.

"I've got Cardak." Kyol's voice cuts through the air. My adrenaline's been pumping way too hard to realize how close he was. He's just entered the back room and is standing a few strides from the false-blood.

I nod, acknowledging Kyol's words, then look at Aren. He's facing Nimael, but his brow is furrowed.

"McKenzie?"

Crap. The *elari* is illusioned.

"Swing!" I shout as Nimael rushes him. I shove a rolling cart forward. Aren's wild swing makes the *elari* twist out of the way, but the cart hits him. A toolbox and a small TV topple over.

Sparks erupt when the TV smashes to the ground. They're blue sparks, bright and sizzling. Aren leaps back, but Nimael falls on his back with a cry.

"Drop the sword!" someone shouts.

I wouldn't pay any attention to the order except that it comes from a human.

I look behind me, see a security guard with a Taser pointed at me. Kynlee's standing next to him.

Kyol sees the Taser, too. He fissures away from Cardak's attack and knocks the device out of the human's hand.

It skitters across the floor, landing by my foot.

"Behind you, Taltrayn!" Aren shouts at the same time I yell, "Kynlee, run!"

Kyol sidesteps, barely avoiding the false-blood's attack.

Aren's back on his feet. He and Kyol close in on the fae. Cardak's glare shifts between the two of them, then, ever so

casually, he raises his sword and slashes through the security guard's stomach.

Kyol and Aren both lunge forward, but Cardak fissures out of the way. Some instinct tells me he's going to appear behind me so I sweep up the Taser, turn, and fire.

The cartridge shoots out, striking the false-blood's cheek. *Edarratae* explode across his skin like a million blue veins. He drops to the ground, shaking, vomiting.

His legs kick out, striking me so viciously I'm knocked off my feet. A surge of electricity flows into me, but it disperses quickly, and I watch Cardak twitch as froth bubbles out of his mouth. I don't feel a twinge of remorse. I remember Sosch and Shane and a countless number of others who are dead because of him and when his body gives one last twitch before it disappears into the ether, I know that this is a death that I will *never* regret.

"Are you hurt?" Kyol kneels in front of me. He searches for an injury.

I grab his hands, hold them still. "I'm okay. Lena?"

"I fissured her to the Realm," he says.

He fissured her to the Realm. She's safe. The false-blood's dead.

My breath whooshes out of me, carrying with it a thousand worries. I squeeze Kyol's hand as I look past him, searching for Aren. I find Nimael instead. He's still here, still alive. His eyes are wide, like he's just witnessed the death of someone he worshipped, and he's still on his back with the TV and the tools and parts scattered around him. I don't think he's a threat, but—

No. He is a threat. The *edarratae* draw my attention first. They're leaping and spiraling and crashing over the hand he lifts. The hand that's holding the Taser I dropped when I fell.

"Kyol!" I scream, but I'm too late. Nimael lunges forward, firing the Taser as he slams it into Kyol's back. Light explodes all around us, then . . .

THIRTY-ONE

•◆•

ALL I SEE are shadows upon shadows. In this emptiness, I should feel nothing, but there are sensations. Sensations of falling. Sensations of burning.

Sensations of loss.

I try to catch hold of something, anything that will ground me and make me whole again.

THERE may be light in the shadows, bolts of blue and white and shades of silver at the edges of my vision, but every time I try to focus on the flashes, they disappear. I think they might be remnants of my soul. It's missing, and I'm a shell of what I was before. Shells can be crushed. They can be ground into powder and scattered in the wind. I feel scattered. I feel lost. The only way to find a path home is to follow the lights. There's a certain color I need to hold on to. It can sew my soul back together, so, blindly, I search the shimmering night . . .

LOW, incoherent murmurs invade the darkness. The shadows fluctuate with the volume of the voices, but I'm still lost. Still cold. Still wandering.

". . . better when . . . together."

". . . loves him."

"Of course . . . Ten years. Not even you can erase that . . ."

The conversation should make sense. If I listen harder, if I climb my way out of the abyss, I can understand.

"I want her to be happy."

"So does he."

He. Kyol. Aren. The names twist through my memory. I *have* to climb out of this abyss. For them.

HOW long has it been?

My question is attached to a voice. Not my voice, though. It's Aren's.

"Long enough that I'm ordering you to leave."

That's Lena. I'm almost there. The fuzziness in my brain is fading, but something's still not right. I don't feel . . .

Kyol. He's lying beside me, his cold arm touching mine. I try to make my hand reach out for him, but I don't have command of my body yet.

I don't have command of my voice either, so I reach out with my emotions. There's no response from him, just emptiness.

"I'm not leaving her," Aren says. "She could wake."

"She may not. And if she does, Aren, she may not be well. The tech . . ."

"She'll pull through this," he says. "*They'll* pull through this."

"You need to prepare yourself for the possibility . . ."

I'M in the Realm. That accounts for some of the lightness I feel. The air has a different quality to it, a different viscousness than Earth's. My head hurts, my mouth is dry, and I feel so weak, like I've been lying here for weeks.

I try to open my eyes. I can't.

Kyol?

"Any change?" Lena asks.

There's no response. I know Aren's here, though. I smell cedar and cinnamon, and I can feel his presence.

"She was angry," he says. "She didn't understand why I claimed to be the *garistyn*."

That's not true. I told him I didn't understand why he didn't leave with me afterward.

"You're an idiot," Lena tells him.

A small snort of laughter. "That's what she told me, but I did what I had to do to protect her, and to secure your seat on the throne. Hison arrested you. If news of that became public . . ."

"We would have found a way to secure the throne despite his interference."

"Would we have?" Aren asks.

I want so much to open my eyes. I think I might be able to now. I should try. I shouldn't lie here and let Aren immerse himself in guilt.

Lena sighs. "If Taltrayn had stepped forward instead of you, he wouldn't have let any harm come to her. He would have fought for his freedom. If he didn't achieve it on his own, he would have left when she found him in Hison's offices."

"She took down half his guard," Aren says, admiration softening his voice. "She thinks so little of herself, but she's strong. She's amazing."

"She's okay," Lena says.

I almost smile.

I *really* should open my eyes now.

"We finished identifying the documents Taltrayn and Caelar found in Jythkrila," Lena says.

"You can link him to Thrain?"

"Yes, not that it matters now. There were letters between Cardak and his brother. There were also several old documents. One was a map of the *Sidhe Tol*. It's old and faded, but the *Sidhe Tol* he gave to Caelar was on it. So was one other we hadn't learned about yet."

There's a long pause. This would be the perfect moment to groggily open my eyes, pretending I'm just now waking. The only reason I don't is that emptiness I'm getting from Kyol. It feels . . . different now. More like a wall than a bottomless chasm. I try chipping away at it.

"She thought I was dead," Aren says.

"We both did. There was no word from you, and Taltrayn heard rumors of your death."

"He was there for her. I'm glad."

"Are you?"

I think he nods. Or shakes his head. I hear some kind of movement. I could open my eyes to very narrow slits. They might not notice. They might not be looking at me at all.

"Staying away from her was the hardest thing I've ever done."

"Oh, come on, Aren." Lena's voice is gently scolding. "You didn't stay away from her."

"I didn't talk to her for three weeks."

"So you never once fissured to her apartment or to the library to check in on her?"

Silence. My ears strain to hear another nod or a shake of his head, something to indicate his response.

"Her friend is here," Lena says after a moment. "She's offered to watch her for a while."

My friend? Paige? That has to be who she's talking about.

"I already told you I'm not—"

"You are," she cuts him off. "You're going to eat and sleep and live. Get out of here now, or I'll have you removed."

I hear Aren sigh, hear him standing, moving away. My thoughts aren't completely centered on him, though. There's a tightness in my chest. I'm not sure if it's mine or an echo of someone else's.

The door clicks shut.

Cautiously, I open my eyes, focus on the ceiling, then—

"If he doesn't fight for you, he's a fool."

"You're awake, too!" I accuse, turning my head and lightly punching Kyol's arm. A smile curves my lips. He's looking at me. I've never seem him so pale and weak, but his gaze is sane. His magic might be fried from the Taser, but it will return. He hasn't turned *tor'um*.

God, he could have turned *tor'um*. He could have died.

My body is under my control again. I roll on top of him, ignore his *oomph*, and hug him tight.

"That was too close," I say.

He wraps his arms around me. "I agree."

Chaos lusters career across me. They're heating his skin, but I don't pull away. He's cold. I saw what happened when I Tasered Cardak. The life-bond is the only reason he's alive.

I move back just a little, lifting myself up enough to look in his silver eyes. "You're okay?"

He reaches up and touches my cheek. The gesture is tender, but it holds no little amount of sorrow. I close my eyes, that emotion cutting through me. I want so much to make him happy.

"I will be okay," he assures me, sensing the pain within me. "I was content during the ten years we worked together. I can be content again."

Oh, Kyol. Don't you know I can feel your lie?

I sit up, help him do the same. He's so much weaker than I am right now. The electrical current that was pumped into him . . . I'm thankful he survived it, but I wish it would have severed the bond. I don't think he'd hurt as much if it were gone. Sure, he would be broken-hearted, but he could take his mind off me more easily.

I have to find a way to sever the bond. Kelia and Naito might have tried everything she could think of to end hers with Lorn, but that was a fae-to-fae connection. Mine is human-to-fae. Surely, that makes it weaker. I'll try everything I can to break it. For now, though, we have to be okay.

"It'll be easier once you move on and find someone else." I'm not sure if my words are meant to assure me or him. He doesn't say anything, doesn't look at me, but I can feel the doubt circling through him.

"You *will* find someone else, Kyol. I'm not the only girl for you."

He doesn't believe me. Not yet, at least.

"Jacia's pretty," I say, attempting to lighten the mood.

His gaze slides my way. "McKenzie."

"So is Lena, but that would be a conflict of interest, I think. Plus, we hate each other."

"McKenzie," he scolds again, but my words have helped. There's a smile in his stormy silver eyes. "We should tell them we're awake."

"Yeah," I agree. "Probably."

The door to our room opens. Paige steps inside, then does a double take when she sees us.

"They said you weren't awake." She grins and rushes forward, throwing her arms around me. Her hair is down, cut into sharp layers, and it's bleached blond except for the ends, which have been dyed red, purple, blue, green. Basically, all the colors of the rainbow.

She grabs my shoulders, putting distance between us. "You are the absolute hardest person I've ever known to get in touch with."

"It's good to see you, too," I tell her. "You're doing okay?"

"Yeah," she says, but her voice takes on an odd note. "I'm fine."

"You know about the Sight serum? That it might not be fatal?"

"It's not," she says. "At least, not the serum I was injected with."

I tilt my head to the side, studying her. "Lee?"

She shakes her head.

Damn. I don't have much love for Lee, but I don't want him to drop dead. And I don't want anyone else who injected the serum to either.

"I'm sorry," I tell her.

"He deserves it," she says. It sounds like she's forcing herself to believe that.

"Where is he?"

"At Naito's. He and Lee are going through some information the vigilantes gave them. Harper and the others captured some fae a while back. They won't say if they're still alive or where they're holding them, but Naito and Lee will figure it out."

"They've captured fae?" Kyol asks.

Paige turns to him, smiles as if she's glad to see him. That's a change. She's never liked Kyol. She always said it was because he strung me along.

"Yeah," she says, then she nods toward me. "Thanks for taking care of her."

"She's taken care of me." He squeezes my hand and stands. "I'll go speak with Lena."

"Good luck with that," Paige says. At Kyol's questioning look, she adds, "Her schedule is beyond full. Nobles and potential nobles and merchants and I don't even know who are lined up and knocking on the palace doors."

I frown. "How long were we out?"

"Just two weeks, but we killed and chased off the *elari*, and Hison immediately put Lena on the throne."

"She's queen?" Kyol asks at the same time I say, "Who's 'we'?"

"Yes," she answers Kyol. "And 'we' is Caelar, Tylan, me, and the rest of the remnants."

I look at Kyol. "We missed a lot."

"Yep," Paige says. "All the pomp and circumstance."

Kyol's presence suddenly softens, and a tension I didn't realize was there eases out of the life-bond. It's startling how different he feels. All that stress and responsibility he's been carrying around, it impacted me despite the wall he tried to build between us. With it gone . . .

A gentle, contented smile spreads across Kyol's normally stony face.

"She's queen," he says, and for the first time in months, there's optimism in his voice.

THE war is over. We won. We survived.

My heart thunders in my chest, and there's an energy, an excitement, under my skin that I need to share. Even my chaos lusters seem to sense it. They zigzag across my body, anticipating Aren's touch as much as I am.

I have to find him. I have to hear him confirm that the violence is over, and we have forever to be together.

I head for his room, don't find him there, then head for Lena's apartments. Paige said she was busy, but maybe she's overseeing his meals and his sleep. He didn't get much of either because he was watching over me. It's so damn sweet.

But I still can't find him. I pass through the sculpture garden for the third time. Maybe he's not in Corrist? He could be at Naito's or—

"You looking for Aren?"

I turn and see Nick sitting on a stone bench.

"Hey," I say in greeting. "What are you doing here?"

"Avoiding the police," he says, leaning forward to rest his forearms on his knees. "They want to know why I fired a gun at my house and left a few bloodied swords lying on the ground."

Oh, hell. "I'm so sorry, Nick."

He shrugs. "I didn't have to let you in."

"But you did, and I appreciate it. I didn't want—"

"It's okay," he cuts me off. "I knew what I was getting into. Plus, she's happy." He nods to the left. There's Kynlee. She's sitting on the edge of a raised flower bed with Lord Garon, her brother. They're both grinning, and it's easy to see the similarities in their smiles. She has a name-cord in her hair. It's made of bright green and white stones and matches Garon's perfectly.

"He's been cool about everything," Nick says. He watches them a moment before he shakes his head and straightens. "Anyway, I saw Aren at the training grounds a little while ago. He's probably still there."

I give him a smile. "Thanks, and I hope all of this works out," I say, indicating Kynlee and Lord Garon. Then I all but run to the training ground.

It's a strip of land that lies between the palace and the silver wall. This morning, it's filled with swordsmen. They're all wearing *jaedric* armor that's engraved with Lena's seal—the seventeen-branched *abira* tree. I try to spot Aren, try to hear his voice but the *clinks* of the practice swords are a steady hum in my ears.

Maybe he isn't here. Maybe he's already left. Maybe—

"McKenzie!" Aren sweeps me into his arms before I'm able to turn. My feet come off the ground as he spins me, and I hold him tight, clinging to him.

"Nalkim-shom," he whispers as he sets my feet back on the ground. He breathes out a thank-you to the *Sidhe*, then holds me half an arm's length away.

My heart flips. Lena must have healed him at some point. His sharp cheekbones and strong jaw are no longer bruised and swollen, and his posture is relaxed. He's not tense and hunched in pain.

Her magic didn't do anything for his hair, though. It's still a disheveled mess.

A sexy, disheveled mess. God, I love him.

I start to move closer, but a pair of swordsmen swing their swords a little too close.

Aren grabs my hand. "Not here."

I expect him to lead me back to the palace, to his room or to mine. Instead, he leads me beneath the silver wall.

"Where are we going?" I ask as we step onto the terrace that separates the wall from the gate that's just ahead.

He runs a hand through his hair, tightens his grip on me. "McKenzie . . ."

He fades off. He seems nervous, and that makes me nervous.

"I . . ." He glances at me, clenches his jaw.

"What's wrong?" I ask, my stomach sinking as I half walk, half jog to keep up with him.

"Nothing, I just—"

"You're practically pulling my arm off."

He immediately slows his pace. "I'm sorry. I . . . I know you said you worked things out with Taltrayn."

"I didn't—"

"And I know you have the life-bond with him, and that he loves you and I've been an ass. I had my reasons for staying away, but I shouldn't have. I should have . . . I shouldn't have made that decision for you, and I regret it." He stops beside the river, turns me to face him. "I'm in love with you, McKenzie. You're the most courageous and beautiful person I've met in either of our worlds, and I want . . . No, I *need* to be with you, and I can't let you go without a fight."

On the inside, I'm doing somersaults and grinning like a fool, but I make myself look at him as sternly as I can manage, and ask, "Are you finished?"

"No." He reaches into the river and opens a fissure.

I start to ask him where we're going, but he cuts me off.

"Your anchor-stone," he says, pressing something into my palm. Something that feels nothing like a small rock.

I frown down at my hand—at the *diamond ring* in my hand—and my thoughts catch. But, no, he can't know what

this means. Diamonds can be imprinted. It's not a well-known fact in the Realm, but Aren imprinted a diamond for me once before. That one was inlaid in a necklace. It was a leap of faith on his part. I could have betrayed him. I could have destroyed the whole rebellion. But I didn't. I didn't because I'd started to fall in love with him.

I clear my throat, not as a nervous gesture or a gimmick to buy me time, but because I really can't seem to form any words.

"Y-You're out of anchor-stones?" I finally manage.

"No," he says, looking into my eyes. Then he takes my other hand in his. "I know I hurt you. I know this is our last chance to be together. Please give me that chance, McKenzie. Please . . ." He seems to remember something. He drops to one knee. "Please marry me."

Lightning strikes between our clasped hands.

"Fae don't marry." I don't know why I say that. My brain obviously isn't functioning.

"Humans do," he says. "And I want to be with you for the rest of our lives. Now that I've been forced into retirement, it could be a very long life, McKenzie."

"But the life-bond. You can live with it? You said . . ."

"It kept us apart only because your life was at stake. The high nobles won't be executing anyone now. I can live with Taltrayn being in your life, but I can't live without you."

"Stand up," I say.

"What?"

"Stand up."

He frowns as he rises. "Naito said I was supposed to kn—"

I silence him with a kiss. Tiny explosions rock through my body, and I swear the air around us glows. I love the feel and taste and the scent of him, and when he deepens the kiss, our connection deepens as well. He's a part of me now, no life-bond needed, and he knows me like no one else ever will.

"McKenzie." He pulls me closer, clinging to me as if I'll slip through his arms.

I'm here to stay, I say with a kiss that promises love and passion. I want that passion now. I want us to find ourselves wrapped in chaos lusters again. I want to wake up every

morning with him at my side, and I want whatever kind of normal we can have together.

Finally, he's mine completely.

He pulls back, breathing hard. "Naito said you're supposed to say 'yes.'"

"That was my yes." I kiss him again, and as he kisses me, he takes my left hand. A cool circle slides over my ring finger, and I smile against his lips.

"Where will it take us?" I ask.

"Anywhere you want."

Ace Books by Sandy Williams

THE SHADOW READER
THE SHATTERED DARK
THE SHARPEST BLADE